Praise for *Millie's Fling*

"A warm and humorous journey... Just reading it makes you feel good. An absolute delight!"

—*Wendy's Minding Spot*

"A charming romp... Love, it seems, is on everyone's mind... Will all find their soulmates? Mansell's dry humor and engaging story make it an undeniable pleasure to find out."

—*BookPage*

"A pleasure to read! ...A super cute and wicked funny book."

—*Night Owl Romance*

Praise for *Miranda's Big Mistake*

"A winning read... Miranda's got more than enough irresistible transoceanic charm to promise that this... should net a passionate new audience eager for the more."

—*Publishers Weekly*

"Mansell's novel proves the maxims that love is blind and there's someone for everyone, topped with a satisfying revenge plot that every jilted woman will relish."

—*Booklist*

"A rip-roaring good time... The sexual tension is electric... The dialogue is sharp and the plot will keep readers... on their toes and cheering Miranda on."

—*Savvy Verse &*

ALSO BY JILL MANSELL

An Offer You Can't Refuse
Miranda's Big Mistake
Millie's Fling
Perfect Timing
Rumor Has It
Take a Chance on Me
Staying at Daisy's
To the Moon and Back

nadia knows best

Jill Mansell

sourcebooks
landmark

Published by Sourcebooks Landmark, an imprint of Sourcebooks, Inc.
P.O. Box 4410, Naperville, Illinois 60567-4410
(630) 961-3900
FAX: (630) 961-2168
www.sourcebooks.com

Originally published in 2002 by Headline Book Publishing, a division of
Hodder Headline, London.

Library of Congress Cataloging-in-Publication Data

Mansell, Jill.
  Nadia knows best / by Jill Mansell.
    p. cm.
  I. Title.
PR6063.A395N33 2012
823'.914—dc23

Printed and bound in the United States of America
VP 10 9 8 7 6 5 4 3 2 1

To Lydia and Cory, with all my love.

And no, this doesn't mean I'll play another game of Monopoly.

Chapter 1

"Ooooohh… eeee…" To her horror Nadia realized she was having a Bambi moment. A scary, drawn-out, Bambi-on-ice moment in fact. Except unlike Bambi, she couldn't make it stop simply by landing with a bump on her bottom.

The car carried on sliding in slow motion across the perilously snow-packed road. Despite knowing—in theory—that what you were meant to do was keep your foot *off* the brake and steer *into* the skid, Nadia's hands and feet were frantically doing all the wrong things because steering into a skid was like trying to write while you were looking in a mirror and—oh God, *wall*—

Cccrunchh.

Silence.

Phew, still alive, hooray for that.

Opening her eyes, Nadia unpeeled her trembling gloved hands from the steering wheel and mentally congratulated herself on not being dead. The car was tilted at a bit of an odd angle, thanks to the ditch directly in front of the wall, but despite the best efforts of the snow, she hadn't actually been going fast enough to do spectacular amounts of damage to either it or herself.

Then again, what to do now?

Pulling her hat down over her eyebrows and bracing herself against the cold, Nadia clambered out of the grubby black Renault and inspected the crumpled front wing. Just as well she hadn't borrowed her grandmother's pride and joy for the journey—the teeniest scratch on Miriam's Maserati would have meant being beaten with a big stick and sent to stand in the naughty corner for weeks.

Her face screwed up against the stinging onslaught of low-flying—and actually quite ferocious—snowflakes, Nadia hopped back into the car. At least she had her mobile. She could dial 999 and ask the police to come and rescue her... except if she did that, chances were they might want to know where she was.

Hmm.

Maybe phone home then, and at least let the family know she was in a ditch, in a blizzard, somewhere in deepest darkest Gloucestershire. Or, more accurately, deepest *whitest* Gloucestershire.

Although it would be dark soon enough.

This dilemma was solved neatly enough by the discovery that her phone was dead, which narrowed the options down to two. Should she leave the car and trudge off through the ever-deepening snow in search of civilization?

Or stay here and hope that somebody else—preferably in a Sherman tank or a helicopter—might come along and rescue her?

Since civilization could be miles away and her feet still ached like mad from dancing last night, Nadia reached over to the backseat for her sleeping bag, wriggled into it like a giant worm, and settled down to wait.

Poor old Laurie, he'd missed a brilliant party. Nadia smiled to herself, thinking back to yesterday morning's phone call. She wondered how hot it was right now in Egypt, if Laurie was remembering to drink only bottled water, and if he'd managed to squeeze in a visit to Tutankhamun's tomb before flying on to Milan.

Gosh, she was hungry. Easing a hand from the cocoon of her sleeping bag, she flicked open the glove compartment. A packet of Rolos and a half-empty bag of gumdrops. Should she ration herself, like people trapped on mountains, to one Rolo a day? Or give in to temptation and guzzle the whole lot at once?

But she wasn't trapped on a mountain and she wasn't going to starve. Compromising, Nadia ate three Rolos and half a dozen gumdrops, then switched on the car radio for company, just in time to hear a DJ cheerfully announcing that there was plenty more snow on the way.

That was the thing about Sherman tanks, they were never around when you needed them.

Less than half an hour later—though it seemed like more—Nadia let out a shriek and abruptly stopped singing along with Sting to "Don't Stand So Close To Me." Actually, it was an appropriate song. The person who had tapped on her window *was* pretty close.

Male or female? Hard to tell with that hat pulled down over their face. Wrapped up in a Barbour jacket, thick sweater, and jeans, it was either a man or a hulking great six-foot-plus woman.

Hoping it wasn't Janet Street-Porter, Nadia opened the window and promptly wished she could have been wearing something more alluring than a green nylon sleeping bag strewn with bits of gold foil Rolo wrapper.

She also hoped she'd been singing more or less in tune.

Not that this was terribly likely.

"Are you OK?"

He had dark hair, light brown eyes, and snowflakes decorating his black, spiky eyelashes.

"I'm fine. Really warm. Skidded off the road," Nadia explained, fairly idiotically given the novel angle at which she was sitting.

He inclined his head. "I noticed."

Nadia peered at the empty road behind him. "Did you crash too?"

"No, I did the sensible thing." He looked amused. "Abandoned the car before that happened. It's at the bottom of the last hill."

"Rolo?" She offered him one through the open window. Not her last Rolo, obviously.

"No thanks. Look, there's a village half a mile ahead. Do you want to walk with me?"

"You live around here?" Nadia brightened, then hesitated. Hang on, a complete stranger offering her shelter in the middle of nowhere, seemingly perfectly normal and friendly right up until the moment he reappeared from the woodshed with madness in his eyes and a sharp ax?

How many times had she seen *that* film?

He shook his head, scattering snowflakes. "No, I live in Oxford."

"So how do you know there's a village?" She didn't want to struggle through the blizzard on a whim.

The mad ax-murderer seemed entertained by the wary look in her eyes.

"I'm very psychic."

Oh God, he really *was* a nutter.

"That's great." Nadia took a deep breath. "Look, have you ever been to this part of Gloucestershire before?"

"No." Smiling, he patted the pocket of his waxed Barbour. "But, unlike you, I do have a map."

"I feel like a refugee," Nadia muttered as they trudged along the narrow lane, the snow squeaking underfoot. Since hopping along like a ten-year-old in a sack race wasn't practical, she was carrying her rolled-up sleeping bag under one arm and her overnight case in the other.

"You look like a refugee." Glancing across at her, he broke into a grin and held out an arm. "Here, let me carry those."

She knew his name now. Jay Tiernan. He'd introduced himself while she'd been struggling to extricate herself from the sleeping bag. In return she'd asked, "What does J stand for?"

"Nothing. It's just Jay."

Hmm, a likely story. It was probably short for something embarrassing like Jethro or Jasper. Or Josephine.

Then again, Nadia could sympathize. School sports days had always been a mortifying experience, with dozens of sniggering boys lined up roaring, "Go, Nad... GONAD... GO, GO, GO!"

But Jay Tiernan didn't need to know that. Thankfully, Nadia handed him her overnight bag. Her nose was a fetching shade of pink, her eyes were watering, and her toes numb. Ranulph Fiennes needn't worry about competition—she'd be hopeless at trekking across the Antarctic.

"You lied," Nadia panted forty minutes later. "That wasn't half a mile."

"Never mind, we're here now."

"And this isn't a village."

"It is," said Jay. "It's just... small."

Nadia peered through the tumbling snowflakes at the deserted single street. There were no lights on in any of the cottages. Nor were there any shops. Just a postbox, a bus shelter, and a phone box.

And a pub.

"The Willow Inn," Jay announced, squinting at the dilapidated sign. "We'll try there."

The front door was locked. After several minutes of hammering on the wood, they heard the sound of keys rattling and bolts being drawn back.

"Blimey," slurred the landlord, enveloping them in a cloud of whisky breath. "Mary and Joseph and the little baby Jesus. Fancy bumping into you in a place like this."

Nadia, clutching her rolled-up sleeping bag in her arms, realized he thought she had a baby in there. Then again, he was so drunk she could probably get away with it.

"Hi," Jay began. "We wondered if—"

"Shut, mate. Closed. Six o'clock we open." The middle-aged

man jabbed vaguely at his watch. "You could try coming back then. No kids mind, this isn't a family pub. Kids? Can't stand 'em."

"Look, the roads are blocked, we've had to abandon our cars, we've been walking for *hours*," Nadia blurted out, "and we need somewhere to stay." Hastily she unraveled the sleeping bag to show him how empty it was. "And we definitely don't have a baby."

As a rule, batting her eyelashes and widening her big brown eyes had the desired effect, but the landlord of the Willow Inn was clearly too far gone for that.

"Don't do board and lodging neither." Wheezing with laughter he flapped his arm and said, "There's a stable down the road, you could try there."

Nadia briefly wondered if bursting into tears would help. Failing that, hitting the landlord over the head before tying him up and locking him in his own cellar.

Jay, his method thankfully more law-abiding, said, "We need somewhere to stay and something to eat. We'd pay you, of course."

The landlord's bloodshot eyes promptly lit up. "Hundred quid."

"Fine."

"Cash, mind. Up front."

Solemnly, Jay nodded. "It's a deal."

The power outage that had left every house in the street in darkness was still going strong at nine o'clock that evening. The pub, illuminated with flickering candles, had gradually filled up with locals driven out of their homes by the lack of TV, as well as half a dozen other stranded drivers in need of a roof over their heads.

By some miracle the landlord, Pete, was still drinking and still conscious. Well, just about. Cindy, the barmaid, confided to Nadia that Pete's latest girlfriend had walked out on him three weeks ago, precipitating this mammoth binge. Now, evidently cheered by the amount of money he was extorting from stranded travelers, he was wavering precariously on a bar stool, leaving Cindy to do all the work.

Dinner, also thanks to the power outage, was thick chunks of bread toasted over an open fire, tinned ravioli, wedges of cheese, pickled onions the size of tangerines, and stale digestive biscuits.

Nadia, who had given the onions a miss, said, "Yum."

"A candlelit meal, what could be more romantic?" Jay indicated their rickety wooden table. "Never let it be said I don't know how to give a woman a good time. Pickled egg?"

Nadia smiled; he had a nice voice. She'd always been a sucker for a nice voice.

"No thanks. We need to sort the room thing out. You can't sleep down here."

Pete's insistence on cash in advance for the only spare bedroom had left Nadia with a dilemma. With only fifteen pounds in her purse, it had been left to Jay to come up with the rest of the money. When Pete had shown them the chilly room, cluttered with junk and taken up almost entirely by a lumpy, unmade double bed (A hundred pounds? Bargain!), Jay had murmured, "It's OK, I'll sleep downstairs."

But that had been before the others had arrived, turning the small bar into a makeshift refugee camp. Two of them had nasty hacking coughs. It wasn't fair to take the room Jay had largely paid for.

"You should have the bed," Nadia told him. "Honestly, I'll be fine down here."

"You might be fine, but you won't get any sleep."

"I'd feel guilty otherwise." She watched him refill their glasses with red wine.

"We could both sleep in the bed," said Jay.

Nadia hesitated. It was the most practical solution, of course. It was just a shame he couldn't have been nice-but-comfortingly-ugly, rather than nice-and-definitely-attractive.

Dangerously attractive, in fact.

Not that she'd be tempted to do anything naughty, but she didn't want Jay thinking she might be tempted. In her experience, attractive men seemed to take this for granted.

"Just sleep." Nadia met his gaze. "No funny business. We'd have all our clothes on. And I'd be in my sleeping bag," she added for good measure.

"Absolutely." Jay's mouth had begun to twitch. Oh Lord, did he still think she fancied him?

"I have a boyfriend," Nadia explained firmly, "and we really love each other."

Jay nodded, to show he understood. "Me too."

Chapter 2

GOSH, WEREN'T GAY MEN lovely? There was just something about them, Nadia thought delightedly as they lay in bed together two hours later. You could relax and chat away about anything at all, secure in the knowledge that there was no underlying agenda. She'd told Jay about her job at the garden center, her family in Bristol, and last night's party in Oxford.

Now he was asking her about Laurie. Only too happy to oblige, Nadia propped herself on one elbow and said, "Oh, he's just brilliant, the best boyfriend in the world. If you saw him, you'd fancy him yourself. He's a model." She added with pride, "Last month he was on the cover of *GQ*."

"I'm impressed." Jay smiled at the look on her face. "So how did you two meet? At some fantastically glitzy party? Did Brad and Angelina invite you to dinner and there he was? Or were you working at the garden center and he just turned up one day in desperate need of a clematis?"

"Ho ho." From inside her sleeping bag, Nadia aimed a playful kick at his leg. "Actually, we've known each other since we were kids, we practically grew up together. Laurie's the original boy-next-door. Well, not exactly next door," she amended, "but he lived over the road from us. We used to go tadpoling together. Laurie taught me how to ride a bike with no hands, I taught him how to shoplift candy from Woolworth's…"

"*Cider with Rosie* meets *Bonnie and Clyde*." Jay raised an eyebrow. "So you've been together how long? Since you were *seven*?"

"Oh no, we were just friends then. I went away to college at eighteen then Laurie was off the following year. When he came back two years ago we took one look at each other and it hit us both like a brick." Nadia clapped her hands together. "*Bam*, just like that. We couldn't believe how fast it happened. And we've been together ever since."

Jay shook his head. "I'm confused. So when did the modeling thing start?"

He certainly seemed interested. Nadia wondered if he was entertaining hopes of moving into the same field himself—not that he could, at twenty-nine. Oh dear, should she gently warn him that he was way past his sell-by date?

"I entered him for a competition," she explained. "One of those daytime TV programs was offering a prize of a contract with a top modeling agency. They interviewed last year's winner and he wasn't a patch on Laurie, so I just stuck a photo in an envelope and posted it off without telling him. A month later they phoned and told him he'd been short-listed for the final."

"Was he shocked?"

"Shocked? He went mental! He thought modeling was for poofs—ooh, sorry, but he did."

"That's OK." Jay inclined his head.

"Anyway, we managed to persuade him that it *wasn't*," Nadia hastily emphasized, "and Laurie finally agreed to go up for the final. Mainly to shut me up, I think. But when he met the organizers and found out how much money he could make, he realized it might be worth making the effort after all. So then he won the competition and that was it, the agency put him on their books and the whole thing took off like a rocket. Before, he'd been training as a stockbroker and hating every minute. Now he's traveling all over the world doing magazine shoots and ad campaigns. It's just brilliant, a whole new career."

"Thanks to you," Jay said mildly. He paused. "Ever regret it?"

Nadia had heard this question before. About a thousand times.

"Why would I regret it? We're still together, Laurie hasn't changed. We might not see as much of each other as before, but he comes back whenever he can. We still love each other. And it's not going to last forever, we both know that. By the time you hit thirty, you're well and truly over the hill." There, slipped it in, just in case Jay was still hankering after a change of career. "If my phone was working, I could speak to him now," Nadia went on. "We talk to each other all the time. He's been in Egypt for the last few days, shooting an ad campaign for Earl jeans."

Jay looked mildly skeptical. "And you trust him?"

It wasn't the first time she'd been asked this one either.

"Of course I do. One hundred percent."

"How about him? Does he trust you?"

"Laurie knows I'd never cheat on him." Smiling to herself, Nadia plumped up her pillow and changed the subject. "Anyway, your turn now. Tell me all about your boyfriend."

The candle on the bedside table flickered, sending an eddy of shadows across the wall.

"Actually, I'm not gay," said Jay.

Oh for heaven's sake.

"So why did you tell me you were?"

"To relax you." His eyes were bright with amusement. "And it worked."

"That's cheating," Nadia groaned. "I trusted you. You lied to me."

"What can I say? I'm a man, it's what we do."

Hang on, was he insinuating something about Laurie? Nadia bristled. "If that's meant to be some kind of dig—"

"OK, I'm sorry." Laughing, Jay held up his hands. "But it did calm you down, didn't it? You stopped panicking about spending the night in bed with a strange man who might try to seduce you."

"And now you tell me you aren't gay after all. Wouldn't it have made more sense to carry it on? You could at least have waited until the morning before telling me you were straight."

"I was going to. Until you asked me about my boyfriend. Anyway, you don't have to worry," said Jay. "I'm still not going to even try to seduce you. So you're perfectly safe."

"Right. Well, that's good." Nadia wriggled down into her sleeping bag, affecting indifference but secretly wishing he could have invented a boyfriend. She preferred him gay. Just because she'd never be unfaithful to Laurie didn't mean she couldn't be attracted to a good-looking man.

"You could ask me about my girlfriend if you like," Jay prompted.

"Go on then, tell me about her."

He winked. "We broke up a couple of months ago."

Typical.

"See?" Nadia heaved a sigh. "You're doing it already. You wouldn't have said that if you'd still been gay."

"Wouldn't have had a girlfriend to break up with," Jay reminded her. "Oh, come on, don't get all defensive. I said I wouldn't try to seduce you, didn't I?"

"But now you're flirting with me," Nadia complained. "And don't tell me you aren't, because you are."

"So? I'm allowed to flirt. You were doing it earlier," he pointed out, "when you thought I was gay."

"I was not." Feeling herself blushing, she was glad of the dim light. "Why would I want to?"

"Because you thought I was safe." Jay's chestnut-brown eyes glinted with amusement.

Oh crikey, was he right? Had she been flirting with him? Something in the pit of Nadia's stomach went *ting* and tightened in alarm. She hadn't even realized.

"And now you aren't doing it," he went on. "You're backpedaling like mad. Which has to mean you like me at least, ooh"—he held out his hand, the thumb and forefinger half an inch apart—"this much."

Not fair, not *fair*.

"If I didn't like you that much, I wouldn't be here." Nadia tilted her head in the direction of the other bedroom, where Pete the landlord was snoring like an elephant seal. "I'd rather sleep in the snow than share a bed with him."

Gravely, Jay nodded. "Well, thank you. I think."

"Then again, you might snore too."

"Not at all. I'm the perfect gentleman in bed." He flashed a wicked grin. "No one's ever regretted spending the night with me."

Nadia's mouth was dry. She didn't doubt it for one second. Anyone would be attracted to him. He was great company, confident and charismatic. If she weren't involved with Laurie, let's face it, she'd be tempted to go for it. Why not, after all? Here they were, cut off from the rest of the world, stranded in a snowbound pub. No one else need ever know…

Oh good grief, she was actually imagining it, picturing the scene in her mind, wondering how it would feel to reach out and slide her hand up beneath that thick dark blue sweater of his… What was the matter with her? She was just a shameless hussy, stop it, stop it, *stop it*.

Delete that fantasy.

She had Laurie. Who could ask for more?

Appalled with herself for even thinking it, Nadia abruptly leaned over and blew out the flickering candle. Passionately thankful that Jay wasn't able to read her mind—and horribly afraid that he could—she said, "I'm going to sleep now. Good night."

Pete, the landlord, was perplexed to wake up the following morning with a violent hangover—well, that was par for the course—*and* a pub full of bleary-eyed strangers. He promptly helped himself to a large Scotch and set about discovering what they were doing there.

Upstairs, Nadia brushed her teeth and sent up a passionate prayer of thanks that she'd managed not to give in to last night's moment of weakness. Not many girls, she wouldn't mind betting, shared a bed with Jay Tiernan and emerged with their morals intact. Then again, not many girls would go to bed with him dressed in jeans, socks, two heavy sweaters, and a less than gorgeous tank top.

Clomping downstairs in her boots, she discovered an arctic wind whistling through the empty pub and the front door gaping open. Everyone had gathered outside to cheer and applaud the snowplow that was shooting great plumes of snow up into the air as it made its stately way along the main street.

Nadia found Jay among the crowd. "We're saved. We shan't have to eat each other, that's a relief. How am I going to get my car out of the ditch?"

"The cavalry have arrived." Jay indicated the tractor, trundling along in the wake of the snowplow. It slowed to a halt outside the pub and a burly farmer type jumped down.

"Passed some cars back there in need of a tow." Spotting Nadia's hopeful face he said, "One of them yours, love? Want some help, do you?"

She could have kissed him. Her fiftysomething knight in a filthy tractor! This was village life for you, Nadia thought gratefully. Everyone pulled together, helping each other out. There were so many kind people around, unsung heroes, prepared to do favors out of the sheer goodness of their hearts.

"Oh, I do," she said with joyful relief. "Mine's the black Renault, this is so *ki*—"

"No problem, love. Any time. That'll be fifty quid."

For heaven's sake, talk about highway robbery. Country people weren't lovely at all.

"Just don't say cash," Nadia warned the greedy selfish mercenary farmer. "Don't ask for cash up front, because I haven't any left." Shooting a meaningful look in Pete the landlord's direction, she added, "I can do a check."

"Got a guarantee card?" The farmer was nothing if not blunt.

Nadia, who could be blunt too, said, "Who shall I make the check out to, Dick Turpin?"

"Have you out of there in a jiffy, love." The farmer winked at her, unabashed. Business was business. Sudden blizzards might cause misery and hardship for many people, but they were always a nice little earner for him.

By the time the Renault had been hauled out of the ditch, dented but otherwise unharmed, Jay had arrived at the scene on his way back to his own car.

"Drive carefully now," he told Nadia as she revved the engine.

"We're only three miles from the motorway. I'll be home in an hour."

"It's been nice meeting you." Jay's eyes crinkled at the corners as he looked down at her. "Could have been nicer still, but never mind. We had fun."

Nadia nodded. In the cold light of day, fun was infinitely preferable to sex. If she'd given in to temptation last night, she'd be feeling twisted with guilt by now. God, she'd be a disaster on a clubbing holiday in Ibiza.

"Thanks for everything. Bye."

The churned-up snow creaked beneath her tires as she turned the car in the direction of home.

"That boyfriend of yours is a lucky bloke." Jay rested his hand briefly on the roof of the car. "Tell him I said so."

For a moment Nadia wondered if he was about to bend down

and give her a goodbye kiss on the cheek; he looked as if he might. She waited, giving him every opportunity to do it, and realized she was holding her breath. Just a sociable peck, not full-frontal snogging, a sociable peck on the cheek was absolutely fine...

Well, it would have been, if it had happened.

"Do the window up," said Jay. "Keep warm. And don't skid into any more ditches."

"Yes, boss. You too." As she buzzed the window shut, Nadia saluted then grinned and waggled her fingers at him. "See you around."

Why did people always say that to each other, when they both knew they wouldn't?

Chapter 3

THE FLIGHT FROM BARCELONA to Bristol Airport had landed fifteen minutes ago and Nadia was hopping impatiently from one foot to the other at the arrivals gate. Any second now, the first passengers would begin to emerge through the sliding smoked-glass doors. There were butterflies in her stomach—huge, excitable tropical butterflies rather than the sedate English kind—and her knuckles were white as she gripped the chrome rail. Adrenaline was sloshing through her body like free beer at a student party. Were there paramedics around? Did lots of people waiting to greet returning loved ones feel like this? Did many of them keel over with heart attacks and—ooh, *door*!

Nadia gazed, transfixed, as an ultra-smart businesswoman tip-tapped out on ultra-high heels, followed by a gaggle of tourists, then some studenty types, several businessmen, and a frazzled-looking girl in her twenties with a screaming baby and a toddler in tow.

At the sound of a shout behind her, the girl turned and let out an exclamation of relief as Laurie raced through the doors clasping a battered toy giraffe.

"I found it on the floor by the luggage trolleys." He waved the giraffe at the baby, who promptly snatched it back and glared at him with breathtaking lack of gratitude.

"That's why she was yelling. I didn't even realize she'd dropped it. Thank you so much." The girl's face was alight with gratitude.

"No problem." Laurie flashed his trademark broad smile and

Nadia, watching them from six feet away, realized that this was why she loved him. He was kind and thoughtful and would help anyone. Plenty of men might have picked up a toy giraffe and chased after a beautiful girl with a wailing baby, but how many would bother to do the same for a girl who was plain and scrawny, with bad teeth and dull, greasy hair?

It would never occur to Laurie not to. That was the kind of person he was.

And here he was now, coming toward her, holding out his arms. "Nad!"

Mushy with love, she threw her own arms round him then felt her feet leave the ground as he lifted her up and swung her round. For a millisecond, before Laurie's mouth found hers, Nadia glimpsed the look of envy on the plain girl's face. Then he was kissing her and she knew they were the center of attention. Everyone was watching them, enjoying the sight of them together. You couldn't beat a romantic airport reunion, it restored everyone's faith in humanity. In fact, they were in danger of getting a round of applause.

"I've missed you so much." Hugging her tightly, then taking a step back, Laurie surveyed her and said, "God, you look fantastic."

"So do you. Messy, but fantastic." Grinning, she put a hand up to his slept-on sun-streaked blond hair, then cupped the side of his gold-stubbled jaw. For a professional model, Laurie had no vanity whatsoever. Anyone else would never get away with it. He was wearing baggy black trousers that looked like yard sale rejects but had undoubtedly cost a fortune. The pale gray sweater with holes in the elbows had once belonged to his father. His trainers were state-of-the-art and filthy. There was a huge purple bruise on his left forearm and what looked like a juice stain on the right sleeve of the sweater.

"I know, I know. I'm a mess." Laurie's green eyes widened with good-natured resignation; he was well used to being fussed over by his booker at the agency, by highly strung editors and frenetic casting agents. "That's just black currant juice," he excused the stain on his sweater. "I was playing scissors-paper-stone with a kid on the plane and he knocked his drink over me."

"And the bruise?" Nadia gently touched it.

"Oh, that's nothing. Fell off a jet-ski and hit a rock." Laurie, who was both fearless and accident-prone, kissed her again. "Let's go. How is everyone? Is that damn parrot still alive?"

Harpo, who belonged to Nadia's grandmother Miriam, had a long-standing love-hate relationship with Laurie.

"Of course he's alive. You're still going to be asking that question when we're eighty." As Laurie expertly heaved his bags over one shoulder, Nadia said, "He's missed you like mad."

"Did he get my card?" Laurie had sent Harpo a postcard of a parrot in a mini deck chair with a tiny knotted hankie on his head.

"We tied it to his cage. He pecked holes in it, said something about gross exploitation and cruelty to parrots."

"That's because he has no sense of humor," Laurie said loftily. "When we get back I'm going to wrap his beak in Scotch tape."

They made their way out of the terminal and headed for the short-term parking lot, catching up on each other's latest news. When they reached Nadia's Renault, Laurie paused to admire the dented front wing she hadn't yet got around to getting repaired.

"Not bad." He bent to take a closer look. "So there you were, upside down in the ditch, when this complete stranger turns up out of the blue and persuades you to spend the night with him. Was it a hobby of his, d'you think? Another kind of bird-watching?"

Nadia, her arm still wrapped round Laurie's waist under the frayed sweater, pinched him beneath the ribs.

"The car skidded in the snow. It wasn't my fault. He came and rescued me. I was so grateful, I thought the least I could do was sleep with him... *ouch*."

"Very funny." Grinning, Laurie pinched her in return. "Come on, let's get out of here."

"Like them." Nadia tilted her head up to watch as another plane soared skyward.

Laurie's eyes followed the plane as it disappeared through the gunmetal-gray clouds. "That'll be me tomorrow. Off to Paris." He sounded resigned.

Nadia gave him a hug. "Not until tomorrow night. We've got a day and a half."

Laurie looked down at her. With a half smile he said, "I know."

Nadia, who was driving, felt her insides begin to churn during the twenty-minute drive back to North Bristol. An ill-defined squiggle of unease was warning her that something was up. On the surface they were both chattering away, talking nonstop as usual, but beneath the surface lay an undercurrent that filled her with fear.

She kept waiting for the feeling to go away, but it didn't. Finally they reached home and she pulled into the driveway of her family's house, having by this time narrowed it down to two possibilities.

"OK, let me just say this. Did you think I was serious when I told you I'd spent the night with that chap at the pub? I mean, d'you think I might actually have had sex with him? Because I didn't, I swear. I just said it as a joke."

"I know that. Of course I didn't think you were serious." Looking distinctly uncomfortable, Laurie raked his fingers through his streaky hair.

Nadia braced herself. OK, now she had to put the second question to him, the one she *really* didn't want to ask.

"So have you? Met someone else, I mean?"

"No." Finally Laurie shook his head. "I haven't. I'd never do that to you."

Phew. Well, that was a relief. Realizing that her fingers had gone tingly, Nadia slowly exhaled.

"But something's wrong," she persisted.

"Nothing's wrong. I'm fine."

The words were great, just what she wanted to hear. Sadly, they were coming from the mouth of the world's poorest liar. Laurie might not be seeing anyone else, but he certainly wasn't fine.

"Laurie, you can't pretend there isn't something wrong, just *tell* me—"

"Here he is, back at last! Darling boy, let me have a good look at you!" Miriam flung open the passenger door and clasped Laurie's face between her thin hands. Huge diamonds flashed on her fingers, there was mud caked beneath her lacquered nails, and for a slender seventy-year-old woman she had a surprisingly firm grip.

But when it came to seventy-year-olds, Miriam Kinsella was hardly par for the course. She could wear couture clothes or ancient corduroy trousers and men's shirts with equal panache. Her glossy black hair was fastened in a bun and, as ever, her dark eyes were heavily accentuated with kohl liner. As the inside of the car filled with Guerlain's L'Heure Bleue, Nadia was reminded that Miriam might spend an entire day gardening, attacking hedges on a stepladder and vigorously demolishing overgrown shrubs, but she wouldn't dream of doing it without first spraying on her favorite perfume.

How many seventy-year-olds had been stopped by the police for speeding at ninety-six miles an hour along the A38? More to the point, how many had batted their long eyelashes at the police and managed to persuade them to let her off?

"Beautiful as ever," Miriam pronounced, having deposited a crimson lipstick mark on Laurie's thin, tanned cheek. "Now come along inside. Are you hungry? Your father's still at the clinic but he'll be back soon. Good grief, darling, aren't they paying you for all that poncing about you do? Surely you can afford a better pair of trousers than that?"

Edward Welch, Laurie's father, was a neuropsychiatrist. Now sixty-six and no longer employed by the National Health Service, he had been unable to face complete retirement and retained a consulting room at one of Bristol's private clinics where he saw patients twice a week. It kept his own brain active, he maintained, staved off boredom, and gave him something to do other than the *Telegraph* crossword.

And lust helplessly after Miriam, thought Nadia as her grand-mother led the way into the house. Following the death of his wife, Josephine, five years earlier—and allowing for the obligatory period of mourning—Edward's feelings for Miriam had rapidly become apparent to all of them. Blindingly obvious, in fact. And what handsome, successful intelligent older man wouldn't be at-tracted to her?

The only fly in the ointment had been Miriam's steadfast refusal to return Edward's feelings. As far as she was concerned, he was a wonderful man, a dear friend and neighbor, and that was as far as it went. They enjoyed each other's company, played canasta like demons, visited the theater, took endless country walks, and were invited everywhere together, but Miriam had made it clear there could be no more to their relationship than that. And since Edward had no say in the matter, he had been forced to accept it. Being Miriam's friend and a sizable part of her life was infinitely prefer-able to not being her friend and being excluded from her life. When other, keener women periodically made a play for him, he simply wasn't interested. Compared with Miriam, there was no contest.

"Now, let's feed you up. I can do steak and mushrooms with fried potatoes." Bustling into the kitchen, Miriam threw open the king-sized fridge. "Or there's some chicken casserole left over from last night, or one of those microwave prawn-and-sole things, but it's only low-fat." The tone of Miriam's voice indicated exactly what she thought of low-fat microwave meals. Not nearly good enough for

Laurie. Checking out the freezer, she went on, "And there's an apple crumble in here, made it myself last week—"

"Miriam, chicken casserole's fine." Laurie was trying not to laugh. "I ate on the plane."

"But you need—"

"And I'm taking Nadia out to dinner, so I don't want to be stuffed. Markwick's," he added when Nadia raised her eyebrows. "Table's already booked."

Markwick's was one of her favorite restaurants. Nadia wondered if it was the equivalent of the guilty husband buying his wife roses and chocolates. From a petrol station. Then again, maybe she wasn't being fair; when he came home, Laurie was always taking her out to gorgeous restaurants.

She just didn't have a good feeling about it this time.

Still, whatever it was would have to wait a few hours. Miriam was here now, and Edward would be back soon, followed by Clare and Tilly—Laurie wasn't just hers, he was a part of the whole family.

Chapter 4

WHEN JAMES KINSELLA HAD married Leonie, it had been possibly the first truly impetuous action of his life. At the age of twenty-one, halfway through his accountancy training, it had been while he was driving home from work one evening that he'd first spotted her walking across the Downs in Clifton, casually thumbing a lift. Appalled, James had stopped his car and informed her in serious tones that hitchhiking was both foolhardy and an incredibly dangerous thing to do.

Laughing at his earnest expression, Leonie had thrown back her long blonde hair and said, "Are you dangerous?"

Realizing that she was laughing at him, probably because he wore spectacles and drove a Morris Minor, James had replied, "Of course not, but the man in the next car to stop might be."

Cheekily, she had yanked open the passenger door, climbed in, and said, "Better give me a lift then, before he turns up."

Three months later, Leonie had announced that she was pregnant. Two months after that, they'd been married. James had never met anyone like Leonie before. He'd never known there were people like her in the world. She was fearless, a true free spirit, with a breathtaking zest for life. And James was utterly enthralled. He was also happier than he'd ever been in his life.

It didn't take long for James to discover that free spirits don't necessarily make great mothers. Nor great wives, come to that. When Nadia was born, Leonie launched into her earth-mother phase, but it didn't last. Shortly before Nadia's first birthday, James came home from work to be greeted by his wife thrusting their daughter into his arms, yelling, "Why did nobody ever tell me being a mother was going to be so bloody *boring*?"

It had taken all James's energy to calm her down and persuade her not to walk out on them. Somehow they managed to stagger on for another year and a half. Then, just as their marriage reached its lowest ebb and separation seemed inevitable, Leonie discovered to her horror that she was pregnant again. Clare was born and the situation went from bad to worse. Leonie felt as if she was trapped in an airless Lucite cube. She loved her children but was unable to cope with their incessant demands. She was twenty-three, married to—of all things—an accountant, and a mother of two. Reality had fallen woefully short of her idyllic pre-pregnancy fantasies of parenthood.

It was while she was in Canford Park one late spring morning that she met Kieran Brown. Having taken Nadia and Clare along to commune with the tadpoles and baby frogs in the pond, she had made the unhappy discovery that Nadia's only interest, at the age of three, was in trying to eat them. Then Kieran, who was there with his own four-year-old son, had engaged her in conversation. He was an out-of-work actor and utterly charming. Bewitched by his attentions, Leonie promptly forgot all about the task in hand—that of persuading Nadia not to cram her mouth with tiny frogs—and arranged to meet Kieran that evening for a drink. When James asked her where she was going, as she flounced past him at the front door, she replied, "To talk to someone who understands me."

A fortnight later she packed her bags and ran off to Crete with Kieran Brown, whose own girlfriend was, frankly, glad to be shot of him.

Witnessing the extent of James's shock and desolation—and having inwardly predicted from the start that her son's marriage would come to a sticky end—Miriam had promptly taken charge and insisted that he and the children move in with her. Widowed but wealthy, her house was large enough and helping to look after Nadia and Clare would give her something to do. At forty-seven, Miriam had the energy of a twenty-year-old. And the children adored her. It was the obvious solution, Miriam had briskly informed her shell-shocked son, so he needn't even bother thinking of other ways he might manage.

Since James couldn't begin to imagine how else he might manage, he had accepted his mother's typically generous offer. The children adapted to the changes in their young lives with gratifying ease. It had, he decided with heartfelt relief, been the right thing to do. In a couple of years, maybe, the difficulties would ease and they would find a place of their own.

Twenty-three years on, it hadn't happened yet, and in the meantime, their unorthodox family setup had expanded to include Tilly, when Leonie had arrived at the house with a fatherless one-year-old and departed shortly afterwards without her.

—⁓—

Nadia felt like a suicide bomber with explosives strapped to her body and somebody else in charge of the detonator switch. She couldn't bear the suspense a minute longer.

"You're not eating," said Laurie. "Come on, try the duck. It's fantastic."

"I don't want to try the duck." Nadia kept her voice low; this was Markwick's after all. "I want you to try telling me the truth."

Laurie reached across the table, his fingers closing around hers. "Can't we just enjoy the meal?"

"Obviously not, if I can't even swallow a mouthful of it." The time had come, clearly, to detonate the bomb herself. "Laurie, either you tell me what's wrong or I stand up on this chair, scream at the top of my voice, and start throwing things."

Laurie smiled. "Go on then."

He didn't believe her. Causing scenes and throwing things wasn't what people did when they came to Markwick's. Sliding her hand from his, Nadia grabbed the basket of bread rolls from the table, pushed back her chair, and rose to her feet.

The look on her face told Laurie all he needed to know.

"OK, stop it, sit down." He blurted the words out as Nadia's left arm—the one clutching the bread basket—began to swing back. "I'll tell you."

The polar opposite of temperamental, Laurie abhorred public scenes.

Nadia froze. Did she really want to hear this? But then, how could she stand not knowing? Jerkily, aware of curious eyes upon her, she sat down.

God, it couldn't be normal for a heart to beat this fast.

"Fire away."

Laurie hesitated, pushing his fingers through his hair. But this time there was no Miriam around to fling open the car door and swoop, like Wonder Woman, to the rescue.

"OK." Another pause. "I think we should call it a day. We hardly ever see each other. It's not fair on you."

It was like plunging into an ice-cold swimming pool that you'd expected to be warm. There was a high-pitched ringing in Nadia's ears. Sadly, not quite loud enough to drown out the words Laurie had just uttered.

Then again, what had she expected? This was what happened when you pressed the detonator.

"Not fair on me or not fair on you?" Nadia couldn't believe she was managing to get the words out.

"Neither of us." Laurie shrugged miserably. "I'm sorry, I'm so sorry. I really don't want to do this."

Don't then.

Aloud, Nadia said, "But you're going to do it anyway."

"It's for the best. Everything's different now. Our lives have changed... You haven't done anything *wrong*," Laurie said helplessly. "It's just... oh Nad, you must know what I mean. This isn't anything to do with you."

Nadia was glad she hadn't thrown the basket of bread rolls at him now. Bread rolls weren't nearly vicious enough. Heavy china plates, that was what was called for. Plates that would crash with a satisfying amount of noise, preferably inflicting pain on Laurie and splattering meticulously-put-together sauces en route.

But would it help?

Struggling to get her bearings, she said, "Why didn't you tell me this afternoon?"

Laurie heaved a sigh. "Basically, I wanted our last weekend to be a good one. What was I supposed to do, call you from Barcelona and tell you over the phone? Get off the plane and just announce it? God, I'm not that much of a shit."

"But you couldn't seriously expect to pretend everything was fine!"

A muscle was twitching in Laurie's jaw. "I wanted to try. I thought we could at least have this last couple of days together. Well, a day and a bit," he amended.

"So when were you planning on actually breaking the news? Tomorrow afternoon, on the way back to the airport? My God, I can't believe we're here having this conversation. I thought we were happy and all this time you've been gearing yourself up to do this." Nadia shook her head in disbelief. "How long ago did you decide?"

"Nad, please, I feel bad enough as it is. Over the last few weeks, I suppose." Laurie was looking thoroughly miserable.

"A few *weeks*? Oh, great. So when I was stranded in the snow a fortnight ago telling that bloke how fantastically happy we were together, you were already planning the best way to dump me! Do you have any idea how stupid that makes me feel? Just think," Nadia rattled on, "if you'd told me in an email, I could have shagged him after all. And I would have, you know, I would have."

"Look, I'm sorry, I thought this was the best way."

"Oh yes, it's perfect, perfect! I'm ecstatic that you chose this way, I'm loving every minute! My boyfriend's very thoughtfully dumping me in my favorite restaurant. I'm fairly sure he's seeing someone else, although he doesn't have the guts to admit it—"

"No one else," said Laurie.

"And best of all, he tells me I haven't even done anything wrong! Which makes me feel *so* much better. Really." Nadia swallowed, she was trembling and her eyes were feeling dangerously hot. "It's just fabulous."

"But we can't carry on like this, never seeing each other. My booker at the agency's got me working nonstop for the next eight months." Laurie struggled to explain. "All over Europe, Australia, Japan, the States…"

"Fine. You don't have to explain. I'm not going to beg, if that's what you're worried about." Nadia had had enough. She felt sick. Then a thought occurred to her that made her feel sicker still. "And you weren't going to tell me until tomorrow." She marveled at Laurie's selfishness. "But we were going to spend the night together. We'd have made…" no, not made love, "…we'd have had sex, and you'd have known it was for the last time, but *I* wouldn't have known that, because *you* wouldn't have told me. Well, that's a really thoughtful finishing touch. What a shame it isn't going to happen now. We're both going to miss out on The Last Time."

It would have been nice, at this point, to have stalked out of the restaurant and disappeared into the black night. If she'd been in a film she would have done it.

But it wasn't a film, this was real life and it was raining outside. Quite honestly, she didn't see why she should be expected to fork out for a taxi.

Damn, she had a git of a boyfriend.

Ex-boyfriend.

Oh hell, this was going to be weird.

"I want to leave. I need a taxi. Give me twenty pounds," Nadia demanded.

"No."

"Bastard."

Laurie shook his head. "I really want us to stay friends."

"Well, I don't. Sod off."

"Nadia, this hasn't been easy. I'm only doing it because it's for the best."

That old line again.

"Oh, do me a favor," Nadia hissed across the table. "You're dumping me because you want to spend the next eight months shagging your way around Paris and Milan and New York and Sydney and Tokyo, because you're a jet-setter now and jet-setters only have sex with It-girls and supermodels."

"It's not that," said Laurie.

"Isn't it? I don't really care anyway." Of course, this was a massive lie, but it was still going to happen whether she cared or not. Her happy life was crumbling before her eyes like sugar lumps dropped in hot coffee and she had no one to blame but herself.

That stupid, *stupid* modeling competition.

Nadia dropped her head. She badly wanted to cry now. Noisily and nose-runningly. Furiously and violently. But she was buggered if she'd give Laurie the satisfaction.

He might look miserable, but he had absolutely no idea how truly awful she felt.

No more Laurie. It was just an unfathomable concept.

Raising her head, Nadia looked at him from beneath her eyelashes. All that mascara, what a waste.

"OK, it's over. But you were still going to sleep with me tonight."

Nadia waited, holding his gaze. "For the last time." Another pause, followed by a tiny playful smile. "Well? Do you still want to?"

It was as easy as asking a five-year-old if he wanted to open his Christmas presents a week early. She saw the spark of relief in his eyes as he reached across the table and squeezed her hand.

"Of course I still want to," said Laurie.

When in the history of the world had any man ever said no?

Feeling powerful for the first time that evening and deciding that sometimes it was worth forking out for a taxi, Nadia rose to her feet and said icily, "Well, that's a real shame, because you *can't*."

Chapter 5

How people's lives could change in the space of fifteen months. Well, some people's lives certainly changed, thought Nadia as she queued up at the supermarket checkout with a basket containing a bottle of hair detangler—yes, it was still uncontrollably curly, no change there—a tube of depilatory cream, and a box of Tampax. This was her precious day off and how was she spending it? Detangling her hair, defuzzing her legs, and watching the woman ahead of her in the queue idly leaf through a copy of this week's *OK!* magazine.

Thanks to her caring sharing sister, Nadia already knew that there was a photograph on page twenty-seven of Laurie in a dinner jacket, arriving at the Oscars hand in hand with one of the nominees for Best Supporting Actress. Clare, who read every glossy magazine going, had spotted the picture yesterday and had thoughtfully rushed downstairs to show Nadia just how much Laurie's life had changed.

"Imagine! The Oscars! At the Oscars with a girl like that! Bet she didn't get that dress in Top Shop. And they describe him as a model-turned-actor. Nadia, I'm trying to show you and you're not even looking."

Nadia had briefly been tempted to batter her sister to death with the iron in her hand. But Clare wasn't being deliberately cruel, she just possessed all the natural sensitivity of a velociraptor. It wouldn't occur to her that Nadia might not want to see her ex-boyfriend pictured in a magazine with some sensational-looking new girl.

Some Oscar nominee, at that.

Oh yes, Laurie was living a whole new charmed life now. Thanks to his hectic schedule, he hadn't been home for months. He had even fallen into acting as flukishly as he'd got involved with modeling, when his agency had sent him to appear in a pop video. At a party several weeks later, he'd met a director who recognized him from the video and promptly declared that he was casting Laurie in his new movie. Hollywood parties are stuffed to the gills with aspiring actors desperate for their big break. Laurie, who didn't even want one, got his. The movie part had been small, but Laurie's English charm and gift for comic timing meant he acquitted himself with honors. People had instantly sat up and begun to take notice. Knowing his luck, Nadia thought drily, by this time next year he'd be the one nominated for an Oscar.

"She used to go out with Johnny Depp." Clare was drooling over the accompanying article. "Hey, how cool is that? You've slept with someone who slept with someone who slept with Johnny Depp."

"I could always singe your ears," Nadia offered, holding up the iron.

"Ooh, *touchy*." Clare turned her attention to Harpo in his cage. "You'd think she'd be flattered, wouldn't you, Harpo? What's Nadia got, eh? What's Nadia got?"

It had taken her hours to teach him this one.

"Brrrkkk," Harpo squawked manically in return. "Nadia's got a fat arse."

Leaving the supermarket, Nadia made her way along Princess Victoria Street past the jewelers, the art gallery, and the scarily expensive shoe shop whose gleaming windows she didn't even dare to look in. Charlotte's Patisserie loomed ahead, their white chocolate éclairs whispering to her, luring her toward them. Of course they were expensive too, but compared with Italian sandals they were a complete bargain.

"Nadia!"

So wrapped up in the heavenly prospect of biting into a squishy, silky-smooth éclair that she barely registered her name being called behind her, Nadia yelped in alarm as a hand came to rest on her shoulder.

Oh God, had she accidentally shoplifted something from the supermarket? Had a burly store detective chased her down the street to inform her that she was about to be frog-marched back to the shop, arrested, and charged with—

"Oh, it's you!" Relief broke over her like a wave. Not that she'd ever actually shoplifted in her life (candy didn't count) but all it took was one moment of carelessness. And when you were as absent-minded as she was, it was always a worry.

Jay Tiernan was shaking his head with amusement. "I saw you walking past the art gallery. Well, I was almost sure it was you. This is amazing, I was just thinking about you the other day."

"Really? Why?" Flattered, Nadia pulled her stomach muscles in.

"My sister-in-law pranged her car. Smashed the front wing, just like you did. She was putting her lipstick on, looking in the mirror, when some wall spitefully jumped out and ran into her. Your face," he went on cheerfully, "when I put my hand on your shoulder. You jumped a mile."

"Yes, well. I thought you were a store detective." Apologetically, she held up her supermarket carrier.

Jay raised his eyebrows. "You've been *stealing*?"

"No! I just—"

"Something decent, I hope. Lobster and caviar at the very least, not economy baked beans and a couple of tins of cat food. If you're going to shoplift you might as well go for the good stuff—*oh*." Having whisked the carrier from her grasp and briskly surveyed the less than glamorous contents, he shook his head sorrowfully at Nadia. "You really don't have any idea how to shoplift, do you?

This is hopeless, hopeless. Why would you even *want* to steal stuff like this?"

"Very funny." Taking the bag back from him—oh well, could've been worse, she could have bought hemorrhoid cream—Nadia said, "What are you doing here anyway?"

"Here in Bristol, or here right-at-this-minute in Clifton?"

"Both."

"OK. Living in Bristol now. Moved down from Oxford a few months ago. And right at this minute—well, up until thirty seconds ago, I was standing in front of two paintings like *this*"—he struck a pose of chin-rubbing indecision—"trying to choose which one to buy."

"In the Harrington Gallery?" Nadia realized that this was where he must have been when he'd spotted her going past the window. "Couldn't you just have paid for the cheaper one and slipped the other one out under your jacket?"

His light brown eyes sparkled with approval. "Nice idea. You're a fast learner. Sadly, the owner of the gallery was *this* far away from me, making sure I wasn't about to try anything rash. Then again, if I had an accomplice we might stand a chance. You could divert his attention, go into labor or something, and all I'd have to do is grab both paintings, stuff them under my jacket, and leg it."

"Both paintings. Now you're getting greedy. Besides," Nadia smugly patted her flat—well, flattish—stomach, "I'm not nearly pregnant enough to be going into labor."

The expression on Jay's face altered by just a fraction. "How pregnant are you?"

"Not at all." She grinned. "Got you."

Did he look relieved? Actually, it was hard to tell.

Jay took her arm. "Come on. I've bumped into you now, this has to be fate. It's your job to help me decide." He paused. "Unless you're in a desperate hurry to get home."

All of a sudden he was sounding concerned. Nadia shrugged and shook her head in a free and easy manner.

"No hurry."

"Quite sure about that? Promise me you're not growing werewolf legs as we speak?" Raising his eyebrows, Jay glanced at the shopping bag containing the offending tube of depilatory cream.

Nadia shot him a sunny smile. "Oh, that's not for me. Whenever I meet a man who thinks he's really hilarious, I like to sneak into his house at night and squeeze depilatory cream into his bottle of shampoo."

She could have told Jay just how well she knew the Harrington Gallery. Not well as in sleeping-with-the-owner, but she'd been dragged along to a fair few preview nights in her time.

Nadia chose not to mention this as he pulled her inside. Werewolf legs indeed.

"This one," Jay announced, stepping in front of the first paint-ing. Moments later she found herself being swiveled by the elbows to her left and planted before a second canvas. "Or this one?"

Nadia opened her mouth to speak, then shut it again.

It just had to be, didn't it?

The painting on the right was the larger of the two, a towering dramatic mountainscape featuring a lot of grape-colored sky with the occasional shaft of sunlight breaking through the clouds. Very moody. Almost biblical. That is, until your gaze was gradually drawn to the bottom left-hand corner of the picture, where a couple were kissing in an old-fashioned red telephone box.

Nadia smiled to herself. Nice touch. The painting, on sale for seven hundred and fifty pounds, was by an artist she hadn't heard of.

The second one, priced at five hundred and twenty pounds, had been painted by Clare, her sister.

If these were the two Jay had been tempted by, he clearly had a sense of humor. Clare's style was quirky, offbeat, and character-led, like Beryl Cook without the acres of fat. This particular work, executed in bold watercolors overlaid with ink, depicted a wedding reception complete with naughty pageboys, lecherous bridegroom, gossiping guests, and the bride's mother passed out with one hand clutching a bottle of Pomagne and her head on the table. The bride, meanwhile, was at the door legging it with one of the waiters.

The painting was titled "Happy Ever After."

Typical Clare.

Not that Clare was especially cynical. She simply delighted in depicting the misfortunes of others.

"Well?" said Jay, at her side.

"Hmm." Thoughtfully, Nadia studied her sister's painting from all angles. Behind his desk at the far end of the gallery, Thomas Harrington put down the phone and spotted her. Catching his eye, Nadia indicated with a faint shake of her head that she'd prefer him not to come over and greet her like an old friend. Or, for that matter, like the sister of one of his exhibiting artists.

Clare had spent her years at art college in typically riotous fashion; it had seemed almost unfair when she had emerged at the end of the course in the upper division, when other students had worked far more diligently and come away with so much less. When Clare had begun selling her paintings—not many, but enough—it had seemed even more unfair. How many graduates from art school, after all, managed to attain such dizzy heights? Ten percent, thought Nadia, if that. This was Clare all over; she had never done a proper day's work in her life.

Still, mustn't be bitter.

"Which one?" Jay prompted in her ear.

"Honestly?"

"Honestly."

Nadia, who was great at being honest, said, "If I had that much money to spend, I'd be in the shoe shop three doors down, buying Italian leather shoes with four-inch diamond-encrusted heels."

Gravely Jay said, "But I'd look stupid in four-inch heels."

"And they can be tricky if you're not used to them." Nadia glanced sympathetically at his feet. "Maybe you're best sticking to paintings."

"I think so too." He paused. "And?"

"It's your money. You should be the one to decide." She recalled Clare's remarks earlier as she'd ogled the photos of Laurie in the magazine. "But since you ask, I prefer the one with the phone box."

"Really?"

"It's unexpected. You don't see it at first. The other one's more all-over funny, a bit slapstick." As guilt belatedly kicked in, Nadia amended, "Then again, it's still good. And cheaper."

"Oh well, that's it then. If I choose it now I'd look like a lousy cheapskate." Turning to Thomas Harrington, Jay said cheerfully, "I'll just have to take the one with the phone box."

Leaving Nadia to wonder if he would have bought Clare's painting if it had carried a price tag of nine hundred pounds.

Chapter 6

When Jay had done the credit card thing and Thomas Harrington had murmured in her ear, "It's no skin off my nose, but your sister's going to beat you to a pulp if she gets to hear about this," Nadia allowed herself to be led away to a pavement café for a drink to celebrate.

To celebrate the fact that she was still whole and unpulped, probably.

Oh well, it was as good a reason as any.

"So tell me what you've been doing with yourself. Are we safe out here, by the way?" Clearly amused, Jay indicated the magazine rack standing outside the newsagents across the narrow street. "Your boyfriend's not likely to leap from the pages of *GQ* and lay one on me?"

Inwardly Nadia squirmed. Oh God, how she had boasted about her wonderful relationship, about the deep love and trust she and Laurie had had for each other.

"That was ages ago. We broke up. And if you say I told you so, I'll pour salt in your coffee. Or if you smirk," she added as the corners of Jay's mouth—predictably—began to twitch. "Smirking's not allowed either. We just aren't together anymore and I'm absolutely fine about it. How about you?"

"I'm fine about it too." Hastily he covered his coffee with his hand. "And I'm not smirking. It's just really nice to see you again."

The next time Nadia looked at her watch, a whole hour, incredibly, had gone by. She had learned that Jay was now living here in

Clifton, just around the corner in fact, in Canynge Road. Still in property development, he was buying up and renovating neglected houses in the area—well, employing a team of people to do the actual dirty work for him—then selling them on at a hopefully spectacular profit.

Although if he could afford to impulse-buy paintings like the one currently swathed in bubble-wrap and propped up against their table, he had to be doing something right.

"And how's your job going? Weren't you working in a nursery or—no, hang on"—Jay snapped his fingers—"a garden center, wasn't it?"

Faintly miffed that he'd had to struggle to recall her line of work, after she'd asked him if he was still in the property business, Nadia nodded and tried not to feel less memorable to him than he'd clearly been to her.

"Out at Almondsbury. Yes, I'm still there. It's great, I love it."

This was a massive exaggeration. Her job was OK, verging on the tedious. The plants and flowers themselves were fine, but when customers came back complaining that the pot of fuchsias they'd bought three years earlier had just died—as if she'd personally doused them with cyanide—well, it was enough to make you wonder if some people should be allowed to buy plants in the first place. And as for the gnomes…

"You love it," Jay echoed thoughtfully. He paused. "That's a shame."

"Why? Why is it a shame?" Nadia sat up a bit straighter, attempting to gauge the meaning of that regretful shake of his head. "I don't love it that much."

"OK. On a scale of one to ten. How much do you love your job?"

"Two," Nadia promptly replied.

Jay let out a low whistle. "Two. You're right, you don't love it that much."

"It's the gnomes. We sell gnomes." Nadia pulled a face, willing him to understand. "Anyway, I didn't want to sound like one of those people who whine on about their boring job but can't be bothered to get off their fat backside and find something better."

Even though, basically, this described her situation to a T.

"But you know a lot about gardening?" said Jay.

"I know everything." Nadia experienced a flicker of hope. "I'm Charlie Dimmock in a bra." How that woman ever managed to work without one was a mystery to her. "Why?"

"Ever designed one yourself?"

"A bra or a garden? Come on," Nadia pleaded, "tell me. What's this all about?"

Jay shrugged. "Maybe nothing. I need a gardener, that's all."

He needed a gardener? Hey, say no more.

"But that's great, I can fit that in, no problem. In my spare time," Nadia explained eagerly. "I mean, how long would you want me for, a couple of hours a week?"

Jay shook his head. "Much more than that."

Blimey, he must have a huge garden. Without thinking, Nadia said, "How big is it?"

Oops. As the actress said to the bishop.

Looking as if he were trying not to smile, Jay leaned back in his chair. "When I buy a wreck of a house and do it up, it generally has a wreck of a garden to go with it. I need someone to start from scratch, transform it into something superb. This isn't just a matter of mowing the lawn and digging out a few weeds. I'm talking clearance, relandscaping, planting, the lot."

"I could do that!" Nadia sat up, her skin beginning to tingle. "I did landscaping at college. I'm a hard worker and I'm stronger than I look."

Crikey, Jay had talked about fate earlier. This really *was* fate.

"I was using a firm from Winterbourne, but they weren't that reliable. Let me down a couple of times."

"I wouldn't let you down." She was dimly aware of not playing it cool, of sounding disgustingly eager. Oh, well… "I'd *never* let you down, I promise!"

Jay hesitated, evidently reluctant to hand her the job on the spot. "I put an ad in the local paper last week. I've had quite a few responses."

"Maybe," Nadia said promptly, "but none of them have slept with you and I have. That has to count for something."

Damn, damn, she *knew* she should have had sex with him.

From the look of amusement in Jay's brown eyes she could tell he was thinking the same thing.

Nadia held her breath and silently cursed her faithfulness. If she didn't get this job it would all be Laurie's fault. Him and his lousy promises that they'd be together forever. God, she wished she could hate him as ferociously as he deserved.

"Please," said Nadia. "I'm a great gardener."

Jay thought for a moment. "Do you have one you could show me?"

His third cup of coffee, half drunk, had grown cold in front of him. He clearly didn't have any pressing appointments for the afternoon, and it wouldn't take long anyway. Feeling quite masterful, Nadia gathered up her plastic carrier, rose to her feet, and said, "Let's go."

Well, this was fate after all. May as well make the most of it.

———

It would have been nice if the house could have been empty, but Nadia's home seldom was. Doing her best to sound businesslike, rather than like a girl bringing her boyfriend back for the first time and shyly introducing him to her family, she led Jay into the kitchen and announced, "Gran, this is Jay Tiernan, he needs a gardener so I've brought him here to show him what I can do. Jay, this is Miriam Kinsella, my grandmother. And Edward Welch, our neighbor."

Miriam and Edward were watching horse racing on TV while finishing a late lunch of garlic bread, Milano salami, and a bottle of Barolo. Betting on the horses was Miriam's latest passion and her language when she failed to win was spectacular. Since Miriam insisted on betting only on horses ridden by jockeys whose colors matched whatever she happened to be wearing that day, her language was frequently spectacular.

Today she was wearing an emerald-green shirt and white trousers. Swiveling round on her chair, Miriam waggled her fingers at Jay.

"Won't shake hands, mine are all messy and garlicky. Well, I can see why Nadia would want to work for you. Will you have a glass of red, Jay? Edward, why don't you open another bottle? Come along, pull up a chair and join us. Darling, *well done*," she stage-whispered to Nadia. "And those *eyes*. Just what you need to cheer you up, wherever did you find him?"

Nadia briefly closed her own eyes and wished the good fairy could have granted her a nice normal apple-cheeked gray-bunned, apron-wearing grandmother. It was a good job she loved Miriam. Otherwise she would have been forced to lock her in the attic years ago.

Jay was grinning broadly.

"And if you think that's embarrassing," Nadia told him, "imagine what it was like for me at fourteen."

"Two more glasses," Miriam instructed Edward, whom she tended to treat like a butler.

"No, don't bother," Nadia shook her head, "we're not staying. Just five minutes in the garden, then Jay has to leave. Your horse just fell," she added, as the racing commentator went into overdrive and a rolled-up ball of jockey in emerald-green narrowly avoided being trampled by the rest of the field.

"Honestly," Miriam exclaimed in disgust—and with remarkable restraint. "I hope he breaks both his legs."

Nadia hastily led Jay through to the garden. "Sorry about my grandmother. She does have her good points, I just can't think of any right now."

"Doesn't bother me." Crossing the terrace, Jay stood with his hands on his hips and surveyed the grounds stretching before him.

The backdrop was provided by a curving amphitheater of mature trees—beeches, ash, and cedar. In the foreground, free-form beds of ostrich feather fern, oriental poppies, and delphiniums bordered the emerald lawn. From the lily pond on the left, a winding stream snaked down to a larger pond in the bottom right-hand corner of the garden. Fuchsia bushes sported pink and violet flowers like twinkle lights. Everything was planted to look as though it hadn't been deliberately planted at all—the gardening equivalent of a supermodel sporting just-got-out-of-bed hair that had actually taken five stylists three hours to achieve. Nadia, covertly watching Jay, crossed her fingers behind her back. She had slogged her guts out to create this garden and as far as she was concerned it was perfect.

But would Jay think so?

Finally he spoke. "You did all this?"

"Absolutely. Flat lawn before, I can show you the photos to prove it. I did this three years ago," Nadia told him with pride. "Every last inch of it myself, down to carrying these flagstones." She stamped her heel against the pale honey Cotswold stone covering the terrace. It had almost killed her, but no need for Jay to know that. Let him think she was Superwoman and be suitably impressed.

"I'm impressed," said Jay.

Phew. Nadia exhaled.

"I knew you would be. Otherwise I wouldn't have brought you out here. So, do I get the job?"

"I still have other people to see. The appointments are all set up."

"Cancel them," said Nadia. "You don't need them anymore. You've got me."

As she said it, a half-remembered snippet of conversation floated into her mind. Janey, one of the other girls at the garden center, confiding over coffee that she'd applied for a gardening job advertised in last week's *Evening Post*.

"I shouldn't." Jay glanced at her, then broke into a grin. "But what the hell. OK."

Yesss! A fast-moving, quick-thinking, executive-decision-maker, unconcerned with breaking the rules and letting other people down. In other words, absolutely not the kind of person to *ever* get romantically involved with.

In fact, the kind who'd cause you nothing but grief. The sensible part of Nadia's brain carefully noted this fact down in her beige leather-bound notebook. The hopeless part gave a happy shiver of anticipation and wondered what her new boss looked like naked.

Because she was almost sure he fancied her. You could generally tell.

"Excellent," Nadia said happily.

Jay smiled. "I'm pleased you're pleased. Now, I've drunk several cups of coffee." He gestured toward the house. "Could you point me in the direction of the bathroom?"

Point him in the direction? Blimey, what did he have in his trousers, a fireman's hose?

But in deference to the fact that he was her new boss, Nadia didn't say this aloud.

Chapter 7

HAVING SHOWN JAY THROUGH to the downstairs cloakroom, Nadia returned to the sunny garden and sat down on the wooden bench to mentally compose her letter of resignation.

> *Dear Mr. Blatt,*
>
> *It gives me great pleasure to inform you that I have been offered a much nicer job than the awful, boring one I've been stuck with for the last two years and I shall also be working for a much nicer—*

"So?" A female voice behind her made Nadia jump. "What have you done with him?"

Damn, Clare had said she'd be out this afternoon.

"Done with who?"

"I've just been told"—Clare's tone was arch—"that you have a man out here with you. In fact, I was told that you had a rather spectacular man out here with you. Naturally, I had to come and see this vision for myself. So where is he? Buried in the compost heap? Tied to a tree? Manacled to the lawn mower and locked in the shed? Nad, how many times have I told you, this isn't the way to stop a man running out on you, they have to *want* to stay."

Nadia knew who she'd like to manacle to the lawn mower.

"He's gone to the loo, and as soon as he comes back we're leaving." She mentally resolved to have Jay out of the house in three seconds flat. "Anyway, I thought you were out this afternoon. You said you were meeting Josie for lunch and the two of you were going to hit the shops afterwards."

"We were, until her boss overheard her on the phone talking about it." Clare, who had never worked office hours in her life, shook her head in disgust. "He said any more three-hour lunch breaks and she'd be getting her pink slip. All she's allowed is fifty minutes. I mean, it's a disgrace, what can anyone do in fifty minutes?"

Nadia, keen to be gone, jumped to her feet and said, "I'd better find—"

"Oh, here he is!" Having leapt up with even more alacrity than Nadia, Clare exclaimed, "We thought you'd escaped! Hi, I've just been hearing all about you."

No you haven't, thought Nadia but it was too late. Clare was already introducing herself, mentally giving Jay Tiernan the once-over and wittering on about handcuffs and lawn mowers. She'd never been what you'd call shy.

Sometimes you do something silly on the spur of the moment then spend the next six months or six years regretting it and praying you won't get found out. Like persuading a virtual stranger in an art gallery not to buy one of your sister's paintings. Because in all honesty, what were the chances of her ever getting to hear about it?

Sadly, in Nadia's case it took about six seconds.

"I've just seen the painting in your sitting room," Jay announced. "Why didn't you tell me you already had one by the same artist?"

Oh fuck.

Right on cue, the words of an old song wafted into Nadia's mind. *Who's sorry now?*

Puzzled, Clare said, "In our sitting room?"

"I wasn't snooping, I promise. The door was open and I spotted it on the wall." Jay smiled at her while Nadia sent frantic telepathic messages instructing him to Stop Right There. "I bumped into

Nadia in Clifton this afternoon and dragged her into the Harrington Gallery. Couldn't decide between two paintings. She told me which one to buy."

Clearly, those telepathic signals hadn't worked. Stumbling over her words, Nadia said hastily, "Oh no, that's not true, I didn't *tell* you—"

"And?" Clare interrupted. Her eyes were glittering, her face dangerously pale. "Which painting did she say you should buy? The one by the artist whose work is hanging in our living room?" Horrible elongated pause. "Or the other one?"

As if she hadn't figured it out already.

"The other one." Now it was Jay's turn to hesitate. "Er, sorry, have I put my foot in it? Is the artist a friend of yours?"

"Yes, Nadia, do tell us." Clare's tone was icy. "*Is* the artist a friend of yours?"

"I… I just—"

"You complete cow!" roared Clare. "How *could* you?" Turning to face Jay, she bellowed, "*I'm* the artist, I painted those pictures and this is the kind of support I get from my own sister! I mean, what did I ever do to deserve this?"

What had she ever done? Ha, only about a million things.

"OK, OK, maybe I should have told Jay I knew you. But then he'd have felt he had to buy your painting. He asked me which one I preferred," Nadia said hurriedly, "and I told him the truth."

"You bitch! And which one *did* you prefer?" Professional rivalry meant Clare was compelled to spit out the question.

"Big mountains. Little telephone box."

"Oh, for crying out loud, that piece of crap!"

"I'll take it back to the gallery," Jay offered. "Swap it for yours."

"See?" demanded Nadia. "Now you've made him feel guilty. He likes the other one best but he's prepared to take it back because you're acting like a big baby. Aren't you embarrassed?"

"Only at having a sister like you." Clare's eyes blazed as she spun back round to face Jay. "She's jealous, that's all it is. Because I can paint and she can't. Nadia spends her days selling plastic gnomes and humping sacks of gravel into the trunks of people's cars. She can't even keep a boyfriend, they all run off and leave her, and who can blame them? That's another reason she's jealous of me. If I were you I'd get out quick, and thank your lucky stars you found out what she's like before it's too late."

And with that she stalked off into the house.

"Well," said Jay finally. "That was... interesting."

"Sorry." Nadia gritted her teeth. She couldn't think of anything else to say.

"Had we better be making a move?"

"Yes."

Keen to avoid any further contact with her family, Nadia led him round the side of the house to where her car was parked on the drive.

As she fumbled with the keys, the sitting-room window was flung open and Harpo screeched, "Nadia's got a fat arse!"

Jay looked startled. "Good grief. Is that your sister?"

"My grandmother's parrot." As soon as the words were out, Nadia wished she'd just said yes.

And then Clare's voice came bellowing through the same window: "She's desperate to get married and have babies, you know!"

OK, enough.

"Excuse me." Nadia abruptly wheeled round. "Won't be a moment."

Aware of Jay's eyes on her back, she crunched up the gravel path and stormed through the front door, slamming it hard behind her.

"Ow!" shrieked Clare, clutching the side of her face. She lunged forward but Nadia was too quick for her. Like the SAS, she was in and out in less than five seconds.

"Sorry about that." Jumping into the driver's seat, Nadia started the engine.

Jay replied with amusement, "I don't think you are."

Thankfully he didn't appear too shocked.

"Well. She deserved it. Sometimes only a really good slap will do." Nadia paused. "We're sisters. It's allowed. Laurie used to call them our Oasis moments."

"Got it." Jay grinned. "You're Noel, she's Liam. She winds you up, you retaliate. But you love each other really."

"I suppose. Anyway, it wasn't true," said Nadia. "About me being desperate to get married and have babies. Not that it's relevant," she added hastily, "but it still isn't true."

This would have been an appropriate moment for Jay to have told her that she didn't have a fat arse either—because she *didn't*—but all he did was nod.

Her heart sinking, Nadia drove him back to his car in silence.

As he lifted the bubble-wrapped painting off the backseat, she said, "I expect you've changed your mind now about giving me the job. Had second thoughts about taking on a mad sister-slapper."

"One thing," said Jay. "Why did you persuade me to buy this painting?"

"Honestly?"

"Honestly."

"I liked it better." Nadia paused. "And also Clare was having a dig at me this morning about my ex-boyfriend. She knew she was getting on my nerves and she was really enjoying it. But I really do prefer that painting."

He nodded. "OK."

"OK what?"

"Better hand in your notice at the garden center."

Nadia exhaled with relief, a huge smile spreading unstoppably across her face. "You're sure?"

"Hey, I have a brother, I know what it's like. We used to fight all the time."

Heroically, she suppressed a wild urge to fling her arms round him. "Used to? You don't still fight?"

Jay shook his head. "Not anymore."

"Oh, thank you!"

"Here, give me a ring in the next day or two." He passed her a business card from his wallet.

Clutching it like a winning lottery ticket to her chest, Nadia said fervently, "You won't regret this. I promise not to slap any of your clients."

"Glad to hear it," said Jay. "And it might be an idea to check the seal on that bottle of hair remover. Make sure it hasn't mysteriously got squeezed into your shampoo."

Nadia knew she was going to enjoy working for him. Still beaming like an idiot, she headed for her car.

"One other thing," Jay called out.

She turned back. "What?"

He'd been watching her walk down the street. "The parrot was wrong."

Chapter 8

THE LETTER HAD ARRIVED this morning. Alone in her bedroom, sitting at her dressing table, Miriam carefully unfolded it and read it for the third time.

This was the trouble with the world today. Too much information technology. Everyone had access to computers and the computers knew too damn much about everything.

It had all been so simple fifty-odd years ago. If you wanted to disappear, you could. You just did it, moved to another part of the country and put the past firmly behind you where it belonged. The world carried on exactly as it had before, and you made a new life for yourself. A happy life.

And it *had* been a happy life, she'd made sure of that.

What was the point of dragging all this old stuff up now?

Raising her head, Miriam gazed impatiently at her reflection in the beveled mirror. It was the eyes, of course. They were what had given her away. She was seventy years old and the rest of her body was showing all the normal signs of wear and tear. But her eyes had remained the same.

Bloody Edward, this was all his fault. Him and his illustrious career in neuro-sodding-psychiatry. When he had been invited to perform the official opening of a new research institute in Berkshire it hadn't occurred to Miriam for a moment that accompanying him to the ceremony would have such far-reaching consequences. When a press photographer had taken their picture together and asked for her name she had given it to him without a second thought.

Who could have imagined that someone might spot her face in the newspaper, put two and two together (as, of course, they had), and actually manage to track her down through some voting register on the Internet?

Miriam heaved a sigh of irritation mingled with fear. Didn't privacy count for anything these days? Did the people who set up these sites ever stop to think how much trouble they could be stirring up?

It had all happened fifty-two years ago, for heaven's sake. One little blip, that was all. After fifty-two years you'd think you were safe from the consequences of a blip.

Tempting though it was to simply rip the letter up and throw it in the bin, Miriam knew she couldn't do that. Carefully she picked up her fountain pen, copied the sender's home address onto the front of the envelope, and crossed out her own. In big capitals she wrote "RETURN TO SENDER. NOT KNOWN AT THIS ADDRESS." Then she slid the letter back into the torn-open envelope and taped it shut.

Better not stick it in the postbox across the road; when their local postman came to collect the letter he might think she'd gone barking mad and insist on giving it back to her. Pleased with herself for having thought of this, Miriam put the letter in her shirt pocket—she'd post it later, somewhere suitably anonymous—and picked up her red lipstick, ready to give her mouth another coat.

The door flew open.

"Can you see a mark on my face?" shouted Clare. "Fingerprints?"

"No, darling."

"*There*," Clare insisted, moving closer and pointing frantically to her left cheek.

There was a very faint mark, a smidgen of redness.

Miriam patted her hand. "You poor, brave child. Let's take you to the ER this minute and demand only the finest plastic surgeon."

"Don't make fun. It hurts." Peering into the mirror, Clare prodded her cheek, encouraging the redness. "Nadia slapped me."

"Did she? Never mind, darling, I expect you deserved it."

"I did *not* deserve it. Honestly," Clare raged, "I came up here for some sympathy and you're taking her side. I should have ripped all her hair out." Her eyes narrowed. "Who was that bloke she brought back anyway?"

"Hmm?" Leaning closer to the mirror, Miriam applied her lipstick then pressed her lips together. "The rather nice looking one?"

"I didn't notice," lied Clare.

"Well, Nadia mentioned something about a new job. He seemed charming, I must say."

"He was going to buy one of my paintings at the Harrington and bloody Nadia persuaded him not to." Clare was still incensed.

"Oh well, I'm sure she had her reasons. Maybe you did something to upset her."

"But I didn't!"

"Like wittering on about Laurie," Miriam said.

"Oh please. All I did was mention that he was at the Oscars."

"You know she doesn't like it."

Clare snorted in disgust. "Not my fault she's touchy."

"You're twenty-three years old, Nadia's twenty-six." Miriam paused to squish L'Heure Bleue on her wrists and throat. "And you still fight like a couple of eight-year-olds. Next time I'll chuck a bucket of water over the pair of you."

"That's because we're dysfunctional. We had a disturbed childhood."

"What rubbish, you were spoiled rotten. And you could make a start on those potatoes—your father and Tilly will be home by six."

Clare gave up. She wasn't going to get any sympathy. And as for peeling potatoes, yuk.

"Want me to post that for you?" Expertly changing the subject, she pointed to the half inch of envelope protruding from Miriam's shirt pocket.

Miriam pressed her hand protectively over the envelope, pushed back her seat, and stood up. At least the return address on it was Edinburgh, a nice safe distance away.

"No thanks."

Twice a week, instead of catching the bus home at four o'clock, Tilly had after-school activities. On Tuesdays she had French club and on Fridays it was netball. Following these, she would walk the quarter mile from school to the offices where James worked as an accountant and get a lift home with him when he finished at around five thirty.

At first when this arrangement had begun, Tilly had waited in the reception area on the ground floor of the office building, where the sofas were leather and squashy and the receptionists coolly professional in their chignons and high heels. The reading matter, immaculately arranged on the glass coffee tables, was a scintillating choice of the *Financial Times*, the *Telegraph* or the latest edition of *Accountancy Today*.

Oh yes, all her favorites.

Nowadays, Tilly much preferred to spend her time loitering in the newsagents on the corner, a hundred yards down from the offices. She always bought something small, chewing gum or Tic Tacs, to give herself authorized customer status. Then, settling down by the rows of magazines she would flip through them, always very careful not to crease any papers or bend any spines.

It was a lovely place to wait, cluttered and friendly, cozy and welcoming. Having decided that Tilly wasn't yet another shoplifting adolescent, the woman who worked in the shop had soon relaxed and allowed her to browse in peace until James appeared fifteen or so minutes later to buy his copy of the evening paper and take her home.

The advice columns were what Tilly liked best. It was always comforting to read about other people's less than perfect lives. Compared to some, she'd actually got off quite lightly.

The other items she was drawn to were the true-life stories in the women's magazines, the ones where mothers revealed how they had risked their lives in some way or another in order to save their children. Masochistically, Tilly devoured these tales of high drama and maternal devotion. On one level she envied them so much she could almost feel the jealousy rising like bile in her tightly closed throat. On another, she was unable to stop herself fantasizing that maybe one day the same thing might happen to her. That if she and her mother were trapped in a smashed-up car and there was only time for the fire brigade to cut one of them free before the engine burst into flames, Leonie would scream, "Just save my daughter, don't worry about me!"

Or, slightly less drastically, say she needed a kidney transplant or something, and her mother was the only match, but because Leonie had some allergy to anesthetics, there was a real danger she wouldn't make it through the operation. But still she'd insist on going through with it, because, "Darling Tilly, you're the most important thing in the world to me, all I care about is getting you well again!" And in this fantasy, Leonie's life could hang in the balance for a bit, but eventually (of course) she'd pull through and they'd live happily ever after, just like the brave, loving families in the true-life magazines.

Well, everyone was allowed to have fantasies, weren't they? Even if all the other girls in her school seemed to center theirs around Robbie Williams.

Tilly carried on carefully turning the pages of *Take-A-Break*, while other customers came and went. She knew that the woman who worked there was called Annie because a lot of the customers were regulars, dropping in to pick up their newspapers, magazines, scratchcards, and cigarettes. A fair number of them greeted her by name and stopped to chat for a minute or two, usually about the weather, the latest scandal to hit the headlines or the fact that the lottery ticket Annie had sold them last week had been a dud; it hadn't won them a thing.

"Try a bit harder this time, Annie," they'd urge when she'd laughingly apologized, and with unfailing good humor Annie would go along with the joke.

She was old, probably in her forties, Tilly guessed, but she had a kind face, a ready smile, and haphazardly tied-back blonde hair that couldn't appear to make up its mind whether to be curly or straight.

Tilly turned as the bell above the door went *ting*, expecting it to be James. But a really ancient woman enveloped in an ankle-length fur coat was shuffling in, peering anxiously across the shop at Annie.

"Hello, dear, I don't know if you can help me. I'm looking for my husband. Has he been in?"

She was carrying a large holdall and wearing frayed slippers. Annie, her expression changing, darted out from behind the counter and made her way over to the woman.

"I'm so sorry, Edna, he hasn't. I haven't seen him all day. Never mind, I'm sure he'll be home soon." Sliding her arm through Edna's, she went on brightly, "Tell you what, why don't I see you across the road? When you get back, you can make yourself a nice cup of tea."

Tilly watched them go, briefly wondering if this was a CCTV trick to see if she'd start shoveling bars of chocolate into her pockets the moment she thought she was alone in the shop. To prove her innocence, she put the copy of *Take-A-Break* carefully back on the rack, stayed rooted to the spot, and kept her hands in full view.

There didn't appear to be a CCTV camera in the shop, but Tilly was taking no chances. Last week there had been a documentary on television about someone in America who'd gone to the electric chair and been found three years later to have been innocent.

Annie was back in less than a minute, panting as she rushed through the door.

"Oh good, you're still here. My boss would have my guts for garters if I left the shop empty! And technically, I didn't." She smiled and shook her head. "Poor old Edna, she breaks my heart. That's the fifth time this week she's been in."

"Where does her husband go?" said Tilly.

"But that's just the thing, he doesn't go anywhere. He's dead."

"*Dead?*" Taken aback, Tilly glanced at the door. "If he's dead, shouldn't you tell her?"

"I have," sighed Annie. "Poor lamb, her memory's gone. But when I do tell her, she gets dreadfully upset. So it's easier not to mention it. Either way she'll have forgotten again by the time she gets home."

How awful. Tilly wondered how the old woman felt, endlessly wandering the streets in search of her husband. She'd got lost in Debenhams once, when she was six, had wandered off while Nadia and Clare were busy trying on feather boas. She could still remember the awful sensation of icy escalating panic as she'd stumbled blindly through Hats and Headscarves, her heart beating faster and faster as she'd wondered if she'd ever see her sisters again. Until about thirty seconds later when, alerted by her shrill screams, Clare had cornered her by the glove rack, given her a swift clip round the ear, and told her to stop making that horrible racket.

Now another customer came into the shop, a jovial man in workman's clothes. Tilly watched him buy an angling magazine and a lottery ticket, and listened to him banter with Annie about last week's ticket being faulty.

"You must get fed up with people saying that," Tilly ventured when the man had left.

"Tell me about it." Annie rolled her eyes in a long-suffering manner. "And they always think they're being so witty and original. Like people bumping into that actor who did *One Foot In The Grave* and going: 'I doooon't belieeeve it!' You just have to smile and play along, and act like you haven't heard it a zillion times before. But they're nice people," she hastily amended. "It's just a bit of fun. Better than not bothering to talk at all."

"I like it in here," said Tilly. "It's friendly. I mean, as long as you don't mind me waiting here?"

"Don't be daft. Of course I don't mind. Better than hanging around outside, especially when it's raining. Here's your dad now," said Annie, glancing up as James came through the door.

"OK, pigeon? Ready to go?"

Tilly loved it when James called her pigeon, almost as much as she loved the way he flung a fatherly arm around her shoulder. She waited at his side while he dug into his pocket for change and picked up a copy of the *Evening Post*.

Innocently Tilly said, "Fancy buying a lottery ticket?"

"I don't buy lottery tickets. Waste of money." James pulled a face. "Tried it once, didn't win."

Tilly and Annie grinned at each other.

"What have I said now?" protested James.

"Nothing."

"Come on then, let's get home and find out what they've cooked for us tonight."

"Bye," said Annie.

Turning, Tilly gave a little wave and said shyly, "See you soon."

Chapter 9

"So who is he?" Clare demanded, appearing in Nadia's bedroom doorway. "Apart from a complete wuss so incapable of making up his own mind that he has to get a girl to do it for him?"

But from her tone of voice, Nadia knew the fracas was behind them. This was Clare's way of indicating that she was prepared to forgive her. Probably because she was going out with Piers tonight and wanted to borrow something to wear.

"His name's Jay Tiernan. He's my new boss." Nadia certainly hoped he was, anyway. Keen not to hang around, she'd already visited the garden center this afternoon and handed in her notice. "And he's not a wuss," she added, since it was important to demonstrate loyalty toward one's employer. "He's a property developer."

"Oh well, you were fed up with the garden place. All those gnomes." Making her way over to the wardrobe, Clare began idly flicking through the clothes hanging there. "Is he married?"

"Don't know. Didn't ask." *Hope not*, thought Nadia.

"Fancy him?"

"No!"

Clare smirked. That was the irritating thing about having a sister, they could always tell.

"I don't," Nadia insisted, going a bit red.

"He's probably married," announced Clare, the expert. "And gets up to all sorts."

A bit like you would if you had a husband, Nadia thought but didn't point out. With her cavalier, treat 'em mean attitude toward the opposite sex, if men were dogs, Clare would have been reported to animal welfare years ago.

"This isn't bad." Clare was pulling out a lime-green top with velvet edging. "New?"

"Yes, that's why it still has the price tag pinned to the label." Nadia watched her hold the Monsoon top up against herself and pretended she didn't know what was coming next.

"Can I wear it tonight?"

Trade-off time. Clare had made the first move, done the reconciliation bit; now in return she had to let her borrow the top.

Nadia sighed. "OK."

"Great. And next time you bump into some bloke in the street who drags you into an art gallery, spare a thought for your family, OK? I'm only a poor struggling artist."

This definitely wasn't true. Clare was a bone-idle artist who'd never struggled in her life. But Nadia let it go.

"He isn't some bloke I just bumped into in the street. Remember when I got caught in that snowstorm last year? He was the one I had to share a room with in the pub."

A slow smile spread over Clare's face. "Get out of here! Ha, so that's how you got this new job. You slept with the boss."

Harpo was shuffling along the window seat in the sitting room when the telephone began to ring.

"Get the bloody phone," he squawked, mimicking Miriam's harassed voice perfectly. "Get the bloody phone!"

"You could try getting it yourself, that'd be a help," Miriam muttered, but there was an air of tension about her as she snatched up the receiver.

Watching from her position on the floor, Tilly saw her hesitate before saying brusquely, "Yes?"

The next moment her grandmother visibly relaxed. Swinging round still clutching the receiver, she said, "Yes, yes, of course she is, I'll put you on. Tilly darling, it's your mother."

Blimey. This had to be the first time Miriam had been relieved to hear Leonie's voice on the phone. Normally she reacted as though a tramp had spat in her face. Mildly intrigued, Tilly wondered if it was Mrs. Trent-Britton her grandmother was so anxious to avoid. The woman was desperate to get Miriam to join the Women's Institute.

—〜〜—

Tilly knew exactly how long the call lasted because *EastEnders* had been just starting when the phone began to ring, and the theme tune was playing to signal the end of the program when she hung up.

Leonie was an erratic communicator, sometimes leaving it as long as three months between calls. At other times, chiefly when she had a new man to rave about, she might ring her youngest daughter twice in a week. To her shame, Tilly regarded these calls with about as much enthusiasm as people who picked up the phone and heard that they'd been specially chosen to participate in a new in-depth survey on household detergents.

This time, running true to form, Leonie was in love again. She had apparently met a wonderful guy (*guy*—ugh, Tilly so wished her mother wouldn't use that word) and she'd never *ever* been happier. His name was Brian, Tilly learned, he was something in the music industry (hmm, probably worked on the checkout at the music store) and he was just a truly amazing person. Best of all, he had a thirteen-year-old daughter, wasn't that just wild? And Brian couldn't wait for the four of them to meet up and all get to know each other.

There was lots more, chiefly the same stuff but recycled. When Leonie got enthusiastic she tended to repeat herself.

It was with muddled emotions that Tilly eventually hung up the phone. Pleasure that her mum actually wanted her to meet Brian and his daughter. Fear that they wouldn't like her. And unease, because her mother's relationships were always so fragile that the slightest knock could cause everything to end up going horribly wrong. Again.

"OK, darling?" Miriam patted the sofa next to her.

"Mm." Tilly nodded and sat down, biting her thumbnail. "Mum's coming down soon with her new boyfriend."

"Lovely," lied Miriam.

"He's bringing his daughter with him. She's the same age as me." Tilly paused. "Her name's Tamsin."

Miriam kept a straight face. "Tilly and Tam. Sounds like one of those American sitcoms."

Tilly smiled, because her grandmother could always make her feel better. Miriam wasn't afraid of anyone or anything.

"Come on, cheer up. I'm sorry I can't pretend to like your mother." Miriam kissed the top of her head. "I'm sure you'd prefer it if I did. But there we go," she added with a shrug, "that's just me."

"I know." Miriam wasn't only fearless, she was honest and Tilly admired her for it. As straight as a die, that was Miriam. Tilly didn't have a clue what a die was, but she'd read the expression in a book.

"And she does have her good points," Miriam went on.

Startled, Tilly said, "Does she?"

"Darling, my son James was always a sensible boy. Then he lost his mind, went completely bonkers for a while, and married your mum. But thanks to her, we have three beautiful girls." Breaking into a smile, she ruffled Tilly's fine, dark-blonde hair.

Yes, thought Tilly, but only two of them are his.

Harpo, losing his balance as he shuffled along the narrow curtain pole, righted himself in a flurry of blue feathers and shrieked, "Oh blimey."

"You daft bird." Miriam gazed up at him with affection.

"Give us a kiss," squawked Harpo. Tilting his head to one side he added bossily, "No tongues."

Miriam heaved a sigh. "I'm going to strangle Clare."

—◦◦◦—

In the taxi on her way home, Clare was forced to admit that things weren't exactly going according to plan. When she'd first met Piers a couple of months ago at a party, he'd definitely been attracted to her. And she'd liked him a lot too.

But all her relationships followed a pattern, one that Clare was happy with. The men liked her more than she liked them. She enjoyed being the one in control. And the fact that her boredom threshold was low meant that she always tired of them first, usually while they were deciding that she was The One for them. Then, when she ended the affair, they were devastated.

Clare was comfortable being in charge. It made her feel strong and desirable. While her exes crumbled, she moved on to the next challenge. Like Madonna.

So why wasn't it bloody well working this time? Why was Piers treating her like this?

And more crucially, why was it having the effect of making her more keen on him, instead of less?

In the darkness of the back of the cab Clare fretfully pulled at the hem of her lime-green top—would those vindaloo stains ever come out?—and ran through the events of the evening. They'd arranged to meet at Po Na Na on Whiteladies Road at eight o'clock and, humiliatingly, Piers hadn't arrived until almost nine. Yet while she'd known exactly what she *should* be doing, which was walk out at eight fifteen, she hadn't been able to bring herself to do it. Similarly, when he did finally turn up, she should have chucked a drink in his face before stalking off. But somehow that hadn't happened either. Instead she'd found herself thinking, "It's OK, he's here now, that's all that matters," and had experienced relief that he hadn't stood her up completely.

Clare bit her lip. It was as if Piers had cast a spell on her or something, with his light, lazy, upper-class drawl, his caustic sense of humor, and that floppy boarding-school hair. Oh, and maybe the electric-blue Ferrari.

Not that he ever seemed to get behind the wheel of the sodding thing, Clare thought darkly. Twice, that was how many times she'd actually traveled in it. Paranoid about being caught drunk-driving and losing his license, Piers insisted they went everywhere in cabs.

From Po Na Na they had moved on to the Clifton Tandoori, even though she wasn't wild about Indian food. When she'd objected, Piers had called her a party pooper and announced that he was in desperate need of a curry.

Then later when he'd playfully flicked a fork at her, spattering beef vindaloo sauce over the front of her top, he'd mocked her attempts to clean it off with a napkin and said, "All this fuss, it's like watching a nineteen forties housewife. Next thing we know, you'll be darning socks."

But it was always said with humor, rather than downright nastiness. And mysteriously Clare found herself making allowances for his behavior, telling herself that he didn't mean it, it was his upper-class upbringing. They were out having fun together, weren't they? That was all that mattered.

Piers was an Old Etonian. He was twenty-five and a financial adviser. He had a chiseled face, wicked navy blue eyes, and extremely wealthy parents in Surrey. He also had an early start at work tomorrow, which was why instead of spending the night at his Clifton flat, Clare had found herself being deposited in a taxi at eleven thirty and sent home.

"Charge it to my account," Piers had casually informed the taxi driver, making Clare feel like a prostitute.

Except they hadn't even had sex.

Well, they had of course. Lots and lots of truly fantastic sex. Just not tonight.

It was one of the reasons he so intrigued her, Clare realized. The fact that he could so effortlessly take or leave her. She'd offered to stay and Piers had turned her down. Which meant that the next time he allowed her to spend the night with him, she'd feel as if she'd won a fantastic prize or something and make an extra special effort to show him he'd made the right decision.

Clare wasn't stupid. She knew Piers was playing a game with her, turning the usual scheme of things on its head to keep her interested, probably because he'd heard all about her reputation with the opposite sex.

Well, it was working. She was interested. And sooner or later she'd redress the balance, show Piers who was really in charge, make him—

"Here we are, Latimer Road. What number, love?"

"The one at the end. Three streetlamps down, on the left."

He slowed to a halt beneath the third streetlamp. "There you go."

"Thanks." The cab's interior light came on as Clare pushed open the rear door.

"A good long soak in Ariel," said the overweight driver.

"What?"

He nodded at her chest. "Curry stains. That's your best bet. Not promising, mind. Probably have to buy yourself a new top."

Clare thought back to Piers's mocking remarks earlier. Taking a leaf out of his book she shrugged and said carelessly, "No problem, it's not my top."

Bloody know-it-all cab drivers. And he needn't think he was getting a tip.

Chapter 10

When Nadia drew up outside the house in Clarence Gardens on Monday morning, Jay Tiernan was already standing on the pavement waiting for her.

Which was deeply unfair, seeing as it was only ten to nine and he'd said he'd meet her there at nine o'clock. She'd wanted to arrive first, create a good impression, and he'd beaten her to it.

Now all she had to rely on was her clipboard.

Stepping out of the car, Nadia tucked the brand-new clipboard efficiently under her arm and made her way over to him. He was wearing a white T-shirt, the usual pair of jeans, and Timberland boots the color of sand… oh, maybe that was why they were called desert boots!

"You're looking pleased with yourself," Jay observed.

Nadia wondered if he knew why his boots were the color of sand and debated briefly whether to tell him. Then again, if he *did* already know, she might sound stupid.

Instead she said brightly, "I'm in a good mood. Can't wait to start my new job."

"Come on, I'll show you round. Just try not to slap anyone, OK?"

The house was a Victorian detached five-bedroomed property that had been owned by a frail old man incapable of looking after either it or himself. Shortly after being moved into a nursing home, Jay briefly explained, the old man had died. The place had gone up for auction two months later. Now it was in the process of being stripped and completely renovated by Jay's team of builders—Bart, Kevin, and Robbie. Nadia was relieved to note that they didn't appear to be the leering, catcalling, whwoarr darlin' types. Bart and Kevin were a father and son act and Robbie, who was in his twenties, seemed painfully shy. As Jay showed her over the house, they continued working away, knocking down walls and clearing small mountains of dusty rubble.

The back garden looked like a bombsite. An overgrown bombsite from the last war. Clearly any form of upkeep had been beyond the capabilities of the previous occupier. If there had once been a lawn, it was no longer remotely visible. The weeds were at waist height and the area closest to the house was littered with rubbish; instead of putting his empty cat food tins, ready-meal containers, and milk cartons into the dustbin, the old man had evidently flung them out of the kitchen window.

As you do.

"Well?" Jay was watching her survey the carnage.

"Well what?"

"Are you scared?"

"You're joking. I love it. This is like being asked to give Hagrid the makeover of his life." And turning him into George Clooney.

Jay smiled. "Not too much for you to handle on your own?"

"Not unless you want it finished by next weekend," said Nadia.

"The aim is to put it on the market in six weeks."

"I can do that." Hoping she could, she wiped her damp palms on her jeans. "Right, I'll make a start. I'll need a truck by Wednesday morning to take away the first load of waste."

"I'll arrange that. If you stack everything by the side gate, they'll load it."

"Once I see what the ground's like, I'll be able to draw up a plan," said Nadia. "Then we'll discuss how much you want to spend."

It was a shame she couldn't use her super-efficient clipboard to knock up a quick garden plan on the spot, but there was no point while it was still in this much of a state.

Which was lucky really, seeing as she'd forgotten to bring a pen.

———

Three hours later, Robbie came out to the garden and mouthed something to her. Switching off the petrol-driven chainsaw, Nadia pushed her goggles to the top of her head, dragged off her protective gloves, and wiped the perspiration from her chin. Who said gardening wasn't glamorous?

"Sorry, couldn't hear you," said Nadia.

"Erm…" Robbie hesitated like a boy in a school play who's forgotten his lines. "Um, we've just boiled the kettle. Bart wondered if you'd like a cup of tea."

"Oh, fantastic." She beamed over at him, willing him to relax.

Inside the house, the kitchen was pretty much gutted but there was a kettle plugged into a socket at floor level. Next to it on the dusty concrete sat a box of tea bags, an opened carton of milk, a bag of sugar, and a grubby teaspoon. Having pointed them out to her, Robbie vanished without another word.

Right.

"OK, love?" Moments later, Bart appeared in the doorway clutching a tobacco pouch and a vast mug of tea. "You've bin workin' your socks off, haven't you? We've bin watching out the window. Blimey, like *The Texas Chainsaw Massacre* out there. Must have worked up a thirst by now."

He was in his mid-fifties at a guess, with very little hair and a friendly face. Having taken a noisy, appreciative slurp of tea, he wiped his mouth with the back of a sausagey hand.

"I have," said Nadia. "Are there any more mugs?"

"Sorry, love, didn't you bring your own? Oh well, no problem." Glugging back the rest of his tea, Bart gave his own mug a brisk upside-down shake then wiped it briefly on the brick-dust-stained T-shirt stretched over his stomach. Holding it out, he said generously, "You can use mine."

It was like sitting down to eat with an Arab sheik and being presented with a dish of sheep's eyeballs. Or was this some kind of test? Bravely Nadia took the chipped mug, dropped a tea bag into it, and filled it from the just-boiled kettle.

She was truly one of the boys now.

Bart nodded approvingly when she fished the tea bag out with the spoon, flicked it into the sink, and put the spoon back on the floor next to the kettle.

"Good little worker, you are. Jay was watchin' you earlier too, before he left. Impressed him, I reckon. He'll be glad of you, after the last lot. Couple of nancy boys, they were, real Julian Clary types." He snorted with disgust. "Happy enough planting out primroses but when it came to anything more strenuous you wouldn't see 'em for dust."

From the tone of his voice, Nadia guessed that he hadn't shared his mug with them. She felt ridiculously flattered.

"Have you worked for Jay long?"

"Four months, me and Kevin. Ever since he moved to Bristol. Robbie joined us two months ago."

"He seems quite… quiet." Nadia privately suspected Robbie of being a bit simple.

"Ah, he's a nice enough lad. Don't have a lot to say for himself, but that's OK. Got a degree in physics," Bart added, almost as an afterthought.

Blimey.

"Couldn't get a job," Bart went on, between puffs of his spindly hand-rolled cigarette. "Between you an' me, I don't reckon his interview technique's all it could be. Still, he's a good worker. Can't ask for more'n that, can you?"

"And Jay? What's he like? I mean, is he a good boss?" Nadia prayed she wasn't blushing.

"Oh, he's all right." From the way Bart nodded, she sensed that this was a term of approval. "You don't mess Jay about, he won't mess you about. Works hard." He coughed and chuckled. "Plays hard too. You know the kind, single bloke with an eye for the girls. That mobile phone of his sees some action, I can tell you. Sometimes they even turn up where we're working, trying to track him down. Oh yes, he's popular with the ladies is Jay. Makes me wonder how my life might've turned out if there'd been mobile phones back in my day. But there you go," he heaved a mournful smoky sigh, "there weren't. I met my wife at the local youth club, we courted for a couple of years—the old-fashioned way, if you know what I mean—and by nineteen we was married with a kiddie on the way."

Not too old-fashioned then.

"He's a good businessman, mind." Bart brightened. "Knows how to make money. That's why he'll be pleased he took you on. Bet you're a lot cheaper than a poncy landscape gardening company with glossy color brochures and a website."

Was she supposed to take this as a compliment? Hauling herself up off the concrete floor, Nadia finished her tea and smiled.

"Thanks."

The top shelf of the magazine rack wasn't Annie's favorite section of the shop. How she hated it when men came in and bought copies of their favorite porn magazines. Then again, she hated it even more when they came in, spent ten or fifteen minutes silently leafing through them, then left without buying anything at all.

But the latest issue of *Playboy* had been delivered and it was her job to put them out on display. Waiting until the shop was empty, Annie hauled the stool out from behind the counter and placed it in front of the magazine rack. Tucking a pile of *Playboys* under one arm, she climbed onto the stool and began stacking them on the top shelf.

The shop door swung open just as the wasp swooped into Annie's field of vision. Letting out a squeak of alarm she batted it away with her free hand. Incensed, the wasp veered round in a circle and promptly dive-bombed her like a mini Spitfire. Annie ducked and took a panicky step back as it headed straight for her cheek.

"Steady on," said a male voice, but Annie was way beyond steadying herself. Her foot groped for support that was no longer there. The pile of glossy magazines slithered from her grasp as she clawed the air like a novice swimmer attempting the backstroke. With an undignified shriek she tumbled to the ground, hitting the sweet display behind her on the way. Mars bars, tubes of Fruit Pastilles, and packets of Tic Tacs came showering down like painful confetti.

Annie flinched as the stool, to add insult to injury, belatedly toppled over and landed on her shin.

"Stay where you are, don't move," ordered the male voice behind her. The same voice which had, seconds earlier, helpfully suggested that she might like to steady on.

Swiveling her head round, Annie saw that it belonged to the father of the girl who sometimes waited in the shop for him to finish work. If it had been Superman, of course, he would have swooshed down in time to save her from an undignified landing.

"I'm OK." Momentarily she closed her eyes. "I think."

"You're bleeding." Stepping carefully through the debris, he crouched down beside her. "Look at your leg."

Opening her eyes, Annie looked and flinched again. Not so much at the sight of the blood seeping from her knee through a hole in her navy tights but at the copies of *Playboy* strewn around her, each one fallen open to display naked women with pumpkin-sized breasts and improbably skimpy knickers.

Apart from the ones who'd forgotten to put any on.

Chapter 11

ANNIE, WHO WAS WEARING extremely sturdy knickers, tugged at her skirt to make sure they remained hidden. Mortified by the nakedness around her, she attempted to wave her helper away.

"I'm fine, really. It's just a scratch. Was it the *Evening Post* you were after?"

A daft question, seeing as this was the man who called in every evening without fail for an *Evening Post*.

"Never mind that, let's get you sorted out."

"The magazines," Annie murmured, her cheeks flushing as she glimpsed yet another model, extraordinarily posed across a laundry basket. That couldn't be comfortable, surely?

"I'll take care of them." Looking faintly embarrassed himself but adopting a businesslike manner, he swiftly closed each gaping magazine, gathered them up, and stuffed them on the bottom shelf of the magazine rack behind a bunch of *Woman's Weekly*s. Next, he set about collecting the scattered Mars bars. The door clanged open and his daughter rushed in.

"Yeeurgh, wasp." With an exclamation of disgust, she swung her schoolbag and expertly dispatched the wasp through the open doorway. Her eyes widened as she spotted her father on his knees, retrieving Fruit Pastilles and Tic Tacs from beneath the sprawled legs of the woman who worked in the shop.

"The wasp tried to get me too." Annie struggled to sit up a bit straighter. "I fell off the stool. Your dad's helping me clear up." To prove it, she picked up the last Mars bar and handed it to the girl's father. At least the *Playboy*s were out of sight.

"Are you hurt?" The girl moved toward them, adding hopefully, "Did you break your leg? I've got my first aid badge."

"Watch what you say," her father murmured under his breath. "She's a demon with the bandages, have you trussed up like a chicken before you can say Jamie Oliver." His dark eyes met Annie's and she broke into a smile.

"My leg's fine," she told his daughter.

The girl looked disappointed. "Not even a sprained ankle? I'm brilliant at cold compresses."

"It's just a graze. I caught it against the edge of the metal shelf on my way down." The hole in her tights was the most annoying part; typically, they'd been new on today.

Having cleared the space around her, the man helped Annie to her feet. Her bottom hurt quite a lot—she'd have a massive bruise there tomorrow—but Annie kept this information to herself. There were some things you couldn't cold compress in public.

Unless of course you were a *Playboy* centerfold.

"It's Monday," said the girl's father. "Why didn't you catch the bus home?"

"I forgot we had extra netball practice. And then it went on longer than I expected. When I reached your office they said you'd just left, so I raced down here to catch you before you drove home." She hesitated. "That's all right, isn't it?"

He ruffled her hair. "Of course it's all right. You know I always pop in for a paper."

Thinking how perfect they looked together, Annie said, "But if I hadn't fallen off my stool, you'd have missed your lift."

The girl beamed at her. "Every cloud has a silver lining."

And every bottom has a huge purple bruise, Annie thought as she limped over to the desk. There was a packet of bandages in the drawer beneath the cash register; with a tissue she dabbed carefully at the blood through the hole in her wrecked tights.

"Here, let me." With the air of a bossy head nurse, the girl whisked the bandage from her grasp, peeled off the backing strips, and placed it over the cut.

Annie was just glad it wasn't deep enough to need stitches. There were mini sewing kits on the shelf next to the till.

"There." The girl stepped back, pleased with her handiwork.

"Excellent, Tilly. You've done a good job." Her father paused, glancing at his watch, then at Annie. "You close up at six, don't you? Are you OK to get home or can we offer you a lift?"

"Oh! That's really kind of you." Annie was touched by the offer, and sorely tempted. Literally. But she shook her head. "No, I'll be fine. But thanks anyway."

By the time Tilly and her father had left the shop, it was time to start closing up for the night. When that was done, Annie hauled her shopping bags through from the back room, triple-locked the door, and set off for the bus stop. Her knee barely hurt at all but her bottom felt like Mike Tyson's punch bag. As Annie hobbled along, wincing as each step sent a jolt of pain radiating out from the base of her spine, she wished the bus stop was nearer. Was this how it felt to be ninety?

A car tooted behind her but Annie didn't look round; it was hardly likely to be an admiring toot for her.

Then the car pulled up just in front of her and the passenger window was buzzed down.

"You're limping," Tilly announced sternly. "You can hardly walk."

Leaning over and reaching behind Tilly's seat, her father pushed open the car's rear door and said, "Come on, jump in."

Jumping anywhere was currently beyond her, but Annie managed to heave both her shopping bags and herself onto the Jaguar's roomy backseat.

"Thank you, but you shouldn't have waited for me."

"We didn't." Swiveling round, Tilly beamed at her. "We had to queue to get out of the parking lot, that's all. When we pulled out onto the road, I spotted you limping along with your bags."

How embarrassing, assuming they'd been lying in wait for her. Feebly, Annie said, "It hurt more than I thought. I think I jarred my spine."

Tilly gave her a told-you-so look. "You should probably have an X-ray."

Annie was distracted. Oh crikey, walking had set the bleeding off again, blood was oozing out from beneath the bandage on the side of her knee. Terrified of it dripping onto the cream leather upholstery, she hurriedly crossed her legs.

"So, where are we going?" Tilly's father sounded cheerful.

"Kingsweston." Annie prayed it wasn't miles out of his way. "Thanks, um…"

"His name's James," said Tilly. Helpfully she added, "Mine's Tilly."

"And I'm Annie."

"Like Little Orphan Annie! Are you an orphan?"

"Tilly!" In the rearview mirror, Annie saw the girl's father raise his eyebrows in despair.

"What? I'm only asking."

"Well, kind of. I lost my father years ago. And my mother died in January. But I think I'm probably too old to count as an orphan."

"Why? How old are you?"

More eye-rolling in the mirror.

"Thirty-eight," said Annie.

"Oh." Tilly sounded surprised. "I thought more than that."

James was by this time looking sorrowful and shaking his head.

"Yes, well." Gravely Annie said, "I've had a hard life."

"I lost my father too," Tilly announced. "He walked out on my mum when I was a baby."

Oh.

"Oh." Annie was taken aback and embarrassed all over again. When she'd talked to Tilly in the shop, she'd definitely referred to James as *your father.* "I'm sorry, I thought—"

"That James was my dad? No." Tilly shook her head.

"So he's your stepfather," Annie said encouragingly.

"Not even that. I used to think he was my stepdad, but he isn't. It's a bit complicated. But he's just like a real dad," Tilly added. "Makes me do my homework, moans about my taste in music, all that sort of thing."

Drily James observed, "Years of practice with your sisters."

Now Annie was definitely confused, but she could hardly start bombarding them with questions. And in typical teenage fashion, Tilly was now digging a CD out of her backpack and persuading James to play it.

The remainder of the journey was spent listening to American rap, with James intermittently complaining that he couldn't under-stand a word and what was wrong with a nice tune you could sing along with?

Swiveling round in the passenger seat, Tilly said, "See what I mean about being just like a real dad?"

"Mine used to say the same about my David Bowie LPs," said Annie.

Tilly frowned. "What's an LP?"

In the rear mirror, James gave Annie a sympathetic, see-what-I-have-to-put-up-with look.

They had reached Kingsweston. Smiling, Annie said, "Just up here on the right, the little row of cottages. Mine's the one on the corner, next to the phone box."

―⁓―

"Oh, for heaven's sake," Miriam sighed, snatching up James's copy of the *Evening Post.* Stalking across the living room to the window, she took aim at the fly that had been bouncing noisily off the glass and—*bam*—killed it.

"Nice to know I haven't lost my touch." Pleased with herself, she handed the rolled-up murder weapon to James. "Darling, I don't know why you buy this paper. Half the time you don't even open it."

"I do," lied James. To prove it he opened the paper. "See? There's a piece in here about… that new restaurant in Stoke Bishop. They're clients of ours." He nodded seriously. "You see, it's all relevant."

"Fine, fine." Diamonds flashed as Miriam made calm-down gestures with her hands. "In that case, why don't we have it delivered? Save you having to call into a shop on your way home every night. It's simple, just get the paper boy to pop it through the letter box."

Rustling through the pages, James hastily buried his head in the obituary column. He didn't want the paper boy to pop his *Evening Post* through the letter box. He liked the routine of calling in to the newsagents and picking up his paper, whether or not he was giving Tilly a lift home.

"Shall I arrange that, then?"

"No thanks."

"But—"

"*No.*" James knew how much he owed his mother, but there were still times when she drove him to distraction. "I'll carry on buying my own paper, OK? It's not a problem."

"If you say so." Miriam's dark kohl-lined eyes flickered with concern; it was unlike James to snap. "I was only trying to help."

Chapter 12

NADIA WAS PLEASED WITH herself. She'd done a really good plan of the garden. She had even bought a brand-new set of top-of-the-range felt-tips in order to create the requisite blaze of color. It had taken her hours last night, stretched across her bed surrounded by discarded ideas and empty potato chip bags. People didn't appreciate quite how much planning went into a plan.

And Jay Tiernan, annoyingly, wasn't here to appreciate it.

He was a busy man, Nadia realized that. As well as organizing the kitchen and bathroom installations, it was Jay's job to make sure the electricians, plumbers, and carpenters were called in to carry out their work at the right times. He was also liaising with estate agents and solicitors, preparing to sell this house when it was finished and already on the lookout for the next house to buy. This meant he was out and about a lot. Which was fine, but it would have been less annoying if he didn't spend so much time with his mobile switched off.

"Still no luck, love?" Bart came outside as she was jabbing at the buttons of her own phone.

Nadia shook her head. She'd already left two messages but Jay hadn't called back. "He said he'd organize a truck." She gestured at the mountain of garden waste piled up next to the side gate. "It's nearly midday and no one's here, and I don't know if he's fixed something up or not."

"If he said he would, he probably did." Bart shrugged and began to roll a cigarette.

"But what if he hasn't? And I've got my plans here for him." Crossly, Nadia prodded her polyethylene folder—also new yesterday. "I need him to see them before I start the next phase. I mean, where can he be? What's he doing?" Her corkscrew hair bounced around her shoulders as she shook her head in disbelief. "Why does he always have to have his bloody phone switched off?"

Bart didn't quite give her a wink and a nudge, but the expression on his face told her exactly what he thought Jay might be up to. Lighting his roll-up, he took a long drag all the way down to his toes.

"Like I told you, he's a busy chap. Popular with the ladies. Had a bit of a thing going with the woman who sold him the last place we done up. Dunno if he's still seeing her, but if he isn't there'll be someone else."

Was Bart warning her not to get her hopes up? Was he subtly letting her know that any hint of flirtation from Jay should be taken with a wagonload of salt?

Speaking of wagons...

"I'm not interested in his love life." Nadia's tone was clipped. "I just want all this rubbish cleared away, and I need Jay to approve the plans so I can make a proper start on this garden."

"Tell you what," Bart said soothingly. "It's twelve o'clock. Why don't you take your lunch break? Maybe he'll be here by the time you get back."

Nadia was away for twenty minutes. By the time she returned from the deli on Henleaze Road with her sandwiches, chips, and Snickers bar, Jay had been and gone.

Allegedly.

"Just missed him, love," said Bart. "He turned up just after you left."

Dismayed, Nadia said, "Are you serious?"

"I told him what you needed. He gave the clearance company another ring and they'll be here by one o'clock. Oh, and he's taken the garden plans with him but he says you can make a start on the terrace."

Nadia felt like a six-year-old beginning to have suspicions about Father Christmas. Had Jay really been here, or was Bart only saying it to humor her? What if Bart had stuffed her painstakingly constructed plans into the bottom of the backpack he kept his packed lunch and tobacco in?

Kevin, Bart's son, was plastering one of the sitting-room walls. Poking her head round the door, Nadia said, "Did you see Jay?"

"What?" Kevin looked taken aback.

"Was he here just now?"

"Um, yes."

Except Kevin would say that, wouldn't he? Bart would have told him to.

Nadia's eyes narrowed. "What was he wearing?"

"Eh?"

Not a clue. *Ha.*

"T-shirt and jeans?" Kevin said hopefully.

Brilliant.

"Actually," Nadia told him, "it was a green polo shirt and black trousers."

"Oh, right." Kevin nodded with relief. "Yeah, that's it, I remember now."

Dear old Kevin. Not too bright, but always eager to please.

When the truck arrived shortly after one o'clock, Nadia wondered if Bart had phoned them himself.

———

Miriam and Edward were sitting in Edward's back garden when he proposed to her. Again.

Miriam briefly closed her eyes, wishing he wouldn't do this to her, wondering why he just couldn't take no for an answer.

"I'm serious," said Edward, removing the folded-up *Daily Telegraph* from her hands and placing her Biro on the garden table. "I don't see what the problem is. I love you and I want you to marry me."

"And I want you to stop asking me." Miriam's spine stiffened instinctively; her shoulders went back. "We're fine as we are."

"I like to do things properly. Properly means getting married."

"Well, that isn't going to happen, so can we please get back to the crossword?"

She would win, of course. She always won, because she'd long ago made up her mind and Edward couldn't force her to change it. But he would make sure she knew he wasn't happy with the situation. He did this now by heaving a sigh, rising to his feet, and moving away from the table. With his hands clasped behind his back he walked stiffly over to the far wall, ostensibly to admire the rambling roses basking in the afternoon sunlight.

Miriam, watching him, wondered how he would react if she told him the real reason why she refused to marry him. Ironically, she suspected he wouldn't even care, once he got over the initial shock.

But the reason she would never marry Edward had nothing to do with whether or not he knew about it. Not allowing herself to marry him was the punishment she had meted out to herself after... well, after *the thing* had happened. And once you made a bargain like that, you had to stick with it.

Even more ironically, Edward was standing in the exact spot where it had happened.

Shielding her eyes from the sun, Miriam picked up the *Telegraph* and called, "Darling, that's enough, come and help me finish the crossword now."

What she actually meant was, *Don't sulk*, but she couldn't bring herself to say it.

Poor Edward. He'd already been through enough.

—~~~—

The next day, Thursday, was hot but showery. Nadia, stripped to a tank top and shorts, worked through the rain to level the ground where the French windows at the back of the house led out onto the garden. Raindrops dripped steadily from the ends of her corkscrew curls. Clumps of mud were stuck to her workboots. She looked appalling but didn't care. All the exercise was doing her good, and there was nobody around to see what a fright she looked. Nobody who counted, anyway.

Jay's mobile was still switched off. For all she knew, he could be in New Zealand now.

He turned up at twelve thirty. Nadia carried on working in the rain while he checked on progress in the house with Bart.

Finally he came outside, carrying her folder of plans in one hand and his mobile in the other.

"These are fine. Go ahead. I've set up an account at the garden center, so you can chalk up anything you need on that."

No friendly greeting. No "Hi, how are you, sorry I missed you yesterday." He wasn't even smiling.

Nadia stopped digging and leaned on her shovel. Somehow she'd expected a more enthusiastic reaction to her plans than just "fine."

"Are you OK?" she asked Jay.

He didn't look OK, he seemed offish and distracted.

"Of course I'm OK," he replied coolly. Not a hint of flirtatiousness about his manner. It was like suddenly being faced with Jay Tiernan's scary bank-managerish twin brother, the one who was in fact a cyborg.

Maybe this was just the way things were going to be, now that she was actually working for him.

"Right." Fair enough, effusive praise might have been too

much to ask for, but Nadia still thought he could have called her garden plan something more constructive than just *fine*. "Can I make a comment?"

Indignation turned to anger as Jay glanced at his watch, then shrugged. "Go ahead."

He clearly couldn't be less interested in anything she might have to say.

"It's none of our business where you go during the day, and it really doesn't bother any of us what you get up to when you aren't here." Skillfully Nadia included Bart and the others in her complaint. "But you can't keep leaving your phone switched off. I was trying to reach you yesterday and I couldn't. I tried again this morning and I *still* couldn't."

"Right."

Rain dripped from Nadia's eyelashes as she stared at him in disbelief. Was that it? Was that his idea of an apology?

"I'm serious. It's unprofessional. We need to be able to contact you."

Jay, his expression as hard and detached as an Indian chief's, said, "There's such a thing as using your initiative. If you were that desperate, you could have organized another truck. Anyway, I have to go. Tell Bart I'll speak to him tomorrow about the electrician."

And without another word he was gone. Nadia, her hands on her hips, watched him disappear through the side gate. Moments later she heard the sound of his car's engine starting up. He couldn't have been less interested in her complaint if she'd been an ant on the heel of his boot.

What the hell was going on here? Was Jay Tiernan a bastard who had formerly masqueraded as a nice person? Was his business in trouble and he was on the verge of being made bankrupt?

Or was he none too subtly pointing out to her that if she fancied him she may as well stop it right now because she was wasting her time?

From the kitchen window, Kevin yelled, "I'm off to the fish and chip shop. Want some?"

It was one o'clock. Nadia, discovering that she could murder a bag of battered cod and chips, felt her spirits begin to rise, just by a fraction.

First rule of employment: if your boss turns out to be a complete pig, you deserve a nice lunch.

Chapter 13

NADIA SCOOPED UP THE just-delivered post on her way into the kitchen the next morning. Clare was already up, which was either an outright miracle or meant that she'd only just come home after last night. Miriam was making her usual blisteringly strong coffee and James was buttering toast.

Dealing the letters out like a poker hand, Nadia recited, "Bill, bill, junk mail, bill."

"Cuthbert, Dibble, and Grubb," said James.

Everyone in the kitchen turned and stared at him.

"Joke," said James. "It was a children's thing on TV."

"Ah," Clare mimicked misty-eyed reminiscence, "the good old days of black and white."

"It was a famous program." James looked defensive.

"More junk mail." Nadia tossed a glossy card over to Clare. "You've won half a million pounds."

"Lovely." Clare turned it over and pulled a face. "Oh, shame. It says here that they *were* going to give me half a million pounds, but then they asked my sister and she persuaded them to give it to someone else instead."

Nadia ignored her. "Something for you, Gran, a fat one. Here, catch."

Miriam caught it, her heart in her mouth. But it was OK, nothing to worry about, just one of Emily Payne's irritating round-robin letters, run off on her computer. At six-month intervals

Emily liked to send boastful my-children-are-better-than-your-children updates to two hundred of her very closest friends. Last Christmas Miriam had been tempted to write back telling her that James had just had a sex change and from now on was to be known as Janice.

"Dad, two more for you. Boring old car brochure and ooh, this looks more exciting." Nadia waggled the heavy cream envelope enticingly under his nose. "Mm, heavy paper and addressed with real ink, talk about posh."

James knew at once what it was. Several other people at work had received theirs in the post yesterday. Taking a cup of coffee from Miriam, he slid the invitation under the saucer and concentrated on opening and studying the glossy brochure from BMW instead.

"Come on, Dad, what's in the other envelope?" Behind him, Clare draped her arms round his shoulders.

"I'll open it later."

"Tell you what, why don't I open it now?" With a grin, she whisked the envelope out from beneath the saucer and danced away from the table.

"That's addressed to me. It's private." James attempted to exert parental control.

"Oh, don't be such an old fuddy-duddy, anyone can see it's an invite." Ripping open the envelope, Clare studied the embossed card inside. She wrinkled her nose in disgust. "I thought it was going to be something interesting. A dinner party at Cedric and Mary-Jane's—God, nightmare. I'd rather eat dog food."

James entirely agreed. Cedric Elson was his boss, the founder and head of Elson and Co. Chartered Accountants. Mary-Jane was his liposuctioned wife. And their dinner parties were the bane of James's life.

"It says James and partner," Clare pointed out.

Cedric and Mary-Jane's invitations always said that.

"I told them I don't have a partner." James sighed. "Mary-Jane said I should jolly well make the effort and find one."

"She may have a point." Miriam wound her dark hair into a knot and secured it with her crossword Biro. "After all, they've been inviting you to these parties for years and you've never taken anyone yet."

"I don't know anyone to invite."

Out in the hall, Tilly was on her knees stuffing trainers and a PE skirt into her already bulging backpack. Pausing for a second, she heard Clare say, "Get someone from an agency. One of those escort girls, a really stunning one. That'll make everyone sit up and take notice."

"Especially if she starts handing out her business card," Tilly heard Nadia retort.

"I'm not hiring someone from an agency." James sounded resigned. "I'm not even going to the dinner party. I'll phone at the last minute and tell them I have the flu."

"You did that last year," said Miriam. "This time you have to go. You can take Eliza."

"Not Eliza." James's groan was audible even out in the hall. It wasn't the first time he'd been threatened with Edward's secretary.

"She's always asking after you," Miriam declared. "You know she likes you. Oh, James, don't pull that face, you don't have to marry the woman. It's only a dinner party."

"I'm going to be late for work." Tilly heard a chair being scraped back.

"You have to take someone," Miriam persisted.

Out in the hallway James picked up his briefcase and car keys before dropping a kiss on Tilly's bent head.

"Bye, pigeon. See you later."

Having finally succeeded in fastening the zip on her backpack, Tilly said, "You're wearing odd socks."

James glanced down at his socks; one navy, one black.

"Don't tell your grandmother." He gave Tilly a conspiratorial wink and pulled open the front door. "Bye."

~~~

"Hi, how *are* you?" Annie greeted Tilly with a warm smile when Tilly came into the shop at twenty past five.

"Fine. Well, muddy." Tilly indicated the mud splashes all over her legs as a result of racing around a waterlogged sportsfield. "Is your knee better?"

"Oh, it's fine." The bruise on her bottom was really colorful, but Annie didn't mention this. "Chewing gum?"

Tilly nodded and pulled her money out of one of the pockets in her backpack. She counted out the coins carefully, passed them over to Annie, and took a deep breath.

"Look, I hope this isn't rude, but do you have another half?"

Annie frowned. Was this about chewing gum? Money? Lager?

"Another half of what?"

"Sorry." Flushing slightly, Tilly shook her head. "I meant *an*other half. You know, like a partner, husband, boyfriend... I never know what to call them."

"Oh." Annie broke into another smile. "Well, no, not really."

"What does not really mean?"

"Um, it means... no." Taken aback by the unexpected interrogation, Annie said, "Why?"

"No reason. Just wondered." Cheerfully, Tilly unwrapped the packet of Wrigley's Extra. "So, in theory, if a man asked you to go along with him to his boss's dinner party next Saturday night, there wouldn't be anything to stop you?"

Annie's heart rate increased, like an ancient car suddenly being urged to break the speed limit.

"Well, that would depend on the man and what he was like."

"But if he was really nice, you'd say yes?" Tilly's eyes were bright.

"Ah... well, I suppose so, in theory."

"That's great. Brilliant." Beaming, Tilly offered her chewing gum.

Behind her, the door swung open and James came in, sending Annie's out-of-practice heart into Ferrari mode. Her fingers gripped the edge of the counter as James picked up his usual paper, dropped the right money onto the counter, flashed her a smile, and said, "Busy day?"

Annie unstuck her tongue from the roof of her mouth. "Um, quite busy."

"Right, we'd better be off." Playfully James tapped his rolled-up newspaper between Tilly's skinny shoulder blades, nudging her toward the door. "Come along, you. Time to go and sit in a traffic jam." Over his shoulder he added casually, "Have a good weekend."

On automatic pilot, Annie called, "You too."

It was like waking up on the morning of your birthday and watching the postman walk straight past your front gate.

The shop door swung shut behind them. Annie ran her fingers through her hair. Oh well, that was that then, so much for getting her hopes up. What on earth had Tilly been on about?

"You didn't." James blanched. "Tell me this is a joke, Tilly. Please."

On their way back to the parking lot, Tilly had casually dropped her bombshell. James abruptly stopped walking; this was awful, just awful.

"It's not a joke, it's perfect. You need someone to take along to this dinner thingy, and Annie said she'd love to go. I think she's a really nice person." Tilly stuffed her hands into her blazer pockets and stood her ground. "And if you don't take Annie, Miriam's going to fix you up with that awful Eliza."

"But... but..."

"Eliza's a horse," Tilly said bluntly. "She laughs like a horse, she has teeth like a horse, and she has hair like a horse. You really don't want to take Eliza. And you can't pull that pretending-to-be-ill trick again. Come on, I've done all the hard work. All you have to do now is officially ask Annie. You already know she's going to say yes."

If there had been a brick wall handy, James would have banged his head against it.

"Tilly, you're thirteen. I know you're trying to help, but this isn't how it's done. I don't even know the woman. She sells me my newspaper, that's all. You can't march into your local newsagents and invite the person behind the counter to your boss's dinner party."

Tilly remained calm. "Why not?"

"Because... oh, for heaven's sake, because you just *can't*." Closing his eyes briefly, James realized that when he'd burst into the shop ten minutes ago, Annie must have been expecting him to raise the subject. What a mess, what a complete and utter balls-up. And now it was up to him to sort it out.

"I'll have to explain to her," James said wearily. "You stay here. I'll be back in five minutes. This is going to be embarrassing," he added. "Never *ever* do anything like this again."

When he arrived back at the shop, Annie was serving another customer. Glancing up and seeing James, she flushed and hurriedly looked away again. Just as the customer finally left and James opened his mouth to speak, a young mother came in with two small children and he was forced to spend the next few minutes pretending to flick through car magazines while the children dithered and bickered endlessly over their choice of penny sweets.

At last they were alone together in the shop. Annie, her cheeks flushed, said hesitantly, "Hello again."

James wished he only had something simple to do, like saw off his own legs.

Mentally bracing himself, he plunged straight in. "OK, look, this is awkward."

"It doesn't have to be." Annie's tone was hesitant.

"Well, obviously Tilly's just told me what she said to you. I had no idea she'd been planning something like this. I'm so sorry," said James, "it must have been incredibly difficult for you. I do apologize. Anyway," he rushed on, before any other customers could come in and interrupt them, "I've explained to Tilly that she can't go around doing things like this, and I'm really sorry she put you in an awkward situation. Please, forget she said anything. Just put it out of your mind. And, um, sorry again."

Annie had been listening to every word. Now, she tucked her unstyled fair hair carefully behind her ears and said, "Right. OK."

"Kids these days." James adopted a hearty tone. "I don't know where they get it from."

"Oh, absolutely." Nodding vigorously, Annie flashed him a wide smile, the kind people adopt when instructed by a photographer to say cheese. "It must be scary, wondering what she's going to come up with next."

"Well, quite." James knew he should be leaving but couldn't quite figure out how to do it without seeming rude. "I mean, I know Tilly's only trying to help, but she doesn't understand. You know how it is with these work-related dinner parties. Everyone else is married, so they expect you to turn up with someone too, because otherwise you'll have completely messed up their seating plan, or some such nonsense. I mean, imagine the horror of eleven guests instead of twelve at dinner; two men might actually have to sit next to each other, it just doesn't bear thinking about."

"Mad," Annie agreed, her smile slightly forced. "Well, good for you, not letting yourself be bullied into taking someone along."

James realized she thought he was a lot braver than he actually was. Hastily he said, "Oh no, I'll still have to take someone. You don't know my boss." He pulled a face, so she'd understand. "Turning up on your own would be like committing professional suicide."

Annie nodded. "Well, I'm sure you'll have a nice time once you're there. Goodness, is it ten to six already?" She began counting busily through the newspapers piled up on the counter.

Taking his cue to leave, James turned and made his way past the racks of magazines. *Horse and Hound* caught his eye, reminding him automatically of horsey Eliza. Damn, he might have solved one problem but there was still the dilemma of who he could actually take along to Cedric's wretched dinner party.

He reached the door, then turned.

Cleared his throat.

"Of course, if you wanted to come with me, that would be great. Not because you're too polite to say no, but because you think you really might enjoy it… um, well, you probably wouldn't… no, don't worry…"

"I'd like to go with you," said Annie. Surprising herself.

"Really?" James couldn't quite believe he'd done it. "Are you sure?"

"Why not?" For the first time since his arrival, her facial muscles relaxed. "If you're sure you want me."

"It might not be much fun." He felt it only fair to warn her.

"We could make it fun," said Annie.

～⁓～

James had been gone for ages, far longer than five minutes.

"I'm sorry," Tilly blurted out when he finally reappeared.

"OK."

They turned and headed for the parking lot.

"Was it awkward?"

"Yes." James was striding along at top speed.

"Was she upset?"

"She did her best to hide it."

Mortified, Tilly said again, "I'm *really* sorry."

"I know."

Her eyes filled with tears. No matter how cross James was with her, he never yelled or lost his temper.

"So who will you invite to the dinner party now?"

"Hmm?" James looked down at her in surprise. "Oh, I'm taking Annie."

Chapter 14

IT WAS SIX THIRTY on Friday evening and the builders were long gone, but Nadia was still working. Taking advantage of the improved weather, she was preparing the ground for the paved terrace. Not glamorous, but necessary. On Monday she would order the paving slabs, hire a cement mixer, and—

The side gate clicked open and Jay appeared, wearing a dark gray T-shirt, black jeans, and dark glasses. He looked like Darth Vader, only less cheerful.

"Hi," said Nadia, wiping soil from her hands. She wondered if he'd forgotten how to smile.

"I thought you'd have left by now."

Like Darth Vader only *much* less cheerful.

"Just finishing off. Is that allowed?" She said it lightly, hinting that it would be fine to make some form of lighthearted comment in return. Jay didn't appear to notice.

"Of course it's allowed. I just dropped by to see how the work was progressing."

He had his hands in his pockets and he was studying the re-painted window frames at the back of the house. Irritated by his dark glasses, which meant she couldn't even tell when he was looking at her, Nadia said, "I'm sorry, have I done something wrong?"

"What?" The opaque lenses swung in her direction.

"Me. Done something wrong. I must have done." She semi-shrugged. "You used to be… different." Almost as if you *didn't* have a poker stuck up your bottom.

"Don't worry about it." Heading back to the house, Jay impatiently jangled his keys. "Just need to check inside, then I'll be off. See you Monday."

"Not if I see you first," Nadia murmured under her breath.

Well, practically under it.

The dark glasses swiveled once more. "What?"

She looked surprised. "Nothing."

Oh dear, turning into a five-year-old, never an attractive trait in a grown woman.

Then again, whose fault was it that she had?

Nadia packed up for the night fifteen minutes later, locking away her tools in the dilapidated garden shed and letting herself out through the side gate. Jay's car was still parked across the road, although she'd assumed he'd have left by now.

Making her way down the short drive, Nadia turned and glanced back at the house. There he was, standing at the living-room window, talking on his mobile phone.

So he did occasionally deign to switch it on. Nadia only hoped the recipient of the call appreciated how honored they were to be actually speaking to him in person. In fact she hoped they were on their knees with gratitude. When Jay looked up and saw her watching him, he didn't smile or wave; just turned a few degrees to the right and carried on talking into the phone.

It would have been nice to think that he was behaving like this because he'd resorted to the treat 'em mean, keep 'em keen strategy of courtship. Sadly, Nadia knew he wasn't.

Oh well, at least it was Friday. Her first week working for Jay Tiernan was over. Or the eerily lifelike cyborg currently passing himself off as Jay Tiernan. If she was still working for him in December, the staff Christmas party was sure to be a riot.

Nadia reached the end of Clarence Gardens before remembering that she was perilously low on petrol. Reversing into a driveway and turning the car round, she set off back up the road and prayed she'd reach the filling station before spluttering to a halt.

It happened completely without warning; they came out of nowhere like two speeding furry bullets zinging across the road. With no chance whatsoever of avoiding them, Nadia let out a shriek of horror and jammed her foot on the brake. A nightmare split second later came the ominous thud of body-on-bumper impact.

With a squeal of tires, the Renault slewed to a violent halt at the side of the road. Sickened and shocked, Nadia stumbled from the car and pressed a shaking hand to her mouth. The cat, a short-haired ginger one, lay on its side in the gutter.

It was quite dead.

"Oh no, oh no," Nadia sobbed, tears streaming down her cheeks as she dropped to her knees. The cat's green eyes were half open. Death had clearly been instantaneous.

"It's OK," said a reassuring voice in her ear. It was Jay crouching beside her, feeling beneath the cat's furry jaw for a pulse.

"It's not OK. I killed someone's cat." Nadia heaved a sob, shaking her head in revulsion at what she'd done.

"Tommy." Jay briefly examined the disc attached to the collar round its neck. "That was his name."

"Is that meant to make me feel better?" Nadia scrabbled up her sleeve for a tissue; she was trembling all over.

"No, I'm just telling you. And you didn't kill him. He ran into the road, chasing after the other cat. I saw it happen from the window."

"He's still dead."

"There was nothing you could do," said Jay. "Come on, don't cry. It really wasn't your fault."

Nadia wiped her wet cheeks with the back of her hand, but the tears were still coming. Quite astonishingly, Jay's arm was round her shoulders and he was actually being concerned and caring.

Almost... *nice*.

"I've never killed anything b-before. Well, only worms and I even hate that. Oh God, it's really dead." Lifting the animal gently onto her lap, Nadia began to stroke it, rocking to and fro as she did so. Poor thing, one minute it had been happily racing after another cat and the next… nothing.

Apart from Jay, nobody had emerged from the neighboring houses in the street. Maybe no one else had seen it happen. Nadia reluctantly turned over the disc bearing the cat's name and saw an address engraved on the other side.

"Felstead Avenue," Jay read aloud. "That's the road behind this one."

"Right." Nadia nodded, feeling sick. She bowed her head and tried to imagine breaking the news to Tommy's owner. Oh, this was a nightmare, she couldn't do it. Right, think about this, think, just concentrate…

"I could say he was already dead when I found him." She looked pleadingly at Jay. "They don't have to know I did it."

Slowly Jay nodded. "You could. Is that what you want to do?"

Nadia's lip began to tremble. She stroked the cat's ears and shook her head. "No. I'll tell them the truth. Oh, look at his dear little face, I can't bear it. What number Felstead Avenue?"

"Fourteen, but you're not doing it now." While she numbly stroked the cat, Jay's fingers were stroking her neck. His arm was still round her shoulders and it actually felt quite comforting, all the more so for being so unexpected.

"They could be wondering where he is."

"A few more minutes won't make any difference. Come on." Taking the cat from her, Jay led the way back to the house. There was no milk left, but he boiled the kettle and made Nadia a cup of black coffee to steady her shredded nerves.

"I can take the cat back if you like," said Jay. "I'll tell them I was driving the car."

Nadia wavered; this was hugely tempting. She kept picturing herself having to break the tragic news to a frail old widow without another friend in the world, or to a cluster of distraught saucer-eyed children who'd doted on Tommy since he was a kitten.

"No." Nadia shook her head, she couldn't wimp out now. "Thanks, but I'll do it."

"I'll come with you."

"OK." She managed a wobbly smile. "You're being really nice."

Jay raised an eyebrow. "Don't sound so surprised. I'm not an ogre."

It was on the tip of her tongue to tell him that, actually, for the past week he certainly had been, but she kept this observation to herself. Clearly, Jay didn't even realize he'd been behaving in a weird and distant way.

"OK, I'm ready." Draining her cup of black coffee, Nadia mentally girded her loins—whatever that actually meant. "Let's go."

"Well," she said ten minutes later. "That's... that."

Jay brushed away a tear that was rolling down her cheek. "You don't have to cry. It's over now."

"I'm not crying for me, I'm crying for the cat! That bloody man couldn't have cared less."

The bloody man, the one who had opened the front door of 14 Felstead Avenue, had been balding, middle-aged, and brusque. Oh right, so the cat had lost a fight with a car, hardly surprising the way it carried on, daft thing had never had any road sense.

By the time Nadia had finished stammering her way through an explanation of what had happened, her heartfelt apologies and a promise to pay for both the funeral expenses and a new cat, the man's eyes had begun to gleam with interest.

"Right, well, I reckon a couple of hundred quid should cover it."

Jay had said firmly, "A hundred."

Hating the man but unable to back down now, Nadia had scribbled out a check. He'd promptly pocketed it, said cheerfully, "Thanks, love," and closed the door on them.

She almost wished now that the cat's owner had been a tearful old lady—anything would have been easier to bear than the man's chilling indifference.

"I bet he won't even have it buried. He'll just chuck the cat in his wheelie bin. Honestly, some people shouldn't be allowed to keep animals." Oh dear, she was getting all worked up again, thinking about reporting the horrible man to animal welfare, except she'd been the one who'd killed Tommy...

"Look, the pubs are open." Jay checked his watch. "How about a brandy to calm you down?"

He was *still* being nice. Grateful to him for understanding how awful she felt, Nadia wiped her eyes with the sleeve of her T-shirt and began to nod. A drink would be lovely, just what she needed—

Jay's phone began to ring. In his hurry to answer it, he missed the nod. With a knot of foreboding in her stomach, Nadia watched his expression change. After several curt whens, yeses, and rights, he hung up.

"Sorry, I have to go. Are you all right to drive home?"

Nadia nodded. Just as well, really.

"OK. Bye."

And that was it, he was gone. Into his car, over the hill, and out of sight.

So was he nice or wasn't he? She still didn't know.

Chapter 15

CLARE WAS IN HER studio, painting and wishing she could stop thinking about Piers. Not permanently, of course. It was just annoying, not being able to concentrate on the canvas in front of you because you kept wondering where he was now, what he might be doing, and when you were next going to see him.

It was Saturday lunchtime and sunlight streamed in through the sloping windows on the top floor of the house. Outside on the drive, Tilly was helping James wash his car. Nadia was still asleep in bed, lazy mare. Miriam was in the bathroom putting the finishing touches to her makeup before Edward arrived to whisk her off to the Painswick Hotel in Stroud for lunch.

Clare sat back on her stool and surveyed the painting so far. The scene was of a gaggle of overexcited women in hugely ornate hats, enjoying a day at the races. She was going to call it "All Of A Flutter." There were no horses in the painting because she couldn't draw horses—they always ended up looking as if their legs were on backward. But in the foreground she had a gloriously seedy-looking bookie leering as he eyed up the ladies in their skimpy skirts.

When Clare was in the mood to paint, she could keep going for hours. But today it just wasn't happening. She was too distracted to enjoy it. Yesterday Piers had been away at a conference in London, and now it was midday and he still hadn't rung her.

Clare gazed moodily out of the window; this wasn't what she was used to. She'd never been the type to wimpishly phone a

boyfriend—in fact she'd positively enjoyed *not* phoning them—
because she'd always known they'd phone her.

And she really didn't want to call Piers, but it was starting to look
as if she might have to, because he didn't appear to be ringing her and
how else could she get to see him? He wasn't leaving her any choice.

She wiped her paintbrush on a piece of old tea towel, swirled
it in a jar of turps, and slid off the stool. Just the thought of calling
Piers and hearing his voice was enough to get her stomach tram-
polining with anticipation. She'd never actually experienced these
kinds of feelings before.

"Yeah?"

"Hi, it's me." *Boing, boinngg* went Clare's intestines as she
gripped the phone. "Just wondered what you were up to."

She'd practiced this line. It was nice and casual, free of whini-
ness, and suitably laid back. Not for her the fretful "you-said-you'd-
call-me" accusations, oh no. Instant turnoff.

"Hi, you." Piers sounded as if he was lying in bed, smiling. She
could just picture him with one arm tucked under his head, his chest
tanned and bare. "I was just thinking about you."

Don't sound flattered, don't simper.

"How was London?"

"Oh, not so bad. Pretty knackering really. How about you?"

"Oh, we were out and about last night. Ended up at a *wild* party
in Failand." Clare was buggered if she'd tell him she'd stayed in and
watched *Frasier*. "I'm fairly shattered myself, don't feel like doing
anything too energetic this afternoon…" She paused, giving him the
opportunity to pick up on the double entendre.

Piers yawned. "Me neither. There's rugby on the telly—that's
enough exercise for me."

"Rugby?" Clare loathed rugby with a passion. "I love rugby!
Tell you what, I could bring over a bottle of wine if you fancy
some company."

Was that pushy, over-keen, pathetically eager? No, of course it wasn't. She was making a relaxed, spur-of-the-moment suggestion, that was all. Watching sports on TV was always more fun when you had company... God, only complete nerds sat at home watching rugby on their own.

"OK. If you like." Piers sounded surprised but not displeased. "Yeah, great, come on over. But don't bother with wine. Pick up some beers instead." He definitely wanted her to be there with him, Clare told herself. He'd said "if you like," not, "if you must." Reassured, she said, "Want to come and collect me?"

"No." Piers chuckled, clearly amused by this suggestion. "I wasn't actually planning on getting dressed today. I'm sure you can manage to make your own way over. Just grab a cab."

Clare switched off the phone with a flourish. There, that hadn't been so hard, had it? She'd called Piers and he'd been delighted to hear from her, and now she was going to spend the rest of Saturday with him. Whereas if she *hadn't* rung him, she'd still be fretting and wondering what he was up to. Which, let's face it, would have been absolutely pathetic.

Clothes, Clare thought joyfully, wiping her hands on her oversized paint-encrusted combats and bounding over to her wardrobe. Clothes for a relaxing afternoon *à deux* in front of the TV. Something casual, of course. But sexy. Jeans? No. Skirt and strappy top? Definitely not. T-shirt and trousers? Boring, boring. What could she wear that would make a real impression on Piers? What did she have that he hadn't already seen her in?

Apart from her dressing gown and slippers.

And her trench coat.

Emerging from the shower, Clare roughly blow-dried her hair, fastened it back with a hair tie, made up her face, and slipped her feet into high-heeled pink leather mules.

Then, letting the towel in which she was wrapped drop to the floor, she sprayed herself with Dior's Eau Svelte and reached into the wardrobe for her trench coat.

Striking a pose in front of the full-length mirror, Clare surveyed herself with satisfaction. Oh yes. Perfect. Saucy but innocent, sexy but fun. She'd never worn it before, but this was actually a great trench coat. Pale pink PVC on the outside, lined with fake fur on the inside, it came to just above the knee. With the buttons done up and the belt tightly tied at the waist, nobody would ever know you weren't wearing anything underneath.

Her mouth turned up at the corners as she pictured Piers's face when the belt and buttons were unfastened. He'd love it. It would become one of those never-to-be-forgotten anecdotes. Twenty years from now, when the kids were driving them up the wall, they'd still be able to look at each other and smile, and Piers would say, "Remember the time you turned up wearing nothing but a trench coat? That was the day I knew you were the girl for me."

OK, fantasizing. But it could happen. That was the thing about men, you never knew what was going through their man-shaped minds.

———

"There you are, love, that'll be eight pounds sixty." The taxi driver spoke with the satisfied air of one who knows he's going to get a tenner.

"Keep the change," muttered Clare. Honestly, ten pounds, talk about daylight robbery.

But she couldn't really get too worked up about it. She was here now, outside Piers's flat, and that was all that mattered. Hefting the Thresher's bag into her arms—lager for Piers, wine for herself—she climbed the steps and pressed the buzzer.

"Yup?" Piers's disembodied voice came through the speaker on the entryphone.

"It's me."

"Hello, you." His voice softened. "Got the lagers?"

I've got better than lagers, Clare thought happily. Aloud she said, "Oh yes."

"So what're you waiting for? Come on up."

The first hint that something was not quite right hit her as she climbed the stairs to his second-floor flat. There was an odd smell, very faint, that she couldn't place.

It wasn't until Piers opened his front door and the full force of the smell rushed out to greet her that Clare recognized it. And if she hadn't, the sound of excitable male voices coming from the living room gave it away.

The air was thick with the acrid stench of alcohol-fueled bodies. Through the open living-room door Clare could see them draped across furniture and stretched out on the floor.

"What's going on? When did they get here?" Horrified, she took a step back.

"Last night. Well, this morning," Piers amended with a boyish grin. "I got back from London around midnight and they persuaded me to meet them at the club. Then we all came back here and crashed out. Here, let me take these." He seized the Thresher's shopping bag and pulled out the lagers. "Just what we need, hair of the dog."

"I thought it was just going to be us." Clare wanted to cry, or stamp her feet in frustration. This was the polar opposite of what she'd been looking forward to. Unless… "Are they going home now?"

"You must be joking. The rugby starts in ten minutes. It's what we've been waiting for."

"OK. Well, why don't I come back later?"

"Don't be daft, you're here now. You're allowed to stay." As he said it, Piers began to nuzzle her neck. "God, you smell gorgeous."

Unlike the rest of your guests, Clare thought sourly. Oh hell, why did this have to happen? She wanted to stay, more than anything. But only with Piers. Why couldn't all his hideously noisy, hard-drinking wanker-banker friends just *go*?

"Come on. You're staying and that's that." Piers pushed her through to the living room and held the Thresher's bag aloft like a football trophy.

"Look what we've got! Lager and... ugh, wine." He turned to Clare, his expression pained. "I said no wine. We're lads, we don't drink wine."

"It's for me," said Clare.

"I'm a woman trapped in a lad's body," announced Eddie, one of Piers's closest friends. Pursing his lips, he blew a kiss at Piers. "Don't fret, petal, I'll have a glass of wine. Clare, come over here and sit by me." He patted the cream sofa across which he was sprawled, still in last night's crumpled clothes. "We'll let the boys watch their nasty rough game on TV, shall we? You and I can have a lovely girlie chat about... ooh, nail varnish."

Eddie was a big groping lech whose hands wandered at the slightest opportunity. Clare may as well have announced brightly, "OK, great, and by the way, everyone, I'm naked under this trench coat," because it would take Eddie less than ten seconds to discover this and declare it to the room at large.

"I'm fine over here." She picked an uncomfortable chair next to the window, well away from Fast Eddie.

"Take off your coat," said Piers, snapping open a lager. "Aren't you hot?"

"Of course she's *hot*." The way Eddie leered made Clare itch to slap him.

"I'm not, actually. I'm cold. I'll keep my coat on, thanks."

The next ninety minutes became a personal battle. Telling herself that as soon as the stupid rugby game was over, everyone would leave, Clare vowed to sit it out. Or, more accurately, sweat it out. The sun poured through the south-facing second-floor window and perspiration trickled down her back. The window couldn't be opened because someone—none of them could remember who—had swallowed the key last night for a bet. The fake fur lining of the trench coat was sticking to her skin. All around her, men were roaring encouragement at the TV screen, knocking back the beers, and calling the referee a pansy every time he granted a throw-in to the other side.

When the match finally ended, Eddie rose to his feet.

"Right, everyone pitch in a tenner and I'll go and pick up some more booze."

No, no, *no*. Scarlet-cheeked with heat and indignation, Clare cornered Piers in the kitchen.

"Can't you make them go?" Her teeth were so clenched she could barely get the words out.

"What, kick them out onto the streets?" Piers looked surprised. "I can't do that."

"I want you to."

"Now you're being unreasonable. Angel, these are my friends. They don't mind you being here."

"They're all drunk. I thought we were going to relax and have some time alone together."

Piers appeared genuinely mystified. "You should have said."

Now she really wanted to cry. "I had a special surprise for you too."

"You did? What is it?"

Clare gave him an are-you-mad? look. "You're not getting it now."

"Ooh, touchy." He grinned. "Never mind, I've got loads of ties."

"It wasn't a tie. Anyway, I'm going now."

Piers shrugged. "OK."

She should hate him. Why didn't she hate him for treating her like this? Even now, if he begged her to stay, she probably would.

Except that was the thing about Piers, he never did beg.

"Hey hey, what's going on out here? Am I interrupting something sleazy?" Eddie barged into the kitchen, waving a fistful of tenners.

"No," Claire said coldly. "I'm just leaving."

"Leaving?" He mimed horror, clasping his big hands to his chest. "But you can't leave, I won't let you!"

Eddie was such a dickhead. To let Piers know how fed up she was, Clare rolled her eyes and said briskly, "Bye," then turned and made for the kitchen door.

"Nooo! I can't bear it, *stay with me*," Eddie wailed melodramatically. His hand, shooting out, grabbed the back of her trench coat. As he yanked her toward him, Clare let out a squawk of fear and tugged the hem of the trench coat back down to her knees.

She was a split second too late. A slow, idiotic grin spread over Eddie's face.

"Oh, wow. Hello, baby!" He leered at her, Austin Powers-style. "Or should I call you Sharon? Tell me, did I really just see what I thought I saw?"

Piers, whose view had been blocked by Eddie, said, "Saw what? And who's Sharon?"

"Sharon Stone." Eddie gave his friend a hefty nudge. "You remember, in *Basic Instinct*." His grin broadening, he turned back to Clare. "So that's why you kept your coat on."

Their laughter followed her all the way down the staircase. Hot tears of humiliation were scalding her eyes by the time she reached the street. A taxi came along and she flagged it down. It was, officially, a disastrous day and the bloody sun was shining more brightly than ever. To add insult to injury, the inside of the cab smelled overwhelmingly of chicken madras and vile dangly air freshener.

"Blimey, love, thought it was gonna rain, did you? You must be boiling in that getup." The driver swiveled round as she cranked open the window. "I'm tellin' you, you'll feel a lot better if you take that coat off."

Chapter 16

THE ANNOYING THING ABOUT electronic organizers was that Nadia didn't know how to work them.

Jay had left behind his Psion on the newly installed worktop in the kitchen before disappearing for the afternoon. Picking it up and turning it this way and that, Nadia thought back fondly to the days of the good old Filofax, when all you had to do to get into them was unpop the clasp. Then you could poke around to your heart's content.

Why did Psions have to be so inaccessible? Honestly, they must have been invented by the world's biggest spoilsport. Who knew what stupendous secrets might be lurking inside this little metal case? Nadia gave it a shake, just in case this was all it needed in order to fall open and magically start spilling out riveting items of gossip about his private life. Then, hearing footsteps on the stairs, she hurriedly stuffed the Psion into her bag. If Bart spotted it, he might volunteer to drop it round to Jay's house on his way home from work.

And there was really no need, she was quite capable of doing that herself.

Nadia pulled into Canynge Road at just gone six o'clock. Jay's car was there, which was good. Not that she had any kind of hidden agenda or anything. It was just always nice... *interesting*... to see where other people lived and what the insides of their homes looked like. She might not be able to get into his electronic organizer but she could get into his house.

Well, it would be a perfectly natural response, wouldn't it? If she turned up on his doorstep with his Psion, the least Jay could do was invite her in for a quick coffee or something. She'd be able to see where he'd hung the telephone box painting, check out the rest of the artwork, discover whether he was obsessively tidy or a complete slob…

Good grief.

Oh help, did this mean she was turning into a stalker?

Except a stalker would surely stop to run a comb through her hair and put on a bit of makeup before calling round to visit her stalkee.

Reassuring herself that she wasn't deranged, merely curious in a perfectly healthy and normal way, Nadia climbed out of the car.

Jay's front door was painted a glossy dark green, with a heavy brass letter box and knocker. When he opened the door he seemed surprised to see her, as if he'd been expecting someone else.

"Oh, hi. What's this about?"

Not the most enthusiastic of welcomes, but Nadia gave him one of her sunniest smiles anyway. He'd changed out of his work clothes into dark blue trousers and a pomegranate-pink polo shirt that not all men could get away with, and he was back to looking harassed.

"You didn't even realize you'd left it behind." Tut-tutting good-naturedly, she held up the Psion. "I found it in the kitchen."

"Right. Thanks." Nodding with relief, Jay took the organizer from her. "Thanks for bringing it over."

For heaven's sake, had the big bad wolf taught him nothing? Why wasn't he inviting her in? Expectantly Nadia said, "That's OK, it wasn't too far out of my way. And it's not as if I needed to rush home."

She was just wondering whether to ask casually how he was

enjoying his phone box painting when Jay cleared his throat and said, "Look, I'd ask you inside but I'm actually just on my way out. There's someone I have to meet."

"Oh no, no, that's fine, heavens, I can't stop anyway." Nadia heard herself begin to babble. "I have to pick up my sister and take her to buy a... a hamster."

It was pretty startling, listening to the words coming out of her own mouth. Jay looked taken aback too.

"Your sister the artist?"

A hamster. Why? Why?

"Not Clare. My other sister," Nadia hurriedly explained. "She's thirteen. You know how thirteen-year-olds are about hamsters. Tilly's set her heart on one and I promised to drive her out to this farm where they're selling them. Anyway, I'd better go, she'll be wondering where I am."

Wondering why I'm such an idiot more like, Nadia thought as she hurried back to the car. The next time Jay left something behind at the house she'd jolly well leave it there. Hamsters indeed.

It was while she was unwrapping a piece of gum that she noticed the taxi pulling up outside Jay's house. Folding the strip of gum into her mouth, Nadia watched as a woman with long blonde hair emerged, paid the driver, and waited for change. From this distance the woman looked to be in her early thirties and beautiful in an unsmiling ice-queen kind of way. Like a bored model sashaying down a catwalk, thought Nadia as the woman flicked back her hair. Honestly, talk about miserable. What she needed was someone to tell her a really fantastic joke.

Then the taxi pulled away, leaving her standing on the pavement in full view, and Nadia saw what she hadn't been able to see before.

The woman was pregnant.

Startled, Nadia watched her turn and climb the steps to Jay's front door, then ring the bell and wait. When the door opened, she looked at Jay and briefly said something before walking past him into the house. The door then closed behind them.

By the size of the bump beneath the woman's flowing yellow dress she had to be seven or eight months pregnant. Nadia sat back in her seat, too dumbfounded to even chew her gum. If the blonde was Jay's girlfriend—especially his pregnant girlfriend—wouldn't they have heard about her before now? He'd never even hinted that he was involved with someone.

Then again, what if she were his ex-girlfriend? That would explain why she wasn't looking too cheerful. God, and who could blame her? She was about to have a baby and it had all gone pear-shaped with the father; that was enough to make anyone miserable.

Stop it. Nadia gave herself a mental telling-off, because she was getting carried away again. Just because a pregnant woman had disappeared into Jay's home didn't automatically mean the baby was his. She could be his cleaning lady, or someone he hired to do his ironing, or a piano teacher who just happened to be pregnant—

The front door opened again.

Even as she scrunched down in the driver's seat, Nadia wondered why she was bothering. If Jay peered down the road in her direction he'd recognize her car in an instant. But he wasn't even glancing to his left. He had his arm round the pregnant woman and was carrying a small overnight case. As he unlocked his own car and helped her into the passenger seat, he gave her hand a squeeze.

Well, thought Nadia when Jay's car had disappeared from view. Probably not his piano teacher then.

———

"But I don't want a hamster," said Tilly the following evening.

"How do you know you don't want one? You've never had one before." Nadia was doing her double-glazing salesman bit. "You don't know what you're missing."

"I think I do. Having to clean hamster poo out of some smelly old cage." Tilly wrinkled her nose. "And it's not as if they ever do anything interesting unless you count sex, and you need two hamsters for that."

Nadia wondered why she had to have such a selfish and uncooperative sister. Last night she'd been so busy envisaging Jay as a father-to-be that all thoughts of hamsters had gone clean out of her head.

When Jay had turned up at work this morning and said casually, "Did you get one then?" she hadn't had the faintest idea what he was talking about.

"A hamster?" Jay had prompted when she'd looked blank.

"Oh! Oh right. Yes, we got one. He's great." She'd nodded with enthusiasm. "Tilly's thrilled."

"Good. What kind is he?"

Kind? Whoops.

"Um, white." Were hamsters white or was that just rats? "Well, whitish. More of a sort of pale brown actually." Nadia had been forced to improvise rapidly. "And really furry. His name's Gerald. He, um, poos a lot."

Jay had seemed happy enough with this information. Tilly, on the other hand, was being decidedly difficult.

"Yuk," she retorted. "I hate hamsters, they're like rats."

"OK." Nadia conceded defeat. "But you have to promise me something. If a strange man ever starts asking about your hamster, just pretend you have a pale brown one called Gerald."

"You're weird," said Tilly.

"I know. But I'm very lovable. Blimey, what's Michael Schumacher doing coming to our house?" Nadia peered out through the living-room window as something testosterone-fueled roared up the drive.

"It's for me." Clare's voice sang out from upstairs. "It's Piers. Can someone let him in?"

This was Clare's way of letting everyone know she was far too cool to be ready on time.

Pulling open the front door, Nadia came face to face with someone who clearly thought he was great.

Irresistible, in fact.

"Hi, Clare'll be down in a minute." Nadia had never seen him before, but she'd met plenty of his type. Confidence oozed from every pore. Instinctively she suspected she didn't like Piers.

"You must be Nadine." He flashed her a boyish grin. "I've heard all about you."

It was on the tip of Nadia's tongue to call him Peter, but she didn't.

"And you're Piers. Come through to the living room, Clare won't be long."

Tilly, twisting round on the sofa, beamed hello at him. "She can never make up her mind what to wear."

"You're telling me." Piers winked at Nadia. "And sometimes she doesn't wear anything at all."

Nadia gave him a blank look.

"Didn't Clare tell you about Saturday?" Piers started to laugh.

"No. Tell me about what?"

There was the sound of thunderous footsteps on the staircase, then Clare breathlessly catapulted into the living room.

"Ready! Let's go!"

—⁓—

As the electric-blue Ferrari made its way down Whiteladies Road, Clare reveled in the fact that they were the center of attention. She adored the way people turned and stared, wondering who she was and what she'd done to deserve a ride in such a crowd-stopper of a car.

After the humiliating events of Saturday afternoon, she had given serious thought to finishing with Piers. But when he'd phoned her on Monday he couldn't have been more charming or apologetic.

Plus, Clare had hastily reminded herself, it really hadn't been his fault. She couldn't blame him for the actions of one idiotic friend.

Which was why she'd agreed to see him tonight and was now extremely glad she had. Piers was on his best behavior, having arrived to pick her up exactly on time and looking sensational in the white shirt and rich-boy navy suit that went so well with his eyes. How could she not feel great when they were together? They looked like a couple out of a glossy magazine, Clare thought joyfully. And he was taking her along to the opening of a new club where everyone who mattered would see them being a couple. Ha, they'd all be so jealous.

"D'you have a brush in there?" Piers nodded at the beaded clutch bag on her lap.

"Yes, do you want to borrow it?"

"I meant for you." He sounded amused. "I prefer your hair down."

Clare bit back the automatic retort that it was her hair and she'd spent ages putting it up. Piers had an eye for these things; style-wise, he knew what was what. If he thought she looked better with her hair down, it probably did look better down.

Taking the small brush out of her bag, Clare began unpinning the carefully constructed chignon.

"Good girl." Piers tooted his horn at a gaggle of students crossing the road too slowly for his liking.

A hideous thought suddenly occurred to her. "Eddie isn't going to be there, is he?"

Piers grinned. "It's OK, you're safe. Eddie's still in a state of shock. By the way," he slid his hand experimentally up her bare thigh, "are you wearing anything under that slinky dress?"

"Big knickers. Very big knickers. And I have to be back home tonight," she added, to show him she wasn't a pushover.

Piers looked hurt. "You can't go home. I want you to stay at my place."

Clare smiled to herself, pleased to be back in charge, her thigh tingling pleasurably beneath his touch.

"Well. We'll see."

Chapter 17

TILLY WATCHED FROM HER bedroom window, a mixture of fear and excitement squirming in her stomach. It was Saturday, it was midday and any minute now her mother would be pulling into the driveway along with her new boyfriend and her new boyfriend's daughter. Brian and Tamsin, mustn't forget their names. They might be complete strangers now but they could end up being her family.

Tilly scratched at the flakes of loose paint on the window frame and prayed she'd like them. When she hadn't seen her mother for months it was easy to mock Leonie and her scatty, rackety ways. But when she was actually here in person it all seemed to matter that little bit more.

As the car came bouncing up the drive, Tilly took a deep, steadying breath. Her stomach was doing that falling-off-a-cliff thing. What was she thinking of, hoping she'd like Brian and Tamsin? What if they didn't like her?

"Oh my baby, come here, give me a hug, look how you've *grown*." Bracelets jangled as Leonie flung out her arms. She was wearing a floaty, pointy-hemmed dress that swirled around her ankles, silver earrings as big as saucers, and woody-spicy perfume. Hugging her, it occurred to Tilly that she'd never known her mother to wear the same scent twice.

Bit like boyfriends.

"Just look at you," Leonie mock-scolded, holding her at arm's length. "Jeans and a funny old T-shirt. And so skinny! I hope you're eating properly."

"Of course I'm eating properly." Tilly tucked her hair behind her ears, feeling mousy and plain. With her long Clairol-blonde hair, heavily made-up eyes, and bright clothes, Leonie looked marvelously exotic in a flashy, fairground kind of way.

"It's so good to see you again. Is anyone else around?" Leonie's gaze drifted toward the house and Tilly braced herself.

"They're in the kitchen."

"I suppose I'd better be polite and say hello. Ooh, introductions first. Darling, this is Brian." Linking her arm through Tilly's, Leonie swung her round to meet the other occupants of the car. "And Brian's daughter Tamsin. You two, this is Tilly, my beautiful baby girl. Now why don't you all get to know each other while I pop inside for a quick chat? Does James have a nose stud yet?"

"A what?"

"Joking, darling. Won't be a minute, then we can go."

Tilly watched her mother's hips sway as she headed for the house. She hated it when Leonie introduced her to people then promptly abandoned her with them. Feeling awkward, she turned back to the occupants of the car. Brian had long hair that was thinning on top and he was wearing a leather vest, as befitted someone who was slightly over the hill and in the music business. Tamsin, who was eyeing her with undisguised curiosity, was startlingly pretty with sparkly green eyes and a heart-shaped face. Her denim jacket was covered in scrawled writing and she was sitting cross-legged on the backseat with an iPod in her lap.

"Hi," said Tilly in desperation.

"All right?" Brian was busy tapping his fingers against the steering wheel, drumming along to an invisible beat.

"Are you a vegetarian?" said Tamsin.

"Um, no." Tilly wondered if this would be enough to make Tamsin hate her.

"Oh." The girl sounded amused. "You look like one."

—᷍᷍—

Things got easier over lunch in a busy pizzeria on Park Street. Leonie was on vivacious form, keeping the conversation going between the four of them. Relaxing, Tilly decided that Tamsin wasn't so bad after all; despite the vegetarian jibe, she was less scary than she'd first appeared. Brian seemed OK too, although he didn't actually say much. He did, however, have a couple of old friends in Bristol whom he was anxious to look up. Tilly was finishing her tiramisu when Leonie explained this.

"So what we thought, darling, is we'd pop off and see them for an hour or two when we leave here. That gives you and Tamsin some time together to really get to know each other, and we'll meet the two of you back here at… ooh, five o'clock?"

It was like being unexpectedly set up on a blind date. Not that she'd ever been on one. With a jolt of dismay, Tilly said, "What do we do until then?"

"Darling, you're teenagers, what do girls your age normally do on a Saturday afternoon?" Leonie stroked Brian's neck as she spoke. "Have fun together. Chat about music! Go shopping!"

"Can't." Tamsin gloomily sucked her ice-cream spoon. "No money."

"We'll give you money," Leonie announced. "And see you back here at five."

—᷍᷍—

"Ten pounds each." Tamsin shook her head in disgust as the two of them emerged from the restaurant. "That won't even keep me in cigarettes."

"It's better than nothing." Tilly actually thought ten pounds was quite a lot.

"Blimey, you're easily pleased. My mother would love you, she was always moaning about how much I cost her. I like your mum, though. She's good fun, isn't she?"

"I suppose." Tilly couldn't help feeling fobbed off. For the last fortnight she'd been mentally building herself up, preparing for her mother's visit, and it was practically over already. At five o'clock they'd all meet up again and find somewhere else to eat. By seven, Leonie would be making let's-go noises, explaining how long it would take to drive all the way back to Brighton. By seven thirty they'd be gone.

"She wants to see how well we get along together." Tamsin offered her a Marlboro Light. "Isn't it a bit weird, you living with some bloke who isn't even your dad?"

"No." Tilly was instantly on the defensive. "I like it."

"So what happened? I mean, Leonie told us about your real dad doing a bunk when you were a baby, but she was a bit vague about the rest."

You don't say, thought Tilly.

"My mum had my sisters first, then she left them with James and went off with some other bloke to Crete. When they broke up, she met another chap, and when *they* broke up she met another one." Bluntly Tilly said, "My mother has a low boredom threshold. Anyway, she was living with a furniture maker called Liam when she found out she was pregnant with me. After my first birthday, Liam took off. Then the lease ran out on the place they'd been renting. Mum didn't have anywhere to live so she turned up on James's doorstep with me in her arms and begged him to let us stay for a few days. James is so nice he didn't have the heart to say no."

"So they got back together?" Tamsin was actually interested.

"No. We were there for three months. Then Mum met the next big love of her life, someone else she couldn't live without. Except *he* wasn't so keen on the idea of taking me on as part of the deal. Mum was distraught, she didn't know what to do, she said she couldn't cope with me on her own… well, by this time I was settled at James's house. I loved being with my sisters—half sisters—and I thought James was my dad. He told Mum he was happy for me to stay with them. I don't know if he only meant for a while"—Tilly's smile was rueful—"but I never left. Mum went off with her boyfriend—I think he lasted a couple of years, which was practically a record for her. And I was happy where I was. I suppose I just got used to her not being around. She was never a mother-type mother."

"You're lucky." Tamsin flicked her cigarette into the gutter as they strode along. "Mine is, and it's a complete nightmare. She's so strict you wouldn't believe it. Nag, nag, nag, do your homework, clean your room, you're not going out wearing *that*—it did my head in. That's why I came to live with my dad instead." She shook back her hair, clearly pleased with herself. "He lets me do whatever I like."

With only ten pounds each to spend, their trawl around the shops didn't last long. When Tamsin discovered that Tilly's school was only fifteen minutes' walk away, and that the varsity team was playing cricket against Bristol Grammar, she insisted they went along to watch the game.

Tilly wrinkled her nose; cricket was unbelievably dull. "What for?"

"Look, it's your duty to cheer them on. And check out the talent."

"You haven't seen the boys in my year." Tilly gave her a pitying look. "We have no talent."

"Ah, you say that, but I'd be viewing them with a fresh eye. And they'd fancy me rotten, because boys always do. Then next time I come down, we can arrange to meet up with them. Oh, come on, it'll be a laugh," Tamsin urged. "I'll do the same for you when you come and stay with us. Boys you don't know are always more fun than boys you do."

On the way to the school, they had to pass the newsagents where Annie worked. When they'd joined the crush earlier in

Claire's Accessories in Broadmead, Tamsin had immediately blown her money on fake tattoos, stick-on glitter transfers, and a toe ring. In order not to be left out, Tilly had spent nine pounds sixty on a nail varnish and two hair ties she didn't even want. Now, with only forty pence left in her pocket, she was regretting it. All this walking had made her thirsty; she could've murdered a can of Coke.

But tonight was Annie's big dinner date with James, the dinner date she'd had such a hand in arranging, and it would be nice to pop in and say hello.

Better still, Annie might let them have a glass of tap water, which meant she could spend her remaining forty pence on chewing gum.

"Want to go in here?" Tilly paused as they drew level with the shop.

"Sure. I like newsagents." Tamsin grinned at her. "We can wave at ourselves on the CCTV."

"I don't think this one has CCTV."

"No? Shame." Jauntily, Tamsin said, "Lead on, Macduff."

Annie was behind the counter, leafing through a copy of *Hello!* magazine.

"You caught me out." Beaming at Tilly, she pointed to the photo she'd been studying, of Jennifer Aniston arriving at some movie premiere with a glamorous new hairdo. "I'm getting mine done straight after we've closed here. This is the kind of thing I'm after, but it's so embarrassing taking a photo along, isn't it? You just imagine all the stylists sniggering with each other in the back room, going, 'Ha, she seriously thinks we can make her look like Jennifer Aniston!'"

"Maybe if you took along a photo of someone more your own age?" Tilly only made the suggestion to be helpful, but the moment the words were out she knew they'd been the wrong ones. Annie was looking determinedly un-upset. Oh God, Jennifer Aniston was probably older than her.

Behind her, Tilly could hear Tamsin quietly snorting with laughter, which didn't help.

"I'm sorry," she muttered. Why did it always have to be her mouth that spouted the embarrassing stuff?

"It doesn't matter a bit. And you're probably right. I'm not going to take the picture along anyway." Annie closed the magazine. "I'll just tell them to put my hair up and do their best to make me look smart. So, what are you doing here on a Saturday?"

"There's a cricket match on at the school. We're going along to watch." Glancing over her shoulder, Tilly said, "This is Tamsin. My… um, friend."

To her horror, as she turned, she saw Tamsin hurriedly stuffing something into her jeans pocket… Tilly couldn't believe it. If she was looking at Tamsin—*introducing* Tamsin, for crying out loud—then surely Annie had to have seen it too.

"Er, I'll have some orange Tic Tacs please," Tilly said, far too loudly, "and a packet of Juicy Fruit."

Ignoring Tilly, Annie said calmly, "Maybe you should put those back."

"Excuse me?" Tamsin raised her eyebrows, apparently mystified. "Put what back?"

Oh God, oh God. Tilly began to sweat.

"Those pens." Annie's gaze didn't waver from Tamsin's face. "The ones you just put in your pocket."

"Pens? Why would I want a bunch of stupid pens?" Tamsin looked at her as if she were mad. "Tilly, ready to go? We don't want to miss the match."

Tilly was rooted to the spot and in a state of anguish. She wanted to cover her eyes like a three-year-old and pretend she wasn't here.

"See this?" Annie gestured to the laminated sign up on the wall behind the counter, announcing that Shoplifters Would Be Prosecuted. "It's true. Now come on, just be sensible and—"

"Who's going to catch me if I ran out of here now? You?" Tamsin smirked. "I don't think so."

Annie said evenly, "I know which school you go to."

"And that's where you're wrong, because I don't even live in Bristol. So you'll never find me." Tamsin's eyes were bright with triumph. "Unless you get the police to do a photofit picture of me and stick Wanted posters up all over the country. Who knows, they might even put me on *Crimewatch*. Can't you just picture it? Thirteen-year-old girl pinches ballpoint pens from crappy corner shop…"

"Put them back," Tilly blurted out.

Tamsin raised her plucked eyebrows. "Excuse me?"

"Put the pens back."

"Oh, for God's sake, this is pathetic." Heaving an exaggerated sigh that was practically a snort, Tamsin dragged the pens from her pocket and flung them back into their box on the stationery shelf. "There, happy now?"

Tilly turned back to Annie. "I'm sorry. I'm so sorry."

"Not your fault," Annie said quietly.

"Could you… um, not mention this to James?"

Annie hesitated, then nodded. "OK."

"Ahem," Tamsin sang out. "Getting *bored* over here. Can we go?"

Chapter 18

"How could you do that?" Tilly hissed when they were outside.

Tamsin pulled a mocking face. "God, what's the big deal? It was only a bit of fun."

"I know her. She's going out with James tonight."

"What, *her*? Ha, that'll give Leonie a good laugh. Oh, come on, cheer up." Tamsin slid her arm through Tilly's and pulled a funny face. "I didn't know you knew her, did I? Look, I promise you never have to take me into that shop again. Next time I'll wait outside like a dog, I promise. And I'm sorry, sorry, sorry... there, can't grovel harder than that, can I?"

By five o'clock, Tilly was officially confused. After the hideous scene in the newsagents, it had become obvious that Tamsin was Seriously Bad News. Except... an hour later, she had flirted so effectively with the boys from school that purely by association Tilly had rocketed into the top ten of girls worth talking to.

This was something that had never happened before. Not that she wanted anything to do with that bunch of sad losers, but entering the league was a seductive prospect nonetheless.

"That was pretty cool." Tamsin sounded pleased with herself as they headed back to the pizza restaurant. In possession of at least a dozen mobile phone numbers, she could afford to be smug. At this rate she'd be kept busy texting for the next fortnight.

"They're dorks." Tilly flicked back her hair as if it was worth flicking back. But secretly she was envious.

"Maybe. Who cares? They fancied me rotten."

"Yeah." This was true. Tilly knew that when she went back to school on Monday, everyone would be asking her about Tamsin.

"Don't tell my dad about the shop thing, OK?"

"OK."

"Cool." Tamsin gave her a nudge. "Hey, if your mum marries my dad, we'll be, like, sisters."

This was it, the sense of belonging she'd been missing for so long. Forcing a smile, Tilly said, "Yeah."

They met Leonie and Brian outside the pizza place on Park Street.

When they dropped Tilly back home at seven o'clock, Leonie gave her a patchouli-scented hug and said, "I *knew* you two would get on."

"Well…"

"Brian's asked me to marry him. Isn't that fantastic?"

Dutifully, but with a sinking heart, Tilly echoed, "Fantastic."

"Darling, this is my big chance. This time it has to work. You'll help me, won't you? You won't let me down?"

Feeling slightly sick and wondering what she meant, Tilly said, "No, Mum, I won't let you down."

Annie Healey wiped the steam from her bathroom mirror and regarded her soft-focus reflection with a mixture of fear and anticipation.

Not fear, that wasn't the right word. Apprehension, maybe. Or just general anxiety.

Actually, no, it was fear.

Scrubbing the mirror clean with her bath towel, Annie pulled a Macaulay Culkin face at herself. She was thirty-eight years old, for heaven's sake. How pathetic to be this scared when all she was doing was going out to dinner with a man.

But she was just so horribly out of practice. Fourteen years out of practice, to be exact. Oh God, don't even think about it. Just brush your teeth, then put some makeup on. Your skin hasn't come out in an embarrassing rash. Everything's going to be fine.

When he arrived at seven o'clock to pick her up, James was looking very smart and not a little uneasy himself. As he helped her into the car, Annie said, "Look, this probably isn't the normal way of going about things, but I feel it's only fair to warn you that I'm very nervous."

Straightening, James adjusted his spectacles. "You are? Oh, I'm sorry. Nervous being with me?"

"Don't take it personally." Annie shook her head. "I'd be the same with anyone. You see, I'm not used to doing this. It's been a long time."

James climbed into the driver's seat and stuck the key in the ignition. "Me too."

"A very long time."

"Same here."

"OK," said Annie, "I don't want to sound childishly competitive here, but I bet my time's longer than your time."

James smiled. "We don't have to be at the Elsons' until eight o'clock. Shall we stop somewhere and have a drink first?"

"Definitely," said Annie with relief.

They sat out in the garden of a pretty pub in Easter Compton, which was en route to Pilning where Cedric and Mary-Jane lived.

"By the way," James cleared his throat, "you're looking very nice this evening. Sorry, my daughter told me I had to say that when I came to pick you up, and I forgot. But it's true," he hastily amended. "You really do look nice. I... er, like your hair as well."

Annie self-consciously touched her hair, which the hairdresser had back-combed and pinned into an ambitious chignon. Like a game of Jenga, she was terrified to move her head in case the whole lot came tumbling down.

Her dress wasn't helping matters either. When she'd tried it on in the shop, it had looked amazing, as glittery and gorgeous as a mermaid's tail. How could she possibly have known that the moment you sat down those triangular sequins would stick into your flesh like knives? Now, every time she shifted position on the chair, it was like being attacked by a shoal of tiny piranha fish.

Oh yes, off to a brilliant start.

"Go on then," James prompted. "Tell me how long it's been since you did this."

Here we go.

"Fourteen years," said Annie, and waited for him to spit his drink all over the table.

But all James did was nod. "Oh well, I can beat that. Seventeen years for me."

Blimey. It was Annie who was shocked. "Look at us, we're a right old couple of dinosaurs! What happened to you, then?"

"Well, it's complicated."

"Sorry, sorry." Embarrassed, she flapped her hands. "That was so rude. You don't have to tell me anything."

James shook his head. "No, not at all, it's fine. You should know anyway, if you're coming to my boss's dinner party. My wife walked out on me and my daughters twenty-three years ago. She's led a fairly chaotic life ever since. When she broke up with Tilly's father she needed a roof over her head so we let her move back in for a while. Then, when she took off again, she left Tilly with us."

"You're kidding," gasped Annie, though he clearly wasn't. "People leave sweaters behind, they leave gloves behind… they don't leave *children*."

"Leonie's in a league of her own. She felt she couldn't cope with Tilly. In fact"—James hesitated—"she gave us the choice. Either we took Tilly, or Tilly went into care. Well, there was no decision to make. We already loved her. Tilly doesn't know this, by the way."

He paused again and took a drink. "As far as she's concerned, we offered to bring her up and Leonie agreed."

Annie was deeply shocked. "Does she still see her mother at all?"

"Intermittently. When it suits Leonie. She saw Tilly today, in fact. Brought her latest boyfriend and his daughter up from Brighton to introduce them to Tilly. The girls are pretty much the same age, apparently."

Right. Annie nodded as all became clear. She was also touched by James's attitude; only a truly decent man would do what he had done, taking on and bringing up a child for whom he was in no way responsible. The simple way he had said, "We already loved her," had brought a lump to her throat.

"Tilly's a credit to you." Annie swallowed the lump. "She's a lovely girl."

"It's been no hardship. Tilly's a credit to herself." James spoke with genuine warmth. "We were the lucky ones. She'd have been a lovely girl whoever brought her up. Anyway, enough about us. Can I be nosy and ask about you?"

"Ask away. But I'm not very exciting." Annie's eyes sparkled. Now that they were sitting down together actually having a conversation, her nervousness had lessened dramatically. She was feeling far more comfortable.

Apart from the sequins, obviously.

"I'm assuming you were married." James cleared his throat apologetically, as if he'd just suggested she was a mass murderer. "Sorry, that's none of my business."

"I've never been married." Annie had to smile. "And I haven't split up with a long-term partner. My mother had a stroke," she said matter-of-factly. "Fourteen years ago. She needed someone to move in with her, and I did. Six years ago she had a second stroke. Last year she died. All the time Mum was ill, I was too busy looking after her to meet anyone who might... you know, become important. Propping up bars and telling men you had to be home by nine o'clock to change your mother's incontinence pads wasn't the greatest chat-up line in the world. I don't regret it, because Mum was brilliant, but this is why I'm what you might call a late starter. Thirty-eight." Annie pulled a face. "Not to mention embarrassingly out of practice."

"Did you really not mind?" said James. "Giving up your life to look after your mother?"

"I didn't give up my life. It just kind of went… on hold. No." Annie shook her head and smiled. "How could I mind? She was my mum."

It was ten to eight and their glasses were empty. Gathering them up, James rose to his feet.

"Another drink?"

"Don't we have to be there by eight?"

"I don't want to go. I'd much rather stay here, talking to you."

It was what Annie wanted too, but she had a highly developed guilt gene.

"They'll be waiting for us. We have to go."

"Why do you keep doing that?" With a crooked smile, James imitated her wiggle.

Damn, he'd noticed.

"Death by sequins." Annie was rueful. "They're digging into my legs. It's all right for you," she complained, "all you have to wear is a suit and—ouch! What was *that* for?"

James had just hit her. *Bam*, right on top of her head.

Chapter 19

CLAPPING HER HANDS TO her smarting scalp, Annie's eyes widened in disbelief. For heaven's sake, and now he was reaching across the table with his own hand raised, getting ready to hit her again.

Economically, James said, "Wasp."

"Oh God, did you get it? I'm allergic to wasps!" Annie let out a squeak of fear as she heard the ominous sound of buzzing emanating from the depths of her hairdo—this was far more alarming than being hit over the head. Practically launching herself at James's chest she shouted, "Get it out, get it out!"

The wasp was trapped in a mass of lacquered back-combing. Squeezing her eyes shut, she felt James yank out the grips and combs, separating her hair like David Bellamy venturing intrepidly through the jungle.

"I can see it."

"Kill it! Kill it!" shrieked Annie, dimly aware that everyone else in the pub garden was by this time agog. The next moment a great wodge of hair flopped into her eyes as James made a grab for the furiously buzzing wasp. Snatching it up, he flung it away into the bushes.

"There, gone."

"Thank God for that." Annie shuddered with relief. "Last time my arm swelled up like the Elephant Man's. Imagine, if I'd got stung on my head I'd end up like some alien out of a sci-fi film. You saved my life."

"But not your hair." James sounded regretful. "I'm sorry."

Gingerly, she put her hands up to her head. "Don't tell me. I look like I've just been in fight."

"You look like you just lost a fight. I'm really sorry about hitting you," James added. "I was trying to stop it getting in."

"You were absolutely right to hit me." Annie smiled, to show she didn't mind being whacked on the head when there was good reason for doing so. "But I don't have a hairbrush." Recalling the incident in the newsagents when she had toppled off her stool, she added ruefully, "Honestly, what is it with me and wasps?"

The drive back to Kingsweston took less than ten minutes, but it was still a painful journey for Annie.

"It's no good, I'll have to change out of this dress. These sequins are killing me."

James looked concerned. "I hope you didn't buy it specially for tonight."

Oooh no, I've got a dozen glittery numbers in my wardrobe, I wear them every day under my overall at work. Men, honestly. They didn't have a clue.

"Not at all," Annie lied as they pulled up outside her cottage. "Come on in. I'll be as quick as I can."

"No hurry." James shook his head. "Dinner is going to be hideously boring."

Annie gave him a look. "Make yourself at home and ring your boss, tell him we're running late."

Upstairs, in the bathroom mirror, she discovered just how much of a disaster her hair was. It was to James's credit that he hadn't burst out laughing at the sight of her. She began brushing away at the sticky tendrils, so solid with megahold styling spray that the brushstrokes made her eyes prickle with pain.

Finally all the hair spray was out, and her hair was back to its normal shoulder-length no-style, not quite curly and not quite straight. Since creating any form of chignon was out of the question, Annie left it as it was and unzipped her dress. Oh, the bliss of freedom from spiky sequins. Never ever again would she be gullible enough to fall for a bit of sparkle.

The only other smart enough outfit she owned was a simple black shift, high-necked and sleeveless. Glad she didn't have a choice to dither over, Annie quickly put it on and added a rope of real-looking pearls.

"You look lovely," said James when she reappeared downstairs.

"Thanks." Annie briefly considered telling him that this was the dress she'd bought to wear to her mother's funeral.

Maybe not.

"Remind me again, why do we have to go to this dinner party?"

"Because your boss will sack you if you don't." Annie pulled open the front door. "Come on, it might be brilliant. Things are never as bad as you think they're going to be."

This was true, of course. Sometimes they turned out worse.

Cedric and Mary-Jane lived in a sprawling brand-new house cunningly designed to resemble an old farmhouse. As Mary-Jane answered the door, it occurred to James that with her it was the other way round. In her late forties, she did her level best to pass for a twenty-six-year-old. With her jacked-in waist and jacked-up face, she looked like Barbie's grandmother. She had such teeny-tiny stiletto-shod feet, James always felt the slightest nudge would send her toppling over onto her back.

Then again, this was possibly what had attracted Cedric to her in the first place.

"At last, at last!" Mary-Jane trilled, ushering them inside. "Everybody, they're here!"

"Sorry we're late. Spot of car trouble." James sensed that Mary-Jane wasn't the type to appreciate the wasp story.

"James, good to see you." Cedric came to greet them. "And this is…?"

"Annie Healey." As he spoke, James became aware that Mary-Jane was sizing up Annie's appearance and finding it lacking.

"*Sweet* little necklace," Mary-Jane murmured.

"Welcome, Annie." Cedric puffed enthusiastically on his King Edward cigar. "Now come along through and meet everyone; it's a pleasure to finally meet one of James's lady friends. Have you been together long?"

James tensed, but Annie said cheerfully, "Oh, for a while. This is a beautiful house you have here."

"Thank you, my dear. And may I say that James has excellent taste too. Now, what can I get you to drink?"

As they sat down to eat, it became apparent that Cedric was charmed by Annie and Mary-Jane wasn't taking it well. She clearly took it as a personal insult that her husband should be smitten with a woman whose hair was unstyled and whose dress was not only a size twelve but chain store to boot. Over their first course, Mary-Jane turned the conversation to jewelry, showed off her latest four-carat solitaire, then asked Annie where she'd bought her pearls.

"Claire's Accessories. Four pounds," Annie said happily. "They look quite real, don't they?"

Mary-Jane smirked at the other female guests, her mouth pursing like a cat's bottom. "Heavens, don't they bring you out in a rash?"

Worse was to come. As they were being served the main course, Ray Hickson snapped his fingers and said, "Got it!"

Ray was a fellow accountant of the sharp-suited, sleazeball kind, whom James had never liked.

"I knew I knew you from somewhere." Ray addressed Annie with a triumphant gleam in his eyes. "It's been bothering me since you got here, I just couldn't figure it out."

Mary-Jane put down her fork and said, "Ooh, do tell!"

"Hang on a sec." Ray made a show of patting his pockets. "Damn, looks like I'm out of cigarettes. Still, never mind." Producing his wallet, he slid out a tenner and waved it at Annie. "Give us twenty Benson and Hedges and a copy of the *FT*."

James suppressed the urge to reach across the table and punch him on the nose. Losing his temper was something he seldom did, but he would happily lose it now. The trouble was, Ray would only protest his innocence and say, "What's the problem? It was only a joke."

"Sorry, I'm afraid we're closed," said Annie. Turning to Cedric, who was looking perplexed, she calmly explained, "I work in a newsagents, not far from your offices."

"How extraordinary!" Mary-Jane started to laugh. "Is that how you two met? James, I had no idea you were involved with a shop assistant!"

James reddened with outrage on Annie's behalf. Intercepting his glance, she briefly shook her head.

Gallantly Cedric said, "My sister worked in a shop once, before she was married."

Mary-Jane snorted with laughter. "Darling, that was Asprey's."

If he stormed out now with Annie in tow, Cedric would be offended. Utterly blind to the wiles of his wife, he would blame James for spoiling the dinner party.

Discreetly, James excused himself and left the room.

He returned two minutes later, clutching his hand.

"Cedric, I'm sorry, we're going to have to leave. There was a wasp in your bathroom and it stung me."

"A wasp?" Cedric looked bemused. Annie put down her knife and fork.

"It's all right, I've killed it. But I'm allergic to wasp stings." Breathing heavily and holding out his hand, palm up, James showed them the puncture mark surrounded by a small raised reddened area. "If I don't take my medication in time, I could be in trouble. Annie, you'll have to drive me home. Cedric, I'm so sorry about this..."

James began to sway on his feet as he spoke. "Oh dear, getting light-headed, we really should be making a move…"

It was pretty scary, driving a make of car she'd never driven before, particularly one that had probably cost more than her own house. As soon as they'd rounded the corner and were safely out of sight of Cedric and Mary-Jane's faux-Tudor monstrosity, Annie slowed the Jag to a halt and said admiringly, "Quick thinking, Batman."

"I'm sorry, I shouldn't have let Ray get away with it. He's beyond belief. I wanted to smack him in the mouth."

Annie shook her head. "It's OK, I'm glad you didn't make a scene. And your boss was nice."

"He liked you too. That's why Mary-Jane was getting so wound up. Are you still hungry?" said James as they both climbed out of the car and swapped seats.

"And Ray's keen on Mary-Jane." Annie fastened her seat belt. "Which could be interesting. Hungry? D'you know, I could murder a prawn rogan josh."

The office was currently rife with gossip about Ray and Mary-Jane. James was impressed that Annie had picked up on it so speedily. He smiled to himself; the evening was about to improve.

"I'm so glad we got out of there."

"Phew, me too. But I still don't know how you managed it." Intrigued, Annie reached for his hand and examined the palm in the dim glow of the interior light. "This is amazing, it looks exactly like a real wasp sting. Did you stick a needle in there to make that bump?"

When she looked up, James's mouth was twitching. "It is a real wasp sting."

"But how could you…? I don't get this." Annie shook her head in disbelief, then ran her fingertips once more over the raised bump. "Oh my God, it's from the wasp that was caught in my hair, isn't it? You got stung when you grabbed it—and never even told me." Touched, she thought what an unbelievably gentlemanly thing that was to do.

"It's no big deal. I'm not really allergic to wasp stings." James looked amused. "And it came in handy."

"Every cloud has a silver lining," said Annie.

"Right. Prawn rogan josh it is then." Assertively, James restarted the car. "I know a great Indian restaurant in Redland."

"Will they mind that I work in a newsagents and my pearls aren't real?"

James, pulling away from the curb, said, "So long as you haven't drunk fifteen pints of lager, they'll welcome you with open arms."

Chapter 20

THE SECOND LETTER HAD arrived this morning. The gist of it, basically, was that he didn't believe he had made a mistake before.

Both irritated and unsettled, Miriam waited until everyone had gone to bed before sitting down at the kitchen table and composing her reply—in handwriting that sloped to the right and bore no resemblance to her own.

> *Dear Sir,*
>
> *I'm afraid this is a case of mistaken identity. You seem to think I am someone I'm not. As I am frail and in poor health, I would greatly appreciate it if you would desist from writing any further letters. I don't know who you are and can state categorically that we have never met.*
>
>

Yours sincerely,
M. Kinsella
>

Miriam addressed the envelope in the same slanty writing then slid the folded sheet of paper, along with his own letter, inside. As she was clicking shut her handbag, she heard the crunch of car tires outside on the drive.

The look on James's face when he put his head round the kitchen door told her all she needed to know.

"What time do you call this?" Miriam demanded, secretly delighted that he'd obviously had a good time. It wasn't as if James was short of female admirers, he'd just never taken them up on their offers. It was as if marriage to Leonie had unnerved him to such a degree that he hadn't been able to bring himself to risk dating again.

Then again, after Leonie, who could blame him?

Checking his watch, James pulled a face. "Ten past one. Don't tell me I'm grounded."

Miriam had written her letter with the aid of a large Scotch. Now, brandishing the bottle, she said, "Nightcap? So you had a good time at the dinner party after all."

"I had a good time," James agreed, sloshing Scotch into a tumbler, "but not at the dinner party."

"You didn't go?"

"Oh, we went. We just didn't stay. Ended up in an Indian restaurant instead. It's been a really great evening."

"With this woman Tilly set you up with? The one from the newsagents?"

Unlike Mary-Jane Elson, Miriam wasn't poking fun. Feeling happier than he had in a long time, James said, "Annie," and felt the back of his neck heat up. It was like coming out of a decades-long hibernation.

"Annie, that's it." Watching him, Miriam was reminded that she had felt the same way once, about the writer of the letter she'd had such trouble replying to tonight.

In a small corner of her heart she still loved him.

The rest of her wished he was dead. Not nastily dead, of course. Nothing violent or unpleasant. Just a peaceful, drifting-away-in-your-sleep kind of death.

Slightly ashamed to be thinking such a thing—but not ashamed enough to stop thinking it—Miriam said, "Tell me what Annie's like."

"Down-to-earth. Straightforward. She's a good person," said James. "Kind. Easy to be with." He paused. "And she's honest. Like you, really."

Honest. And a good person.

"Oh, that's me all right." As she flashed a smile, Miriam wondered how James would react if he knew the truth. "I'm just an all-round saint."

"I'm not stupid, you know," Tilly announced. "I know exactly what you're up to."

Nadia looked bemused as Tilly chucked her schoolbag into the back of the car and jumped into the passenger seat.

"What? All I did was offer to pick you up after school while Dad's away. It's practically on my way home and I knew I was finishing early today." Big lie. "What's wrong with that?"

Tilly raised her eyebrows. "Remind me again, which of us is thirteen?"

Precocious little brat.

"I just thought you'd be glad of a lift," Nadia protested.

"Take a tip from me." Tilly looked smug. "Never try and smuggle drugs through customs. That look-at-me-I'm-innocent thing's never going to fool anyone."

"Fine. So do you want a lift or not?"

"Lift please."

"And how about an ice cream?"

"What for?" said Tilly.

They were by this time heading in the direction of James's office building. Nadia flapped the neck of her T-shirt.

"I'm hot, I've been working my socks off, and I fancy a white Magnum. What's wrong with that?"

"You've got white Magnums at home in the freezer," Tilly pointed out. "Hidden under the broad beans so Clare won't find them."

"I want one now. And an evening paper." Casually Nadia said, "Where's that newsagents you usually go to?"

Equally casually, Tilly said, "There's a garage just up here on the left."

"Oh, come on," begged Nadia, "don't be so mean, I just want to see her! Is that it?" Brightening, she pointed to a small shop with a gaggle of schoolboys with skateboards loitering outside.

"No. Does this mean you'll buy me a Magnum?"

"If that's what you want."

"Actually," said Tilly, who was saving up for the new Eminem CD, "I'd rather have the money."

"Just tell me which one she works in."

"Up past the traffic lights, on the right."

Over the years Nadia had seen James being set up on blind dates against his better judgment and, true to form, nothing had ever come of them.

This time, clearly, things were different. Following his initial outing with Annie Healey on Saturday night, they had seen each other on Sunday afternoon, then again on Sunday evening and *again* on Monday evening. This morning, Tuesday, James had driven up to Liverpool for a two-day conference, having already arranged to meet up with Annie when he arrived back on Thursday night.

Bursting with curiosity and far too impatient to wait, Nadia had hatched her cunning plan and finished work early. She was longing to see her dad's new girlfriend for herself.

In honor of the occasion she even stamped the clods of earth from her wellies before entering the shop.

The woman serving behind the counter had wavy fair hair loosely tied back in a pony tail, friendly blue eyes with a trace of blue shadow melting into the creases, and plump ringless hands.

Tilly said, "Nadia, this is Annie Healey. Annie, meet Nadia, my sister."

Thinking how much less stressful for Annie a chance encounter would be than a deliberately pre-planned one, Nadia put on her surprised-but-delighted face and said, "Really? Well, hello! How lovely to meet you!"

"You too." Annie flushed slightly, but she was smiling.

"We came in because Nadia was desperate for an evening paper and a white chocolate Magnum." Tilly counted the reasons off on her fingers, frowned, then added happily, "Oh yes, and to check you out."

Fantastic.

"She wasn't supposed to say that," Nadia apologized to Annie. "I'll beat her up when we get home."

"It's OK, I don't mind. He's your dad." Annie was sympathetic. "I'd be curious too."

Hugely relieved to discover that she liked Annie Healey, Nadia said, "It's one of those weird situations. Our mother's had so many boyfriends I can hardly be bothered to meet them anymore. But with Dad it's different, he… um…"

"I know, he told me. And here I am." Annie pulled a face and gestured self-deprecatingly at her green nylon overall. "I hope you weren't expecting Nicole Kidman."

"Here you go." Tilly, who had been delving into the chest freezer, pushed a Magnum into Nadia's hand. "And don't forget your paper."

Nadia didn't want a paper, but she took one anyway. Tilly added helpfully, "You can give me my ice-cream money when we get home."

"When Dad's back from his conference, you must come round for dinner one evening," Nadia told Annie. "Meet everyone properly. But now we really have to go," she added, because the poor woman was still looking apprehensive, like an interviewee about to be grilled by Piers Morgan. "I've parked on double yellows—just my luck to get clamped."

"I don't get this. You tell me that it's bad to lie and then you go and do it," Tilly complained as they made their way back to the car. "We're not parked on double yellows."

"It was a white lie, to get us out of there. Sometimes it's easier to fib." Meaningfully Nadia added, "Like pretending I didn't know who Annie was until you opened your big mouth. What's that noise?"

Tilly glanced over her shoulder. "Boys from our school, mucking about."

As the shouts intensified, Nadia recognized the group of skateboarders she'd seen outside the other newsagents earlier.

"Somebody's on the ground. Are they playing or fighting?"

"Don't know." Tilly didn't care; they were Year 10s. Everyone knew Year 10s were a law unto themselves.

Everyone except Nadia.

"They're hitting him!" Outraged, Nadia grabbed Tilly by the sleeve.

"So? They're always hitting people. Come on, the car's this way."

"Now they're kicking him!" Nadia ignored Tilly's attempt to drag her away. "Right, that's it."

"Just leave them. Don't interfere," begged Tilly. "It'll be embarrassing."

"Even more embarrassing when you hear on the news that a schoolboy was kicked to death in the street and no one bothered to do anything about it. HEY!" shouted Nadia, breaking into a run and dragging Tilly along in her wake. "You lot, what d'you think you're doing? Leave him alone!"

"Ooh, I'm so scared," mocked one of the teenagers, grinning insolently at Nadia as she raced toward them. "Watch out, boys, it's Batman and Robin."

Tilly was mortified. The half-dozen fourteen-year-olds might not know her by name but they would undoubtedly recognize her from school. It was all right for Nadia, piling in where she wasn't wanted, she wasn't going to have to face them in the cafeteria tomorrow.

"I said STOP IT," roared Nadia, when one of the Year 10s aimed another kick at the boy sprawled on the ground.

"It's not Batman and Robin," one of the others jeered, "it's Clint Eastwood. Look, he's got his Magnum."

That cracked them up. They promptly began licking imaginary ice creams and snarling, "D'you feel lucky, punk? C'mon, make my day."

Nadia shoved the uneaten Magnum into Tilly's hand, glared at the ringleader, and said, "You should be ashamed of yourself."

"Look who's talking." With a smirk, he indicated her muddy wellingtons. "I wouldn't be seen dead in gear like that. What is it, all the rage down on the farm?"

"I recognize this one." His second-in-command jabbed a finger at Tilly, who by this time was puce with embarrassment and had ice cream trickling down her arm. "She's in my brother's class."

Tilly wanted to die.

"So who are you?" The ringleader leered at Nadia. "Her mother?"

"I'm her sister"—Nadia controlled herself with difficulty—"and you need a good slap."

"Oh dear, more violence? Is that really the answer?" The boy stood there with his hands on his hips, cockily chewing gum. "Sure you wouldn't rather just shoot me with your big scary Magnum before it melts?"

"Get out of here, all of you, or I'll call the police," bellowed Nadia and, laughing, they turned and scooted off on their skateboards.

"Did he really think I was your mum?" Nadia looked worried. "Maybe it's time to start buying proper moisturizer. It's OK, they've gone," she told the curled-up heap on the ground. Bending down, she rested a hand on his trembling shoulder and felt him flinch. "Sshh, you're safe, nobody's going to hurt you now."

"Go away." It came out as a muffled groan. "Leave me alone."

"I will not. Come on, let's take a look at you. Up you get." Nadia wrapped her arms round the boy and heaved him into a sitting position. He was of smallish build with rumpled dark hair, a thin face, and a rip in the knee of his school trousers. There were a couple of grazes on his arm, struggling to bleed, and he had a swollen, cut lip. "Here, it's OK, I've got a clean tissue." Digging in her shirt pocket, Nadia found it and tried to dab the wound, but the boy twisted out of reach. "Honestly, those thugs, how could they do this to you?"

"How could *you* do this to me?" hissed the boy, whom Tilly now recognized. He was new to the school. She had noticed him at break times, sitting on his own. Now, pushing Nadia away, he rose painfully to his feet and used his shirtsleeve to wipe the blood from his mouth.

"Look, you were trying to help," he muttered, "but you weren't, OK? I'm never going to live this down now, being rescued by a couple of *girls*. Can you imagine how humiliating that is?"

Nadia gazed at him, openmouthed. "But… they were—"

"Kicking me, I know. And it would have been all over in a couple of minutes. But not anymore, oh no." Vehemently the boy shook his head. "They won't let me forget this in a hurry. Thanks to you, they'll still be taking the piss out of me when I'm forty."

Nadia looked as if she'd just been slapped. Since it seemed a pity to waste it, Tilly took a big bite out of the almost melted Magnum. The boy, perilously close to tears, wiped his sleeve across his face and muttered, "Next time, just leave people alone, OK? Don't interfere."

Then he turned and limped away.

"That's OK, no problem, my pleasure," said Nadia when he was out of earshot. "Any time."

Tilly gave her a what-did-you-expect shrug. "Told you not to get involved."

Chapter 21

ONE MINUTE PIERS WAS being fantastic, the next he was back to playing silly buggers again. It was driving Clare mad. When they were clearly so great together, why did he have to do it? Why couldn't he just admit to himself that it had finally happened, he'd met the one he was meant to be with and he didn't need to play these ridiculous games anymore?

Because he was a man, probably. Scared of having the mickey taken out of him by his mates—who were only jealous anyway because they didn't have gorgeous girlfriends of their own.

It was one o'clock in the morning and Clare, too agitated to sleep, was painting instead. Sadly she was also too agitated to paint and it wasn't going well, but jabbing her brush at the canvas, like sticking pins into a wax effigy, was quite cathartic.

Sunday had been so brilliant, she'd been convinced Piers had come to his senses. They'd spent the day with old friends of his in Cheltenham, a brilliant married couple who lived in a glorious rambling Cotswold farmhouse. Clare had liked them immediately and they in turn had taken to her. After a vast lunch, they'd all walked for miles together through the stunning countryside surrounding their home. Piers had been cheerful, relaxed, and effortlessly affectionate, sliding his arm round her shoulders and planting jokey kisses on her face, which was something he never did when his Bristol friends were around. She'd felt loved and secure, and ridiculously happy. All the way back to Bristol on Sunday evening she had fantasized about them moving to the country and living in a stunning *Ideal Home*-style farmhouse like that.

When Piers had dropped her home, he'd kissed her lingeringly before murmuring in that full-of-promise way of his, "I'll give you a ring on Tuesday."

And—get this—she'd actually been idiotic enough to believe he would.

Jab, jab, *jab* went the paintbrush as Clare attacked the canvas with renewed irritation. All evening she'd waited for him to call and he hadn't.

When she'd phoned his flat, there'd been no reply. His mobile was switched to the answering service. Pride had only allowed her to leave one message, but Piers still hadn't got back to her.

Why, *why* was he doing this? It was all so unnecessary. And this painting was in danger of being completely ruined; if she couldn't sell it, it would be all his fault.

Like an addict desperate for just one more fix, Clare snatched up the phone and pressed out his number again.

It went straight to the answering service.

Closing her eyes, she pictured Piers lying dead in the ER somewhere, with hospital curtains drawn round his cubicle and nurses sobbing helplessly at the tragedy of it all. His jacket lay across a chair and inside one of the pockets his mobile began to ring again. The nurses looked at each other, knowing that one of them had to answer it and break the terrible news to whoever was on the other end of the line. So young, so good-looking, such a waste...

Clare switched off the phone. Well, you could always live in hope.

It was the hottest day of the year so far and Nadia was stripped to a cropped white halter-neck tank top and denim shorts, with her hair tied up in a messy topknot. The sun was blazing down and her tan was coming along nicely, but it would never be a glamorous tan. Since a professional gardener couldn't work in a bikini and bare feet, the middle sections of her legs were always going to be browner than the bits at either end. Which meant, basically, that you ended up looking pretty damn gorgeous with your shorts and trainers on, but a bit of a twit the moment you took them off.

Leveling the soil before laying down the patio stones was back-breaking work. Thirsty too. Pausing to uncap her bottle of water, Nadia glugged back a couple of tepid mouthfuls and pulled a face. Yeeurgh, disgusting. Never mind, there was more in the house, stored in the mini-fridge that Jay had brought along for them to use now that summer was properly here.

She was standing at the kitchen window guzzling down proper ice-cold water when she saw the taxi pull up outside.

The passenger got out and Nadia abruptly stopped drinking. It was the pregnant woman she'd seen arriving at Jay's house the other day.

This time she was wearing loose white maternity trousers and a man's dark blue shirt. Nadia wondered if the shirt belonged to Jay.

The woman wasn't looking very happy, that was for sure. And she was keeping the taxi waiting while she approached the house.

Bart and the boys were working upstairs in the bedrooms. Nadia opened the front door and came face to face with... well, with whoever she was. Blimey, at close quarters she looked even more miserable, pale and drawn, and her shoulders were slumped in defeat.

Had Jay dumped her, was that it? Had he told her he'd do his bit financially, but that any kind of relationship between them was out of the question?

Frankly, Nadia couldn't blame him. She felt sorry for the woman of course, but at the same time she wasn't exactly making much of an effort. If she just looked more cheerful and wore some makeup, that would be a start. OK, it couldn't be much fun being hugely pregnant and dumped by your boyfriend, but where was the incentive for Jay to change his mind? What she needed to do was disguise those dark circles under her eyes, dress herself up a bit, smile like mad, and show him what he was missing.

Damn, I'm good at this, thought Nadia. I really should be a therapist.

"I'm looking for Jay. Is he here?"

Nadia realized she'd been staring. This woman would look *so* much better if she washed her long stringy hair.

"Sorry, he isn't."

"Any idea where he is?"

Nadia shrugged and shook her head. "He doesn't always tell us. I think there's a property auction going on in Bishopston, but to be honest he could be anywhere. Have you tried his phone?"

"It's switched off." The woman's expression was bleak and Nadia felt a surge of compassion.

"Tell me about it. That thing's always switched off. Look, can I take a message?"

Nosy? Moi?

The woman checked her watch. She looked absolutely wretched. "No. I'll just keep trying his phone. But if you do see him, tell him it's urgent. I'm on my way to the hospital now." As she spoke, the woman's ringless left hand moved to her stomach. "He has to get there as soon as he can."

Oh God, don't say she was actually in labor!

"Of course I will." Nadia nodded vigorously. "And your name is…?"

Well, she could hardly refer to her as the stringy-haired pregnant one.

"Belinda."

"Belinda." Nadia's smile was reassuring. "No problem, I'll

definitely tell him. You get off to the hospital. And don't worry, Jay'll be there in no time at all."

For what it was worth.

"Thanks." The woman didn't smile. She turned and made her way back to the waiting taxi.

Urrghh, imagine your water breaking on the way to the hospital and having the baby on the backseat.

Jay turned up an hour later. By the time Nadia had rushed in from the garden, he was deep in conversation with Bart and the boys, discussing the schedule for the rest of the week.

"Jay, could I—"

"Hang on a sec." Jay held up a hand to stop her. "Let me just get this sorted out first."

Agitated, Nadia said, "But—"

"*Please*." Jay glared at her. "I need to speak to Bart."

"You need to get to the hospital," Nadia blurted out. "Belinda was here. It's very urgent, you have to go right away."

That got his attention. She watched the color drain from Jay's face.

"Belinda was here?"

"Looking for you. Your phone was switched off. She was desperate to find you."

"I was at the auction." Jay raked back his hair, visibly shaken. "It had to be switched off."

Was that guilt in his eyes?

"She's gone straight there in a taxi. You'd better hurry," said Nadia. "Or you might be too late."

Bart let out a low whistle when Jay had left.

"What was that all about? Who's Belinda?"

"She's nine months pregnant," Nadia told him. "And not very happy with our boss."

"Bugger me," whistled Bart.

"Maybe we won't throw in together for a congratulations card," said Nadia.

"See? Let that be a lesson to you." Bart turned and wagged a stubby index finger at Kevin and Robbie. "Messing about with girls, not takin' proper care—this is the kind of trouble you'll end up in. You want to take my advice and keep it zipped."

Kevin, never the brightest sparkler in the packet, nodded sagely at his father. Then he frowned and looked puzzled. "Keep what zipped?"

Chapter 22

TILLY SAW HIM IN the afternoon as they passed each other in the corridor on the way to their respective classes. Glancing up and accidentally catching her eye, he hastily looked away. One of the boys behind him, also recognizing Tilly, whacked him on the shoulder and jeered, "Hey, Davis, aren't you gonna say hello to your girlfriend?"

Appalled to realize she was blushing, Tilly shot the boy a filthy look, which only amused him all the more.

"Oi, Robin, where's Batman today?" Darting across the corridor he aimed a skillful kung-fu-style kick at the hem of her pleated school skirt. "Got your pants on over your tights, I hope, Boy Wonder. Phwoarr, very sexy"—Tilly's skirt flew up to reveal sturdy navy knickers—"NOT."

Any attempt at retaliation was pointless. The boy was a Year 10 and there was nothing Year 10s enjoyed more than reducing Year 9s to puree. Making sure her skirt was covering her knees once more, Tilly gave him another killer stare then extended it to include Davis, letting him know he wasn't the only one suffering here. Davis glared back at her, indicating that he still blamed her and her sister for causing all the trouble in the first place.

Tilly stalked off down the corridor in disgust. Honestly, it was times like this that made you almost look forward to double physics.

———

He was loitering casually, waiting for her when school finished at three thirty. Tilly knew this because of the way he ignored her totally as she walked past him at the school gate.

As she made her way down the road to the bus stop, Tilly sensed him behind her. Finally, when there was no longer anyone else from school in sight, he caught up to her.

"Look, I'm sorry."

"What?"

"You heard." He loped along beside Tilly, hands stuffed into trouser pockets, narrow shoulders hunched. "It wasn't your fault, OK? I do know that. And I'm sorry Moxham's having a go at you now."

Tilly shrugged. "He'll get bored soon enough, find someone else to pick on." She paused. "How's your face?"

"Not so bad." He touched the livid greenish bruise along his cheekbone, then the cut below it. "And nobody beat me up today, which has to be good news."

He'd only arrived at the school a week ago, Tilly remembered. He barely knew a soul. It couldn't be very nice, being new.

Transferring her overstuffed schoolbag from one shoulder to the other, she said, "What's your name?"

"Me? Davis."

Tilly hid a smile. "I meant your first name."

"Oh. Calvin."

"*Calvin?*" Crikey, talk about embarrassing. She'd thought hers was bad enough.

"My friends call me Cal. Well," he amended, "the friends I *used* to have. Since we moved down here, everyone's called me Davis." Pause. "I keep asking my mum to stop it, but she won't listen."

Tilly realized he was making a joke, actually laughing at himself and his rotten situation. When his eyes lit up like that he looked so much better. Still thin of course, and on the disheveled side, but a lot less nerdy than before. It couldn't be much fun, having to start all over again at a new school; people saw you observing from the sidelines and forgot you had a personality. It didn't occur to them that at your last school you might have been Mr. Dazzlingly Popular, the life and soul of the party.

"You can call me Cal if you like," Calvin announced. "Or Calvin. Or Davis. Up to you." For a moment it seemed likely that he might actually smile. "Multiple choice."

"OK." He wasn't what you'd call fantastically good-looking or anything, but he wasn't ugly. Just... average, verging on not bad, Tilly concluded. Plus he'd be better when the cuts and bruises had gone. "I'm Tilly." Glancing over her shoulder as a familiar rumbling noise reached her ears, she added, "And this is my bus."

"Right." Cal's gray eyes crinkled at the corners as he watched her jump onto the bus. "See you around."

—⁓—

Nadia was feeling pleased with herself as she arrived for work early the next morning. It was going to be another stunning day and to celebrate she had stopped off at the mini supermarket on the way. Nestling in a bag on the passenger seat beside her were four Galaxy truffle ice creams. Thanks to the fridge Jay had supplied, with its minuscule freezer compartment, she had been able to treat the workers. Oh yes, she would definitely be popular today. An ice cream each for herself, Bart, Kevin, and Robbie. And nothing for Jay because... well, to be brutally honest, she didn't think he deserved one. Then again, there was every chance they wouldn't see him. Babies didn't pop out like bars of chocolate from a vending machine; at this very minute Belinda could be panting and screaming and gouging fingernail-shaped wedges out of Jay's hand. Crikey, you heard about some women being in labor for *days*.

Eeeuw. Imagine that.

But as she climbed out of the car clutching her brown paper

bag, a double-parked post van pulled away revealing Jay's car parked behind it.

So, he was here after all. Indicating that either Belinda had already had the baby, or it had been a false alarm.

Hugging the bag of ice creams possessively to her chest, Nadia decided that either way, he still wasn't getting one.

Noiselessly, she unlocked the front door and let herself into the hall. On tiptoe she made her way through to the kitchen. The fact that Jay's car was outside meant he had to be somewhere in the house, but so far there was no sign of him. Holding her breath, Nadia inched open the fridge door and prepared to slide the bag into the freezer section without—

"What are you doing?"

"Ouch!" yelped Nadia as the spring-loaded door of the freezer compartment snapped back, catching her fingers. The Galaxy truffle ice creams tumbled to the ground. Guiltily, she swung round to face Jay. "Are you trying to give me a heart attack?"

"Just wondered what you were up to."

"I was putting stuff in the fridge, that's all. It's allowed, isn't it?" Dropping to her knees, she began to scoop up the ice creams.

"All for you?"

"No. One for each of us. I wasn't expecting to see you today." Nadia hesitated, because it was all very well having a dig, but Jay did actually look terrible. His face was drawn, his eyes heavily shadowed. Dark stubble covered his chin and he didn't appear to have slept. The clothes he was wearing were the ones he'd had on yesterday. "Um… is everything all right?"

"Is everything all right?" echoed Jay, rubbing a hand over his face. "To be honest, no."

In the time she'd known him, he'd always been In Control, capable of handling anything at all. Now, for once, he appeared defeated. It was quite scary.

Unnerved, Nadia said, "Did she have the baby?"

"What? Oh... no." He shook his head. "It's not due for another month."

Right.

When he didn't elaborate, Nadia said cautiously, "Look, it's none of my business, but if you want to talk about it..."

"Yes." This time Jay nodded. Slowly he repeated, "Yes, I think I do."

"Does she want you to marry her?" As she said it, Nadia stuffed the ice creams into the freezer section, shut the door, and straightened up.

Jay smiled briefly. As if he'd forgotten how to.

"Belinda is my sister-in-law."

Blimey. He was in deeper trouble than she'd imagined.

"It's not my baby," said Jay. "Belinda's married to my brother, Anthony." He paused and glanced out of the window, visibly collecting himself before carrying on. "She *was* married to my brother Anthony," he amended. "He died last night."

~~~

They sat outside on the stone steps leading down to the garden. Seated next to her so he wasn't forced to make constant eye contact, Jay explained about Anthony's earlier brush with cancer, the radiation therapy, and punishingly aggressive doses of chemo.

"It was rough, but he came through it. The doctors warned him not to raise his hopes but Anthony was convinced he'd beaten it for good. Six months later, even more of a miracle, Belinda found out she was pregnant. They'd thought the treatment would leave him infertile. You've never seen a happier couple."

Picking up a small stone, Jay turned it over and over between his fingers before lobbing it into the leveled earth where the patio would be built. "Then a few weeks ago the cancer came back with a vengeance. This time it was everywhere, in his bones, in his liver, in his lungs. Anthony didn't have a chance. He knew he was going to die, but he was desperate to see the baby. The doctors were planning to take Belinda into the hospital next week for a Caesarean, but Anthony went into a coma yesterday. That was when Belinda came here, trying to find me. Anyway, it was clearly too late to do the Caesarean. And then Anthony died at eleven o'clock last night. He was thirty-two," Jay said steadily, "and now he's gone."

Silence.

Nadia felt as if she'd refused to give money to a beggar in a wheelchair, convinced that not only was the man not really a beggar, but that he was only pretending to need a wheelchair. Now, belatedly, she was discovering that the beggar was a homeless old soldier who had lost both legs during some heroic action in the war that had earned him the Victoria Cross.

"I'm so sorry." She meant not just the usual condolences, but for thinking bad things of Jay all this time. He'd spent every spare minute of the last few weeks visiting his brother in the hospital—no wonder his phone had been turned off. Desperately ashamed, Nadia said, "We hadn't any idea. You should have said something before now."

Above the treetops, a yellow and red hot-air balloon glided into view. Shielding his eyes from the sun, Jay watched it float through the cloudless sky.

"I probably should," he agreed. "But I didn't want to. I made the mistake of telling my neighbor a while back. Since then, every time I've pulled up outside my house, she's been there with her caring face on, asking me how everything is, how Anthony's doing and how poor Belinda's bearing up. I started to dread the sight of her. In fact, that's why I haven't been home yet. When we left the hospital at five o'clock, I came here instead. It's been easier," he explained, "knowing that you didn't know anything about it. Being treated like a normal human being."

"Sometimes I treated you like a bastard," Nadia said bluntly. "Especially yesterday." She went hot and cold all over again, just thinking about it.

"It's still been better than everyone being unnaturally nice because my brother's dying of cancer."

Nadia picked at the frayed ends of her cut-off shorts. It was good to know he hadn't minded, but her conscience was working overtime. Toe-curlingly, she remembered thinking yesterday that Belinda's hair could have done with a wash.

God, that poor woman.

"Where is Belinda now?"

"Her parents drove up from Dorset last night. They've taken her back to stay with them until the funeral. I'm organizing everything," said Jay. "So if you can't get hold of me, that's what I'll be doing."

"And I had such a go at you," Nadia groaned, "because we could never get hold of you. I can't believe you just let me do it."

"I'll be more reachable from now on. I won't need to keep my phone switched off. Apart from when we're actually in the church, of course."

He was trying to cheer her up, which only made Nadia feel worse. Humbly, she said, "Um... do you want an ice cream?"

The hot-air balloon was drifting out of sight now. As the gas burners opened, a whoosh of neon-blue flame illuminated the inside of the balloon and it disappeared behind the rooftops. Jay, lifting his head to watch it go, said, "No, I have to get to the register office."

Of course, register offices weren't only places to get married in. They were where you had to go in order to register your brother's death.

"And you need something on these," Jay went on, tapping her shoulders. It might only be eight thirty, but the sun was already beating down on her bare skin.

"I have sunscreen." Like David Blaine, Nadia magicked a tube of Ambre Solaire from her jeans pocket.

"D'you want a hand?" Jay indicated the low-cut back of her white tank top.

She hesitated, then shook her head.

"I'll be fine. I'm very bendy."

"Sure?"

"Sure." Nadia watched him stand up, brushing the dust from his trousers as he prepared to leave. If she had to twist her arms right out of their sockets, she'd manage without Jay's help. Rubbing in sunscreen would feel way too intimate right now. It had just occurred to her that at last she knew why he'd been so offish and abrupt ever since she'd come to work for him, and so completely unlike the Jay Tiernan she'd first met in the wilds of Gloucestershire in a decrepit snowbound pub.

Everything suddenly made sense.

As if reading her mind, Jay said drily, "You never know, once things get back to normal I might turn out not to be the boss from hell after all."

"I won't count my chickens."

Nadia only said it to make him smile. The trouble was, things weren't likely to get back to normal, were they? Not for a while at least.

Belinda hadn't even had the baby yet.

Chapter 23

It had been James's idea to hold a barbecue in the back garden. He wanted to introduce Annie to the rest of his family, and this seemed the best way to do it. The weather had been fantastic all week. Barbecues were casual, informal affairs. Everyone could relax and enjoy themselves. Far better, James thought happily, than a sit-down dinner in the dining room. Nicer for Annie and easier for the rest of them too.

At least that had been the plan before Leonie had turned up and James found himself faced with the prospect of having to introduce Annie to rather more of his family than he'd had in mind.

Hearing a car pull up outside and thinking it was Piers, Clare raced across the hall and yanked open the front door.

"Mum!" She stared in alarm at Leonie, who was stepping out of a brand-new Renault Clio—goodness knows how she'd managed to mistake *that* for a Ferrari. "What are you doing here?"

More to the point, how had Leonie managed to get her hands on a brand-new car? By smuggling it out of some showroom under her coat?

"Nice, isn't it?" Intercepting Clare's look of disbelief, Leonie said gaily, "Brian bought it for me."

"But what are you doing here?" Clare was puzzled. She knew Tilly was due to be spending the weekend in Brighton, but the plan had been for her to catch the train down there tomorrow morning.

"It's a surprise, darling! Tilly mentioned on the phone that you were having a little get-together this evening and there was me dying to try out my new car… and Brian had to take Tamsin to some ghastly school function, so I just thought why not pop on down? Come along now, give your mother a kiss. There, that wasn't so bad, was it? And Nadia as well, look at you! Honestly, it's like being given the once-over by a couple of nightclub bouncers. It wouldn't kill you to be a tiny bit more welcoming."

Clare was torn. Their mother was a hopeless case—she and Nadia were in complete agreement on that—but if she'd come all this way, could they actually refuse to let her in?

Plus, Clare wasn't particularly looking forward to meeting this Annie person. Apart from the very occasional blind date, James had been single as far back as she could remember and in a purely selfish way she was happy with that. When you were used to having your dad all to yourself for practically your whole life, the thought of him suddenly finding someone was… well, a bit yucky, to be frank. OK, maybe she shouldn't be feeling like this at twenty-three, but she couldn't help it. What's more, everyone else might be pretending to like the woman, but hadn't it even occurred to them that she might be after his money? James had a good job, financial acumen, and a hefty shares portfolio. He also drove a top-of-the-range Jaguar and wore expensively tailored suits.

As far as Clare was concerned, you had to keep your wits about you these days. Annie Healey worked in a newsagents and clearly wasn't in the higher tax bracket. She was bound to regard their father as a catch.

And speaking of catches, where was bloody Piers?

Behind her, Nadia said flatly, "This isn't a good idea, Mum. Dad's bringing his new girlfriend over. She might feel a bit awkward—"

"Oh, that's ridiculous, why on earth should it be awkward?" Leonie trilled with laughter. "I left James over twenty years ago, for heaven's sake. I'm hardly likely to be jealous, am I?"

Behind Nadia and Clare, Tilly's footsteps sounded across the oak floor. "Gran says the barbecue's ready to start cooking stuff and can someone fetch the steaks marinated in bourbon from the kitchen—oh!"

"My' *baby*," Leonie exclaimed, pushing past her two elder daughters and enveloping Tilly in a hug. "Isn't this a lovely surprise? I couldn't wait to see you, so I drove down early. Tamsin's *so* excited about this weekend—she hardly stops talking about you. Steaks marinated in bourbon," Leonie added, eyeing Nadia over Tilly's shoulder. "Mustn't keep Miriam waiting. Where is James, anyway? Why don't I have a quick word with him? I'm sure he wouldn't begrudge me a steak sandwich."

At that moment they heard another car slow down in the lane before turning into the drive. Make this be Piers, make this be Piers, Clare silently prayed. But it wasn't, of course. It was James's dark blue Jaguar. He'd been to pick up Annie and now they were back.

Nadia saw the look of barely contained horror on her father's face as he spotted his ex-wife in the doorway. His lips moved and then it was Annie's turn to look dismayed.

"So this is the girlfriend?" Leonie stood with her arm round Tilly's narrow shoulders watching with amusement as they emerged from the car. "Darling, what did you say her name was again?"

"Annie." Tilly sounded torn, as if she wasn't quite sure whose side to be on. Nadia guessed that she'd mentioned to Leonie on the phone that Annie would be coming to the barbecue tonight.

"James, you're looking wonderful, just as handsome as ever." Leonie threw out her arms and left her daughters standing in the doorway. Greeting her ex-husband with enthusiasm, she then turned and said gaily, "And you must be Annie, I've heard so much about you, how lovely to meet you at last! And what gorgeous earrings you're wearing!"

"Leonie, what are you doing here?" James's voice was level.

"I was missing Tilly. She mentioned the barbecue. The girls said I might make things awkward for Annie, but I told them we'd be fine. And now we are fine, aren't we?" Leonie gazed brightly from James to Annie. "Heavens, there's not even anything to be awkward about!"

Nadia sighed, realizing that, like it or not, they were going to be stuck with Leonie for the rest of the evening. She had skin thicker than a brontosaurus and absolutely no shame.

Oh well, served James right for marrying her.

"It's gone seven." Nadia gave Clare a nudge. "Are you sure Piers is coming?"

Clare, through slightly gritted teeth, said, "Of course he is."

Up in her room a couple of minutes later, she rang Piers to check he was on his way.

Déjà vu. Phone switched off. Taking deep breaths, Clare told herself that he'd be here by seven thirty. She'd kill him if he let her down again.

Out in the garden, chiefly for Tilly's sake, everyone was behaving in a civilized fashion and acting as if Leonie was an invited guest.

Well, fairly civilized.

"What would you like on your steak, Leonie? Tomato sauce? Mustard? Herbicide?"

Beaming, Leonie took the plate from Miriam.

"Just as it is, thanks. Everything looks gorgeous." As unflappable as ever, she went on, "Did Tilly tell you I'm getting married again?"

"Poor man," said Miriam.

"He's not poor." Leonie's bracelets jangled as she pushed her dyed blonde hair back from her face. "Actually he's quite rich."

"That's good." Miriam nodded. "I'm happy for you. Just promise me one thing, OK? Don't have any more children."

Even this wasn't enough to make Leonie take offense. Calmly she said, "I did what was best for my daughters. I couldn't give them the kind of upbringing they needed. Mm, this steak is tender. Anyway, they were far better off staying with James. Clare? Over here, darling, you've got a face on you like a wet Wednesday in Wigan. Whatever's wrong, my angel? Come on, you can tell me."

"Nothing's wrong." Clare allowed Edward to refill her wineglass.

"Boyfriend was supposed to be turning up," Miriam cut in, "and he hasn't. Mr. Unreliable," she added, with a pointed glance at Clare. "If you ask me, he's giving you the runaround. Men like that don't suddenly improve. This one needs getting rid of."

"He isn't unreliable." Clare felt bright spots of color spring to life in her cheeks; she hated it when Miriam launched into one of her lectures. "He's probably just been held up."

"Could have phoned," said Edward, who was busy pouring drinks. "If I'm held up, I let people know. Another one *already*?" He looked shocked as Clare held out her just-emptied glass. "Shouldn't you eat something first?"

Clare rolled her eyes because Edward could never quite forget he was a doctor.

"I'm fine. I'll have some food later." Draining the measly half glass Edward had poured her, she said brightly, "Bathroom first, then I think it's time I got to know Annie."

In the deserted living room, Clare used the ordinary phone to dial her mobile. With the windows open, those outside would be able to hear it playing its jaunty tune. After several bars, Clare hung up the landline and pretended to answer her own phone, wandering back out onto the terrace as she did so.

"Oh no, that's *such* a shame. Your poor mother, how awful for her... Piers, how can you even think that? Of course I don't mind. You stay there as long as you have to. And give my condolences to your family. Yes, yes, I love you too. OK, ring me tomorrow. Bye."

There, ha. Gwyneth Paltrow, eat your skinny heart out.

"That was Piers," Clare said pointlessly. "He's in Surrey. His grandmother died suddenly this morning and his mother's in a complete state. He tried to ring me earlier but he was stuck on the motorway and the battery was flat on his phone. It was a heart attack, apparently. All very sudden. Poor Piers, he's trying to comfort his mother and apologizing to me for not turning up… he sounds pretty upset as well. He was very fond of his grandmother."

"Oh darling, that's such a shame, I was so looking forward to meeting him," said Leonie. "Honestly, old people are so selfish, aren't they? You never know when they're going to drop dead."

Chapter 24

ANNIE WASN'T HAVING A great time. Beforehand, the prospect of meeting James's family had been scary, if only in a five-out-of-ten kind of way. Now that she was actually here, it was turning out to be more of an eight-out-of-ten level of scariness. Tilly, whom she'd thought she could count on to be on her side, was clearly torn by the arrival of her mother. Leonie, whilst perfectly polite on the surface, had a disconcerting habit of saying things in a jokey fashion then glancing at people so as to signal that she hadn't been joking really. Nadia, who would have been an ally, was busy helping Miriam with the barbecue. Edward seemed nice enough but Annie couldn't begin to imagine what kind of conversation she might hold with a consultant neuropsychiatrist—unless he'd like to hear her recurring dream during which she jumped from a great height into a child's plastic bucket and all her teeth fell out.

Annie hated it when that happened. Upon waking, she always had to leap out of bed, race to the mirror, and check her teeth.

But Dr. Welch—sorry, Edward—would no doubt be bored to tears by this. Happily, she hadn't had the chance to ask him about her dream.

Less happily, this was because she was being interrogated by Clare. And not in a relaxing way.

"Annie, you *must* try the kebabs, they're fantastic. Ooh, careful, bit hot. So whereabouts exactly *do* you work?"

This was what Clare had been doing, urging Annie to try the

kebabs, or the king prawns, or the roasted peppers, then asking her a question the moment her mouth was full. Anxious not to appear rude, Annie was then obliged to frantically chew and swallow far too soon, so that she could feel the lumps of food fighting their way down her throat. She just hoped it didn't look as painful as it felt, like in *Tom and Jerry* when Tom gulped down a fish sideways and you could see the head and tail bulging out either side of his neck.

"It's the newsagents on Quorn Street," she finally managed to say.

"That's it, a newsagents." Clare pulled a rather-you-than-me face. "God, is it awful?"

"I like it there," said Annie.

"And you live in Kingsweston? Is yours one of those big houses by the village green?" There was a glittery look in Clare's eyes. She was a pretty girl, enviably slim in jeans and a midriff-baring black T-shirt, and with her long dark hair falling like a waterfall down her back. But she was definitely having a dig.

"No," said Annie. "One of the small cottages next to the phone box."

Clare raised her plucked eyebrows. "Have you tried the scallops yet? Here, you must try a scallop. So why did Dad have to come and pick you up this evening? Is there something wrong with your car?"

Not falling for the scallop trick, Annie said calmly, "I don't have a car."

"No car? Heavens, you poor thing! Still, it must be nice being driven around in Dad's Jag."

Even James, just back from switching on the lights around the terrace, couldn't miss the insinuation this time.

"Clare." He shot her a look of warning.

"What?" Apparently mystified, she shook her head. "I'm just saying it must be nice. Better than having to catch some smelly old bus, surely."

"Buses don't bother me. I'm used to them." Annie steadfastly refused to rise to the bait. "This mayonnaise is brilliant, by the way. I must ask your grandmother where she bought it."

Clare snorted with laughter. "Bought it? She'd throw you onto the barbecue if she heard you say that. Miriam wouldn't allow shop-bought mayonnaise in the house."

Now that the lights were on, the garden was looking even love-lier. What a shame the same couldn't be said for Clare's personality. Wondering if anyone had ever given her the slap she deserved, and preparing to move away, Annie said, "In that case, maybe she'd give me the recipe. I think I'll just ask her."

But Miriam was nowhere in sight and a phone was ringing some-where inside the house. Moments later Miriam emerged clutching a bowl of potato salad in one hand and the cordless phone in the other, into which she was saying sympathetically, "…and I'm so sorry to hear about your grandmother."

Annie watched the color drain from Clare's face.

"I can't hear you, dear, you'll have to speak up." Miriam raised her own voice. "Say that again? Oh, right. Well, that's good. Here's Clare, I'll pass you over to her now."

Mutely Clare held out her hand for the phone.

"Darling, fantastic news, Piers's grandmother has been miracu-lously resurrected. She's absolutely fine, not dead at all. You might need to shout though, it's a dreadful line. Almost sounds as if Piers is ringing from some crowded pub."

Clare couldn't believe it. Her palm was so slippery with sweat she almost dropped the cordless phone. Bloody Piers, how could he do this to her? He'd never even called her before on this number; until now he'd always rung her mobile.

"Yes?"

"Clare, hey, sorry I couldn't make it, got held up in Clifton. We're all at the Happy Ferret if you fancy joining us."

"No thanks." Clare spat the words out like pebbles; she'd never been so ashamed.

"Suit yourself." It came out as shoot yourself; Piers had clearly been held up in the Happy Ferret for a while. "Anyway, what was all that about just then? My grandmother isn't dead."

Actually, shooting herself might not be such a bad idea.

Annie had cheered up considerably. The way Miriam had winked at her as she'd passed the phone over to Clare had helped a lot. Miriam, she guessed, was perfectly aware of what Clare had been up to.

Now, with the sky darkening and the citronella candles flickering away in their water bowls, Annie settled back into her chair on the terrace and surreptitiously undid the button on the straining waistband of her trousers. She had eaten a huge amount, to Miriam's evident pleasure. She'd also learned that the secret ingredient in the mayonnaise was fresh tarragon. She'd even managed, by some miracle, to hold a lively conversation with Edward, who'd turned out to be a lot less intimidating than she'd imagined. He might know everything there was to know about brains, Annie had discovered, but he could also talk entertainingly about TV quiz shows, the bizarre selection of magazines stocked in hospital waiting rooms, and wild parties he had attended during his time as a medical student, including the one where a pickled brain had somehow tumbled out of its bucket and fallen into the host's swimming pool.

"Edward, that's disgusting," Miriam had protested. "You're putting me off my lamb cutlets." She'd paused, her kohled eyes bright with curiosity. "Did it sink or float?"

Now, music was drifting out through the living-room windows and Miriam and Edward were dancing on the terrace. James was turning the last of the kebabs on the glowing barbecue. Leonie kicked off her shoes, grabbed Clare's wrist, and dragged her up to join in the dancing. Tilly, sitting on the stone steps with her arms wrapped round her knees, watched them and tapped her feet in time with the music.

"Top up," Nadia announced, pouring wine into Annie's almost empty glass. Shaking back her curls and collapsing onto the chair next to her, she said, "So, are we not so scary as you thought?"

Annie smiled. "I've enjoyed myself." Well, most of it.

"Miriam likes you. That's always a good start."

"I think your sister thinks I'm a gold-digger," said Annie.

Nadia looked astonished. "Tilly?"

"*No.* I meant Clare." Too late she saw Nadia's teeth gleaming in the candlelight. "Oh, right, joke. But she does, and I really wish she didn't." Earnestly Annie added, "I promise you, I'm not interested in your dad's money."

"Don't take any notice of Clare, she's in a state because of this so-called boyfriend of hers. Posh Piers." Nadia pulled a face then said mischievously, "Posh *rich* Piers, from what I hear. Unlike the rest of us, Clare isn't used to being mucked about by men."

It occurred to Annie that she wasn't used to it either, but only because she'd been so busy nursing her mother that no men had had the opportunity to muck her about. Now, at the deeply embarrassing age of thirty-eight, she had all this to look forward to.

"How about you?" said Annie.

"Oh God, heaps of experience! All the way back to my school days when the boys laughed at my braces and my acne and my sweet little moustache." Nadia grinned at the look on Annie's face. "Not to mention my puppy fat and my hairy legs, because Miriam wouldn't let me shave them. Oh yes, I was a scary sight. And then I hit sixteen. The braces came off, the spots went away, I got taller and thinner and, best of all, discovered the joys of depilatory cream. So I thought, wow, this is fantastic, from now on all the boys will be completely in awe of me, I look so gorgeous they'll never be horrible or treat me badly again."

"And?"

"Well, of course I was wrong." Nadia smiled and shook her head. "They carried right on being horrible and treating me as badly as ever."

Annie laughed. "That's boys for you. But how about now?"

"My last proper boyfriend dumped me almost eighteen months ago. Edward's son," Nadia added, nodding toward Edward and Miriam. When they'd first broken up and the subject had arisen, she hadn't been able to stop herself explaining to strangers who Laurie was, just so they understood she hadn't been dumped by anyone ordinary or middle-of-the-road. Nowadays she didn't bother. Since the breakup, Laurie's flying visits to his father had been few and far between and she'd always made a point of making herself scarce during these times. It wasn't that she was still bitter, she just didn't see why she should feel obliged to be amicable and pretend they were still jolly good friends.

Because it did still hurt, deep down. Of course it did.

"Edward's son. Gosh," said Annie. Sympathetically she went on, "Must be awkward."

"Not really. Edward doesn't talk about Laurie when I'm around. Nobody talks about Laurie when I'm around except Clare sometimes, because she likes to wind me up. Anyway, he's in America now, which makes things easier."

"And you've not met anyone else since then?"

Suddenly feeling like Miss Havisham, Nadia mentally brushed away a few cobwebs. "Well, no, but I haven't given up yet. They can just run faster than me, that's all. Once I learn to use a lasso, they won't be able to get away." She mimed twirling a lasso above her head and aimed it at James as he headed toward them, bearing yet another plate piled high with lamb cutlets.

Anxious not to look as if she was part of the catch-a-man plan, Annie said hurriedly, "Tilly's going to be gorgeous when she grows up."

The song that had been playing came to an end. Leonie, her

gypsyish velvet skirt swirling around her ankles, murmured something to Clare and disappeared through the French windows into the house. Clare, her mood evidently improved, danced over to Tilly and dragged her to her feet as the next track began.

Plenty of thirteen-year-olds wore more makeup than Lady Gaga, but not Tilly. She didn't even own so much as a lip gloss. Her baby-fine blonde hair hung loose and unstyled around her shoulders and she was wearing a gray T-shirt over baggy green shorts that flapped around her bony knees. But for all her apparent gawkiness, she could dance. Maybe not at the school dance when everyone was judging her and she became paralyzed with shyness, but out here on the candlelit terrace, surrounded by her family…

Watching with pride, Nadia said, "She'll be fine."

———

Leonie had been to the loo and was on her way back outside when the front doorbell rang.

From the sitting room Harpo squawked, "Somebody get the bloody door."

Since there was no one else around, Leonie did as Harpo suggested.

Blimey. And very nice too.

Smiling playfully up at the visitor, Leonie said, "Let me guess. You're the bad boy."

The visitor said, "I'm sorry?"

"The naughty one." Leonie stepped to one side and ushered him into the hall. "Oh yes, I've been hearing all about you." She wagged a finger at him. "Still, at least you're here now. Better late than never. I'm Leonie by the way. Clare's mother. Come along through, everyone's outside."

"I think we may have our wires crossed," said the visitor. "I just wanted a quiet word with Nadia."

Since he wasn't moving, Leonie said, "Aren't you Piers?"

"No. Jay Tiernan."

"And you're a friend of Nadia's? Now this *is* interesting," Leonie teased, "because I've heard absolutely nothing about you. Were you supposed to be here earlier as well? Honestly, what is it with my daughters and reliable men? And why so *formal?*" she went on, brushing her hand against the lapels of his dark suit. "I mean, it's a very *nice* suit, but not what most men would wear to a barbecue."

"It was my brother's funeral this afternoon," said Jay. "I haven't—"

"Stop! Foul! Repetition," Leonie shouted in triumph. "We've already had death-of-a-close-relative, you can't just copy someone else's excuse," she chided with a playful prod to the chest. "That's *so* unoriginal and boring. Come on now, try and think up one of your own."

"Sorry," said Jay. "OK, just tell her my watch stopped and that's why I'm late. Now could you go and find Nadia and let her know I'm here?"

Chapter 25

ANYONE ELSE WOULD HAVE been mortified, but all Leonie did was shriek with laughter when she learned the truth. Leaving her in the back garden, Nadia made her way through to the hall. Pausing en route to check her reflection in the living-room mirror and to give her hair a quick comb-through with her fingers, she saw that she was harboring a blob of garlic mayonnaise in her cleavage.

See? This was why it was always important to check.

In the hall, Jay was looking handsome but strained, as though the day had taken its toll. Thanks to several glasses of wine, Nadia was able to give him a hug. Nothing erotic, just one of those brief poor-you ones.

"I'm sorry."

"About what?"

"Everything. All of it. Especially my mother. When I was young, I used to be embarrassed that she was never around. Nowadays I'm embarrassed when she is."

"Don't be. No need." Jay half-smiled. "When she told me who she was, I assumed you'd already told her about my brother. Otherwise I'd never have mentioned the funeral."

"I don't talk to my mother about that kind of stuff." Nadia waggled her hands in apology. "We don't have girlie chats. She wasn't even invited here tonight, she just turned up."

"Anyway, it's OK. If Anthony could hear her, he'd think it was funny. Anyway"—Jay glanced up as a burst of laughter filtered through from the garden—"I didn't realize you had a party going on. I'll just leave—"

"No you won't." Nadia put a hand out to stop him as he moved toward the front door. "What made you come here?"

Jay hesitated, then shrugged. "After the funeral we all went back to the Kavanagh Hotel. I've spent the last six hours being suitably solemn and not drinking and accepting condolences from a load of people I've never met before. The last guests left half an hour ago. Belinda's parents have taken her back to Dorset. I just gave a couple of people a lift home and it turned out they live not far from here, in Druid Avenue. So when I'd dropped them off I practically had to drive past your front door. I just stopped by on the off chance that you might be free to join me for a much-needed drink."

It was horribly inappropriate, but Nadia couldn't help it. A little knot of lust was busily forming in the pit of her stomach, because with those shadowed eyes and that dark stubble and the sexily loosened tie around his neck, Jay really was looking fantastically attractive.

Of course he didn't want to be at home on his own after the traumas of the day. He needed someone to take his mind off all that and cheer him up.

And she was just the girl to do it.

"I'm free," said Nadia, "and I'd love to go for a drink."

"But what about—?"

"They'll understand. Just give me two minutes and I'll be right out."

In the event, Jay came through to the back garden with Nadia while she told her family she was leaving. Miriam threw her arms round him and said, "My poor boy, what a rotten thing to happen. I'm so sorry."

Leonie, in a whisper that wasn't far enough under her breath, said to James, "I can't keep up with the shenanigans in this family. Clare's chap was supposed to be here tonight and he didn't make it.

Now this one appears when no one was even expecting him. So is he Nadia's boyfriend or not?"

Clare said encouragingly to Jay, "You know what would make you feel better? Buying a painting from a struggling but very talented artist."

"Please excuse my sister, she has no shame." Hurriedly Nadia steered him back toward the French windows. "Come on, let's go."

———

"You look different," Jay commented as he led the way through to his kitchen. The lights flickered and came on, and he reached into the fridge for a bottle of Meursault.

"That's because you've never seen me in a dress before. Thanks," said Nadia as he handed her a brimming glass. Pouring an equally large one for himself, he downed half of it in a matter of seconds.

"Blimey, are you sure that's the way the wine experts say to do it?"

Jay shrugged. "Right now, I'm not bothered with what it tastes like. I just want to blur the edges of a truly godawful day. Sorry, I don't suppose I'll be great company tonight. I won't be able to drive you back home either."

"That's why we have cabs. And I don't mind a bit," said Nadia. "So long as you're paying for it."

Jay smiled. Dangling the already half-empty bottle from his fingers, he showed her into the living room. "Have a seat. Sorry about the mess."

Like a lot of men, he really didn't have a clue.

"Call this a mess?" Nadia surveyed the room. Presumably he was referring to the sweater thrown across the back of a chair, the newspapers on the coffee table, and—oh *horror*—the dirty cup on the floor next to the sofa. "Crikey, you should take a look at my sister's bedroom. When you haven't seen your carpet for six months because it's knee-deep in clothes and CDs and magazines and empty potato chip bags, now that's a mess."

"True, true. My bedroom used to be like that too. So did Anthony's when we were teenagers. Pigsties, our mother used to call them." Jay pulled a face. "I got tidy without realizing it. I don't even remember it happening."

The sitting room was huge, high-ceilinged and unfussily decorated. The walls were covered with dark blue wallpaper, the carpet and curtains were cream, and the navy sofas squashily comfortable. Above the fireplace hung the telephone box painting. Other less imposing pieces of artwork adorned the walls. Nadia, sinking into one of the sofas, watched Jay shrug off his jacket, remove his tie, and fling them onto the back of another chair. Then he topped up his glass and drank some more, his tanned throat moving as he swallowed.

Blimey, at this rate she may as well order the taxi now. He'd be out cold in thirty minutes.

"Come and sit down," said Nadia, feeling sorry for him but still not quite able to ignore the squirrely feelings in her stomach. She meant come and sit down in the general sense, i.e., on any chair or sofa in the vicinity, but Jay took it as an invitation and joined her on the sofa to the left of the fireplace.

"D'you know what gets me? It's all so fucking unfair. Two brothers, more or less the same age. One's single, the other one's married with a baby due any time now. The single one used to smoke, the married one never did. The single one enjoys a drink, doesn't go to the gym, and has eaten more than his share of junk food. Needless to say, the married one's always taken good care of his body. So which one of them dies of cancer? The married brother of course."

Taken aback, Nadia said, "Are you telling me you wish it had been you?"

Glug glug, another refill.

"I'm not that noble. I don't wish it was me. I'm just saying that, statistically, it should've been." Jay held up the empty bottle. "Guilt trip, I suppose. I'm still here and Anthony's gone."

"That's normal." Nadia nodded wisely. She'd watched enough episodes of *Oprah* to know that.

"I know. But it doesn't stop me feeling guilty. Bet you're glad you came here now," Jay added drily.

"I'm fine. Don't worry about me."

"You're not drinking." He indicated her almost full glass, and Nadia obligingly knocked it back. Actually, it was really nice wine.

"Better." Jay nodded his approval. "Could you find your way back to the kitchen, d'you think?"

"Why?"

"There's another bottle in the fridge."

Over the course of the next hour, Jay slowed his rate of consumption and they talked about Anthony. And death. And what it was like to have a sister, and whether brothers were better than sisters. And what heaven would be like if you could design it yourself. And where the corkscrew had disappeared to. And whether the same landlord was still running the pub where they'd stayed when they had been snowbound, because if anyone deserved to be dead it was him.

By eleven o'clock the second bottle was empty. Well, Nadia reassured herself, it had seemed rude not to join in. She hadn't been invited over to sit there like a prune sipping water.

"Shall I tell you the good news?" said Jay, resting his head back against the sofa cushions and tilting it to one side.

"Definitely. Always glad to hear a bit of good news." Nadia nodded and found it quite hard to stop, which was always a clue that she'd had a bit too much to drink. "Tell me your good news this minute."

Another sign was repetition.

"I might be nicer to work for. I know I haven't been in the best of moods recently. It's been tough, not wanting Anthony to die and knowing deep down that he was going to. At least that part of it's over now. Give me a while and I should get back to normal."

"You told me that before." Nadia dimly recalled him saying something similar the other day.

"And now I'm telling you again. When I hired you, you came to work for someone you thought you knew and got a completely different person instead. I did feel guilty about that." Jay touched her bare arm and all the little hairs on the back of it instantly leapt to attention; luckily he'd had far too much wine to notice. "But things should start to improve."

"You mean you'll stop being an ogre?" Nadia thought about easing her arm away, but it didn't seem to want to move.

"Was that what I was? Really, an ogre?"

"No. Well… no." She shook her head, because to be fair he hadn't been. "But you're right about not being what I was expecting."

"I'm sorry." Jay's smile was rueful, his hand still in contact with her forearm. Idly, without even realizing it, his fingers were stroking her overheated skin. Now would definitely be a good time to move away, Nadia thought fuzzily. Oh, but it was such a heavenly feeling. And it would be churlish to move, surely. The man had just buried his brother. Well, not personally, of course. He was in a state of grief. She was here to cheer him up.

Crikey, thought Nadia, and I *could* cheer him up.

"What are you thinking?" said Jay.

Ha, not going to tell you *that*.

"Nothing."

"You must be thinking something. Go on," Jay prompted, taking another drink.

Nadia's gaze was drawn to the hand holding the glass. "Nice watch."

"Wrong. That wasn't it."

"I was just wondering what it must feel like to have hairy wrists."

Jay's mouth twitched. "No you weren't."

Oh yes, this was more like the old flirtatious Jay Tiernan she remembered so well.

"OK, cleverclogs, why don't you tell me what I'm thinking?"

This time he smiled properly. Their eyes met.

"Fine. I'll tell you. But only telepathically."

"That'll be useful."

"Trust me. We can do this. I'll tell you what you're thinking, then I'll tell you what I'm thinking, then you can tell me if I'm right."

"And we do all this telepathically?"

Jay nodded, his gaze fixed on hers. Dark brown eyes with wickedly long black lashes. Tanned skin surrounding them, showing paler laughter lines at the outer corners. Shadows like faint bruises beneath his eyes. Crooked nose separating them. Unable to tear her gaze away, Nadia knew exactly what was going through his mind:

You want to sleep with me.

I don't.

Oh yes you do. And I want to sleep with you, so why are we wasting time?

Bloody hell, you're a bit sure of yourself, aren't you?

Just being honest. We like each other, don't we? We're both adults. And we're unattached.

I suppose so.

You don't sound very enthusiastic. OK, never mind, forget I mentioned it...

Nooo!

Chapter 26

"WELL?" JAY'S MOUTH WAS twitching once more at the corners, his eyebrows lifting inquiringly as he spoke. "What's the verdict?"

Not giving him the chance to back off again, Nadia reached over and hooked her hand behind his neck. Pulling him toward her, she kissed him gently at first, then harder. Joyfully, she felt Jay respond. Making the first move wasn't something she was familiar with, but this time he'd provoked her, he'd *made* her make it.

Gosh, and was she glad she had. He was a gorgeous kisser. His arms were round her, his warm hands moving against her back—

Rrrrring rrrring, sang the phone on the table in front of them and Nadia froze.

"Bloody hell," Jay muttered under his breath. Heaving a sigh he broke away. "Any other day, I'd ignore it…"

"But not today. Go on, pick it up. It's only a phone call," Nadia reminded him, and Jay smiled.

"You're right. Don't go away."

He'd meant it as a joke, but this was actually a lot easier said than done. Half sitting, half lying on the couch, pretending not to be listening to the phone call, Nadia's discomfort increased by the second. While she lay sprawled like some wanton trollop with her pink dress halfway up her thighs and her lipstick smudged, Jay paced around the sitting room and spoke on the phone to some distraught relative.

After a couple of minutes he said loudly, "Hang on a moment, Aunt Maureen, I just need to switch something off in the kitchen…"

Covering the mouthpiece, he turned to Nadia. "It's my mother's sister, Maureen. She's eighty-three and lives in a nursing home in Toronto. Her doctors wouldn't allow her to fly over for the funeral. She's very deaf and extremely upset about Anthony."

A lump sprang into Nadia's throat. She shook her head, picturing a distraught old lady in a Canadian nursing home, desperate to hear about the funeral of her beloved nephew.

"Don't worry about me," she told Jay as he headed for the door. "You go ahead, I'll be fine."

No longer smiling, he shot her a look of gratitude and left the room.

Was this how mating dogs felt when they got a bucket of cold water unceremoniously chucked over them? Nadia sat up straight and pulled the hem of her dress down as far as it would go. Every ounce of desire had drained out of her, melted away along with the heady loosening effect of all that Meursault.

How could they have even considered doing anything so selfish? Jay's brother was dead, his funeral had taken place just a few hours ago. Romping around on a sofa was… God, it was practically sacrilegious, like seducing someone in the vestry while the vicar was taking Sunday School.

Nadia cringed, deeply ashamed of herself. It was all wrong. Jay was in a vulnerable state. God, why did it have to be so quiet in this room?

Straining her ears, she was just about able to hear the murmur of Jay's voice as he carried on talking to the ancient aunt. He was either at the far end of the hall or in the kitchen. Unable to bear the silence, Nadia reached for the remote and flicked on the TV. Typical late Friday night shows were on, featuring over-excited girls in bikinis cavorting in Spanish bars, swigging from bottles of beer, and declaring their intention to sleep with as many boys as possible before they passed out unconscious. The boys, clearly up for the challenge, bared their backsides for the cameras and went *Whooaar* a lot.

Hideously aware that what she and Jay had been on the verge of doing hadn't been a million miles from what she was now seeing on the screen—minus the puddles of vomit—Nadia hit the Off switch.

More silence.

It really was very quiet in here.

The desire may have gone, but the four glasses of wine were still swimming around in her veins. Nadia briefly pictured them doggy-paddling along in their water-wings. That was the incredible thing about alcohol; if you were excited it heightened the excitement. If you were sitting there doing nothing, the effect was soporific.

Since getting up and going home would be plain rude, Nadia kicked off her shoes and curled her legs up on the sofa. It was a really comfortable sofa, which helped. And the velvet cushions under her head were blissfully squidgy…

Crikey, imagine if they'd actually been *doing it* when Aunt Maureen had struggled along on her walker to the pay phone and rung Jay to talk about Anthony's funeral…

Nice comfy sofa, mmm…

Nadia woke up at seven o'clock on Saturday morning with an aching head and a bladder fit to burst.

Urrgh.

Having visited the downstairs loo, she stumbled back to the living room and took in the rumpled blanket on the sofa. Jay had covered her with a crimson blanket, which wouldn't have gone with her pink dress at all.

The house was still silent.

Phew, thank goodness they hadn't done it.

Feeling commendably pure, Nadia phoned for a cab.

Arriving back home at seven thirty, she had banked on the rest of the household being asleep. Her breath caught in her throat as she saw Tilly on the driveway, loading an overnight bag into the back of her mother's new car.

"Seven pounds fifty," yawned the cab driver, who had been on duty for the last twelve hours and was just glad Nadia hadn't thrown up in the back of his car.

Mindlessly Nadia passed him a twenty and murmured, "Keep the change."

Leonie, emerging from the house, exclaimed, "Darling, there you are, we were all wondering where you'd got to. Oh dear, I hope you realize how cheap you look. Last night's clothes… Saturday morning… act like a pushover and men will treat you like a push-over. It's not the way to gain their respect."

Sometimes, Nadia marveled, her mother really was beyond belief.

"I didn't act like a pushover."

Leonie glanced significantly at her crumpled pink dress. "Of course you didn't, darling. But I do think the least he could have done was drive you home. I always think it's so tacky when men pack last night's conquest off in a taxi." Lowering her voice she added reprovingly, "Nor is it setting a good example to your sister."

There were so many cutting ripostes jostling around in Nadia's brain (Me! No, me! No, no, let me say mine!) that she couldn't manage to get any of them out. Which, since Tilly was listening, was probably for the best.

"I slept on the sofa," said Nadia, and Leonie, laughing merrily, pointed up at the sky.

"Ooh, look, flying pig."

"Mum," Tilly groaned. "Please don't."

"Don't what? I'm just trying to give Nadia some perfectly sensible advice. I don't like to see my daughter looking cheap."

Nadia was tempted to remind her mother that since walking out on them over twenty years ago, she hadn't been around to see her daughters looking *anything*. But what would be the point? She hugged Tilly instead and said, "Have fun. See you tomorrow night."

"Come here, darling, give me a kiss." Settling herself into the driver's seat, Leonie beckoned Nadia over. "I'm sorry if I've offended you, but I am your mother and I really am only trying to help. This chap of yours is a good-looking fellow, he can have his pick of girls. A man like him doesn't want a clinging limpet."

Through gritted teeth Nadia said, "I'm not a clinging limpet."

Oh God, she wasn't, was she?

"Don't ring him and ask when you're going to see him again," advised Leonie. "They can't stand being pestered like that."

"I know when I'm going to see him again," Nadia reminded her mother. "He's my boss. I'll see him at work on Monday morning."

"That's something else you should never do. Get involved with your boss." Leonie switched on the ignition and fastened her seat belt. "That's just asking for trouble, sweetheart. Before you know it, you'll be dumped *and* out of a job."

———

"It's for you," said Miriam, handing the phone to Nadia.

Nadia wondered if it was Leonie, calling to remind her not to ring Jay.

"You left."

Not Leonie after all. Her stomach tightening with pleasure— See? I didn't phone him, he phoned *me*—Nadia replied, "And they said you weren't observant."

"You should have woken me. I would've driven you home."

Hear that, Mother?

"I was up early. Sorry about falling asleep on your sofa."

"And I'm sorry I abandoned you. Poor old Aunt Maureen," said Jay. "She was on the phone for over an hour. I couldn't not speak to her."

"Of course you couldn't. Really, it's OK."

"Anyway, thanks for last night."

"Thanks for what? I didn't do anything." The phone rang, remember? The damn phone rang just as things were starting to get *interesting*.

"You know what I mean." Jay sounded as if he was smiling. "Look, what are you doing tonight?"

Nadia's heart broke into a canter. Ooh, crikey, a repeat performance? A repeat performance, only this time with the phone left off the hook?

"Um…" A vivid mental image of Leonie flashed into her mind, tut-tutting and shaking her head in disapproval. Irritated, Nadia took a deep breath and attempted to banish the unwanted image.

But… but… hadn't she made her own executive decision last night? Admittedly only after Jay had taken the call from Aunt Maureen, but all the same. She'd realized that sleeping with him so soon after Anthony's funeral would be a mistake. Seeing him again this evening would still be too soon.

Nadia closed her eyes and saw her mother again. Men like Jay could have anyone they wanted, they were used to girls flinging themselves at them with all the subtlety of a custard pie in the face. It never hurt to keep them hanging on.

Finding it hard to believe that she was actually taking Leonie's advice, Nadia said quickly, "I'm busy tonight. And tomorrow."

There. She'd done it. *Yes.*

"Oh right. That's a shame."

Beginning to panic, she tried to gauge whether Jay was heart-broken, disappointed, or at this very moment flicking through the pages of his little black book. When all he'd uttered were five words, it was hard to tell.

"This weekend's difficult. Um, but maybe next weekend… I'm free then." Out of the corner of her eye Nadia saw Miriam smiling broadly. "I mean, I think I'm probably free then… I'd have to check my diary."

Just in case that's when I'm having dinner with Robbie Williams and it's completely slipped my mind.

"OK. Well, we'll talk about it later in the week," said Jay, which sounded a bit too casual for her liking. "And when I see you on Monday I'm paying you back for that taxi."

"No need."

"Every need. How much was it?"

"Oh well, if you really insist," said Nadia. "Three hundred and fifty pounds."

Chapter 27

THE PHONE RANG AGAIN twenty minutes later as Nadia was polishing off a doorstep of toast and Marmite. Clare, who had belatedly surfaced and was moodily stirring a mug of coffee, leapt up as if she'd just sat on an electric fence.

"I'll get it!"

Nadia hoped it wouldn't turn out to be Piers.

Snatching up the phone, Clare said eagerly, "Yes?"

Her shoulders sagged as someone who clearly wasn't Piers replied. "Hang on. I'll get her."

As though the phone had suddenly grown fifty times heavier, Clare waved it feebly at Miriam. "Gran, for you."

Miriam, wearing slim black trousers and a black jersey top, was at the sink scrubbing last night's barbecue racks with her customary vigor. She glanced over her shoulder. "Who is it?"

"Don't know." Clare shrugged, uninterested. "He didn't say."

As Miriam peeled off her wet rubber gloves, Nadia wondered if she was tempted to swipe Clare round the head with them. Diamonds glinted as Miriam seized the phone.

"Hello?"

Pause.

"I'm sorry, who is this?"

Looking up, Nadia saw her grandmother's spine stiffen.

Miriam switched off the phone.

"What was *that* about?" Nadia demanded.

The rubber gloves were back on. Miriam, returning her attention to the metal racks in the sink, said, "Hmm? Oh nothing. I ordered some bath towels from John Lewis and they've come in."

Clare and Nadia exchanged glances. Bathroom towels. Of course.

"If Piers phones you up," Nadia addressed Clare, "you want to tell him to take a running jump." Into a cesspit, preferably. "Jay rang earlier asking to see me tonight and I said I was busy all weekend." She couldn't help sounding smug.

Clare raked her fingers through her uncombed hair and rattled irritably through the pages of the newspaper in search of the horoscope.

"I'm fine. Just let me handle things my way, OK? Piers isn't going to get away with this."

Honestly.

"Excuse me," said Nadia. "I think he already has."

The metal barbecue racks clattered onto the drainer. Miriam, snapping the rubber gloves off once more, turned and stalked out of the room.

"Whoever that was, he's rattled Gran." Clare raised her eyebrows. "You don't think she's been having an affair, do you?"

This wasn't likely. Miriam didn't have enough spare time for an affair.

"Bookmaker?" suggested Nadia. "Maybe she's been gambling and owes loads on her account. Did he sound like the kind of man who might send the heavies round?"

"Just sounded a bit Scottish." Clare had a brainwave. "Ooh, how about a long-lost relative? Miriam's illegitimate son?"

"Son! How old was he?"

"How would I know? Next time he rings I'll ask him his date of birth, and if he could send a photo of himself along with a DNA sample, even better."

"Anyway, don't change the subject." Nadia was stern. "You and Piers. I'm serious now. Isn't it time you binned him?"

Clare hesitated, clearly torn between maintaining a brash facade and needing to confide in someone, even if it was only the sister she spent most of her life bickering with.

"The thing is, I really like him." Helplessly she shrugged. "I can't help it, I just *do*."

"Even when he treats you like a pile of old dog poo?"

"He doesn't," Clare flared back. "He forgot about the barbecue last night, that's all."

"Dog poo," Nadia repeated. "He's messing you about."

"Oh God, I *know*." With a howl of despair, Clare abruptly buried her face in her hands. "But it just makes me like him *more*."

———

Upstairs, Miriam sat on the bed and dialed the number she'd obtained by calling information. The strings of pearls round her neck rattled as she straightened her shoulders then leaned forward to triple-check that the bedroom door was shut.

He picked up on the first ring.

"Miriam? Is that you?"

"Now listen to me. I never want you to call this number again, OK? That was my granddaughter who answered the phone. You have your own life and family, and I have mine. I don't want to see you or speak to you. It's all in the past. I'm serious." Miriam heard her voice begin to crack and waver. "Just leave me *alone*."

———

"Yay, brilliant, you're here." Tamsin hugged Tilly like a long-lost best friend. "Welcome to the house of no-fun. I've been bored out of my skull." She cast a sly glance in her father's direction. "Come on, I'll show you where you're sleeping. This is going to be so cool!"

Tamsin's bedroom was large and south-facing, with two single beds and posters of pop stars on every wall.

"Dad bought the second bed the other day, specially for you." Bouncing onto her own, Tamsin slid a packet of cigarettes out from beneath the pillows and flung open the window. "Want one? Oh, go on, live a little. I've got a bottle of vodka for later, as well. God, aren't parents the pits? I've been grounded since Monday. One minute they're moaning that I'm under their feet the whole time. Then last Sunday I went out with some friends and came home a bit late and they went completely mental, said I wasn't to mix with people like that. I mean, does it make any sense to you? Their trouble is they don't know what they *do* want. Most of the girls in my class are so boring you just want to stick pins in them but the minute you meet a few who seem like a real laugh, you get told they're a bad influence. I'm telling you, it's doing my head in. Still, never mind, you're here now."

"Right," Tilly said uncertainly.

"*Bloody* right," declared Tamsin.

"Look at the two of you." Leonie gazed fondly at them from the doorway. "Getting on like a house on fire, just like a couple of sisters."

Tilly thought of Nadia and Clare, who spent most of their time fighting. Tamsin, kneeling behind her on the bed, fashioning her hair into intricate plaits, gave her a prod between the shoulder blades.

"Um, could me and Tam go and get a McDonald's later?" Tilly said it as though the thought had just occurred to her.

"Well… did Tamsin tell you she'd been grounded? She was supposed to be back by eight o'clock last Sunday and she didn't come home until half past one in the morning."

Half *one*? Good grief, thought Tilly.

"I could stay here," Tamsin helpfully suggested, "while Tilly goes to McDonald's. But then I don't suppose she'd want to go on her own. Poor old Tilly, it's like she's being punished when she didn't even do anything wrong."

"Ha, worked like a dream," Tamsin crowed, kissing the ten pound note as they headed toward the town center.

"We have to be back by two o'clock."

"Don't fuss! As long as we're together, they won't mind if we're a bit late. You're my chaperone." Tamsin tucked her arm cozily through Tilly's. "My very own Mary Poppins."

Except Mary Poppins was in control, thought Tilly. She wasn't secretly quaking in her lace-up boots, wondering what the hell her wayward charges might do next.

"You're late," said Brian, and Tilly felt her palms grow sweaty.

"Tilly wanted to look around the shops," Tamsin lied easily. "Dad, relax, we're here now. It's only half past three."

"They're fine, darling," Leonie chimed in. "Didn't I tell you there was nothing to worry about? Look at them, they've had a lovely time."

A lovely time sitting in the not-very-clean studio apartment belonging to one of Tamsin's new-found friends. One of the friends her father disapproved of, it went without saying. Jif—*Jif!*—sported beige dreadlocks, many tattoos, and a quite staggering amount of facial jewelry. What with his tongue stud getting in the way, it had been quite hard to guess what he was talking about at times, and he didn't smell that great but he'd seemed all right in a grungy kind of way. And Tamsin liked him.

They hadn't really done much at the bedsit, just listened to music and smoked a lot. It had actually been rather boring, not that Tilly had told Tamsin this. Jif was seventeen and—according to Tamsin—like, totally cool.

"Are there any doughnuts left?" Tamsin was now rummaging through the fridge.

"You've just been to McDonald's," Brian protested.

Tamsin, the ten pound note safely tucked away in the back

pocket of her jeans, rolled her eyes at the stupidity of fathers. "We're growing girls, Dad. That was two hours ago. We're both starving again. Here," she tossed a doughnut at Tilly, "catch."

That evening they went out to a family-friendly pub where an Abba tribute band was playing on stage and children danced with their parents. The younger children anyway. "You must be joking," Tamsin exclaimed when Brian teasingly suggested a twirl on the floor. "God, music for old fogies." She wrinkled her nose in disgust. "Wouldn't catch me doing that."

Leonie wrapped an arm round Tilly's thin shoulders. "Enjoying yourself, darling?"

Tilly nodded and smiled, and Leonie gave her a hug. Tilly, flushing with pleasure, thought, look at us, me and my mum having a nice time together. It gave her a warm glow in her stomach and she rested her head for a moment against Leonie's chest.

"Oh, *sweet*." Tamsin was grinning broadly. "Quick, where's my violin?"

"Don't make fun," said Leonie, squeezing Tilly's waist. "This is my baby."

Tilly's throat ached with happiness.

"Come on." Brian reached for Leonie as the band broke into "Waterloo." "Time the old people had a dance. Here." He dug a handful of pound coins from his pocket. "You two have a few games of pool. Stop you laughing at us."

Jumping to her feet, Tamsin said cheerfully, "Haven't you old fogies ever heard of multitasking? We can play pool *and* laugh."

Nadia picked Tilly up outside Bristol Temple Meads station when she arrived back on Sunday evening.

"Was it awful?"

"No, it was nice." Tilly bundled her weekend bag onto the

backseat and climbed into the car. "We had a great time. Mum bought me this." She plucked at her black cropped top, then held up the silver necklace she was wearing. "And this."

"'St ends.'" Nadia studied the right-hand half of the silver heart. "Who's he, the patron saint of jewelry?"

Tilly flushed. "She bought Tamsin the other half. Together they make Best Friends."

Right.

"So Tamsin's one says Be Fri." Nadia put the car into gear. "You definitely got the better half."

"And we won a competition at the pub this afternoon. The family quiz," Tilly said with pride. "It was general knowledge, us against six other families, and we beat them all! I got a prize for that too."

Nadia glanced sideways at her. There was no mistaking Tilly's joy in repeating the *F* word. Her heart sinking, Nadia wondered what Leonie was up to now.

"That's brilliant, what kind of prize?"

"A CD." Tilly tugged her top down over her exposed tummy button, which was sporting a stick-on tattoo. At least Nadia hoped it was stick-on.

"Which CD?"

They looked at each other. Tilly said neutrally, "Hear'Say."

Nadia gave her knee a consoling pat. "Oh well. Never mind."

Chapter 28

ON WEDNESDAY MORNING, MIRIAM announced to Edward that she was going shopping. She drove across town to a suburb of Bristol she'd never visited before, found the address she was looking for, and parked the car outside the firm of solicitors she'd picked out of the phone book.

"Christine Wilson," she told the receptionist. "I have an appointment at eleven with David Payne."

The offices were dull and in need of redecoration. David Payne, in his midforties, matched them perfectly. He was also, mystifyingly, in possession of very little hair yet copious amounts of dandruff. The shoulders of his gray suit were liberally dusted with it. Miriam wondered if the suit jacket in fact belonged to somebody else. She was attempting to distract herself from the problem that had brought her along to these grotty offices in the first place.

"Right, Mrs. Wilson. Perhaps you'd like to tell me why you're here."

Trying hard to ignore the dandruff, Miriam explained her situation. When she'd finished, David Payne sat back in his chair and shook his seal-like head.

"Oh dear," he sighed, tapping his pen on the desk. "Oh dear, oh dear."

"And?" Miriam prompted tightly.

"This could be messy. Very messy indeed."

She wondered if it could be as messy as going with her initial instinct and hiring a hit man.

"Well, give me a clue. Could I go to prison?"

David Payne's expression was grave. "I'm afraid prison can't be ruled out. It's a… ah… possibility."

Miriam nodded. Prison, imagine. Glancing down at her fingers, tightly laced together in her lap, she said, "So what do you suggest I do?"

"Not a lot you can do at the moment. As far as you and this gentleman are concerned, the ball is pretty firmly in his court." Clicking and unclicking his pen, David Payne said, "Frankly, Mrs. Wilson, I wouldn't like to be in your shoes."

Miriam tried hard not to feel sick; she almost wished she hadn't come now. This was turning out to be scarier than she'd thought.

"Bleeuurgh." Nadia shuddered and jerked away, scrunching her eyes shut and stumbling on the rocky ground. Behind her on the terrace she heard sounds of unconcealed amusement.

Turning, she saw the plumber, the council planning officer, and Jay, all laughing at her.

"Not funny." Nadia clutched the handle of the spade she'd been using to loosen the earth. Worms were the bane of her life. Why did people automatically assume that when you were a professional gardener you stopped being squeamish about worms? She didn't like them much at the best of times, but she *really* didn't like accidentally chopping them in half with her spade.

Why did worms—especially when they were cut in two—have to be so *wriggly*?

Actually, it probably had something to do with playing in the garden as a child, when Clare had dropped a handful of the things down the back of her T-shirt.

"Worm?" Jay called out; it wasn't the first time he'd witnessed the shudder of revulsion. "Big scary one?"

"Rattlesnake," Nadia called back. Down by her left foot, both halves of the worm wriggled out of sight.

Brushing her hair out of her eyes, she gingerly resumed digging. Up on the terrace, Jay and his companions disappeared inside the house. Willing herself not to look at her watch—damn, too late— Nadia wondered if she'd blown her chances with Jay. It was ten past five on Thursday afternoon and there had still been no mention of their date. If he hadn't forgotten about it, or changed his mind, he was officially cutting it very fine indeed. She'd been waiting for him to say something for four whole days now. And it wasn't restful.

Worst of all, she was beginning to understand why Clare refused to give up on Posh Piers, and why she'd agreed to see him the instant he'd phoned her on Monday. The more Jay didn't ask her out, the more Nadia wanted him to.

Frustrated, she shoved her heel down on the spade and carried on turning over the soil in what would eventually be a flowerbed. And now—her watch was almost taunting her—it was quarter past five. What if Jay *had* changed his mind? How dare he! Bloody hell, sixteen minutes past, and she was due to finish at five thirty. Men shouldn't be allowed to say they were going to ask you out then go back on their word. They should be arrested for doing that, it was downright unfair; couldn't they be charged with breach of promise or something? And now it was *seventeen* minutes past five.

Nadia slammed the spade into the ground, exhaled impatiently, looked back at the house, and decided there was only one sensible course of action to take.

She took off her watch and stuffed it in her bra.

———

Jay's voice behind her made Nadia jump. Well, not really, because she'd heard him making his way across the terrace, but she pretended he'd made her jump. It never did any harm to give your boss the impression you were so engrossed in your work you wouldn't notice if Russell Crowe ran through the garden naked.

Except he might hurt his feet on the stones, so maybe he should wear wellingtons…

Anyway.

"What?" She raised her head.

"I said it's almost six o'clock. Everyone else has left."

"Almost six?" Reaching inside her bra—but in a ladylike way—Nadia pulled out her watch. "Sorry. I just wanted to finish this bed."

"Dinner on Saturday?" said Jay.

"Sorry?" Inside her chest, her heart did a tiny victory hornpipe.

"Saturday evening. Unless you have other plans." Jay raised his eyebrows. "Because if you have, that's OK, I'll just—"

"Saturday's great! No other plans," Nadia blurted out, "no other plans at all!" She wasn't about to make *that* mistake again.

"Fine." Jay nodded. "I'll pick you up, shall I? Eight o'clock OK with you?"

"Eight o'clock, perfect." Nadia paused. "I thought you'd forgotten."

"What made you think that?"

"It's Thursday afternoon." Honestly, was he thick?

"Oh right. Well, you've kept me waiting." Jay's look of amusement sent lustful quivers darting down her spine. "I thought it was my turn to do the same to you."

———

"Will you two please be quiet?" With a sigh, Tilly flung open Nadia's bedroom door. "I'm trying to watch *Blind Date* downstairs and I can't hear the TV."

"Yes, boss, no, boss, sorry, boss." Clare mock saluted before breaking into song once more.

"You can't sing. You're tone deaf. It's just horrible," said Tilly. Hands on hips, she turned to Nadia. "And you sound worse than Harpo. He's cringing downstairs with his wings over his ears."

"Don't blame us, blame Cher." Nadia pointed to the CD player, from which Cher was warbling that she belieeeved in life after loooove. "She's singing so loudly we can't hear ourselves. It's all her fault."

"And who was that yelling just now?"

"Clare. I had the hair dryer first." Nadia waggled it triumphantly.

Tilly shot them both a look of long-suffering disdain. "God, I'm so glad I don't have a boyfriend. Just turn the music down a bit, will you?"

"Aye aye, boss. Nad, turn the music down." Clare was pouting like a goldfish, applying lip gloss to her already glossy mouth. Spotting Nadia in the mirror she yelped, "Those are *my* earrings. I was going to *wear* those earrings."

"They look better on me. Anyway, I let you borrow my belt. Ooh, is that a car outside?"

As a diversionary tactic, it worked like a charm. Clare shot over to the window. Tilly, rolling her eyes, left the room. Cher carried on warbling at maximum volume. Nadia, smugly finishing off her hair in the mirror, experienced that warm glow of anticipation you get when you just know a truly great night lies ahead.

In honor of the occasion she had even—sluttishly but sensibly—slipped a spare pair of knickers and her toothbrush into the side pocket of her handbag.

It was seven thirty and Miriam had already left with Edward for the theater. James was out too, with Annie. Piers, on his best behavior (this week at least), had already rung to let Clare know he was on his way over. And at eight o'clock—give or take a few minutes either side—Jay would be here.

Oh yes, this was definitely going to be a night to remember. Smirking at her reflection—because she was looking rather stunning, if she did say so herself—Nadia wondered which restaurant Jay was taking her to, and if it was actually compulsory to go there. Would the maître d' really be that distraught if they phoned and canceled their table, and went straight back to Jay's house instead?

"Hoooo!" Clare let out a squeal of excitement at the sound of tires on gravel. This time a car really had arrived. She again launched herself at the window. "It's Piers! Yay, we're in the Ferrari!"

"Break a leg," said Nadia as Clare skipped to the door.

"Break both yours," Clare gaily called back, already on her way down the stairs.

In those heels, it was a miracle she didn't.

Having primped to the limit, Nadia made her way down to the living room ten minutes later. Tilly was stretched out across the sofa, peeling a tangerine and watching *Blind Date*. On the TV screen, Cilla Black was pulling comical faces while the couple who'd been last week's date hurled increasingly lurid insults at each other.

"So it was true love then." Nudging Tilly's feet out of the way, Nadia sat down.

"Absolutely." Neatly lobbing a piece of peel into the wastepaper bin, Tilly added, "Just like Clare and Posh Piers. Except Piers only loves himself."

"Sure you're going to be all right here on your own?" Nadia gave Tilly's bony ankle an affectionate rub; only since her thirteenth birthday had she been allowed to stay in the house alone. Tilly raised her eyebrows.

"And if I'm not sure? What'll you do, cart me along to the restaurant like a big third wheel so I can sit and watch you do your flirty stuff with some ancient old man? No thanks."

"Jay's thirty!"

"OK, maybe not ancient. Middle-aged," Tilly conceded.

"If he was here now, he'd throw *you* into the wastepaper bin. Thirty isn't middle-aged."

"Fine, don't get your knickers in a twist."

My teeny-tiny silky lacy irresistible knickers, Nadia thought smugly.

"Anyway, you don't have to worry about me." Tilly tore off another strip of peel. "I'm looking forward to some peace and quiet. I'm going to finish up the tub of Snickers ice cream and watch whatever I want to watch on TV without being interrupted."

About to offer to bring petits fours wrapped in a napkin back from the restaurant for her, Nadia remembered in the nick of time that—fingers crossed—she wouldn't be back tonight.

"OK. But no cocaine, no bingeing on tequila, and no wild parties."

"Are salt and vinegar chips allowed?"

"No more than two packets." Reaching over, Nadia ruffled her hair. "Oh, we're lucky to have you. Come here and give your big old nearly middle-aged sister a kiss."

"Phew, you stink." Tilly wriggled out of reach. "What're you trying to do to the man, chloroform him?"

Instantly Nadia scrambled into a sitting position. "Oh God, is it too strong? I couldn't smell it so I put a bit more on, then the bottle kind of slipped as I was doing it—bugger, it *is* too strong." She sprang to her feet, panicking slightly as the giveaway tick-tock sound of a cab outside reached them. Once you'd accidentally splashed on way too much perfume, it wasn't easy to undo the damage. Apart from attacking your skin with a Brillo pad, nothing ever seemed to work. But if she greeted Jay now, she would reek of both Amarige *and* eagerness. Not a good start.

Rushing to the downstairs cloakroom—because a Brillo pad would be reckless—Nadia seized the nailbrush Miriam used to clean her hands after gardening. Dragging it through the bar of Cussons Pearl in the soap dish, she frantically brushed her wrists then ran them under the tap. Now that Tilly had pointed it out, the smell of Amarige *was* overpowering. Gingerly she scrubbed at her—ouch—neck, then splashed on cold water to rinse away the soap and vigorously toweled herself dry. Well, not quite; the front of her white top was splattered with water—but on such a warm night it would evaporate soon enough.

Rrrrrinnggg.

"The man of your dreams is here," Tilly sang out, a bit too loudly for Nadia's liking. "Is it safe to let him in or has the smell not gone yet?" Feigning concern she added, "Want me to find a clothespin for his nose?"

"I'll get it." Since it clearly wasn't safe to let Tilly answer the door, Nadia skidded across the hall. She pulled the door open and prepared to tell Jay he was ten minutes early.

Her mouth failed to form the words.

Oh good grief.

"Nadia." Laurie's green eyes surveyed her with affection. He shook his blond head at her in long-time-no-see admiration. "You look fantastic. Is this a private wet T-shirt competition or can anyone join in?"

Chapter 29

THE GRANDFATHER CLOCK WAS still ticking in the hall, but the seconds seemed to stretch into hours. Nadia tried to breathe and found she couldn't; the air was stuck in her lungs. Not Jay. Laurie. *Laurie*, whom she'd spent the best part of eighteen months trying to forget. And if she hadn't been able to forget him—because let's face it, who *could*?—she'd certainly made every effort to put him out of her mind. Damn, she'd practically turned not thinking about Laurie into an art form.

And now here he was. The ex-love of her life, turning up out of the blue on her doorstep and giving her the kind of look she remembered so well.

Was it any wonder she couldn't breathe?

Laurie didn't kiss her or hug her. It was just all there in his eyes. Finally he said, "Who else is in?"

"Um… nobody."

Behind her Tilly wailed indignantly, "Oh, thanks a *lot*," before running across the hall and throwing herself into Laurie's outstretched arms. "It's so great to see you again!" She had idolized Laurie since babyhood. "What are you doing here?"

As he hugged her, Laurie's eyes met Nadia's over the top of Tilly's head. "I'm back. For good."

Nadia couldn't think where her knees had gone to. She couldn't speak.

"Everyone else is out," Tilly told him. "Your dad's taken Gran to the theater."

"I saw there weren't any lights on over the road. That's why I came straight here." Laurie kissed Tilly's thin cheek. "All my stuff's outside in the porch. OK if I bring it in?"

Tilly, flushed with excitement, helped him lug the various bags into the hall. Then, glancing at Nadia's shell-shocked expression, she said chirpily, "Well, better leave you to it! I've got geography homework. If anyone needs me, I'll be in my room."

They watched her run up the stairs, heard her bedroom door slam shut. As they went into the living room, the grandfather clock whirred, clunked, and began to chime. It was eight o'clock.

"Well," said Laurie. As he paused, Nadia realized there wasn't time to pause.

"Well what?"

"OK. I've been planning this all the way across the Atlantic, so can I just say it? Nad, I'm sorry. I can't believe what I did and I'm really, truly sorry." His expression was deadly serious. "I missed you after we broke up, I missed you a lot. But there was so much else to do… work was crazy… and I honestly thought I'd done the right thing for both our sakes."

He took a step closer. Nadia's fingers and toes were now numb. "And?"

"I was an idiot. I made a horrible mistake." Laurie shrugged. "I can see that now. Hollywood's a shit place to live. The film industry's crap. I couldn't stand it a minute longer, the people out there just aren't *real*, they're *hollow*."

"Does this mean they stopped giving you jobs?" Nadia couldn't help it; the question popped out.

"Brrrrkk," squawked Harpo, beadily eyeing his old sparring partner. "Gillette, the best a man can get."

Laurie smiled, ignoring him. "The opposite. They're offering me bigger and better jobs. I'm just not interested in doing them anymore. I don't want to be there, because none of it means anything." Reaching into his jeans pocket, he pulled out a crumpled fax. "Here, you big doubter."

Nadia read the fax from his agent. Addressed to Laurie, it said, "Kid, big mistake. You're kissing goodbye to a terrific career. Get in touch if you change your mind. Hyram."

"I'm not going to change my mind. Hyram wanted to send me to his shrink." Laurie's mouth twitched. "Can you see me going to a shrink? Although I left you," he added with a shake of his head. "Maybe I should have seen one then. What's happened to your neck anyway? Has Clare been trying to strangle you?"

The nailbrush had left its mark.

"Too much scent. I was scrubbing it off." Jay would be here any minute now. Nadia began to panic.

"Girls' night out?"

Bloody cheek!

"What makes you so sure it's not a man?" Pink with indignation, Nadia prayed that Jay wouldn't stand her up.

Or did she?

"Don't get mad. I rang Dad last week," Laurie said easily. "He told me you weren't seeing anyone."

Nadia felt her short fingernails digging into her palms. "Well, I'm seeing someone tonight. And he's a man." Oh yes, definitely a man.

"Do you want to ring and cancel?"

"No!"

Anyway it was too late.

"No." Laurie shrugged in good-natured agreement. "Of course you can't do that. It's fine. I'll just wait here until you get back."

Oh, fantastic.

"Don't look at me like that." Laurie was pushing his hair off his face, smiling again in that heart-melting, rueful way of his. "Nad, I know this has all been a bit of a shock. No pressure, obviously, but we do have to talk. You go out on your date. Have a great time. I'll keep Tilly company until you get home." Turning his head slightly toward the door he added, "Sounds like this could be him now."

Tilly, who'd been eavesdropping shamelessly *and* peeping out of the landing window, came galloping down the staircase.

"He's here! Off you go. Me and Laurie'll have a brilliant time." She looked eagerly at Laurie. "Do they have Monopoly in America?"

"They do. They also have geography homework." He grinned and hustled her toward the living room.

"I don't really have geography homework." Tilly tut-tutted at his naivety. "I was being discreet."

"Nobody in this family knows the meaning of the word. Come on, I'll teach you now. You and me have to hide and pretend we aren't here. No noise, OK? We don't want to scare off Nadia's date."

Nadia, her heart in her throat, waited until the living-room door was firmly closed behind them. Although she knew it was coming, the front doorbell when it rang still made her jump. Oh God, how could this be happening to her, how *could* it?

And then Jay was there on the doorstep, smart in a suit and eyeing the luggage on the floor behind her with amusement.

"Somebody leaving home?"

"Harpo." From somewhere, Nadia dredged up a flip remark. "He says we drive him mad and he's going back to Madagascar."

"Never mind, he'll be able to ring you." Jay looked more closely at her neck as she reached for her handbag. "What are those marks? You and Clare been fighting again?"

Through the closed living-room door, they heard Harpo squawk raucously, "Have a break, have a Kit Kat."

"Come on." Jay moved to one side, ushering her out through the front door. "I think we can do better than a Kit Kat."

———

Nadia's brain was too full to concentrate on anything—she felt like an apprentice shepherd struggling to control a flock of sheep that were scattering in all directions. The restaurant Jay took her to was buzzy and fun, but even ordering from the menu was beyond her. Laurie was back, Laurie was back and he was telling her he'd made a terrible mistake. It was all too much to take in.

"Nadia?" Jay raised his eyebrows at her and she realized the waiter was waiting with pad and pen poised.

"Um… I'll have the same as you."

Big mistake. Nadia flinched when their first courses arrived. How could Jay even think she'd like whitebait?

"So, are you going to tell me what this is about?"

"Sorry?" Oh God, those dear little silvery fish, still with their heads on and their eyes in. Nadia couldn't eat them, she couldn't even bear to look at them. Did Laurie seriously expect to walk back into her life and be greeted with open arms? And what was Tilly telling him right now? Dammit, couldn't he at least have waited until next week to turn up?

Or even tomorrow?

Jay sat back in his chair. "Listen, much as I'd like to put it down to the excitement of being here with me, I somehow don't think it's that. Are you OK?"

Nadia nodded vigorously. This wasn't his fault. "I'm sorry, I just forgot they served whitebait with the eyes still in."

Jay clearly didn't believe her. His dark eyes were fixed on her face, silently daring her to fob him off again. "What's really wrong?"

"Nothing."

"Nadia." There it was, the third and final warning.

Exhaling, she pushed the scary whitebait away. "The suitcases. They belong to Laurie." Oh, the relief of finally saying it. "He came back tonight."

Silence. At their table, if nowhere else. All around them, laughter and lively conversation and the clink of cutlery carried on regardless.

"He came back," said Jay. "To *you*?"

"No. Back from the States. But he says he's sorry. He seems quite, um…"

"Keen?"

Nadia shook her head, then nodded, then shook it again. Just as well it was firmly attached.

Helplessly she said, "I don't know. He only turned up ten minutes before you did. I'm a bit…"

"Confused?"

"Could you stop finishing my sentences?" said Nadia.

"Somebody has to."

She nodded at her pushed-away plate. "Do you want my whitebait?"

"No. Do you want me to take you home?" countered Jay.

"Yes please." Nadia waited for him to catch the waiter's attention, then settle the bill. What there was of it. Oh well, nobody could say she wasn't a cheap date.

"Not my home," she told Jay as they left the restaurant. "Yours."

Chapter 30

"No," said Jay, when they reached the car.

"Please," Nadia begged. Despite the heat of the evening, she was shivering.

Within seconds they were roaring up Park Street.

"Look." Jay sounded resigned. "This isn't how I expected tonight to turn out. I was looking forward to it." With a brief sideways glance in her direction he added, "I think you were too."

Unable to speak, Nadia nodded. There was a huge lump in her throat. Fumbling in her bag for a hankie—oh God, *mustn't cry*—she pulled out the spare pair of knickers by mistake and hastily shoved them back in.

"But you need to sort yourself out. Make up your mind what you want. I prefer my houseguests to give me their undivided attention. If I took you home with me now, you'd be thinking about him." Jay paused. "You have a big decision to make and you can't put it off."

He was right. Nadia's vision blurred with tears. Crying seemed a weird thing to be on the brink of doing, under the circumstances. She'd never imagined that Laurie might do anything like this. But he had, and he loved her, and he really and truly wanted her back, which meant she now found herself torn between two men, because Jay wanted her as well.

Although for how long was anybody's guess.

But she should be happy, surely? As far as dilemmas went, this had to be one of the less traumatic variety. Hardly on a par with having to decide whether to be eaten by the lion or leap into the crocodile-infested lake.

Stupid, I'm being stupid. Nadia cleared her throat, blinked hard until the lights of Park Street swam back into focus, and said, "So what do you think I should do?"

"You can't ask me."

"I am asking you."

"Fine." Jay's tone was curt. "In that case, I think you should tell your ex-boyfriend he has a fucking nerve, and you can't believe he has such a low opinion of you that he thinks you'd even *consider* taking him back. I think you should tell him to fuck off back to LA and never bother you again."

"OK, OK, I get the message." Nadia held up her hands to stop him. Maybe asking Jay's advice had been a mistake—in all honesty, what had she expected him to say? "But I can't do that."

"Of course you can."

"I *can't*."

"Only because you don't want to."

"Look, you don't *know* Laurie."

"I don't need to. I just wish *you* didn't know him."

"But he's…"

"Oh, come on"—Jay was scornful—"stop defending him. Where's your pride? He dumped you once. What's to stop him doing it again?"

"Who says I'm going to take him back?" Nadia's voice rose; they were having an argument and she didn't think Jay was being fair. "I haven't said I will! He just turned up tonight."

"He certainly did that. Perfect timing." Jay shook his head in disgust. "OK, I've said my piece. What you decide to do now is up to you."

"Thank you so much."

"Don't be grumpy. You asked me what I thought and I told you."

Maybe, thought Nadia, but it doesn't mean I have to like it.

They drove the rest of the way in chilly silence. Jay pulled up outside the house and kept the engine running.

"Sorry," Nadia said awkwardly.

"Not your fault." The curtness of his tone managed to indicate that actually it was.

"Right. Bye then."

"Have fun."

She climbed out of the car, feeling dismissed. Jay roared off. In the manner, Nadia couldn't help feeling, of someone escaping from a girl who'd told him she had an unpleasant sexually transmitted disease.

She straightened her shoulders. Right. Phew. Next.

"Go away," Tilly wailed in outrage as she entered the sitting room. "You're too early. We were having *fun*."

Oh well, soon put a stop to that.

"Too bad, Cinderella." Nadia gave her scruffy ponytail a tug. "One of your ugly sisters has come home, and it's time you were in bed."

Tilly and Laurie had been playing Pictionary; the carpet was littered with discarded, scribbled-on sheets of paper. Pulling a face, Tilly lightning-sketched a miserable-looking face.

"Go on." Laurie gave her a hug. "I'll still be here tomorrow."

"Unless Nadia chops you up into tiny pieces and buries you in the garden."

"Keep your fingers crossed," said Laurie with a grin. "I don't want to be plant food."

They got on so well together, they always had. Nadia knew that Tilly would want her to carry on with Laurie exactly where they'd left off, just get back together as if the split had never happened.

As Tilly put her arms round Nadia and kissed her good night, she stage-whispered, "Isn't it great? You're so *lucky*."

Nadia managed a brief smile. Lucky wasn't how she was feeling right now.

"We weren't expecting you back before midnight," said Laurie when they were alone in the living room.

"I nearly didn't come back at all."

"Come on, sit down." He patted the sofa next to him. "But you changed your mind."

Nadia didn't sit down. Or tell him Jay had refused to let her stay.

"Hey." Laurie's voice softened. "I'm sorry if I messed up your date. I didn't know, did I?"

"Suppose not." He'd phoned his father last week, Nadia reminded herself. A week ago, as far as Edward was aware, she'd been one hundred percent single.

"Tilly told me it was your boss."

"That's right."

"Maybe not the best idea." Laurie pulled a face, much as Leonie had. "Could make things complicated."

"Thanks for that." Nadia wondered if it had occurred to Laurie that he was the one making things complicated. Incapable of sitting down, she said, "I'm having a cup of tea, d'you want one?"

But that didn't help either. Laurie followed her into the kitchen and leaned against the dresser, watching her faff about with mugs and spoons and tea bags. He was wearing a crumpled white shirt and typically battered jeans that sagged low over his hips. His hair was blonder, his tan deeper; even his eyes were greener than she remembered.

"Are you wearing colored contact lenses?" Nadia blurted out.

Laurie looked appalled. "You're not serious. *Me?* Here, check for yourself." Moving toward her, he gazed into Nadia's eyes. "No colored contacts. No botox. No dodgy implants." He sounded amused. "Anywhere."

"Glad to hear it. Good to know you haven't turned into a woolly woofter." Turning back to the tea-making, which felt as complicated as putting together a seven-course dinner and simultaneously carrying out open heart surgery, Nadia managed to spill sugar all over the worktop. Damn. "Do you still take…?"

"Oh yes." He was grinning at her now. "I think I was the only person in Hollywood who did. You should have seen the look on people's faces. Funny how it's fine to shove cocaine up your nose, but"—he mimed horror—"to actually put *sugar* in your *tea*…"

"So they wouldn't have been too impressed with your deep-fried Mars bars," Nadia remarked. She'd managed to get the sugar into the mugs without spilling any more of it, but was still acutely aware of how close to her Laurie was.

"One more reason to get out of there." He shrugged. "So have you made up your mind yet?"

"About deep-fried Mars bars? Well, I couldn't eat more than three in one go, but—"

"You know what I'm talking about," Laurie interrupted, and a shock of electricity zip-zapped down Nadia's spine. It was far easier to pretend she didn't. OK, just concentrate, stir the tea, scoop out the tea bags, drop the tea bags into the sugar bowl…

"Us," said Laurie. "I'm sorry. I know I shouldn't pressure you. But I just wondered if you'd decided anything yet. Now that the initial shock's worn off, kind of thing."

Worn off? Good grief, she hadn't even *begun* to get to grips yet with the initial shock. Marveling at Laurie's high opinion of her, Nadia thrust one of the mugs at him.

"If I told you to go away and leave me alone, would you do it?"

"No." Laurie smiled and shook his head. "I'd stay and try to change your mind." Pausing, he added, "Actually that's not true. I'm going to stay *until* you change your mind."

"What makes you think I would?"

Laurie put down his tea, untouched—after all the trouble she'd gone through to make it.

"I just do."

"Confident," said Nadia.

"I wouldn't be here if I wasn't. And I don't mean that in a big-headed way," Laurie hurriedly explained. "I have confidence in *you*. We were brilliant together, Nad. You know we were. As soon as you forgive me for being a twat, we can be brilliant again. Spoon?"

"Sorry?"

"Spoon." Laurie indicated the one on the worktop behind her. "You left the tea bag in my mug."

———

"I don't believe it!" exclaimed Miriam, when she and Edward arrived back at ten thirty.

You and me both, Nadia thought as Miriam flung her arms round Laurie and greeted him like… well, the proverbial long-lost grandson-in-law.

This really wasn't how she'd been expecting her Saturday night to turn out.

"Dad." Having disentangled himself from Miriam, Laurie turned to give his father a hug. Touched, Nadia saw tears glisten in Edward's eyes.

"Well, this is a surprise." Edward cleared his throat. "How long are you home for?" Due to pressure of work, Laurie's last few visits had been fleeting.

"I'm back for good, Dad."

Miriam raised an inquiring eyebrow at Nadia. Nadia shrugged, feeling wrung out and shattered. When this kind of stuff happened to people in soap operas, they always seemed to handle it so much better than she was doing.

"Bit of a surprise," Miriam said gaily, making possibly the understatement of the year. Then again, Miriam took everything in her stride.

"Back for good?" Edward frowned, sounding concerned. "Is anything wrong?"

"Something *was* wrong," Laurie agreed. "Dad, don't worry, I'm not in any trouble. I just came to my senses." He turned to Nadia. "As soon as this one here forgives me and takes me back, everything will be all right."

Nadia squirmed, aware of all eyes upon her. This was what she'd dreamed of for so long.

Simply, Laurie added, "I love her."

Oh dear, all getting rather Hollywood now. Nadia was tempted to mime sticking her fingers down her throat.

"Sorry." Laurie broke into a grin. "Bit rubbish, like the closing lines of some terrible movie."

"You're back in Bristol now," Nadia reminded him.

"OK. You're my bird an' I quite fancy you, so how about it, darlin'?"

"*Much* better. Exquisitely put." Laughing, Miriam gave him another hug. "And how does Nadia feel about this?"

Nadia was feeling like a pincushion; stick a load of pins in her and she knew she wouldn't feel them. Annoyed that they now appeared to be discussing her as if she wasn't even there, she said, "Nadia isn't making any decisions right now. In fact, Nadia's going to bed."

"Stubborn," whispered Miriam. "Always been stubborn. Remember when she pushed over the Christmas tree because she couldn't get the fairy to sit properly on the top? Oh well." She squeezed Laurie's tanned arm. "If anyone can talk her round, darling, it's you."

Nadia couldn't believe it.

"This has *nothing* to do with Christmas fairies."

There was a flash of diamonds as Miriam, unfazed, wagged a finger at her.

"Sweetheart, admit it, you can get temperamental. You'd spent two hours decorating that tree. When you knocked it down you smashed all the baubles."

"I remember that," Tilly chimed in from the living-room doorway. Released from bedroom exile by Miriam and Edward's return, she added brightly, "I was six. There was glass everywhere and Nadia cried and cried."

"*So?*" Nadia spread her arms in despair.

"Darling, I'm just saying that sometimes you do something impulsive and live to regret it." Miriam's tone was soothing. "It's called cutting off your nose to spite your face."

———

Nadia had a terrible night's sleep. Having gone off to bed in a bit of a huff, she'd spent the next few hours tossing and turning and listening to the noisy celebrations continuing downstairs. James, returning at midnight from his evening out with Annie, had joined in. Harpo, clearly overexcited, was happily trading insults with Laurie. The boy was back and everyone was delighted. When he and Edward finally left at around three, she'd heard Miriam saying reassuringly, "Don't worry about Nadia, she'll come round soon enough. She's missed you dreadfully, you know."

Gritting her teeth in exasperation, Nadia had only just resisted the urge to yell out a Harpo-style epithet. If anyone else had treated her that badly, her family would have done the decent thing and united against him. But the fact that it was Laurie apparently meant all was forgiven.

Did that mean she was supposed to forgive him too?

Did she *want* to?

Doooff, Nadia flipped over her pillow and punched it into shape. The rest of the house was silent now, and still she couldn't sleep.

Four o'clock came and went.

Then five.

What was Jay doing now?

Well, nothing at all. He'd be out for the count, obviously. Like any normal person.

Let's face it, the chances that he was lying awake fretting about *her* were an unequivocal nil.

Chapter 31

"I JUST HEARD," BELLOWED Clare, flinging open the bedroom door and launching herself onto the bed.

"Owww," Nadia groaned as her legs were pinned to the mattress. They'd better not be bent out of shape for good.

"I just got home and Dad told me. Come on, wake *up*." Clare prodded her annoyingly in the ribs. "Tell me everything! How can you sleep after something like this?"

Rolling over, Nadia shielded her eyes from the sunlight pouring through the window. "What time is it?"

"Ten o'clock. And according to Miriam, Laurie's going to be here at ten thirty."

"Why?"

"Apparently you're going shopping with him."

"Shopping." This was all far too much, far too soon in the day. "To buy what?"

"What do runaway boyfriends generally buy when they want to win you back? A bloody great engagement ring with a stone the size of a grape."

"*What?*" Jack-knifing into a sitting position, Nadia experienced early-morning headrush.

Clare flashed a triumphant grin. "Only joking. He's after a house."

Nadia didn't need Clare to regale her with details of the night she'd spent with Piers—the spark in her eyes and her irritating

Tigger-on-springs demeanor were more than enough to let Nadia know it had been fantastic.

But Clare told her anyway, perching on the window seat in the bathroom and shouting above the roar of the shower. Even with her ears full of shampoo suds, Nadia discovered, there was no escaping it.

"...he's so gorgeous... we had such a brilliant time... he's taking me up to Scotland next weekend... I can't wait," Clare bellowed happily.

Hmm.

"Did you hear all that?" she double-checked when Nadia emerged from the shower, just in case she'd missed a bit.

"Loud and clear." And bubbly, thought Nadia as she vigorously towel-dried her hair.

"He's really turned over a new leaf." Clare hugged her knees. "Realized he can't mess me about anymore. I told him, any more bullshit and I'd be off. That brought him to his senses."

"Well, good." Life at home was certainly easier when Clare was happy.

"So how did it go with thingy last night? Jay."

"Not good." Nadia began rubbing de-frizzing serum into her ringlets. She'd been trying hard not to think about Jay.

"Oh well, never mind. You've got Laurie now." As far as Clare was concerned, it was as simple as buying a new parakeet when your old one dropped off its perch.

"What if I don't want Laurie now?"

"Are you mad? Why wouldn't you want him? Coming back like this." Dramatically, Clare spread her arms. "It's just so romantic! Don't you realize how lucky you are? Laurie's giving you a second chance. You'd be mad not to grab it."

When Laurie arrived twenty minutes later, Clare hurled herself at him like an overexcited puppy.

"Ha!" Triumphantly she pulled away. "I've just kissed someone who's kissed someone who's kissed Johnny Depp."

"Blimey." Laurie looked impressed. "Who'd you just kiss?"

"You, you idiot!" Clare punched him on the arm. "You were at the Oscars with that actress who used to go out with him." Her eyes lit up. "Did you and her… you know, *do it*?"

"Clare," Miriam remonstrated mildly.

"What? I like to know these things."

Grinning, Laurie shook his head. "Our agents set it up. We'd never even met before. I didn't touch her—and I mean literally didn't touch her. Our job was to pose for the press like *this*." Using Clare to demonstrate, he placed the palm of one hand an inch from the small of her back, tilted his head toward hers and flashed his teeth at an imaginary camera lens. "Her dress was on loan from some wanky designer or other. No physical contact allowed in case I marked it with my nasty sweaty hands."

"Don't look nasty to me." Clare beamed. "Actually, I'm quite partial to a bit of sweat. God, I still can't believe you're back. How on earth could you not enjoy being in LA?"

"I had an apartment overlooking the beach," said Laurie. "That meant when I woke up in the morning I could see the ocean and the water-skiers and the windsurfers and the paragliders."

Clare rolled her eyes. "Poor you."

"I also had a clause written into my contract by my agent, forbidding me from taking part in *any* activity that could *possibly* injure or scar me. He put that in after I came off my motorbike," Laurie explained, "and had to have stitches in my cheek. I messed up an ad campaign doing that. Anyway, so by the time I'd signed the new contract, about the only thing I was allowed to do was peel oranges. It was a joke. I'm telling you, living that lifestyle isn't all it's cracked up to be."

"But you must have met loads of famous people." Clare still thought he was barking mad.

"Of course I did. But just because they're famous doesn't make them fun. Besides, I missed Nadia. Well, you already know that." Laurie paused. "That's why I'm back. Where is she, anyway?"

Nadia, who'd been loitering in the hall, took a deep breath and stepped into the kitchen.

"I'm here."

~~~

"Definitely going to have to get a new car." Laurie swung the steering wheel of his father's Volvo station wagon and turned right into Over Lane. "Now, half a mile down here, and it's on the left. Barrel Cottage."

Nadia had the bundle of estate agent's details balanced across her knees. It was eleven thirty on Sunday morning. If yesterday had gone ahead according to plan, she might still be lying in Jay's bed now, getting up to goodness knows what.

Well, actually, she had a pretty good idea.

But that wasn't happening. She was here instead with Laurie on the outskirts of Almondsbury, about to check out a property that, if he took a fancy to it, he was threatening to buy, more or less on the spot.

They pulled up outside Barrel Cottage, a long, low, four-bedroom property with diamond-leaded windows, a whitewashed exterior, and—surprise!—oak barrels overflowing with geraniums on either side of the front porch.

"How much?" said Laurie.

Nadia checked the details. "Three hundred thousand."

"What d'you think?"

"Bit chocolate-boxy."

"You don't like it?"

"Laurie, what am I doing here?"

"Helping me choose."

"But you're the one buying the house. You have to decide."

He winked. "It has to be somewhere you like, though. If we get back together, you'll be living there."

Oh well, ask a silly question. That was the thing about Laurie, he'd always tell you what was on his mind.

"What are you doing?" Nadia protested as he restarted the engine. "You're not wild about it."

"But it might be gorgeous inside!"

With a grin, Laurie switched off the ignition. "OK. Let's go and find out."

"*Ooof,*" Nadia gasped as she lost her footing at the top of the staircase. Next moment she was tumbling down the stairs. "Ouch, bugger, that *hurt*."

They were looking round the third property of the day, an empty four-story house in Redland whose agent had given them the keys. Laurie, rushing down behind her, said urgently, "Don't move. Lean back against me. Shit, where are we? I can't remember the address."

Nadia batted the mobile phone out of his hand before he could dial 999. "You big Hollywood Nancy, I don't need an ambulance. I just slipped, that's all."

"Nothing broken?" Laurie's face was white with concern. "Are you sure?" He was crouching beside her, his crumpled white trousers streaked with dust.

Nadia nodded and slowly flexed her hips. "Jarred my back a bit, but the rest of me's fine."

"I could have told you that." Unable to resist the quip, Laurie placed her arm round his shoulders. "Come on then, let's get you up. Lean on me." Carefully he hauled her upright. "Are you sure you're OK?"

"I'm sure. Don't make a fuss." Nadia turned her head away; disconcertingly, his face was only inches from hers.

"Was the carpet loose? Is that why you slipped?"

"I slipped because I wasn't looking where I was going."

Laurie's smile was rueful. "If we were in LA, I'd be calling my lawyer now, telling him to sue the ass off whoever owns this house."

"Maybe, but it was my fault."

"You see? That's why I love you." Laurie cheered up. "Nobody in LA ever admits they might be to blame for anything. So how much does it really hurt?"

Quite a lot, actually. But Nadia determinedly dusted herself down. "I'm fine. You can let go of me now."

His green eyes fixed on hers, as honest and heart-wrenching as ever. "Do you have any idea how much I want to kiss you?"

Not fair, not fair. Nadia felt her stomach wrestling itself into knots.

"I didn't kiss you last night," Laurie murmured. "Did you notice?"

He was so close to her. She concentrated on the barely visible scar on his cheek. Funnily enough, she *had* noticed.

"I wanted to, more than anything," Laurie went on when she didn't reply. "And I do now."

OK, this was becoming farcical…

"But I'm not going to," said Laurie.

Oh.

"Not until you really want me to."

His breath was warm and sweet. She could feel his heart beating through his thin, slate-gray T-shirt.

Nadia took a step back. Being kissed was one thing; actually admitting you *wanted* to be kissed was quite another.

"We haven't seen the ground floor yet."

Laurie's mouth twitched. "How did I know you'd say something like that?"

The rooms on the ground floor were huge and airy, helped along by the lack of furniture. Standing at the drawing-room window overlooking the garden, Laurie consulted the battered sheet of details and said lightly, "Eighty-foot garden. Big enough for you?"

"Too big for you," Nadia retorted, because Laurie was to horticulture what Princess Anne was to pole-dancing. And this house was priced at three seventy-five, for crying out loud. It was a ludicrous amount of money for him to shell out on a whim.

"I like this place," said Laurie.

"Oh, stop it. Why can't you just rent a flat?"

"Because that would look temporary, and I'm back for good. If buying a house is what it takes to make you believe me, that's what I'll do."

"But you can't—"

"Nad, don't get your knickers in a twist. Now that I'm back, I may as well have somewhere decent to live."

"And you can really afford it?"

"I can really afford it."

Gosh.

"OK." Nadia gave up.

"And I like this place."

"Even though it's too big for you."

"You see? That's *such* a pessimistic outlook. Can't you ever look on the bright side? I mean, picture this garden in five years." Laurie gestured expansively through the window. "A swing over there, under the apple tree. A slide going down into the paddling pool. One of those baby trampolines, a couple of tricycles…"

"Aren't you a bit old for a tricycle?" said Nadia.

"It could happen. It's what I want to happen. You, me, and a houseful of kids." Laurie broke into a grin at the look on her face. "OK, three kids. Three's fine, if that's all you want."

"What are you going to do, now you're back?" Abruptly she changed the subject. "Job-wise, I mean. Would you go back to stockbroking?"

Laurie pulled a face. "Something else, preferably. I hated stock-broking. But I suppose I'd do it again if I had to. Anyway," he went on carelessly, "I'm not even thinking about that yet. There's money in the bank and I'm taking the rest of the summer off to enjoy myself."

Nice work if you could get it.

"You must have enjoyed yourself over there too," said Nadia. Well, the question had been niggling away at her all morning, waiting to be asked. Actually, make that the last fifteen months. "You had girlfriends, didn't you?"

"A couple." Laurie grew serious. "What are you asking, how many girls I slept with? OK, three. Which is a pretty modest number, especially by LA standards. None for the first five months, by the way. I just wasn't interested. Then I realized I couldn't live like a monk for the rest of my life. But no serious relationships. Just casual flings. How about you?"

"God, hundreds. A different man every night," said Nadia. Well, she'd almost slept with Stevie Grainger from the garden center after last year's Christmas party. In Santa's grotto, no less. That had to count as point seven five of a conquest, surely? They would definitely have done it if someone hadn't set the fire alarm off.

"Hundreds? Now I'm getting worried. Were any of them as good as me?"

Nadia gave this some thought. "About eighty."

"Right. And were any of them... you know, serious relationships?"

"Only a couple of dozen."

"A couple of dozen," said Laurie. "Well, that's not so bad. That's manageable competition. So I'm still in with a chance, then?"

"Mr. Modest-as-ever," Nadia observed, pushing her hair back from her face. She really should still be in bed now. Either Jay's or her own, she couldn't decide which.

"Not modest," said Laurie. "Just optimistic. I have hope. After all"—he flashed his irresistible smile—"you haven't said no yet."

Chapter 32

THE PATIO AT CLARENCE Gardens needed laying, which as far as Nadia was concerned, was both good and bad news.

It was Monday morning, and the opportunity to escape the Laurie Welch Appreciation Society was a welcome one. On the other hand, her back was giving her serious bother. Clattering down a flight of stairs like a wayward pinball, bashing her spinal column against every step, had resulted in pretty spectacular bruising. Even tucking her T-shirt into her jeans had been so painful it had made her yelp. Surveying the stacked up paving stones without enthusiasm, she unscrewed the top of her Evian bottle and took a swig of water. That hurt too.

And there was no sign of Jay, which was a disappointment. Seeing him again, Nadia had felt, would help her with her dilemma. She'd planned to compare her reaction the moment she saw him with her reaction when Laurie had come over to take her house hunting yesterday morning. Rely on her body's instincts to tell her what she needed to know. Except her body was probably going to be too busy going *ooh, ouch* to tell her anything helpful right now.

Oh well, hey ho. On with the job she was being paid to do. Maybe after the first few paving stones her muscles would stop behaving like big crybabies and loosen up.

When the side gate clicked open an hour later, Nadia turned—creakily—and felt her heart begin to gather speed. Color rushed to her cheeks and her stomach clenched tighter than a three-year-old clutching a sweet.

"For heaven's sake." With difficulty, she straightened up and wiped her dusty, perspiring hands on her shorts. "What are you doing here?"

Laurie removed his sunglasses and indicated his crumpled T-shirt and jeans. "I asked Miriam how you were this morning and she said you crawled down to breakfast on all fours."

"That's not true." Nadia was indignant; she'd only *wanted* to crawl down to breakfast on all fours.

"Anyway. I thought you might appreciate a hand, and I'm free." He made free-type motions with his hands. "So here I am, dressed for work and ready to help."

Laurie's total indifference to clothes and famously casual wardrobe meant it was hard to tell. Today's gardening jeans were indistinguishable from Saturday's just-flown-back-from-LA ones. If he was off to a film premiere, he'd probably choose whichever were cleanest.

"But this is *my* job," said Nadia.

"I can still help, can't I? You don't have to pay me."

"I don't think this is a good idea." The word *help* was insinuating itself lovingly through Nadia's brain. Oh God, but what if Jay turned up?

"Makes sense to me." Laurie shrugged. "May as well do something useful with these muscles while I've still got them."

One of the other clauses in his agent's contract, Nadia had learned, was that Laurie had been obliged to spend a minimum of fourteen hours a week working out in a trendy LA gym.

"If you want to be useful," she said, "you could go to the pharmacy and pick up some Tylenol."

"Hey, I nearly forgot." Laurie delved into the front pocket of his bashed-up jeans. "Miriam found this after you'd gone. She thought you might need it."

He had brought a tube of Deep Heat. Nadia's nose wrinkled at the thought of its powerful smell, but Laurie was already squeezing the cream into his hand and advancing toward her.

"Come on, pull your T-shirt up. It'll help."

Was he doing this on purpose? Nadia's mouth went dry.

"I'll do it."

"Don't be a baby. Anyway, you couldn't reach." Taking hold of her T-shirt, Laurie lifted it to bra level and surveyed her bruised back. He shook his head in sympathy. "OK, don't worry. I'll be gentle."

That was what Nadia was afraid of.

He was gentle. While she held her breath, closed her eyes, and thought of... well, something else, he carefully smoothed the musty-smelling cream into her skin. Standing there in the sun-drenched garden, Nadia thought how intimate it felt, like being massaged by a lover with baby oil.

"There, all done." Stepping back, Laurie dropped the T-shirt back into place and re-capped the tube. "Now, what needs doing? Laying the paving stones? I can do that."

"Tylenol," Nadia repeated.

"Why don't you go and get the Tylenol? And pick up something for lunch? I'll get on with laying the stones."

It made sense. The ground was all ready, painstakingly leveled and marked out. Laurie was more than capable of laying the stones; he'd make a good job of it.

But... but...

"Look, forget why I came back," Laurie said patiently. "Just think of us as friends. If we were friends and I needed help, you'd help me, wouldn't you?"

"Maybe." Nadia tried to imagine them as just good friends. As they had been once, years ago.

"Right, so that's all we are. And now it's your turn to need help, so stop being so bloody stubborn and let me get on with the job."

"OK. Thanks." A thought belatedly struck her. "How did you know where I was working?"

"Miriam told me you were in Clarence Gardens. I looked for the house with the builder's van outside."

"Right. OK, Tylenol."

Laurie, already picking up the first paving slab with ridiculous ease, said, "And lunch."

"Who are you?"

Looking up, Laurie saw a young, scruffy lad with sticky-up hair and a smattering of acne.

Not Jay, he cleverly surmised.

"I'm Nadia, the gardener."

"No you aren't." The boy paused. "I've seen you somewhere before."

"I'm Nadia's friend," Laurie explained. "She's gone to the shops. I'm helping her out."

"Right." The boy nodded. "I'm Kevin."

"Kevin. Hi. Laurie."

Kevin frowned, the cogs moving slowly. "Where do I know you from? Do you drink at the Prince?"

"Um, no."

The cogs finally caught and slipped into place. Kevin burst out laughing. "I know what it is! You look just like the bloke in that video they've been showing on MTV. You know... you know..." He rattled his silver identity bracelet at Laurie. "Cassie McKellen's video, the one where she's drowning in the sea and the bloke dives in and saves her... you're the bloody spitting image of him!"

"Am I?" said Laurie.

"Christ, yeah. Brilliant video, that is. Cassie McKellen in a bikini, now she's a bird and a half—ha, wouldn't kick her out of bed, would you?" As he said it he glanced over his shoulder, checking that his dad wasn't within earshot. Cassie McKellen was a serious drug user.

Laurie, who had turned down an offer to climb into bed with her, said, "I should be so lucky." With a wink he added, "Just as well I prefer brunettes."

"So you and Nadia...?" Kevin hesitated, unsure how to phrase it. "Sorry, I mean, we didn't even know she had a boyfriend."

"Oh, I'm not her boyfriend." Separating the next paving stone from the stack and carrying it easily across to the marked-off patio area, Laurie said, "Not at the moment, anyway." As he lowered the stone into place and lined it up against its neighbors, he added cheerfully, "But I'm working on it."

Unlike Kevin, Jay knew at once who the stranger was. For a minute he watched unobserved from the French doors as Laurie Welch got on with the job in hand. Finally, straightening up and pulling his T-shirt over his head, Laurie turned and spotted him.

"Where's Nadia?" said Jay.

"Gone to pick up a few things. She hurt her back yesterday. I'm helping out." Laurie's voice was friendly, his eyes startlingly green. "If that's OK with you."

"Fine with me," Jay lied.

"You're the boss, I take it."

"That's right." There was a spade propped up against the wall. Jay wondered if bashing Laurie Welch over the head with it and burying his body in the garden would be an option.

"I'm the ex-boyfriend. Laurie Welch." Wiping his palms on his jeans, Laurie came over to shake hands.

"So I gathered."

"Look, I'm really sorry about Saturday. Hope I didn't mess up your night."

Since there was no polite answer to this, Jay said, "How did

Nadia hurt her back?" and immediately regretted it. Did he really want to know?

"We were looking at houses. I took her to see one in Redland and she fell down the stairs. Frightened the life out of me," Laurie admitted, "but she'll be OK."

"Right." Pushing him down a flight of stairs was another possibility, and far less messy than a spade. Jay said, "Which house in Redland?"

"Clarendon Road. Five bedrooms, fantastic garden. It's standing empty."

"The one on the corner. I know it." Jay kept up with what was happening on the property market.

"Really?" Laurie's face lit up. "We liked it. Plenty of room for… well, you know. We both know we want kids, so not much point in buying a penthouse flat. So, d'you think it's a good buy?"

"Up to you." Jay was buggered if he was going to hand out professional advice.

Laurie was enjoying himself hugely; having arrived back in England in the nick of time, he had no doubt at all that Nadia would come round before long. OK, so she had undoubtedly developed a bit of a crush on this boss of hers, but he and Nadia had years of history between them. Laurie was confident that he'd win in the end; he didn't regard Jay Tiernan as a serious threat.

And it was such fun, subtly letting him know that.

"I don't think it's overpriced," Laurie went on easily. "You know, I was all ready to put in an offer yesterday afternoon. But falling down the stairs might have put Nad off the place." The gate clicked and Laurie's gaze shifted away from Jay. "Here she is now."

Jay turned and saw Nadia carrying two Waitrose bags. Laurie, heading over, swiftly relieved her of them.

"I was just telling Jay about your accident yesterday. Did you get the Tylenol?"

"Um, yes."

"Good. Show him your bruises."

"There's no need, I'm sure he believes—"

"See?" Before Nadia was able to protest, Laurie had swiveled her round and pulled up her T-shirt. His tanned fingers moved lightly over her back, tracing the outlines of the swollen, purple bruises.

"I'm fine," Nadia protested, flushing as she covered them once more with her T-shirt.

"Did the Deep Heat help?"

Deep Heat. Jay imagined Laurie massaging the cream into her skin.

"It helped. Look, I need to get the rest of this stuff inside." Wincing slightly as she reached to retrieve the Waitrose bags, Nadia glanced at Jay. "Could I have a word?"

Jay didn't move. "Fire away."

She gave him a don't-muck-about look. "In private."

Chapter 33

BENDING DOWN WITH DIFFICULTY, Nadia put the snacky lunch food and drinks into the fridge and prayed the blast of cold air would remove the heat from her cheeks. The meeting between Jay and Laurie had been more or less inevitable, but she'd still found it an ordeal. Letting herself into the back garden, her insides had been doing a Baz Luhrmann-style can-can. She hadn't known whether this was a reaction to seeing Jay again or to seeing the two of them together.

And now Jay was standing behind her in the kitchen doorway.

Slowly straightening up, Nadia turned and mumbled, "Sorry."

"Again," said Jay.

"I didn't ask Laurie to come here and help me. He just turned up."

"Just as well he did. He's making a pretty good job of that patio."

"I know. But it's an awkward situation."

There was a pause. Upstairs in the master bedroom, they heard Bart and Kevin hammering away at the skirting boards and singing tunelessly along to "It's Not Unusual" by Tom Jones on the radio.

Finally Jay spoke. "It's not awkward. We're all adults. Look," he said evenly, "you work for me. We get on well. You know as well as I do that if Laurie hadn't come back when he did on Saturday night, things would have gone further."

Nadia's arms prickled with goose bumps. Phew, talk about coming straight to the point.

"Possibly."

"Bullshit." Jay's eyes glittered with amusement. "Definitely."

"But—"

"But how long would we have lasted? A week? A month? A decade?" He shrugged, presenting her with a *fait accompli*. "That's the trouble, isn't it? We just don't know. And now we're not going to get the chance to find out, because your old boyfriend came back. It's slightly disappointing, but it's not a catastrophe."

"Right." Nadia felt the goose bumps subside in defeat. So, not pistols at dawn then.

"If you didn't want him back, you'd have told him by now. The two of you have a history," Jay went on. "Long term, you've decided, he's probably a safer bet than I am. The devil you know versus the devil you only work for. And there's no need to look at me like that, I'm just being honest. Basically, you've made your decision, and that's fine. I can handle it. I'm not going to lock myself in my house and drink myself to death."

Since he was clearly teasing her, Nadia ventured a smile and said, "Well, good."

"Meeting girls is easy. All it takes is a trip to a wine bar. You see someone you like the look of, you get chatting, they give you their phone number. Mission accomplished."

"Wine bars? That's where it all happens?" Nadia was finding it increasingly difficult to sound natural; her breathing had gone to pot.

"Not always. You can meet girls anywhere. At the gym," said Jay. "Or the squash club. Or at auctions, parties, art galleries…"

Was it really that easy? Nadia pictured girls flinging themselves at him everywhere he went. Locking himself in his house and drinking himself to death was beginning to sound preferable.

"Once I even found one crashed in a ditch."

Oh humor, very droll. Now he was making jokes about the situation. Nadia was inwardly miffed; clearly she was far less important to him than she'd imagined.

Then again, as Jay himself had pointed out, he was the devil she didn't know.

"I'd better get back to work," Nadia said awkwardly. "The turf's being delivered tomorrow."

"I won't be around. There's a property auction at the Aztec Hotel. Will he be here to give you a hand?" Jay tilted his head in the general direction of the garden.

"I don't know."

"Well, take care of yourself. Don't strain that back of yours."

Did he mean in a turf-laying way or sexually? For a moment Nadia was tempted to blurt out, "I haven't slept with him."

But she didn't. Telling Jay that would be a bit silly now. Reassuring a jealous rival of your affections was all very well, but it was a pretty pointless exercise if he wasn't jealous.

"And you watch yourself tomorrow." Remembering what he'd said about meeting members of the opposite sex at auctions, Nadia went on flippantly, "No winking or waving at pretty girls or you might end up accidentally buying the wrong house."

⁓

Tilly arrived in the school cafeteria in a state of shock. As she queued up with her tray, she spotted Cal sitting on his own in a far corner, reading a textbook and eating his way through a mountain of chips.

When the tray was filled, Tilly made her way over. Warily Cal looked up; sharing a table for two with a girl was asking for trouble of the heckling kind. But Tilly was too preoccupied to care. Plonking her tray down opposite him—watery spaghetti bolognese, chips, chocolate sponge pudding, and peony-pink custard—she breathlessly announced, "You'll never guess what."

"My mother says that. It drives me nuts when she does it." Cal smiled slightly to soften the accusation. "It can mean one of the neighbors has dropped down dead in the garden, or the cat fell into the fish tank or the price of carrots has gone up by two pence."

"Sorry. My mother does it too. Only when she says it, you know it means she's fallen in love with some new bloke."

Cal raised his eyebrows in mock-horror. "Is that what's happened to you?"

Tilly gave his skinny leg a kick under the table. "No, you dope. Suzy Harrison's in hospital. She had her appendix out last night."

"Blimey," said Cal. "I really hope you aren't going to tell me you're in love with Suzy Harrison."

This time he moved his legs out of reach before Tilly could kick him again.

"She had the leading part in next week's school play. You know, Sandy in *Grease*? And Gemma Porter, who was understudying her, broke her ankle really badly playing tennis yesterday. Mrs. Durham auditioned for a new Sandy this morning, and I've got the part!"

"Wow, that's great." Cal was duly impressed.

"It's scary." Tilly attempted to fork up a twirl of wet spaghetti but it splashed back down onto her plate. Her stomach was in knots anyway; the school's drama productions were well attended and generally a big deal. She still couldn't believe she'd actually plucked up the courage to audition.

Cal, meanwhile, was peering at her plate. "Why's there rutabaga in your spaghetti bolognese?"

He was new to the school. He didn't know. "There's always rutabaga in the spaghetti bolognese. They put rutabaga in everything, even trifle. Oh God, I'm going to be *Sandy*." Tilly shook her head and shivered with a mixture of elation and fear.

"You'll be fine."

"It's only eight days away. I've got so many *lines*. What if I can't learn them in time?"

Cal calmly dunked a chip into the pool of tomato ketchup on his plate. "If you like, I could help you."

"Really? That'd be brilliant." Reaching down for her schoolbag, Tilly said, "I've got the script right here—"

"Not now." Cal jerked his head meaningfully in the direction of one of the rowdier tables, where a group of his classmates had just spotted him with Tilly. As they began bawling out the theme tune to *Batman*, he lowered his voice. "After school, OK? I'll meet you at the gates."

—⁓—

Cal had a real talent for voices.

"You should be playing Danny." Tilly was deeply impressed. "Why didn't you audition?"

They were in the park, lying on their stomachs under one of the chestnut trees bordering the public tennis courts. The script lay open on the grass between them and Cal was reading all the other parts, changing his voice according to whichever character he was playing. All Tilly had to concentrate on were Sandy's lines.

"Can't sing. Can't dance," Cal told her. "Well, technically I can dance, but I look as if I'm being electrocuted."

"I'm scared everyone will laugh at me." Tilly squashed an ant that had crawled onto her forearm. "I don't look anything like Olivia Newton-John."

"I should hope not. She's prehistoric by now," said Cal. "At least fifty."

"You know what I mean. What if they all start sniggering because I'm not pretty enough?"

He paused and looked at her, and Tilly realized she sounded as if she was angling for a compliment. She cringed, not wanting Cal to humor her and say that of course she was pretty. God, that would be so humiliating.

"You'll have the costume on, and your hair up in a ponytail, and heaps of makeup. You'll scrape through." Cal broke into a grin. "Or you could make all the audience wear blindfolds."

The butterflies in her stomach melted away. Tugging a single stem of couch grass out of the ground, Tilly waggled it in his ear. In retaliation Cal snatched up one of last season's wizened chestnuts and lobbed it at her. The conker shot straight down the front of Tilly's school shirt.

"Sorry!" Rolling into a sitting position, Cal abruptly stopped laughing. "Oh shit, people from school."

Following the line of his gaze, Tilly saw a group of Year-10 girls sauntering in their direction. Year-10 girls weren't as alarming as Year-10 boys, but it was a close-run thing.

"I'd better go," muttered Cal.

"No, don't." Without meaning to, she laid a hand on his arm.

"What are you two up to?" The leader of the girls approached them, her friends trailing in her wake. Her name was Janice Strong and she wore an astonishing amount of mascara. With her streaked hair pulled tightly back from her face she always reminded Tilly of a drag queen in the making.

"Cal's helping me learn some stuff."

"Cal? You mean Davis? Is that what you call him?" Janice's tarantula eyelashes shielded her eyes as she lit a cigarette. "What kind of stuff anyway? Homework?"

"I'm in the school play. I need to learn my lines." Tilly was determined not to be intimidated.

"Aren't you supposed to know them by now?" On the verge of sneering, Janice peered down at the script lying open on the grass, with Tilly's lines highlighted in Day-Glo pink. "Bloody hell, you got the part of Sandy? You're taking over from Suzy Harrison?"

Tilly nodded, tensing up inside and waiting to be scornfully informed that she wasn't pretty enough. But Janice started to laugh.

"Ace! That cow Colleen Mahoney went up for it this morning. She was so certain she'd get the part. So you actually beat her to it—bloody good for you, serves the silly bitch right!"

The next moment, Janice and her acolytes had dropped down onto the grass next to them. Tilly found herself being offered a cigarette.

"Cheers." Since a refusal would undoubtedly offend, Tilly took it and prayed she wouldn't splutter.

"So, *Cal.*" Janice emphasized the name. "How are you helping her with her lines?"

Cal hesitated.

"He's reading all the other parts," Tilly explained. "He's great at it."

Playfully, Janice nudged Cal's thigh with her outstretched toes. "Come on then, *Cal.* Let's hear you."

Tilly saw him mentally weighing up the available options; either run away and risk ridicule or stay and read and risk more ridicule.

Finally Cal turned the page of the script and launched into Rizzo's attack on Sandy, his American accent spot on and his tone suitably bitchy.

At the end of the exchange, Janice and her friends whistled and clapped.

"Bloody brilliant," Janice exclaimed. She was gazing at Cal with new respect.

"Of course," Tilly said playfully, "I taught him all he knows."

An ice-cream van had trundled into the park. As it came to a jangly halt fifty yards away, Cal said, "I'm going to get an ice cream."

"One for me?" Janice batted her eyelashes as he rose to his feet.

"Sorry, I've only got a pound."

The occupants of the playground had raced up to the van ahead of Cal. By the time he'd queued up and returned with two Magnums, Janice and her gang had left.

"I thought you only had a pound," said Tilly as he handed her one of the Magnums.

"I lied."

"You've won them over."

"I think you did that."

Tilly sat up and ripped off the wrapper. Cracking the outer layer of chocolate with her teeth, she took a heavenly bite.

"I think Janice fancies you. She told me you were cool."

"I have my moments." His eyes sparkling, Cal said, "Do you think I'm cool?"

Tilly felt a hot sensation flower inside her rib cage. Was this flirting?

Happily the chestnut chose that moment to roll out from under her untucked shirt. Scooping it up, she threw it at Cal and watched it bounce off the top of his tousled head.

"You bought me a Magnum. Can't get much cooler than that."

Chapter 34

WITH WORK FINISHED FOR the day and the patio completed, Laurie was keen to see the rest of the house. This time Nadia made sure she didn't lose her footing on the stairs.

"How long before it's finished?" He inspected the en suite bathroom on the first floor, ran his hands over the marble tiling, then came back into the master bedroom.

"Another three weeks." Nadia was over by the window, gazing down at the garden. From this angle the shapes of the dug-out flowerbeds were more apparent; it helped to have a fresh perspective.

"How much is he asking?"

"Not sure. When the valuer was round last week, he said it should fetch four fifty." She would plant hollyhocks against that sunny, south-facing wall. Everyone liked hollyhocks.

"We could buy this place," said Laurie. He moved up behind her, his breath warm on the back of her neck.

We? Nadia visualized her last bank statement. "I can't afford it."

"That wasn't what I meant. I've got the money. Oh, come on"—Laurie broke into a grin—"don't take it so seriously. Buying a house should be fun."

The turf was arriving tomorrow. Concentrating hard on the prospect of laying eighty square meters of lawn, Nadia said, "I need a bath. My back's too achy to even think about fun."

Laurie's tone was playful. "Want me to put some more Deep Heat on it?"

Yes.

Oh God.

Turning away, Nadia said, "No."

———

"Darling, that's fantastic news." Miriam gave Tilly a hug. "But next Tuesday, what a *shame*. We'll be away."

Tilly's face fell. She was beginning to feel like a five-year-old gleefully handing out invitations, only to discover that nobody could come to her party. On the way home in the car, James had regretfully broken the news to her that on Tuesday and Wednesday next week he would be stuck at some work conference in Sheffield. And now Miriam and Edward wouldn't be able to come along to the show either, because on Tuesday evening they were flying off to Venice for a week's vacation.

"I've got six tickets," Tilly fretted. Suzy Harrison's family, no longer interested in coming to see the show now that their daughter wasn't in it, had donated them to Tilly.

Nadia, fresh from her bath and bundled up in her dressing gown, helped herself to a handful of cold sausages from the fridge and said, "Well, I'll definitely come. I love *Grease*."

"That's why you've got such a big bum." Clicking her tongue at Harpo, Clare said cheerfully, "What's Nadia got, Harpo? What's Nadia got?"

"Gotta pick a pocket or two," cackled Harpo.

"That bird's losing it." Clare shook her head. "He's got Alzheimer's."

"And Laurie will want to come," Nadia persisted.

"Oh Lord, Laurie's driving us up to Heathrow on Tuesday." Miriam shook her head in apology. "Well, look, that's not a problem, he doesn't have to."

"It's OK." Tilly swallowed a lump in her throat. At this rate she was going to be about as popular as the bride who arranges her wedding for the day of the World Cup final.

"Clare's coming," said Nadia, widening her eyes meaningfully at Clare. "Aren't you?"

"Wouldn't miss it for the world. I'll just chuck away my ticket to see Robbie Williams in concert, shall I?"

Clare didn't have a ticket to see Robbie Williams in concert. Not having spotted Tilly's trembling chin, she was making one of her ill-timed jokes.

"How about Annie?" Nadia was getting desperate now.

"I already asked her." Tilly's voice wavered. "But she can't close the shop before six, and that's when the show starts. Last year Mrs. Durham went mental because people kept coming in late and disrupting the performance, so this year anyone who doesn't get there in time has to wait outside the hall until the second half." As she pictured her personal allocation of six seats in the front row, with only Nadia and Clare there to support her, Tilly's eyes brimmed with tears. Her voice rising slightly, she said, "Suzy Harrison's dad works in New York and he was flying back specially for the show. But that's fine, don't worry about it, I'll be—"

"Tilly." Miriam couldn't bear it. "Sweetheart, it's OK, we'll come to the show."

"You can't." Tilly wiped her wet cheeks. "You're going to Venice."

"We'll cancel it."

"You can't c-cancel a v-vacation."

"If it means this much to you, I will." Miriam's dark kohl-lined gaze didn't falter. She paused. "OK?"

Nadia slipped unnoticed from the room. Upstairs, she looked up her mother's number and punched it out.

"Tuesday, Tuesday," mused Leonie, when Nadia had finished explaining. "Hmm, I don't see why not. Sounds like fun!"

Hooray. Nadia heaved a sigh of relief. She couldn't remember ever feeling grateful toward her mother before.

"Fantastic. Could you ring Tilly in five minutes? Just ask her how her day's been, then take it from there?"

Cheerfully, Leonie said, "OK, darling. Bye!"

The transformation in Tilly was instantaneous. Coming off the phone, she erupted into the kitchen and threw her arms round Miriam, clinging to her like a baby koala.

"It's OK, Gran, you and Edward can go to Venice. Sorry if I was a pain before."

"You're never a pain." Miriam's heart contracted with love. That was half the problem where Tilly was concerned; unlike most pubescent teenagers, she didn't have tantrums or shouting matches or endless raging sulks.

Her blue eyes bright, Tilly tilted back her head and said, "Mum's coming to see me in the show! As soon as I told her I'd got the part, she asked if she could. They're going to drive up on Tuesday afternoon, Brian, Tamsin—all three of them! Isn't that brilliant?" Tilly looked as if she might burst with pride. Miriam fondly stroked her uncombed blonde hair and pulled out a shred of dried grass.

"Darling, you'll be a sensation. I'm so glad your mum's going to be there."

"I just hope I don't forget my lines and mess everything up." Tilly couldn't stop beaming now. The six seats would no longer be humiliatingly empty. She wouldn't be the only one on stage without her family watching.

"I love you," Miriam told her.

"They'll probably want to stay here for the night." Tilly was busy conjuring up happy family images. "I expect they'll take me out to dinner after the show, then it'll be too late to drive back. It's OK if they stay, isn't it?"

"Here, you mean?"

"Why not? You'll be away. Tamsin can share my room, I'll sleep on the floor."

Leonie and whatsisname could have the spare room, Miriam decided. The thought of the two of them cavorting together in her own far more beautiful bedroom in her absence made her feel sick.

"Of course they can stay," she told Tilly, because what else could she say, under the circumstances? "That's absolutely fine."

Five people, Tilly thought joyfully. Six seats. She would give her last ticket to Cal.

Tamsin would be so impressed.

~~~

The next morning dawned grayish but dry, perfect turf-laying weather. At nine o'clock the lorry arrived, the turf was swiftly unloaded and Nadia prepared to get down to business. No sign of Laurie, she couldn't help noticing. No sign of him last night either. Did that mean he was tiring of his attempt to win her over? Had her refusal to fall into his arms, not to mention his bed, caused him to lose interest?

Nadia, her mouth dry, wondered if he'd gone out last night and found himself a more accommodating girlfriend, one who didn't back off every time he went near her and flatly refused to believe a word he said.

Oh good grief, had he?

Sorreee, sang a spiteful little voice in her head, clearly not sorry at all. Laurie came back, he told you he wanted to be with you. You had your chance, darling, and you blew it.

The disembodied voice probably belonged to the girl who'd succeeded in attracting Laurie's attention last night. Tart.

Lining up the first strip of turf, Nadia knelt and prepared to unroll it.

Bastard.

It was actually really unfair. Like telling someone they'd won Miss World then snatching the prize away because they hadn't raced out onto the stage to be crowned quickly enough.

If she'd *known* there was a time limit—

"Are you stuck?"

The truck driver who'd delivered the turf hadn't shut the garden gate behind him, which was why she hadn't heard Laurie arrive. Turning, Nadia felt a rush of—what? Relief? Love? *Don't get carried away.*

He was here, that was all that mattered for now.

Chapter 35

"So you can move." Laurie broke into a grin. "When I saw you there freeze-framed, I thought maybe you'd slipped a disc."

"I was just thinking about something." Leaning back on her heels, Nadia slowly rotated first one shoulder then the other.

"Where's that packet of Tylenol?"

"Actually, my back's loads better today, it hardly aches at all."

"Not for you. For me." Touching his head, Laurie winced. "Hangover."

"Oh." Stumbling to her feet, Nadia fetched her haversack, slung over the low wall, and dug out the Tylenol and a bottle of water.

Laurie swallowed the tablets, rinsed them down with the water, and wiped his mouth with the back of his hand.

"Fancy a wedding on Saturday?"

Nadia felt as if she'd been plunged into a pool of ice-cold water. Her heart was clattering against her ribs.

"Meaning what?"

Not what she thought he meant, surely.

"I rang Nick Buckland last night. You remember Nick?"

Nadia nodded. Laurie and Nick had trained together to become stockbrokers and had remained good friends. With his average looks and ebullient character, Nick had always maintained that if he was ever going to land himself a gorgeous woman, he'd need to make a serious pile of cash.

"Is he still working at the same place?"

"Yep, and loving every minute. Doing brilliantly, by all accounts. And—can you believe it?—he's getting married on Saturday."

"Good for him." Nadia's cheeks reddened fractionally. "I always liked Nick."

"Oh dear." Laurie surveyed her with wicked amusement. "Did you think I was asking you to marry me on Saturday?"

Energetically unrolling the first strip of turf and patting it into line, Nadia said, "I could always wallop you with my level and make your headache worse."

"OK." Grinning, he held up his hands. "Anyway, last night was his bachelor party. Timing or what? When I rang him he was just setting off for the Alpha Bar, so he insisted I joined them. Did you wonder why you didn't see me last night, by the way?"

"No," Nadia lied. "Get on with it."

"Well, we met up and had a few drinks. Then we had a few more drinks. And after that, quite a lot more drinks."

"Who's Nick marrying?"

"A girl called Sophie. I met her when she and her friends turned up around eleven. She's great," said Laurie. "Tall, thin, pretty, and blonde, of course. Nick always had a thing about blondes."

When Nadia had known him, Nick's chief ambition had been to land himself a girl with hair. Success, clearly, had bred choosiness.

"It was a fantastic night," Laurie went on happily. "Well, apart from the hangover afterwards. They make a great couple. And they invited us along to the wedding. Nick sends his love, by the way. He can't wait to see you again."

It would be nice to see Nick too. Nadia wondered if Laurie had been chatted up by any of the girls at the Alpha Bar last night. It was a glitzy, upmarket place whose female clientele weren't renowned for being shy.

"You'll have to wear a suit."

"I'll grit my teeth and think of England. I do own a suit, you know."

"You'll need to press it."

"Oh well, I'll buy another one." Laurie shrugged. "Don't worry, I won't embarrass you. I can look smart when I have to."

Nadia knew Laurie would look jaw-droppingly stunning in a suit. He sent jaws dropping wherever he went, even when he was wearing his customary scruffy T-shirts and jeans.

"Was it busy at the Alpha Bar?"

"Heaving."

"So you had a good time?"

Damn, he'd already told her he had. And now Laurie was giving her one of his looks. That was the trouble with old boyfriends; he knew her too well.

"You mean did I get flirted with and chatted up while I was there?"

"Just interested."

"Was I flirted with and chatted up by girls who were far nicer to me than you are?"

Yes!

Nadia shrugged. "You don't have to tell me."

"Of course I was flirted with." Laurie rolled his eyes. "Of course I was chatted up."

A wasp landed on Nadia's arm. Irritably, she flicked it away.

"But I'm not interested in being hit on by girls in bars," said Laurie. "There's only one reason why I came back here. And you know what that is."

"OK." Out of the corner of her eye, Nadia saw Bart's portly figure moving about behind the French doors leading out onto the terrace. Hardly the moment for a romantic... um, moment. Pushing her hair back from her forehead, she said, "Bart's watching us. I think he's wondering why it's taken me forty minutes to lay three feet of turf."

"But you'll come to Nick's wedding on Saturday?"

"Yes." Nadia smiled; of course she'd go to Nick's wedding. "So what's this suit of yours like, then? Where did you get it?"

"God knows. Top Man, I think." Laurie scratched his head. "Top Man-ee?"

"What?"

"No, that's not it. I remember now." He winked at her. "Our Man-ee."

Armani.

"Careful," said Nadia. "Wouldn't want my sides to split."

Together they began unrolling the lengths of turf. After a minute or two, Laurie said, "Speaking of Our Man…"

"Oh God, not more designer jokes." Nadia let out a groan. "If I laugh any more, my head might fall off."

"Actually, I was talking about our man Jay. Your boss." Laurie tossed his head like Simon Cowell in a huff. "But now you've made fun of my joke, I'm not going to tell you."

It was like being sixteen again. How many times, all those years ago, had he done this, safe in the knowledge that he was teasing the world's nosiest person?

Giving her impression of someone who really couldn't care less—it was a very poor impression—Nadia said, "Hmm? Tell me what?"

"Nothing."

"Tell me."

"No really, you wouldn't be interested."

"He's my boss. It's your duty to tell me."

"Sorry." Laurie nudged a bale of turf with his foot, unrolling it like a red carpet.

Nadia played her trump card. "I've got a worm here."

"Really, it wasn't even that interesting."

"A big old daddy worm, all twisty and squirming."

"OK." Laurie held up his hands in defeat. "It's just that I saw him at the Alpha Bar last night."

Nadia dropped the worm. It wriggled away in relief.

"What was he doing there?" Her voice came out a bit higher than she'd planned.

"The usual." Laurie was busy pressing the edges of the turf together to disguise the join. "Why do single men generally go to places like the Alpha Bar? Apart from me of course," he added with a grin. "I only went along because Nick made me."

Nadia was now unrolling turf at a rate of knots. It was completely irrational to feel betrayed, but somehow she did. Jay had done what he'd said he'd do and it felt like a kick in the gut.

"Who was he with?"

"On his own. Well, to begin with," said Laurie. "The next time I looked he seemed to be getting on pretty well with a couple of girls."

A couple!

"What were they like?"

"Ugly. A right couple of dogs." Laurie kept a straight face.

"Really?"

"Duh, joke. Why would Jay waste time talking to dogs?"

"So what happened?"

"Haven't the foggiest. We left just after midnight, went on to the Alexander Club. Nick ended up dancing on one of the tables with a feather bra tied round his head."

"Some things never change." Nadia mentally resolved not to think about Jay; he was free to do whatever he liked, with however many women he liked.

"Pete got a photo of him."

"Of…?" Who, Jay?

"Nick, with the bra wrapped round his head. He looked like a Spitfire pilot with feather goggles. Pete's planning to slip copies into every Order of Service booklet in the church. You can sleep with him if you want."

Nadia thought she must have misheard. But from the way Laurie was waiting for a reaction, she knew she hadn't.

"Sleep with Pete? I don't even know him!"

"He's Nick's best man. He's good fun, you'd like him." Laurie paused. "But that wasn't who I meant."

Nadia swallowed. This was definitely a weird conversation to be having on a Tuesday morning. Not your run-of-the-mill chat about the weather at all.

The sun chose that moment to come out from behind the clouds, illuminating the greenness of Laurie's eyes and bouncing off his disheveled gold-blond hair.

"Jay Tiernan?" he said helpfully. "The chap you work for? The one you were on the verge of getting involved with when I came back and threw a wrench in the works?"

"Who told you that?" Nadia's fingers were tingling, a sure sign that she was breathing too fast.

"Oh, come on, I'm not stupid. I have eyes in my head." With a brief smile Laurie added, "Plus, Clare may have mentioned it in passing."

Sisters, who'd have them?

"But that's not—"

"She just filled in the details. I'd already guessed most of it. But now you're torn. You can't help wondering what you might be missing if you choose me. So find out," said Laurie. "Sleep with him, then decide."

"This is ridiculous." Nadia shook her head. "You can't be serious."

"If that's what it takes, I'm completely serious. Because if you don't, you'll never know. I think I'll win in the end." Laurie broke into an unrepentant grin. "Sorry, I just do. But I don't want to spend the rest of my life with someone who's always going to be wondering, deep down, if she made the right choice."

Nadia was lost for words. Was Laurie mad? Or so super-confident that he simply didn't believe he could lose?

"And if I did this… this *thing*? What would you do if I decided I'd rather be with him than with you?"

Him. She couldn't even bring herself to say Jay's name.

"That's a risk I just have to take. But at least then we'd know."

"I can't believe you want me to sleep with another man."

"I don't *want* you to. I just know it's the only way, otherwise you'll never be able to decide." Laurie waited. "That is, if he's still interested in you. After last night he may not be. You see, that's the thing about men like him, they don't exactly sit at home and mope. If it doesn't work out with one girl, they move on to the next. Still," he added encouragingly, "you could always ask."

Nadia was just thankful that Jay was attending an auction today. If he turned up now, Laurie was liable to ask him on her behalf.

Bart, flinging open the kitchen window, bellowed, "Kettle's on."

"Shall I get on with this?" Laurie indicated the rolls of turf at his feet. "I could murder a mug of tea."

Never mind tea, thought Nadia as she headed up the stone steps. I could murder a vodka and tonic.

Chapter 36

Cal met up with Tilly at the school gates.

"Janice smiled at me in the corridor today."

"That's nothing." Tilly smirked. "She stopped me in the toilets at break and told me you're cute."

Cal looked horrified. "Cute? That's terrible! How *dare* she call me cute? Yesterday she said I was cool! How can anybody be cool *and* cute?"

"Don't knock it. She fancies you."

"Now you're starting to scare me."

Daringly, Tilly said, "Don't you fancy Janice?"

"No, I do not." Cal spoke with feeling as he slung his schoolbag over his bony shoulder. He paused. "So what are you up to now?"

"Me? Just waiting for Janice. I fancy her even if you don't."

He broke into a grin that definitely managed to be cool and cute. "Want some help learning your lines?"

Thanks to Janice, word about Cal's attributes had evidently spread; girls streaming past them were glancing at him with renewed interest. Flushed with pride, Tilly said, "OK."

Cal shook his head. "Sorry, not enough enthusiasm. Not nearly enough."

"You mean you'd do that for me?" Clutching his arm, Tilly widened her eyes and gave him a look of incredulous delight. "Oh my God, *really*? That is *so* fantastic. Thank you, thank you, I can't believe this is happening to me!"

"Much better." Cal's gaze was locked on hers, his amusement unconcealed. Two Year-10 girls going past nudged each other.

"That's him, the one Janice was going on about," hissed the darker haired of the two.

"Hmm, she's right, you know. Definitely something about him."

"See?" Tilly teased, when they were gone. "There's definitely something about you."

Cal's eyes twinkled. "Has to be better than cute."

The wedding ceremony was proceeding without a hitch. Beautiful blonde Sophie had arrived bang on time, her sleek ivory dress uncreased and her smile dazzling. Nick, paunchier than the last time Nadia had seen him, was looking uncharacteristically smart and had remembered to peel the price stickers off the soles of his new shoes for the kneeling bit. Everyone had sung along, more or less in tune, to the jolly hymns. Nobody had burst in at the crucial moment to object to the ceremony taking place.

Nadia marveled that outside, the rest of Clifton was carrying on as usual. It was one o'clock on a Saturday afternoon and people were shopping, drinking in bars, taking their children to the playground, and filling their cars with petrol. Yet here inside the church, Nick and Sophie were plighting their troth, promising to love and honor each other in sickness and in health until death did them part.

Extraordinary, thought Nadia, when so many marriages these days didn't even last as long as the guarantee on a washing machine. Gullible, that was the only word to describe people who got married and actually expected to live happily ever after. And it cost thousands to hold a wedding like this, talk about money down the drain, why *did* people bother?

"Stop sniffing," Laurie murmured out of the corner of his

mouth. "Oh no, not again," he added, glancing at Nadia and passing her the handkerchief from his top pocket.

Cursing her inability to cry without sniffing—well, she *could* cry without sniffing, but her nose would run in a most unattractive manner—Nadia wiped her eyes and dabbed at her mascara. Why, why did this always have to happen to her?

"You big wuss," Laurie whispered, squeezing her arm.

It was the triumph of hope over bitter experience, she knew that now. Combined with the look of naked adoration on Nick's ruddy face as he'd gazed into Sophie's eyes and slipped the platinum ring on her slender finger. It was the unwavering inner belief that, OK, other people's marriages might not work, but theirs would. When you loved each other this much, nothing could go wrong...

"You may kiss the bride," proclaimed the vicar.

"Whmmph." Nadia muffled the sob by burying her face in Laurie's hankie. She couldn't help it; Nick and Sophie were in love. Nick, normally so bawdy and cynical, looked as if he might be on the verge of tears himself. This was all he wanted in the world. Oh bugger, and now her mascara really was starting to run.

"We could do this." Laurie's mouth was millimeters from her ear.

A shiver zipped down Nadia's spine. "Do what?"

"This. The whole church bit. All you have to do is say yes."

Nadia gazed straight ahead at Nick and Sophie ecstatically kissing each other. She couldn't breathe.

"I want to marry you," Laurie went on.

Talk about shameless, thought Nadia. He was taking advantage of her while she was in a vulnerable state.

"I mean it." Laurie squeezed her hand. "You wouldn't regret it, I promise."

The organ was striking up; Nick and Sophie were no longer kissing, just grinning idiotically at each other like a couple of... well, newlyweds.

That could be us, Nadia thought.

Aloud she said, "Have you ever thought about becoming a door-to-door salesman?"

When the service was over, the bride and groom led the exit from the church. The people in the front pews peeled off row by row, following them outside into the blazing sunshine. Nadia and Laurie, five pews back, left their seats when the time came and made their way down the aisle.

Nadia admired the posies of white rosebuds and stephanotis attached to the ends of each of the pews. Spotting a woman in an ornate orange hat the size of a satellite dish, she wondered how much it had cost—anything more than a fiver, basically, and the woman had been had. Oh, but there in the row behind her was someone with far better taste, a tall redhead wearing a knee-length old-gold silk jacket over a peachy-yellow dress of the same material. The colors were stunning together, complementing the girl's auburn hair perfectly, and her amber necklace exactly matched her shoes. Now that was the way to make a good impression on—

Oh, *good grief.* As she'd been thinking nice things about the redhead's way with accessories, Nadia's attention had wandered idly to her companion. Now she faltered, utterly poleaxed to discover that it was Jay.

How? How could he be here? *How?*

"What?" said Laurie.

"Nothing."

The redhead was chattering away in a vivacious fashion. Next to her, Jay nodded and smiled as if agreeing with whatever she'd just said. Then his gaze shifted and came to rest on Nadia. He nodded again briefly, this time in acknowledgement, then carried on listening to the redhead at his side.

He'd spent the last hour sitting two pews behind her. No wonder he wasn't as shocked to see her as she was to see him. Nadia really hoped he hadn't heard her sobbing embarrassingly into her hankie.

Laurie, following her line of vision, said, "Hey, look who's here!" Grinning, he waved at Jay. "How did this happen? You didn't invite him along, did you?"

"Of course I didn't invite him." Feeling hot all over, Nadia realized too late that Laurie had been teasing.

"Losing your sense of humor." He gave her a playful nudge. "It's OK, I've figured it out. That's one of the girls he was with at the Alpha Bar the other night."

Nadia's stomach did a clumsy double back-flip. "And?"

"Well, she must be one of Sophie's friends. She was out for her bachelorette party."

The reception was being held at the Holborn Hotel, famed for its views over the suspension bridge. It was a really nice hotel, rather posh, quite grown-up.

Nadia, in contrast, wasn't feeling nice at all. What's more, she was having a hard time behaving like a grown-up. Everyone else was mingling in the hotel garden, drinking champagne and socializing in time-honored weddingy fashion. On the surface, this was what Nadia was doing too. But inwardly she longed to stick out her foot next time Redheaded Girl wandered past, and trip her up.

It wasn't logical, but it was happening anyway. She couldn't help it; Redheaded Girl was annoying her intensely. The way she threw back her head and laughed whenever Jay said something even remotely amusing. The way she kept picking invisible bits of fluff off the lapels of his jacket. And as for the way she ran her tongue over her lips before speaking, well, that was the most irritating mannerism of all. Talk about obvious. Any woman doing that porn-star-in-training thing with her tongue absolutely deserved to be tripped up.

"Nadia! Brilliant to see you again. You're looking fantastic!" Nadia found herself enveloped in a bear hug that quashed all the air out of her lungs. Nick had never known his own strength.

But he was right, Nadia thought with a trace of smugness; for once, she *was* looking fantastic. The dark blue spaghetti-strapped top Clare had bought last week went brilliantly with her own indigo-and-silver long floaty skirt from Monsoon. For once her hair had done as it was told. Miraculously, even her high-heeled sandals were comfortable enough for her not to be longing to kick them off.

She just hoped Nick wasn't the only person here who'd noticed how completely gorgeous she was looking today.

"You too," Nadia told him. "And now you're married! I can't believe it." Over Nick's sturdy shoulder she watched Jay refilling Redheaded Girl's glass. He was wearing a dark gray suit, a purply-blue shirt, and a tie that was—oops, quick, look away.

"You'll be next." Beaming all over his face, Nick said, "When Laurie told me the two of you were back together—"

"We aren't back together," Nadia interjected. Bloody hell, what had Laurie been telling him?

"I didn't say that." Next to her, Laurie shook his head. "I didn't. I just said we were seeing each other again. In a purely platonic way. Until I can persuade Nadia to change her mind."

"He did. Absolutely right." Nick nodded vigorously. "That's what he told me. But you will change your mind, won't you?" He clutched Nadia's hands. "Give him another chance? I know he's an ugly bugger, but he's not so bad, deep down. Go on, give him the benefit of the doubt. If you two tie the knot we'll be able to have married-couples dinner parties like proper grown-ups. With matching cutlery, the works."

"That's a great reason to get married." Nadia nodded thoughtfully. "Thanks, I'll bear it in mind."

Leaning in for another clumsy kiss, Nick whispered, "He really does love you, you know."

This was definitely a case of the confetti talking. Under normal circumstances, Nick would be more likely to dance in *Swan Lake* on stage at Covent Garden than discuss—yeeugh—*love*. He clearly wasn't himself today. Spotting Sophie's mother heading their way, Nadia said, "Your mother-in-law's coming over."

"Jean!" Letting go of Nadia, Nick said cheerfully, "You won't believe this, but I actually like my mother-in-law. Weird or what?"

Chapter 37

"Do I know you?"

At the sound of an unfamiliar voice, Nadia turned and came face to face with Redheaded Girl.

Oh shit.

"Sorry? No, I don't think so." She'd just said sorry. How British.

"Do you know me?"

"No." I just really want to trip you up.

"Oh. That's odd." The girl's tone was challenging rather than friendly. "It's just that you keep looking over at me. All the time. If you don't even know me, I was wondering why you'd do that."

"I don't keep looking over at you." This was actually true. She was looking over at Jay. The problem was, every time he turned his head in her direction, she was forced to hastily glance away and pretend to be gazing transfixed at something or someone else instead. It wasn't her fault if the someone generally turned out to be this girl with her flame-red hair and ridiculously licky lips.

God, how could Jay like her? Surely he could see through someone like that?

"Well, if I've been looking at you, it wasn't deliberate. I didn't realize I was doing it." Nadia was tempted to add, "Would you like me to wear a blindfold for the rest of the day?" but held herself back. How embarrassing if the girl said yes.

Where was Laurie anyway? Now that she could actually do with having him around, he'd disappeared to talk to his old workmates.

"OK." Redheaded Girl waited and tilted her head to one side. "I hear you work for Jay."

"That's right. Who told you that?"

"Jay."

"So you do know who I am." Nadia didn't normally dislike people practically on sight, but for Redheaded Girl she'd make an exception.

"You're a gardener. Jay employs you to sort out the gardens of the houses he's renovating." Another pause. "Do you have a thing for your boss?"

Oh, for crying out loud, where *was* Laurie?

"No." Perspiring, Nadia shook her head.

"It's just that I thought it might explain why you keep looking over. Because you want Jay and you're jealous that I have him and you don't."

Nadia was outraged. How dare this horrible girl be right?

"That's not true." With a huge effort she kept her voice calm. Going squeaky with indignation would only make her sound riddled with guilt.

"Well, I'm very glad to hear it." The girl's smile didn't reach her cold, slanting eyes. "Because I've spent a long time waiting for a man like Jay to come along. He's just what I'm after, and I plan to hang on to him."

Unable to resist it, Nadia smiled. "Really? Does he know about this?"

"I'm thirty-three," the girl replied evenly. "It's no laughing matter. Once you reach thirty-three, there aren't that many decent men around. It's all right for you," she added, "you've already got one of your own."

⁓

Nadia bumped into Jay in the corridor on her way back from the loo.

"Why didn't you tell me you were coming to Nick and Sophie's wedding?" Three glasses of Moët had loosened her tongue. "If you saw Laurie with the bachelor party at the Alpha Bar, you must have known we'd be here."

Jay looked mildly surprised. "I guessed he'd been invited. I didn't know you'd be coming too. Does it matter?"

They'd hardly seen each other this week. Jay's visits to the house had been brief and the only time he'd stayed longer than five minutes had been when she'd been at the garden center.

"Of course it doesn't matter." Nadia wondered if he really liked Redheaded Girl. "It just would've been polite to mention it. How did you get invited anyway?"

As if she hadn't already worked it out for herself.

"I bumped into the girls at the Alpha Bar. Andrea used to share a flat with Sophie. She didn't have a partner for the wedding, so she asked me if I'd like to come with her."

"She's thirty-three," said Nadia, hoping for a glimmer of shock.

Jay looked amused. "I know. She told me."

Bugger.

"She's been waiting ages for someone like you to come along." Nadia wondered if they'd already slept together.

"Thanks. The garden's looking good, by the way."

Bastard. Nadia tried to imagine picking a bit of invisible fluff off his jacket. Maybe running her tongue over her lips in a provocative manner. Except, knowing her, she'd only end up with lipstick on her teeth.

Irritated, she said off-puttingly, "Andrea likes you. A lot."

"Really?" Now he was being downright annoying.

"I'd have thought it was pretty obvious."

"Well, good." Jay's brown eyes shone with amusement. "I didn't go along to the Alpha Bar to meet women who'd hate me. What would be the point of that?"

Outside, a gong sounded.

"Saved by the gong," said Jay.

Nadia bristled. "Saved from what?"

"I'm sorry, I thought this was an interrogation."

She gave up. The trouble with sparring with Jay was that you never actually won. He had an infuriating habit of always having an answer for everything.

The gong rang out again.

"People are going in to eat. I'd better get back to Laurie."

"And I'll go and find Andrea," Jay said easily.

Andrea and her shrieking, thirty-three-year-old ovaries, Nadia thought with derision. She wouldn't mind betting that Andrea was desperate for babies.

God, if they were sharing a table with Andrea and Jay, it would be pepper shakers at twenty paces.

"See you later," said Jay.

Great.

They weren't sharing a table. Thankfully, the next couple of hours whizzed by. Meeting up with Laurie's old stockbroking pals and their other halves was great fun. Their table, one of the rowdi-est in the room, indulged in some good-natured heckling during the best man's speech. The food was excellent. Bottles were emptied with a flourish and speedily replaced. Nadia had a stitch in her side from laughing at Nick's boss's impression of Nick making his own speech, complete with trembling chin and askew tie.

Actually, when you were laughing this hard, a stitch was the least of your worries. Keen not to disgrace herself—because leaving a wet patch on your plush velvet chair seat was never sophisticated—Nadia stood up and said, "Back in a minute."

"Again?" Tania, who was married to Nick's boss, took a great slurp of wine. "Blimey, not pregnant are you?"

No chance of that, thought Nadia as, snorting with laughter, Tania gave Laurie a nudge and almost toppled sideways into his lap.

"Let's hope not," Laurie said with a wry grin that only Nadia understood.

She was in much-needed mid-wee when the door to the ladies' loo opened and closed. Expensive sounding high heels clattered across the red and black marble-tiled floor. Two lots of heels. One set tap-tapped into the cubicle two down from her own, while the other set headed for the sink. Nadia heard the sound of a makeup bag being unzipped, followed by the rattle of cosmetics.

"So who's Hannah seeing now?" This question came from the girl in the cubicle.

"She went out with Toby the other night. He took her to dinner at that new place on Chandos Road."

Dinggg, Nadia's ears pricked up. Was that Andrea's voice?

"The Mexican? I heard it's crap. No sign of her getting back with Piers then?"

Piers? Piers who?

"Ha, she wishes! Piers is up to his old tricks again." The voice that possibly belonged to Andrea was scornful and slightly distorted; she sounded as though she was stretching her mouth in order to put on a fresh coat of lipstick.

"When did he ever stop? Hannah was mad to ever get involved with him in the first place." The girl in the cubicle peed noisily, pulled the flush and click-clacked over to the sink to wash her hands.

"He's been seeing this girl, some arty type apparently. Total pushover, according to Piers." *Was* it Andrea? Pssh, pssh, went a perfume atomiser. "But when I saw him at Boom on Sunday he was all over Felicity Temple-Stewart."

Nadia's brain was racing. Sunday, Sunday… Clare hadn't seen Piers on Sunday. He'd told her he was visiting his sister in Oxford and Clare had spent the day at work on her latest painting. Slowly, silently, Nadia tugged up her knickers then lowered herself to the floor of the cubicle. Good job it was a spotlessly clean floor.

"Anyway, how are things going with you two?" This from the girl washing her hands. "Very nicely, by the look of things."

Nadia held her breath. Now she really had to know. Crouching on her hands and knees, she ducked her head down and to one side.

"Very nicely indeed." The voice that possibly belonged to Andrea was smug. "I'm telling you, I really think my lottery ticket's come up. It just goes to show, there's a whole load of losers out there, but if you keep on going, you can always find a good one in the—*aaarrgh!*"

Hell. Nadia banged her forehead on the cubicle door as she tried to jerk away. Peering through the four-inch gap between the bottom of the door and the marble floor, she had found herself gazing at Andrea's bony, pale-stockinged legs.

Andrea, having glanced in the mirror and spotted a pair of dark eyes peering out from under the closed cubicle door behind her, let out another high-pitched shriek and spun round, sending her make-up bag flying into the sink.

"What the fuck's going on? I don't believe this! Get up," Andrea shouted, "get up and get out here! What the bloody hell d'you think you're playing at?"

Nadia briefly considered doing what Ewan McGregor had done in *Trainspotting*, diving head first into the loo.

Well, maybe not. Awkwardly, she stumbled to her feet.

"You!" jeered Andrea, when Nadia reluctantly emerged from the cubicle.

Her friend said, "Andy? Who is this?"

"She works for Jay. She's a… gardener." Andrea made it sound like maggot-eater. "She won't admit it, but she's jealous of me because I'm with Jay and she isn't. And now she's in here, crawling around on a toilet floor, eavesdropping on us." Her mouth twisted into a triumphant smile. "Classy. I can't wait to tell Jay about this."

Sophie seemed so nice, Nadia couldn't imagine what she'd been thinking of, sharing a flat with someone as poisonous as Andrea.

Then again, maybe that was why Sophie had been so keen to get married.

The deeply annoying thing was, if Andrea had been a nice person, she would have been able to tell her the real reason for the eavesdropping. She could have found out all about Piers. But she'd rather cut out her tongue than ask Andrea now.

Raising her chin, Nadia headed for the cloakroom door. "Tell Jay what you like. Doesn't bother me. Except I wouldn't get your hopes up too high if I were you. He's pretty crap in bed."

Pleased with herself, Nadia swung the door open and prepared to make a dignified exit.

Andrea's friend began, "Oh, your skirt's tucked into your knick—"

"You idiot," Andrea snapped furiously as Nadia—phew, relief—remedied the situation. "Why'd you have to go and tell her that?"

Well, what could she do now, other than launch into the rest of the reception with a vengeance and show Andrea, by actions rather than words, that she did indeed have a man of her own?

By this time the DJ was already playing Duran Duran's greatest hits. Determinedly not looking—even for a millisecond—in the direction of Jay and Andrea's table, Nadia danced with Laurie, then with Laurie's ex-boss, then with Nick's sweatily eager best man, then with Laurie again.

The DJ, slowing down to give the older contingent a breather, began to play something hideous by Celine Dion. When Laurie turned automatically toward their table, Nadia hauled him back.

Understandably he looked shocked. "You don't want to dance to this."

"I do." Nadia swung herself against him, and Laurie grinned.

"Blimey, you must be drunk."

Nadia wound her arms round his neck. Laurie was a good dancer, loose-limbed and in possession of that ability so sadly lacking in men to actually move in time with the music. What was it called? Oh yes, natural rhythm.

And he was looking great in his suit, now that it had been unearthed from the bottom of a backpack and paid a much-needed visit to the dry-cleaners. In fact Laurie was looking great, period. He was by far the most beautiful man in the room. He had the best hair, Nadia decided, running her fingers through it as they danced together. The best eyelashes. And the very, *very* best cheekbones...

Hmm, maybe she was the tiniest bit tipsy.

Leaning her head on Laurie's shoulder, Nadia risked a speedy glance in Jay's direction. OK, bit juvenile, but she so wanted to know if he was watching her. In an envious fashion, preferably.

Except he wasn't. He was bloody writing something on a napkin while Andrea sat beside him with her body language on show. She was smirking away like a *Countdown* winner.

If Nadia's legs had been twenty-five feet long, she could have kicked her. She really hoped Jay wasn't giving Andrea his mobile number.

Celine Dion gave way to Michael Bolton. It was that kind of wedding DJ. I'm so lucky, Nadia thought, to be dancing with Laurie. So, so lucky. Ooh, Jay's standing up, hooray!

Damn, so was Andrea. Boo hiss.

"You know," Laurie's tone was conversational, "a lesser man than me might think his luck was in."

Mortified, Nadia realized that she'd been indulging in some shameless hip-grinding.

"It's not you, it's Michael Bolton. He has that effect on me."

"I know what you mean." Laurie nodded sympathetically. "I'm just the same with Eminem."

Nadia ordered her hips to behave themselves. After Michael

Bolton they danced along, rather more decorously, to something by Westlife. When they eventually returned to their table, Laurie disappeared to the bar in search of more drinks.

There was no sign anywhere of Jay and Andrea.

Nadia was hot, her face undoubtedly pink and shiny. In search of a tissue, she reached for her bag and encountered a napkin folded and laid over the zip.

Unfolding it, she saw that the napkin had been written on. There, in Jay's unmistakable slanting scrawl, were the words: "No I'm not."

Chapter 38

JOSH, ONE OF THE workers at the garden center, harbored dreams of becoming a stand-up comedian. When he had begun going along to the open-mike sessions at the Comedy Club off Whiteladies Road, he had insisted on dragging along as many friends as possible to masquerade as adoring fans, cheer him on during his ten-minute sets, and drown out any detractors who might try to boo him off the stage. Because, frankly, Josh was rubbish at stand-up.

Nadia still went along; she enjoyed the club's rowdy, irreverent Sunday night atmosphere and it gave her the chance to keep up with all the goings-on at her old workplace. Janey, arriving back at their table with a round of lagers—this was the Comedy Club, after all—plonked herself down and assumed her role of gossip-in-chief.

"Right, here goes. Mandy's been seeing one of the barmen from the Old Duke—his name's Ryan and he's a total jazz freak, which jolly well serves her right for going to a jazz club in the first place. And he's only got a moped, so she has to drive him around in her car whenever they go anywhere. He found all her S Club 7 CDs in the glove compartment the other night and she had to pretend they were her brother's. It'll never last," Janey confidently predicted. "Stevie Grainger can't stand his new job, by the way. When he decided he'd earn more working as a security guard, it didn't occur to the silly sod that night shifts would play havoc with his social life. Ooh, and that cross-eyed actor who used to be in *EastEnders* came in last week to buy a gazebo. He's living in Easter Compton now. Got ever so cross when another customer asked for his autograph then looked at it and said, 'Oh, I thought you were that carpenter bloke from *Changing Rooms*.'"

"What's Bernie doing here on his own?" Nadia was peering through the smoky gloom to the bar. "Why isn't Paula with him?"

"Ah." Janey was triumphant. "That's my next item of news. They broke up three weeks ago!"

"Never. Blimey." Suitably astounded, Nadia gazed at Bernie Blatt, son of the owners of the garden center. Bernie, who worked on the financial side, had been engaged to Paula, a nurse, for the last two years. "I thought they were together forever. What happened?"

"Paula left him. Turned out she's been having a thing with an orthopedic surgeon at the hospital where she works. Bernie couldn't believe it, he was in total shock. Still, you know what men are like—he's getting over it now. Bitter and twisted, of course, but recovering. Oh, there's Suzette! Suze, over here," Janey bawled, waving madly. "Suzette just started with us last week, she's great. Even if everyone does fancy her," she added as Suzette joined them. "God knows why, what with her being so ugly."

Suzette grinned and squeezed in beside them. She was tiny and enchantingly pretty, with rippling white-blonde hair and dancing green eyes.

"Bernie thinks he's died and gone to heaven, of course." Janey rolled her eyes in despair. "Why does it never occur to completely average, overweight men with very little hair that someone like Suze might not find them irresistible?"

"Hi," said Suzette cheerfully. "You must be Nadia. I've heard all about you."

Nadia liked her at once.

"Hey there, girls." It was Bernie, clapping a hefty hand on each of their shoulders in turn. "Suze, love the outfit." He cast an admiring glance at Suzette's green halter-neck and low-slung jeans. "And Nadia, how the devil are you? Did Janey tell you what happ—?"

"Sshh," said Janey as the announcer appeared on the tiny spotlit stage. "Yes, I told her, now sit down and keep quiet, it's time for Josh to do his thing."

Squashing himself in next to Nadia, Bernie said cheerfully, "Righty-ho. Give me a nudge if I fall asleep."

"Was I OK?" Josh was desperate, as ever, for reassurance.

Nadia gave him a hug. "You were great. We weren't the only ones clapping, were we? And hardly anyone booed."

"Is it all over?" Bernie pretended to wake up. "Am I allowed to talk again now?"

"I don't know why the bouncers let you in," said Josh. "I told them not to."

"Ah, but I'm a heartbroken man. My fiancée chucked me. I need cheering up, and where better to come than a comedy club? Besides," Bernie said expansively, "my favorite girls are here, on hand to do just that. C'mon, Nadia, cheer me up, tell me you're still single."

"She's the opposite of single," Janey countered importantly. "Nadia's got two men after her. There's her new boss, who sounds pretty damn gorgeous. And Laurie's back from LA, chasing her all over again."

"*Laurie?*" Spluttering into his pint, Bernie said, "Nadia, tell me you're joking! You wouldn't seriously consider getting together again with that bastard?"

"I haven't made up my mind yet." Trapped within spraying distance, Nadia wiped drops of lager from her jeans. "Anyway"—she felt compelled to defend Laurie—"he isn't a bastard."

"Excuse me! Do you remember how gutted you were when he dumped you?" Bernie clearly thought she was mad. "Because I bloody do! How could you ever trust him again?"

"But you have to admit he's lovely," said Janey, who had met Laurie plenty of times. "Funny and charming and—"

"Liable to run off with any pretty girl who catches his eye." Bernie snorted with disgust.

"But he didn't do that," said Nadia, beginning to wish they weren't having this conversation.

"Are you telling me he wouldn't, given the chance? If you think that, you're living in cloud-cuckoo land."

"Just because Paula did it to you," Nadia told Bernie, "doesn't mean everyone's the same."

"Bet *he* is, though," said Bernie with satisfaction. "He's just the type."

Crossly, Janey said, "You're only saying that because he's good-looking."

"Is this the one who's a model?" Suzette looked at her. "You showed me a photo of him in that magazine."

"Can we change the subject here?" said Josh plaintively. "Couldn't we talk about… ooh, I don't know. Me?"

"Laurie isn't like that," Nadia couldn't resist telling Bernie, by way of wrapping the matter up.

"Oh no?" Bernie shrugged, then said idly, "Prove it."

—◦◦◦—

Nadia wasn't doing this to prove anything to Bernie Blatt. Bernie wasn't even going to know about it. She was doing this to prove it to herself.

Because maybe, deep down, she did actually need to have it confirmed.

"Peace of mind," said Janey, next to her in the passenger seat. She nodded with satisfaction. "You're right, it makes sense. What's the time, anyway?"

"Just gone seven." Nadia jumped as her mobile began to ring, almost exactly on cue. Oh God, what if this was a terrible thing to be doing? What if it all went horribly wrong? "Hello?"

"Hi, it's me," said Suzette. "It's OK, he's here. He ordered a bottle of red and he's sitting at the bar. I just came outside to ring you. I can see him through the glass."

"Good." Picturing Laurie waiting for her in San Carlo, Nadia felt her heart quicken. "Better go back in now. Stay by the bar."

Suzette giggled. "I feel like an FBI agent. OK, boss, over and out."

The line went dead. Nadia waited less than a minute, then rang Laurie's number. He answered on the second ring.

"Laurie? Listen, I can't make the restaurant," said Nadia. "We're going to have to cancel dinner. Janey just rang, her boyfriend's chucked her and she's really upset." Next to her, Janey made boo-hoo faces and pretended to slash her wrists. "I promised I'd go over there, is that OK? Sorry to mess you around, but you know what Janey's like when she gets into a state. You aren't at San Carlo yet, are you?"

She heard Laurie sigh.

"It's seven o'clock. You said be here by seven. Of course I'm at the restaurant. I've bought a bottle of wine."

"Oh. Well, sorry. But I can't let Janey down. Maybe we could have dinner tomorrow instead?"

"Perfect," said Janey, when Nadia had ended the call. "I'm feeling less suicidal already."

"I feel sick," said Nadia.

"Come on, this is Laurie, he won't do it."

Hoping Janey was right, Nadia said, "By the way, he sends his love."

"What did I tell you?" Janey gave her a reassuring grin. "He's a gem."

"Not you as well," said Suzette, finishing her glass of wine.

"Sorry?"

"I couldn't help overhearing. You sounded as if you were being stood up." She smiled ruefully across at Laurie. "Me too. My friend just rang to tell me she has to work late."

Laurie stuffed his phone back inside his jacket pocket. The girl was startlingly pretty, with laughing green eyes and a full, curvy mouth. She was wearing a faded denim jacket over a simple white cotton shift dress that showed off her slim hips, and flat gold sandals on her feet.

"Mine has to go and comfort a friend who just got ditched," he said wryly. "Looks like it's our unlucky night."

"Typical." The girl rolled her eyes. "Here I am, starving hungry, in a restaurant that smells of fantastic food… oh well." She checked her watch, picked up her empty glass, then put it down again. "Looks like it's going to be microwaved lasagna at home instead."

Laurie watched her pay for her drink and prepare to leave the restaurant.

"Look, I've got this whole bottle here. You could help me out with it if you don't have to rush off." He picked up the bottle of St. Emilion and gave her an encouraging smile. "In fact, I'm pretty hungry too. Seeing as we're here, there's nothing to stop us having something to eat. Only if you'd like to, of course."

The girl looked surprised, then pleased. "Are you sure?"

"Why not?" Laurie grinned at her, then beckoned to the barman to bring a fresh glass.

"OK then. Thanks. But we split the bill," the girl insisted.

"Fine. I'm Laurie, by the way."

She smiled and shook his hand. "Suze."

───※───

Oh my God, thought Suzette, that wasn't supposed to happen, that really wasn't supposed to happen…

She still wasn't even sure quite how it *had* happened.

"Hey," said Laurie, his hand reaching out to brush her hair back from her face. "Don't tell me you've gone to sleep."

Awash with shame, Suzette kept her eyes closed. They had had dinner together at San Carlo. Laurie had been as charming and wonderful as Janey and Nadia had told her to expect. The electricity had crackled between them throughout the meal; this was one gorgeous, irresistible man. Nevertheless, she hadn't thought for one moment that she would actually end up in bed with him. She had simply gone along with the game, enjoying herself, wondering if he was really thinking what she thought he was thinking...

Laurie had insisted on paying for dinner. Just as he had insisted on driving her home to her tiny flat in Redland. When he had said, "You could invite me in for coffee if you like," Suzette had almost managed to convince herself that he actually meant coffee. And by the time he'd gently closed the front door behind them and taken her into his arms, it had been all she could do to manage to stay upright.

Her cheeks flamed as she remembered how he had kissed her, the way he had slowly unzipped her dress and removed the rest of her clothes. Suzette wondered if she'd ever felt more dreadful in her life. It was never meant to go this far. When she'd met Nadia, she had liked her at once. When Janey had jokingly suggested that if anyone was capable of testing Laurie's morals it was Suzette, and then Nadia had said, "Well, why don't we do it then?" she had found herself agreeing to go along with the plan. If Laurie overstepped the mark, she would rebuff him, simple as that.

It hadn't occurred to her for a moment that she might be swept away on a tidal wave of lust and... oh God, she couldn't believe she'd actually *done it*...

"You *are* asleep," teased Laurie. "Damn, now you've really hurt my feelings. I had no idea I was that boring."

Tortured by the thought of hurting Nadia's feelings—and realizing in an instant that she must never *ever* find out—Suzette opened her eyes and sat up, clutching the duvet around her chest. Laurie was watching her with amusement. All their clothes were scattered across the bedroom floor. A glance at the alarm clock on her bedside table told her that it was nine thirty. In two and a bit hours she had managed to meet a total stranger, share dinner with him, and end up in bed with him. That alone would have been enough to earn her the title of Slut of the Year. Even if he hadn't been the kind-of-boyfriend of a girl she genuinely liked.

"You have to leave," Suzette blurted out. "Now. Right away. Just put your clothes on and go."

Laurie raised an eyebrow. "Why?"

"Look, I've never done anything like this before in my life," said Suzette. "I'm not that kind of girl. But my boyfriend could be here at any minute. I didn't realize it was so late. *Please*," she urged, mortified. "We can never see each other again. You've got a girlfriend, I've got a boyfriend. Promise me that what happened here tonight will be our secret. No one must ever find out."

Laurie smiled and held up his hands. "Fine, fine. No problem. I wasn't exactly planning to broadcast it from the rooftops. It was just a bit of fun."

"*Clothes*," hissed Suzette, jabbing a finger at his shirt and jeans. "On. Now." She might not really have a boyfriend, but she still had to get Laurie out of her flat.

Laughing, Laurie got himself dressed. "I was going to ask for your phone number. But maybe I'd better not."

"Bye," said Suzette, unable to look at him. "I'm sure you can see yourself out."

"Relax." Laurie reached for his car keys and headed for the door. "Easy come, easy go."

~~~

Nadia's mobile rang again at nine forty-five.

"Hi, I'm home."

"And?" said Nadia, gripping the phone so tightly it was a wonder it didn't crack.

"Just like you said. He was the perfect gentleman. We had dinner, we split the bill, he insisted on dropping me home."

Nadia exhaled slowly. She'd guessed that Laurie would invite Suzette to have dinner with him—that was the kind of spontaneous, innocent thing he would do. But…

"Did he say anything? Do anything, um, you know…?"

"Nothing," Suzette told her firmly. "Nothing at all. Didn't ask to see me again or try and get my phone number. I didn't even get a peck on the cheek. To be honest, I was almost offended! He's just a genuinely nice person who doesn't play around."

"Thanks, Suze." Nadia realized there was a lump in her throat. She hadn't seriously thought that Laurie would do anything like that, but it was a relief to have it confirmed.

"Listen, you won't ever tell him we arranged this, will you?" Suzette imagined the whole sordid truth coming out. Her reputation would be in tatters, nobody at the garden center would ever speak to her again. "I mean, you won't admit it in a fit of gratitude, because I can't see it going down well. Men don't like to think you're checking up on them."

"God, no," Nadia exclaimed happily. "I know Laurie's easy-going, but he'd go berserk if he thought we'd set him up."

Chapter 39

"Right. Have I got everything? What's the time? Don't forget, you have to be there by six or they'll close the doors and you won't be able to get in."

"For heaven's sake," Miriam rolled her kohl-lined eyes, "will someone give this girl a gin and tonic."

It was eight o'clock on Tuesday morning and Tilly was all of a jitter. Today was her Big Day. School, followed by final rehearsals, followed by makeup and preparation, followed by The Show Itself.

Tilly had been up since six, pacing the kitchen like a caged leopard, going over and over her lines.

"You'll be brilliant." Nadia gave her a squeeze. "I can't wait for tonight."

"You won't be late, will you?" Tilly's eyes were huge in her pale face. Ten hours before curtain up and she was already in the grip of acute stage fright.

"We'll be there. *Early*," Nadia added, before Tilly could remind her for the hundredth time about the doors.

"All ready?" James came into the kitchen carrying his overnight case. He was dropping Tilly at school before setting off for Sheffield.

"Ready." Tilly leapt to her feet in anguish. "Oh God, I forgot the flowers for Mum's room! I meant to pick them this morning."

"I'll do it," Nadia said firmly, before Tilly had a full-blown panic attack. "I'll pick them now, before I go to work."

Miriam kissed Tilly. "Off you go, darling. I'm so sorry we're going to miss the show. You'll be a sensation, I just know it."

"Especially if I forget my lines and fall off the stage." Tilly hauled her haversack over her shoulder. "Anyway, you and Edward have a great time."

Miriam hugged her hard, her conscience jabbing at her like a sharp stick. Needing to escape the anxiety of further letters and phone calls was what had prompted her to book the holiday. She had persuaded Edward that a week in Venice would be fun, when in reality all she was doing was running away from the problem, like a child sticking its fingers in its ears and closing its eyes to shut out the world.

"We'll be thinking of you," she told Tilly.

"Come on, Liza Minnelli," said James, checking his watch.

Tilly looked perplexed. "Who's that?"

James was pleased with himself. "You might think I'm a hopeless old fogey, but I'm not that out of touch. Liza Minnelli starred in *Grease*."

———

Nadia's car was booked into the garage in Westbury to fail its Ministry of Transport test. At eight thirty, Miriam was following Nadia to the garage, then giving her a lift into work. At three o'clock, Laurie was driving Miriam and Edward up to Heathrow; thanks to major roadworks on the M4, the journey was set to take three hours. At five o'clock, Nadia would finish work for the day, change into the clothes she had brought with her, make herself generally presentable, then wait for Clare to pick her up at five fifteen and drive her to Tilly's school.

It had all been planned like a military campaign.

Having glugged back her coffee, Nadia ran outside to the garden at twenty past eight and picked armfuls of flowers—as stipulated by Tilly—for the spare bedroom. Preparing for Leonie, Brian, and Tamsin's visit was proving as arduous as hosting an overnight stay for the Queen; Tilly had been fussing over the details all week, intent on making sure everything would be perfect.

Resentfully clipping the stem of a perfect deep-pink peony—such a waste, seeing as Leonie didn't even care much for flowers—Nadia was forced to remind herself that she had been the one to phone and persuade her to come down for the show.

In the kitchen, Miriam was jangling her car keys.

Nadia filled two huge bowls with water and hastily divided up the blooms, jooshing them around to look as if they'd been carefully styled in *au naturel* fashion rather than plonked in by someone with no arranging skills at all.

The telephone shrilled as she was wiping her hands on a towel. Since Miriam showed no sign of answering it, Nadia snatched up the phone.

"Darling, it's me. Now listen, this show thing of Tilly's. It is tonight, isn't it?"

Exasperated, Nadia gritted her teeth. How absolutely typical of Leonie not to be sure.

"Yes of course it's tonight. The show starts at six and we all have to be there *before* six, otherwise—"

"The thing is, darling, we're not going to be able to make it after all, so could you just let Tilly know and wish her good luck?"

Nadia froze. Was her mother *serious*?

"You can't do that. Tilly's expecting you there. You *have* to come."

"Oh, stop it, don't go all disapproving on me. We've just been asked to a party and it's really not the kind of invite you turn down! This chap used to be a member of Status Quo, darling, can you imagine? So of course Tamsin's *desperate* to go along. If you explain everything to Tilly I'm sure she'll understand."

"She won't." Nadia was discovering the true meaning of the

expression "making your blood boil." "Mum, I'm telling you now, Tilly *won't* understand. You promised to come and see her."

"And we will! We'll pop up and see her next weekend," Leonie said gaily. "How about that?"

"You promised to come and see her tonight! In the show! You *have* to be there." Nadia felt sick, chiefly because she knew Leonie wasn't going to change her mind. She never did.

"Nadia, you're making a big fuss over nothing." Leonie began to sound irritated. "Let's face it, we're talking about a tin-pot little school production here. It's hardly the London Palladium."

"You'll break Tilly's heart." Nadia paused. "Again."

"Oh please, listen to yourself. Now you're just playing the drama queen."

"You seriously want me to tell Tilly that you won't be coming to see her in the show because you'd rather go along to some long-haired has-been's party?"

"He isn't a has-been," Leonie retorted crossly. "He toured Japan *very* successfully last year. And he's an absolutely charming person. But OK, if it'll make you any happier…"

Nadia held her breath.

"…we won't tell Tilly that's where we're going. We'll make up some other excuse instead. I know," Leonie went on cheerfully, "we'll say the car broke down. Ooh, though she might think we should've caught the train. Right, got it. Stomach upset. We've all gone down with a really nasty bug—that's better, isn't it? Tilly can't argue with that."

⁓

"God, what now?" Clare groaned and buried her head further under the pillows, but the hideous shaking wouldn't stop. Rolling over onto her side, trying to pull the duvet with her, she muttered, "Don't do it, please don't—oh, I *hate* you."

"Listen to me." Whisking the duvet into the air matador-style,

Nadia leapt back to avoid Claire's foot as it kicked out. "And pay attention, because I have to go to work."

"Hooray," muttered Clare.

"Leonie isn't coming to the show. Basically, she's had a better offer. So it's just you and me tonight."

Clare kept her eyes closed. Since Nadia was sounding absolutely livid, it seemed safer.

"OK."

"I'm serious. It's Tilly's big night and we're all she has. Just make sure you aren't late picking me up from work."

"I won't be late. Give me back my duvet."

"You'd better not be. In fact," Nadia ordered, "be early. Meet me at five."

"Blimey, love, you scrub up a treat." Bart bumped into Nadia as she emerged from the newly refurbished bathroom with her scruffy work clothes stuffed into a shopping bag. Having fastened up her hair, done her makeup, and changed into a strappy red dress and high heels, she certainly wasn't looking gardener-like anymore.

"Thanks, Bart. You're looking very lovely too." Nadia grinned because Bart was covered from head to toe in brick dust and was sweating freely through his grubby gray T-shirt.

"Got a hot date then?" As he expertly rolled a cigarette, Bart glanced out of the landing window and broke into a nudge-nudge leer. "Hmm, looks like you have. Better not tell Laurie about this, eh? Don't worry, love, we won't let slip. Mum's the word."

Mum's the word? What did that mean? If it meant reliable and discreet, thought Nadia, it hardly applied to Leonie.

Peering out of the window, hoping to see Clare, she watched Jay emerging from his car. No Clare yet, but it was only ten past five. Being ten minutes late was Clare's version of early.

"I'm not waiting for Jay. We don't have a hot date. My sister's picking me up."

Bart looked disappointed. He was partial to a spot of intrigue. "He must be here to check on the fitted wardrobes. I'll show him what we've done, then we're off. *Kevin*," he bawled up the stairs, "get a move on with 'oovering up that brick dust. The boss is on his way."

The next second, the Hoover was switched on. Downstairs, the front door banged. Aware that her last contact with Jay had been the note he'd left, informing her that actually he wasn't rubbish in bed, Nadia nipped back into the bathroom. He wouldn't be here long.

At five twenty, the builders trooped off home. Jay was still upstairs. Nadia, by this time in the kitchen drumming her fingers on the worktop, rang home and listened to the phone go unanswered. Well, that was good. It had to mean Clare was on her way.

"What are you doing? I didn't know you were still here." Jay appeared in the kitchen doorway. "Your car isn't outside."

Nadia had already rung the garage. Her car needed new brake shoes. She'd told the mechanic that she could do with some new shoes too, but apparently the Renault needed them more.

"It's in the garage, getting an evaluation. Clare's picking me up."

Except she's *late*.

"Off somewhere nice?"

"School play. Tilly's starring in *Grease*. Excuse me." Getting seriously twitchy now, Nadia fumbled in her bag for her mobile and pressed redial. At home the phone continued to ring unanswered.

"I can give you a lift," Jay offered as she punched out the number of Clare's mobile. It was switched to the answering service.

"It's me. Clare, call me back. It's nearly half past."

"Really, it's no trouble," said Jay.

"She should be here any moment. I *told* her not to be late." Nadia began to feel sick; surely Clare wouldn't let Tilly down. "Leonie was meant to be coming as well, but she canceled this morning. Bloody hell," she burst out, "I told Clare to be here by five o'clock. I can't believe she's doing this."

By twenty to six there was still no sign of Clare, and no answer from either phone.

"Come on." Jay ushered Nadia into his car.

"I'm going to kill her."

"But not until after the show."

Nadia's hands were shaking so much she could barely fasten her seat belt. She pictured Tilly, peeking through the curtains up on stage, anxiously awaiting the arrival of her family.

"I've got five tickets," she fumed, "for the front row. And I'm going to be the only one sitting there."

"Would it help if I offered to go with you?"

Too wound up to care how she sounded, Nadia heaved a sigh and said, "I suppose you're better than nothing."

The corners of Jay's mouth twitched. "Thanks."

Chapter 40

By TEN TO SIX the school hall was buzzing and crammed with people. Clare wasn't there. Nadia decided she'd never forgive her for this. Easing their way to the front row through the crowds, they found their allotted seats with Tilly's name on them. The end one was already occupied by Cal Davis, with whom Tilly had recently become so friendly.

As Nadia greeted him, a hand touched her arm. Swinging round, she saw Annie looking out of breath but triumphant.

"Oh, thank God." Nadia hugged her. "But how did you get here?"

"Your grandmother phoned James. James rang me. I closed the shop at five thirty and ran all the way. Poor Tilly, I know it's not the same as having her mum here, but at least I can fill an empty seat."

Annie wasn't supposed to close the shop early. If her boss found out, she'd be sacked on the spot.

"I need to let Tilly know," said Nadia, realizing that she couldn't allow Tilly to make her entrance on stage expecting to see Leonie and Tamsin and Brian in the audience.

"Hi, Cal!" a chirpy voice sang out, and Nadia turned to see two girls looking delighted to see him. "Exciting, isn't it? Lucky you, in the front row. We're stuck right at the back."

Something about the girl's heavily mascaraed eyelashes rang a bell in the back of Nadia's mind. Tilly had relayed the story of her and Cal's encounter with her in the park.

"Are you Janet?"

"Janice." The spidery lashes batted with pride as she indicated her silent friend. "And this is Erica. We're mates of Tilly and Cal."

"We've got two spare seats. Want to sit with us?"

"Hey, cool!" Brightening, Janice immediately bagged the one next to Cal.

It was five to six.

"I'll be back in two minutes," Nadia told Annie and Jay as she headed for the stairs at the side of the stage.

"What are you doing?" squealed Tilly, who was warming up in the wings. "You'll get me into trouble!"

With no time to break it to her gently, Nadia said, "Tilly, Mum isn't here. She couldn't make it."

It almost broke her heart to see the look on Tilly's face.

"Or Tamsin? Or Brian?" It came out as a whisper.

Nadia shook her head. "Stomach bug. They've gone down with a really nasty virus. Sorry, darling, they're really upset about missing the show. But the school's videoing it, so we'll be able to send them a DVD."

"I told everyone my mum was going to be here." Tilly's bottom lip began to wobble.

"I know, but she can't help being ill." Nadia hated lying.

"Who's this?" bellowed a teacher, marching across the stage and jabbing a stubby, accusing finger. "Off! Off! Leave the performers alone! Curtain up in one minute."

Teachers. Why did they always have to be so scary? Nadia raced back down the wooden steps and took her seat between Annie and Jay.

"I think I just made Tilly cry," Nadia whispered to Annie.

Annie gave her hand a comforting squeeze. "Not you."

Eighty minutes later, the final curtain fell and the audience rose to their feet as one, clapping and cheering and whistling so loudly that the whole hall seemed to vibrate.

The applause carried on. The curtains lifted once more and the cast stepped forward to take their bows. There was a lump in Nadia's throat the size of an egg as Tilly was invited to step forward and the roars of approval rose to a climax. From the stage, Tilly beamed down at Nadia and her fellow guests in the front row. The scary teacher, emerging from the wings, presented her with a huge basket of flowers, causing Tilly to go bright pink. Apart from the opening moments of the show, when her eyes had been red-rimmed and she'd flubbed a couple of lines, she had played the part of Sandy to perfection. The evening had been a triumph.

Nadia, clapping until her hands were sore, briefly fantasized about killing Clare when she got home. She could squeeze her neck until her head exploded.

"I only came along to fill an empty seat." Next to her, Jay had to raise his voice in order to be heard. "But I'm glad I did. Tilly was brilliant." He paused, then said, "I feel like a proud father."

The scary teacher, who had legs like a rugby player beneath her stiff floral skirt, reappeared on stage once everyone had taken their bows, to announce that as soon as *all* the chairs had been stacked *neatly* at the back of the hall, the bar would be open. Within sixty seconds, every chair had been stacked. Parent volunteers began serving warm white wine and an assortment of soft drinks. Nadia was relieved to discover that after being in the hall-cum-gym for over an hour and a half, you became accustomed to the smell of sweat and adolescent trainers.

"You don't have to stay," she whispered to Jay. "You'll hate this bit. Tilly and I can get a cab home."

He looked astounded. "You must be joking. This is Tilly's big night. I wouldn't miss it for the world."

By the time Tilly reappeared, changed back into her own clothes and lugging her basket of flowers, Jay had bought a round of drinks. Much to her disgust, Janice was forced to settle for fruit punch. This hadn't, however, put her off Jay.

"Cheers." Clicking her plastic cup against his, she beamed up at him like Lolita. "You're all right. How old are you?"

Gravely, Jay said, "Absolutely ancient."

"You were fantastic," Nadia swung Tilly round, "the star of the show."

"I wish Mum could have been here. And Tamsin. What happened to Clare?"

The six-million-dollar question. Nadia couldn't bring herself to tell any more lies. "I don't know, sweetheart. She just didn't turn up."

Tilly looked worried. "D'you think she's had an accident?"

Not yet.

"You were ace," Janice said enthusiastically. "Wicked. Wasn't she, Cal?"

"Oh yes." Cal smiled his quirky smile at Tilly. "Totally wicked."

"And your teacher certainly thought so," Annie chimed in, "giving you those gorgeous flowers."

"Oh, they weren't from *her*." Tilly pulled a horrified face, then held up the vast basket and said with pride, "They were from my mum."

"How lovely," said Annie valiantly.

"I know. Even though she was really ill, she still managed to organize flowers. That was thoughtful of her, wasn't it?"

Don't say a word, don't say a word.

"Terrific." Knocking back her mouth-shriveling wine, Nadia exchanged a glance with Jay. "I'd love another drink."

"Thanks for the lift," said Annie, when they dropped her off at the cottage at nine thirty. She smiled at Jay, then at Nadia in the passenger seat. "And for tonight. I loved every minute."

"I'm just glad you could make it," said Nadia. "I hope you don't get the sack."

"Well," said Jay, when they'd watched Annie disappear into her house. "One down, one to go. Do you want to go somewhere for a drink or get home?"

Nadia had slipped Tilly twenty pounds and left her to celebrate with her new-found friends and fellow cast members over a pizza on the Gloucester Road. Tilly had promised to share a taxi with Cal and be home by eleven.

"I need to see Clare." And tear her hair out by the roots.

"OK. I didn't ask earlier," Jay went on easily as he swung the car round in the narrow lane. "Where's Laurie tonight?"

"London. He drove Miriam and Edward to Heathrow, then arranged to meet up with an old friend from the agency. He'll be back later." Realizing that she hadn't yet apologized for Saturday, Nadia said warily, "Are you still seeing thingy? Andrea?"

"Yes, thanks." Jay looked amused. "Despite what you told her, it hasn't put her off."

Shame.

"Sorry. She annoyed me."

"So I gathered." He was still smirking.

"She made assumptions I didn't like." Nadia pleated the red silky material of her dress between her fingers. "And they weren't true either."

"I hate it when that happens. People making assumptions about me. Especially when they're not true."

Oh dear. Touché. Feeling her pulse beginning to accelerate,

Nadia recalled something else about Saturday. If she wanted to sleep with Jay, she could. She had Laurie's permission to do so. Not that she needed his permission, seeing as she was still officially single and free to sleep with whoever she liked. And if she did decide to go for it, what better time than tonight? They could head on over to Jay's place. Laurie wouldn't be back from London for hours. Best of all, it would drive Andrea insane…

"I need to get home," Nadia said firmly.

It was true. Some things were more important than annoying somebody else's annoying new girlfriend. She had to beat the living daylights out of Clare.

———

"OK," Jay announced, ten minutes later.

Nadia surveyed the driveway. Clare's car was there, parked at a different angle than it had been this morning.

"I'd invite you in," she said, "but…"

"I know. I might not be able to handle the sight of all that blood."

The ground floor of the house was in darkness but there were a couple of lights on upstairs. As Nadia let herself in, all the rage came flooding back and adrenaline rushed through her veins. If Jay hadn't been around to give her a lift, she might have missed the show herself. Had Clare even bothered to think about how Tilly would have felt if *none* of her family had turned up?

Flinging her shopping bag of gardening clothes into the corner of the hall, Nadia stormed up the stairs.

Clare's room was messy but empty.

The bathroom door was shut.

What if Clare had slipped in the shower and spent the last five hours lying unconscious with a fractured skull?

Dry-mouthed, Nadia tried the handle. The bathroom door was locked.

"Clare? Are you in there?" Stupid question. "CLARE? OPEN THE DOOR."

Nothing. Oh God. You read about accidents like this in the papers.

Rattling the handle again, as if it might miraculously unlock itself, Nadia bellowed, "CLARE!"

Oh dear God, what if she really was dead?

Chapter 41

MORE SILENCE. THEN...

"Go away."

"*What?*" Nadia stared at the door in disbelief, terror instantly replaced by boiling rage.

"Leave me alone."

"You bloody selfish little *cow*," Nadia roared, hammering on the door with both fists. "Where the *fuck* have you been? You were supposed to pick me up from work, you missed Tilly's show, and you couldn't even be bothered to fucking *phone* me! You're unbelievable, you know that? You just don't care about anyone else. I don't know how you can live with yourself—and you'd better open the bloody door this minute, because I'm not going anywhere until you do."

More silence. At last, Clare said slowly, "Who else is out there?"

"No one. I'm on my own." And oh so ready to teach you a lesson you'll never forget.

Moments later the key turned in the lock and the door swung open. About to reach out and grab a handful of hair, Nadia was stopped in her tracks by the pitiful sight before her. She'd never seen Clare looking so awful, puffy-eyed, pinch-faced, and... well, a complete mess.

"Don't tell me, this is about Piers. It just has to be," Nadia sneered.

Clare stumbled past her out of the bathroom, heading back to the sanctuary of her room. On a roll now, Nadia followed close behind before another door could slam shut between them.

"He's dumped you, hasn't he? You've never been dumped before and you can't handle it." Her voice was accusing and tinged with satisfaction. Now, at last, Clare knew how it felt. "You spoilt, self-centered bitch, you could still have phoned me. Piers is just a waste of space, he's not important! Tilly's your own *sister*. You said you'd pick me up at five o'clock. You promised *faithfully* not to miss the show…" The words were tumbling out faster and faster now, turbo-charged by rage and Clare's breathtaking selfishness. "You know what? I'm glad he's dumped you! It serves you right! You *deserve* to be miserable—"

"Shut up!" screamed Clare, hurling something small at her. It bounced painlessly off Nadia's chest and dropped to the floor.

Nadia peered down at it. "What's that?"

She said it, although she already knew.

"What d'you bloody think it is? I'm pregnant." Clare buried her face in her hands and collapsed on the bed.

Oh fuck.

Bending, Nadia retrieved the white plastic stick thing. One blue line. Two blue lines. She'd never actually seen one before in real life, only on TV. Turning it over in her hand she realized that it was wet, and quickly put it down on the bedside table.

"Don't worry, I did wash it," Clare muttered. "It's not catching."

Nadia felt as if all the breath had been knocked out of her. Taking the anger with it.

"Does Piers know?"

"Of course he bloody knows." Clare snatched a handful of tissues from the box next to the pregnancy stick. Fresh tears began to roll down her cheeks. "Why else would I be looking like this?"

"He's not happy." Nadia sank down on the bed next to her.

"He went berserk. He doesn't even think it's his." Roughly wiping her swollen eyes, Clare said helplessly, "He thinks I've been sleeping around, but I haven't. He also thinks I did it on purpose, to trap him. But I *didn't*."

"How long have you known?"

Blearily Clare peered at her Wallace and Gromit alarm clock. "Seven hours? God, I can't believe this is happening. At lunchtime today, I was actually happy. Working away." She gestured wildly at the canvas propped on her easel. "Tom rang from the gallery to tell me he'd sold another painting. The bloke's a collector and he seemed really interested in my stuff, asking Tom loads of questions about me. So Tom said he could arrange a meeting if he liked. Fix up a date for next week or something. That was how it happened. When I was flicking through my diary, I realized my period was a couple of days late. Only two days, but I'm never late. I told myself it didn't mean anything, but after that I couldn't concentrate. In the end I thought I'd pop to the pharmacy and pick up a testing kit, just to put my mind at rest." Clare paused, then shrugged and said brokenly, "Except it didn't."

"God." Nadia picked up the testing stick again and examined it. She couldn't imagine how Clare must have felt, first finding out she was pregnant, then having to relay the news to someone as loathsome as Piers. All in one afternoon.

"I'm sorry, I'm really sorry about not picking you up or getting to Tilly's school thing. And I know I should have phoned you. But I just couldn't." Clare began to tremble. "I rang Piers at work, but he wasn't there. They said he'd taken the afternoon off, so I went round to his flat but he wasn't at home either. So then I drove round all the bars in Clifton until I found him."

"With a girl," guessed Nadia.

"No. With his horrible friend Eddie. Well, there were girls there," Clare amended. "But they weren't *with* them. Just chatting at the bar. Piers is a good-looking bloke," she went on defensively. "Wherever he goes, he'll always get chatted up."

Nadia couldn't believe Clare was still defending him. She hadn't mentioned the conversation she'd overheard at the wedding. But all she did was nod. "OK. Go on."

"I told Piers I had to talk to him. He didn't want to leave the bar. I wanted us to go back to his flat, but he wouldn't. In the end I managed to get him to come and sit in my car. And that's where I told him." Clare took a deep, shuddering breath. "Oh God, it was a nightmare. He went berserk. He called me a tramp and a liar and… all sorts of vile names. He said he never wanted to see me again. I couldn't believe it, I just couldn't believe he was saying all these terrible things. He tried to write me out a check for an abortion and when I ripped it up he called me a stupid little tart. Then just as I was getting really hysterical, a traffic warden came along and started banging on the window. He said I was parked on double yellows and I had to move my car. So that was it. Piers jumped out, told the traffic warden I was a raving nympho, and legged it back into the pub."

"He's a tosser." Nadia shook her head. "A complete and utter tosser."

"I know. But it might have been the shock. Maybe when he's had a chance to think about it, he'll change his mind. I mean, it must have been a terrible shock," Clare pleaded, "coming out of the blue like that. He might wake up tomorrow morning feeling completely—"

"Like a tosser," Nadia said firmly. "Because that's all he is, and you know it. Let's face it, he isn't going to change his mind."

"Oh God." Clare started crying again, hopelessly and noisily. "What am I going to do? I don't know what to *doooo*. I don't want this to be *happening* to me… I just want it to GO AWAY."

Nadia put her arms round Clare, who clung to her, sobbing and shivering and dripping hot tears down her front.

"Sshh, come on, it'll be OK," murmured Nadia. When had she last done this, comforted her distraught sister? She honestly couldn't remember; Clare had never been the in-need-of-comforting type. Apart from the time her pet frog, Eric, had died when she was eleven—accidentally mowed to death by Miriam—she never cried either.

"How can it be OK?" Clare sniffed and wiped her nose on the

front of Nadia's dress. "I'm pregnant and my boyfriend's dumped me. It can't get any worse than this."

Nadia manfully ignored the mark on her favorite red dress. What with all the tears, she looked as if she'd been out in the rain anyway.

"Look, we'll sort this out. If you don't want to have this baby, you don't have to." Despite squirming inwardly as she said it, Nadia forced herself to sound matter-of-fact. Surely in these circumstances it was the only sensible thing to do.

"Get rid of it, you mean? Have an abortion?" Dully, Clare shook her head. "No."

No?

Astounded, Nadia said, "You want to have the baby?"

Clare was running her fingers through her tangled hair, over and over again.

"Of course I don't want to. I'm twenty-three, for crying out loud. But I couldn't get rid of it, I just can't do that." She sniffed again. "Like mother, like daughter. Leonie had kids she didn't want. Now I'm about to do it too. Maybe it's genetic."

Piers opened the door and said coldly, "What do you want?"

"To talk."

He rolled his eyes. "Sounds boring. Do we have to?"

Clare knew he wasn't about to change his mind. If a tiny part of her had hoped he would pull her into his arms and say passionately, "I was such a git yesterday, I'm so sorry," the moment she saw that eye-roll she realized it was never going to happen.

Luckily, most of her hadn't expected it to.

Clenching her fists, she dug her nails deliberately into her palms in order to stay calm. Nadia had been right, Piers was a tosser.

"It may be boring, but we still need to talk. I'm going to have this baby and you're going to pay for it."

This time Piers raised an eyebrow in laconic James Bond fashion. Except James Bond would never be such a git.

"Sure about that? Shouldn't we wait for the results of the DNA tests first?"

She wasn't going to cry. She wouldn't give him the satisfaction.

"It's yours," Clare said steadily. "I haven't slept with anyone else."

"Look, you've had your fun. We both know you aren't going to keep this kid. You want money for a trip to the clinic? Fine, I told you yesterday, I'll pay for it. Wait here and I'll get my checkbook."

Realizing that he was about to shut the door in her face, Clare stuck her foot in the way.

"Can I come in?"

"Can you come in?" drawled Piers, mimicking her. "I don't think so, do you?"

God, he was loathsome. How had she never realized it before?

In fact Piers was turning out to be surprisingly easy to hate.

"Why not? Got another girl up there?"

"Maybe. Maybe not." Piers smirked unpleasantly. "Either way, it's not actually any of your business."

Since she'd been waiting in the car for him to arrive home from work and had watched him enter the flat alone, it was highly unlikely there was anyone else inside.

"You know what?" said Clare. "I feel sorry for you. You're actually quite pathetic."

"Now I'm really starting to get bored." Piers pretended to yawn, in that laid-back, upper-class way of his, then glanced at his watch. "Look, why don't I just get you that check? Will a grand cover it?"

Clare said nothing. She was gazing into his eyes, those beautiful navy-blue eyes she'd always loved so much.

All she wanted to do now was gouge them out with a sharp stick.

"Give me two minutes," said Piers, and this time Clare moved her foot away from the door, allowing him to close it. She turned and made her way down the steps.

Laurie buzzed down the car window and called out, "Is that it?"

"He's gone to get his checkbook." Clare was tempted by the thought of the thousand pounds but concerned that taking it might prejudice any future claim for child support.

"Are you OK?"

Clare nodded. Much to her own amazement, she actually was OK. She leaned against the side of the car and said, "Can I have some of that?"

Laurie passed her his can of soda and gave her hand a reassuring squeeze. "You did well. I thought we were in for another shouting match. You aren't even crying."

The moment he said it, she felt a lump expand like cotton wool in her throat.

"I'm probably in shock. You know, this was never how I pictured it. I thought I'd carry on painting and partying and having fun. Then, about ten years from now, I'd meet someone amazing and get married. And we'd really love each other, you know?" Clare paused, blinking back tears. "Then one day when I was about thirty-five or something, I'd wait for my husband to come home from work and say, 'You'll never guess what?' And then I'd tell him I was pregnant and he'd be so *happy*, because a baby was what we both wanted more than anything else in the world." She heaved a wobbly sigh. "Oh well, serves me right for watching too many old Doris Day movies when I was bunking off school. But I really thought that was the way it would happen. God knows, it was never supposed to turn out like this."

"You and Piers. Nadia and me. Look at the mess I made of that," said Laurie. "Nothing ever goes according to plan." He retrieved his can of soda and nodded at Piers's house. "Here he comes."

Clare turned, wiping her hands on her jeans, as Piers sauntered down the step holding the check. He paused on the pavement and surveyed Laurie before returning his attention to Clare.

"Who's he? New boyfriend?"

"No. This is Laurie, Nadia's friend. He drove me here."

Casting his eye over Edward Welch's gray Volvo station wagon, Piers drawled, "Nice car."

Clare thought longingly about pouring paint stripper over Piers's nice car.

"Here you go, then." He held out the check. "I wish I could say you were worth it, but frankly I've had better."

Snatching the can of soda back from Laurie, Clare tossed the fizzing contents in Piers's face. He regarded her with derision. "How original. About as original as you were in bed."

"You wanker," said Laurie furiously.

"Oh dear. Struck a nerve, have I? Don't tell me you're shagging her too." Amused, Piers glanced at Clare. "Is that what you've been doing? Shagging your sister's ex behind her back? Maybe he's the one who should be writing out the check."

Clare had never seen anyone move so fast. Before she even had a chance to blink, Laurie was out of the car. *Crrrackk* went Piers's nose as in a blur of movement Laurie's fist made contact with his face. Letting out a roar of pain, Piers staggered backward, lost his balance, and landed in an awkward heap on the pavement.

Clutching his face as blood gushed out, Piers bellowed, "You broke my nose! You broke my fucking nose!"

"Excellent," said Laurie. "That's just what I was aiming for."

"I'll sue you for this," Piers shouted as blood trickled through his fingers onto his blue and white striped shirt.

"Think yourself lucky." Clare smiled sunnily down at him. "Imagine if he'd broken your dick."

Chapter 42

Nadia was impressed.

"You actually broke his nose? Fantastic."

"It was," said Clare, hugging her knees and grinning across at Laurie, who was trying to look suitably modest. "He was like a superhero—*bam*—and it made a noise like ripping into an old chicken carcass. Oh, you should have seen the look on Piers's face. Not to mention the blood all over his shirt. Ralph Lauren," she added with satisfaction. "And then, the best bit of all, as we were leaving, this sweet little old lady who lives in the flat next to Piers flung open her window and yelled out, 'Bravo, bravo,' just like she was at the opera. When she'd finished clapping, she shouted, 'I've been waiting years for someone to do that!'"

"Bit of a nightmare neighbor then," Nadia remarked.

"Actually, I've spoken to her a few times. She seemed really nice."

"Not the little old lady." Nadia raised an eyebrow at her sister's stupidity. "I was talking about Piers."

Clare appeared to have cheered up. Nadia wondered how long it would last.

She found out three hours later when she took a mug of tea upstairs and knocked on the door to Clare's room.

"I hate him, I hate him." Clare was sitting in front of her easel, slashing away at the canvas with a brush. The painting wasn't something that would ever sell; it was the kind a monkey might produce if he'd been on the Guinness. Lots of black sloshed around with gashes and streaks of bottle green and gentian blue and purple. Even a serious fan of modern art might turn his nose up at this one.

Oh well, it was probably cathartic. You couldn't put a price on that.

"Tea," said Nadia. Clare had been crying again; quite a lot, by the look of her eyes. "Come on, you'll be OK. You deserve so much better than Piers."

"I *know* that. I just feel so stupid. He's made me look like an idiot. I want to hurt him like he's hurt me," Clare raged.

"Didn't Laurie do that when he broke his nose?"

Clare jabbed at the canvas with a brushful of crimson acrylic, splattering it like ketchup.

"I've been fantasizing about smashing up his flat. Doing the prawns-in-the-curtains thing. Cat food under the floorboards. Graffiti on the walls, trashing his precious DVD collection."

"Getting done for breaking and entering," said Nadia.

"Ooh, and then there's that brilliant thing about planting mustard and cress seeds in people's carpets."

"They'd need watering. He might notice if his flat's turned into a paddling pool. And he might set his solicitor on to you," Nadia pointed out. "You could get sued. You'd end up having to pay for a new carpet. You'd lose, he'd win. Come on, drink your tea."

Clare sighed and picked up the mug. Gazing out of the window, she saw the lights on in Edward and Laurie's house across the road.

"You know, Laurie was brilliant this afternoon. He only offered to come along to give me some moral support. You don't realize how lucky you are."

Lucky that my boyfriend buggered off to America for a year and a half, thought Nadia. Getting up to all sorts, no doubt, while he was over there. OK, so she hadn't been pregnant, but what Clare didn't seem to grasp was that if it hurt being dumped by a bastard like Piers, it was fifty times more painful being chucked by someone who everyone agreed was wonderful.

"He's not going to hang around forever," Clare went on. "If you're not careful, someone else'll snap him up."

"Don't nag." Nadia felt her stomach muscles tighten automatically at the thought of Laurie being snapped up by someone else. Like Jay had been by the predatory Andrea, except she'd vowed not to think about that.

"Then you'd be sorry," said Clare with a shrug.

"Snapping up. You make him sound like a bargain in the sales."

"But he *is*. Laurie's a perfect Versace suit in an Oxfam shop. You can't dither around and think he'll probably still be there next week. Because he won't," Clare concluded bluntly. "He'll be gone."

Miriam had issued strict instructions that any post arriving while she was away and addressed to her should be left in the top drawer of the dresser in the hall. Now, she took a deep breath and slid open the drawer. Everyone else was out; she had the house to herself. Across the road, Laurie was lifting Edward's cases out of the boot of the Volvo. The holiday had been wonderful but Edward was still pressing her to marry him. Once or twice she'd been tempted to tell him everything. But she couldn't bring herself to go through with it.

There was quite a stack of mail. Miriam sifted through each item in turn, her spirits rising—for once—at the sight of electricity bills, endless junk mail, bank statements and letters from the various charities she supported. No handwritten envelopes, however, and nothing from Edinburgh. Maybe he'd given up at last.

Then she reached it, beneath the glossy cellophane-wrapped car brochures and a catalog from La Redoute. Feeling momentarily light-headed, Miriam stared at the padded envelope bearing her name and address in that all-too-familiar handwriting. A padded envelope containing something that felt like a book. Oh God, what now? Surely he hadn't sent her a Bible with the relevant passages underlined?

It wasn't a Bible. It wasn't even a book. It was a DVD, Miriam discovered when she'd managed to unfasten the sealed envelope.

Leaving her cases in the hall, she made her way through to the living room, slotted the tape into the video, and pressed Play.

Her heart began to gallop as the TV screen flickered, then cleared. Black and white, not color.

Old cine film, recorded over fifty years ago, now transferred to video.

Miriam watched, almost in disbelief, as the film switched jerkily from one scene to the next. She remembered the day—how could she ever forget it?—yet she'd never seen this film before. She couldn't even recall the name of the person who had been wielding the bulky cine camera. Was it Geoffrey? Gerald? At the time it had been something of a novelty, and they had looked forward to seeing the results. But Geoffrey or Gerald had been called up shortly afterwards, had disappeared to carry out his stint of National Service, and that had been that. They hadn't heard from him again.

And now, fifty-two years later, here was the result. Twisting the diamonds on her fingers, swallowing with difficulty, Miriam watched the day unfold, chopping inexpertly from scene to scene like a slightly too fast silent movie. There she was, wearing a dress that looked pale gray on the video but which had in fact been a glorious lime green. Laughing into the camera without a care in the world. Wearing dreadful shoes, of course—well, that was post-war rationing for you. And carefully darned stockings beneath the narrow, below-the-knee skirt of the dress.

But it was so obviously her. The eyes were just the same, even if the wrinkles around them had been absent then. Her smile was instantly recognizable. Even her hairstyle was unchanged.

It had been such a happy day, crisp and autumnal but still warm for September. Carefully Miriam identified everyone else captured by the camera. Most of all, she studied the man who had sent her the video, the man who had turned her life upside down once before and was now threatening to do the same again.

It was impossible not to wonder how the years had treated him, what he looked like now.

With a shudder, Miriam hoped to God she wouldn't find out.

Feeling like a boxer psyching himself up before a fight, Clare made her way downstairs. Miriam was back and dinner was about to be served. Tonight was the night Clare was going to make her announcement. To Miriam and her father and Tilly. Getting it all done in one fell swoop, with Nadia there to back her up.

About to head out to the garden, where she could hear voices, she glanced out through the French windows and promptly shot into reverse.

Bursting into the kitchen where Nadia was mashing potatoes, Clare hissed, "What's *she* doing here?"

"Who? Annie?" Pouring in a carton of double cream, Nadia's bottom wiggled as she resumed her energetic mashing. "Tilly's brought back the video of the school show. We've all got to watch it after dinner. When they called in to the newsagents on the way home, Tilly persuaded Annie to come along with them and see it too. Don't look at me like that," she went on, because Clare was scowling like a teenager. "Annie's nice."

"I'm telling Dad and Gran about the baby. It's none of her business. Why can't it just be *us*?"

Nadia sighed. Clare was still wary of Annie, reluctant to welcome her into the family. It was irrational and frustrating, particularly when their father was clearly so happy.

"You might be glad of her. Dad's less likely to go mental."

"Tuh. And she's always sucking up to Tilly."

"She's kind to Tilly. What's wrong with that?"

"What's wrong with that?" Clare mimicked. "She's nearly forty and never been married. We don't need someone like her worming her way into our family. Ask yourself what's wrong with it when Dad dies and he leaves everything to her in his will."

When Dad died. For heaven's sake, he was only forty-eight. Nadia finished piling the mashed potato into a dark blue serving dish, plonked it into Clare's hands, and shook her head sorrowfully.

"Hormones. It's the hormones getting to you. Now take the dish through to the dining room and call everyone inside. I'll bring the rest of the stuff through. And… try and break it to them gently," Nadia pleaded. She didn't see how this could be achieved, but Clare had a talent for making an awkward situation worse. Subtlety had never been her strong point.

"Oh, don't nag." Clare tried to sound irritated, but her insides were in too much of a knot. She managed a weak smile. "It'll be OK. It's only a baby, after all, not the end of the world."

Chapter 43

NADIA SERVED UP THE chicken casserole, everyone helped them-selves to broccoli and buttered carrots, and James poured the wine. It was, on the surface, a normal, happy, noisy gathering. Miriam was regaling them with tales of Venice, proudly showing off the antique amber and silver bracelet Edward had bought for her in a narrow street off St. Mark's Square.

"What have you done to your arm?" Nadia was distracted by the large bandage on Miriam's tanned forearm.

"Oh, nothing. Slipped and grazed it on a beam as I was putting the cases back in the attic."

"You should be careful. Next time, let me put them away." Nadia frowned, because climbing the rickety pull-down ladder wasn't something a seventy-year-old should be doing.

Miriam, who had hidden the incriminating DVD inside the smaller of her two cases, said cheerfully, "Darling, I *was* being careful. I always am."

Nadia flinched and glanced across at Clare, wondering if she'd take this as her cue. ("Speaking of being careful, what a shame I wasn't!")

"It's gorgeous." Annie was admiring Miriam's bracelet. "Amber's so pretty, I just love it."

"Imagine if it was diamonds instead," Clare said idly. "Be even better then, wouldn't it?"

Only Nadia picked up on the dig. She narrowed her eyes warn-ingly at her sister.

"Clare, more chicken?" Noticing that she'd almost cleared her plate, James pushed the dish toward her. "You must be hungry."

Nadia's toes scrunched up in hideous anticipation. ("Well, that's probably because I'm eating for two now!")

"Starving." Clare beamed at him and helped herself to more casserole. "Thomas Harrington rang me this afternoon. He's putting on a show next week and one of the other exhibitors has had to pull out." She spread her arms, ta-dah style. "So I'm in! Isn't that fantastic? Twelve paintings and loads of media coverage. I just know this is going to be my big break."

Nadia breathed out slowly. Clare was doing the good news, bad news routine, softening them up before delivering the killer blow. James, beaming with pride, ruffled Clare's hair and said, "There, we always knew you could do it."

Equally delighted, Miriam exclaimed, "My darling, this is brilliant news."

Clare was basking in their approval, visibly happy, then Nadia saw her take a deep breath.

"And there's something else," Clare began, her voice trembling slightly.

Nadia felt the urge to dive under the table.

"Isn't everything just great?" Tilly exclaimed. "First me in my show, and now Clare has one too! Gran, can we watch my DVD as soon as dinner's over? I'm so excited, I can't wait for all of you to see it!"

Clare glared at Tilly.

"Darling, of course we can," said Miriam. "The very moment we finish eating."

"I've already ordered my own copy," Annie chimed in with enthusiasm. "Honestly, they were all so good, so professional. None of the others were as good as Tilly, of course."

Clare shot Annie a look of disdain. Almost under her breath she muttered, "Pass the sick bag."

Nadia tensed. Annie went red. James said icily, "*What* did you say?"

"Nothing." Clare pressed her lips together, sensing she wasn't doing herself any favors.

But Tilly was furious. "You couldn't be bothered to turn up for the show. Now you're not even interested in watching the video. Well, that's fine, *don't* watch it," she shouted. "See if I care!"

Nadia took a gulp of wine. Under the table seemed like an increasingly desirable place to be.

"I wasn't talking about the show," Clare said tightly. Turning to Tilly, she went on, "When I said that, I didn't mean you."

"Then you're even more horrible than I thought." Tilly's voice rose.

"Yes, Clare," Miriam joined in, "you're being extremely rude."

With an edge of sarcasm, Clare said, "I wonder why."

"I know why." Tilly looked at Clare, then at Annie. Finally she turned to Miriam at the head of the table. "It's because she's pregnant."

Stunned, Miriam saw Tilly's thin hand resting protectively on Annie's plump one. Around the table, all eyes swung round to gaze in disbelief at Annie.

Hastily recovering herself, Miriam said, "Well, that's... that's wonderful news. Con-congratulations!"

James looked as if he might keel over.

As astounded as the rest of them—more, possibly—Annie blurted out, "But I'm not! I'm not pregnant."

"Not Annie." Tilly shook her head vigorously, despairing of her family's stupidity. "I didn't mean Annie. I'm talking about Clare."

A fork clattered onto a plate. Nadia drained her glass. If this had been *EastEnders*, the end-of-episode dum, dum-dum-dum music would have been reverberating through the room. Like Wimbledon spectators, everyone's gaze swiveled in unison across to Clare.

"Oh no." Her heart sinking, Miriam said, "Tell me this isn't true."

Tossing back her long hair in defiance, Clare glared at Tilly. "It is true. And how the bloody hell did *you* find out?"

"I overheard you and Nadia talking about it yesterday. You were in the kitchen and the door wasn't closed."

James looked at Nadia. "You knew about this?"

While Nadia squirmed, Clare snapped, "I had to tell someone. And I was about to tell all of you, until Bigmouth here stuck her oar in. Anyway, it's done now. Everyone knows. Can someone pass the mashed potato?"

Her words were casual but her blue eyes glittered with unshed tears. Annie, the unwilling catalyst for all this mayhem, was looking mortified.

"Oh Clare, how could you be so stupid," Miriam sighed. "What were you thinking of?"

Phlummph went the serving spoon as it landed back in the mashed potato.

"Oh great, thanks very much," Clare shouted. "When you thought Annie was pregnant it was wonderful news! You congratulated her, for God's sake. But as soon as you find out it's me, it's a complete disaster."

Since James was clearly too shell-shocked to speak, Miriam said, "Are you telling me this isn't a disaster? Clare, you couldn't take care of a cat, let alone a baby. Who's the father, anyway?"

Clare lowered her voice. "Piers."

"Ferrari boy?" Miriam's eyes narrowed with distaste. "I should have guessed. And how happy is he about this?"

"He's not." Clare was defiant. "We broke up. I don't need him anyway. I didn't mean this to happen, but it has. And I'll manage."

"You're going to have the baby?" said James.

"Yes."

"Why?"

"Because it deserves a chance, OK? Think back, Dad. When

Leonie found out she was pregnant with me, I don't suppose she was too thrilled, was she? It would have been easier for her not to have gone through with it. But she did. And I'm glad about that." Clare's eyes swam. "Because I'd rather be here than not here. Even now," she added, her voice starting to waver. "And I wouldn't call this the best night of my life."

There was a long silence. Then Miriam said gently, "Oh, darling."

Clare burst into tears.

As Miriam jumped up from her chair and enveloped her in a hug, Clare sobbed, "I'm s-sorry, it was an accident. I'll look after it, I p-promise."

"Sweetheart, don't cry. Everything's going to be fine. We'll manage. Sshh, there there, it's all right."

Clearly ashamed of her earlier outburst, Tilly said bluntly, "I never liked Piers. I'm glad Laurie broke his nose."

"Laurie?" Over the top of Clare's head, Miriam looked questioningly at Nadia. "Dear God, what else has been going on that I don't know about? One week away from this place and all hell breaks loose."

"Piers was being vile to Clare, so Laurie punched him." Tilly shrugged. "Just something else I overheard while they were in the kitchen. Anyway, sounds like he deserved it."

Clearly feeling horribly out of place, Annie rose to her feet and said, "Why don't I clear away the plates?"

"I can't believe I was so stupid," Clare sobbed. "I really loved him. I thought he loved me. I've been such an idiot."

"Everyone makes mistakes." Miriam's tone was soothing, her capable hands rubbing Clare's heaving shoulders.

"Give us a kiss," squawked Harpo, doing his careful sideways shuffle along the curtain pole.

"You never make mistakes. I wish I could be like you." Clare wiped her eyes.

If only you knew, thought Miriam.

"And I won't be a nuisance, I promise. I'll move out."

Everyone knew this was about as likely to happen as Rod Stewart announcing he was gay.

"Plenty of time to think about that," James said gruffly.

Annie had finished clearing the plates. Hovering in the doorway she said hesitantly, "Shall I... um, bring in the pudding?"

"Pudding." Clare heaved a sigh, clearly disgusted that anyone could think about food at a time like this.

"Oh great," Tilly burst out. "Now we're not even allowed to eat! I suppose we won't be watching the video either."

For a split second Miriam thought she meant the incriminating DVD that had arrived through the post from Edinburgh. No, panic over, it was safely hidden away in the attic.

"Don't be so silly." Her tone brisk, Miriam nodded at Annie and gave Clare a buck-up pat on the back. "Of course we're having pudding. And after that we'll all watch Tilly's video."

A plane was droning overhead. Pointing skyward, Clare said, "Shouldn't we wait until Steven Spielberg gets here? He'll go berserk if he misses it."

Chapter 44

THE GARDEN WAS REALLY taking shape now. Wiping her hands on her jeans and straightening up, Nadia surveyed the border she had just planted with mahonia, nicotiana, and mignonette. (How she loved those names; they sounded like a troupe of can-can dancers at the Moulin Rouge.) Behind them, Himalayan honeysuckle covered the stone wall. She still had boxes of Hidcote lavender waiting to go in, then a serious amount of watering to do if the plants weren't about to keel over and die in the current heat wave.

Speaking of keeling over and dying, she could do with a drink herself.

"Looking good." Jay, who had just rolled up, greeted her in the kitchen.

Aware that she was hot and sweaty and streaked with soil, Nadia said, "Hardly, I'm a mess."

"I meant the garden."

Oops. Serves me right.

"Tea?" Jay grinned to soften the blow. He filled the kettle and switched it on, then watched Nadia scrub her hands in the sink.

"Actually, I've got something for you." When she'd finished, Nadia dried her hands on a grubby towel and dug into her jeans pocket. "It's a bit embarrassing, but Clare made me promise. Here." Retrieving the glossy invite with difficulty, she passed it over. "Sorry it's crumpled. You don't have to go if you don't want to. She just said it would be really nice if you could come along."

Jay studied the invitation.

"And buy a painting, I imagine." Drily he added, "Preferably something of hers this time."

"That's up to you. Anyway, it should be a good show. Hi, Robbie." Nadia broke off, realizing that Robbie was hovering uncertainly in the doorway. "I'm just making tea. Want some?"

Robbie nodded. Still as shy and awkward as ever, he far preferred to communicate nonverbally. He waited. Nadia, who knew the score by now, said, "Shall I make three cups?"

Another nod.

"Thursday," said Jay. "I think I can manage that."

"Look, don't feel obliged to buy anything. And don't let Clare bully you." Nadia busied herself flinging tea bags into not terribly clean mugs. "She can get a bit carried away sometimes."

"Can't we all?" Jay grinned. "Anyway, don't worry. I can look after myself. I'm not scared of your sister."

You haven't seen her since she got pregnant, thought Nadia. In the last week Clare had turned into a human tornado, having convinced herself that the only way forward was work. If she painted more pictures and sold enough of them in the show, she would be able to support her child.

"Besides," Jay went on easily, "you never know, I may want to buy something. She's a talented artist. I like her work."

"Robbie, here you are." Nadia had made the teas, piled in the sugar and milk, and mashed the tea bags repeatedly against the sides of the mugs in true builder's fashion before flicking them into the bin. Tea the color of Idris Elba, that was how they liked it.

His thin cheeks aflame, Robbie ventured into the kitchen. Jay's invitation lay on the worktop next to the assorted mugs. Gazing intently at it, then turning to Nadia—but managing not to actually catch her eye—Robbie said awkwardly, "Um… could I have one of those?"

It was like Hillary Clinton sidling into a sex shop and asking for a leather G-string.

Jay, glancing at Nadia, clearly thought so too.

"You mean an invite to the private view? Well, it's my... um, sister's show," Nadia prevaricated. This was awkward. When Clare had given her the invitations she had specified that only wealthy, glamorous, and preferably highly photogenic people should receive them. No freeloaders, no time-wasters, Clare had bossily instructed. And absolutely *no* tongue-tied, socially inept builder's laborers even if they had—somewhat astoundingly—managed to gain a degree in physics.

"The thing is," Nadia said apologetically, "I don't have any more invitations."

"Yes you do." Robbie pointed. "There's one sticking out of your pocket."

"Oh!" It was Nadia's turn to blush. Stalling for time, and realizing that Jay had no intention of helping her out—he was laughing, the bastard—she stammered, "I d-didn't know you were interested in art, Robbie."

Oh God, if she ended up being forced to give him an invite, would he turn up in his disreputable work clothes and steel-capped boots?

"I'm not. Art's boring. But my brother likes it. He's always going round art galleries."

Robbie's brother. Nadia pictured him, as painfully shy as his sibling, slipping through the glittering crowd, hoovering up all the canapés and free drinks. Then, mercifully, melting away again. No harm done.

Bugger it, how could she refuse Robbie? Especially when he was still standing there gazing fixedly at the invitation protruding from her jeans pocket.

"OK. Of course he can have one." Overcompensating for her

guilt with a bright smile, Nadia handed him the invite with a flourish. Luckily she wasn't expecting a thank you.

"Right." Reaching past her for the three steaming mugs, Robbie reverted to monosyllables. "I'll take the tea."

"Well," said Jay, when Robbie had shuffled out of the kitchen, "I thought that went very well."

He was still laughing at her.

"Clare's going to kill me," Nadia groaned. "It's supposed to be a glittering occasion, packed with beautiful people."

Jay raised a dark eyebrow. "Was that a compliment?"

"Actually, Clare said beautiful if possible." Nadia smiled sunnily at him. "Failing that, filthy rich."

—⁓—

Being pregnant and single had a way of making you feel horribly alone. It didn't help, Clare discovered, that the rest of the world seemed to be going around in pairs. Like socks, she thought with irritation. And guess who was the odd sock out?

Checking through the invitation list, she counted the couples. Even her own family were at it. Miriam was coming along with Edward. Nadia with Laurie. James was insisting on bringing Annie, which was annoying, but when she'd tried to persuade her father that it might not be Annie's thing, he'd got quite cross.

When Tilly had tried the same trick, however, Clare had put her foot down.

"No, you cannot bring Cal," she'd told Tilly bluntly. "It's an art gallery, not a school dance. He's fifteen years old. He's not going to be buying anything, is he? It's just a waste of a ticket."

Tilly had gone off in a fit. Later, when Leonie had phoned, Clare had heard Tilly huff to her mother about how unfair it was. Since Leonie wasn't likely to shell out for a painting, Clare hadn't bothered to invite her either.

Returning to the kitchen some minutes later, Tilly had announced, "Mum's asked me down to Brighton for the weekend. School finishes on Thursday so I'm going on Thursday afternoon."

"Fine." Was she meant to be distraught? Clare picked up her pen and said, "So you won't be coming to the exhibition."

"No, you can cross me off your list." Tilly sounded pleased with herself.

Great. Clare happily ran a line through Tilly's name. She'd only invited her in the first place because she was family.

Stung by Clare's relief, Tilly couldn't resist having a dig. "So what happens if nobody wants to buy your stuff? If you don't sell a single painting, what then?"

The other thing about being pregnant was that it didn't automatically turn you into a lovely saintly person. The urge to give Tilly a slap when she provoked her was as strong as ever.

"That's not going to happen. I'm going to sell loads." Sarcastically, Clare added, "But thanks for the support."

~~~

Thursday night. Seven o'clock. The Harrington Gallery was lit up and bursting with guests. Clare and the two other exhibiting artists were being photographed for the local paper and interviewed by various journalists.

With her glossy dark hair swinging loose around her shoulders and her high-necked, sleeveless pink dress skimming her tanned body, Clare was easily the most photogenic of the three. As she carelessly flicked back her hair and flashed a dazzling smile for the camera, anyone could be forgiven for envying and admiring her talent and stunning looks. Nadia, watching from a distance, marveled at the facade Clare was able to present. The last week at home hadn't been what you'd call plain sailing. Clare had been working punishing hours upstairs. She had also been alternately grumpy, tearful, sharp-tongued, and at times downright irrational. She'd even shouted at Laurie, yelling that it was all his fault Piers hadn't been in touch and that everything would have been sorted out by now if only he hadn't broken Piers's nose.

Now, leaning against a white pillar at the far end of the gallery, Nadia sipped her drink and checked out the throng of guests. As instructed, they had dressed for the occasion. Everyone seemed to be chatting animatedly, exchanging greetings and helping themselves to canapés. Some of them were even bothering to glance at the paintings on view.

Taking advantage of the distance between them, Nadia used the opportunity to study Laurie. There he was, looking scruffily gorgeous as usual in his dark suit, conversing easily with a stern, rather plain, middle-aged woman who was examining one of Clare's works. As he said something else and gestured toward the picture, the woman looked at him and broke into a delighted smile. No one was capable of resisting Laurie's charms.

Except me, thought Nadia. So far, at least. Seeing him still had that overwhelming effect on her, the disappearing-stomach sensation coupled with the familiar rush of adrenaline. But how much longer could she hold out, keeping him at arm's length like this? As Clare had already pointed out, he wasn't going to wait forever. And when she did finally give in, would it change things? Would the thrill of the chase be over for Laurie? How long might it be before he began to lose interest?

Never, according to him. But how could she know that for sure? What if he—

"Spotted him yet?" murmured a voice in her ear, and Nadia jumped, almost spilling her drink.

It was Jay. She'd been so busy observing Laurie, she hadn't even seen him arrive.

"Spotted who?" Heavens, it was hard to sound casual when you didn't feel it. The thing that had almost happened between them still hung in the air, unspoken but as tangible as ever. If Laurie hadn't burst back into her life with typically careless lack of timing, where would she and Jay be now? Together and serious? Together and casual? Would it have turned out to be nothing more than a brief fling? God, it was frustrating, not knowing the answer.

"Robbie's brother. I thought you'd have been on the lookout for him."

"Oh, right. Well, I am. No sign so far." Nadia pulled a wry face. "I had to tell Clare in the end. She said if he's even remotely embarrassing, it's my job to kick him out. Basically, I'm tonight's bouncer."

"He might not be embarrassing. See that chap over there? It could be him."

Jay was pointing to a handsome, extremely smartly dressed man in his mid-forties.

"Nice try. Except that's Marcus Guillory, he's an antiques dealer."

"OK. Him, then."

"HTV newsreader." Honestly, didn't Jay ever watch television?

"Right, what about that one?"

"God, you're hopeless at this." Nadia gave him a sympathetic look. "I'm telling you now, Robbie doesn't have a brother who wears a purple velvet suit and a gold lamé waistcoat."

Undaunted, Jay said, "How about the one talking to Miriam?"

"That's a woman."

"How do you know? Could be Robbie's brother in drag."

"It's the antique dealer's mother." Her attention diverted by a glamorous brunette sporting a football-sized bump under her lilac shirt, Nadia said, "Speaking of mothers, how's Belinda?"

"Not too bad. Looking forward to being able to see her feet again." Jay paused. "Missing Anthony, of course."

"You must miss him too."

He nodded. "Sometimes I forget. When Anthony's soccer team

got beaten three nil on Saturday, I actually picked up the phone to ring and tell him what a bunch of pansies they were." With a wry smile, Jay added, "Actually, he'd probably be glad he didn't live to see their pitiful performance."

"Come on," said Nadia, "let's get you another drink."

Jay stayed where he was. "One more thing. Why are you over here and Laurie's over there? Have you finished with him?"

B-bump b-bump went Nadia's heart. She breathed in Jay's aftershave, fresh and tinged with lime.

"You have to be a couple in the first place before you can finish with someone."

Jay's gaze didn't waver. "And? What are you going to do?"

"I don't know." Nadia shook her head. God, this was like being on *The Weakest Link*.

"Isn't it about time you made up your mind?"

Of course it was. But it wasn't as simple as that.

"I want another drink." Discovering that her glass was empty, she pushed away from the pillar. "Are you going to buy a painting?"

Pause.

Finally Jay said, "I'm not sure."

"Why not?"

"The thing is, there are a couple I like, but I can't decide. Over there." With his glass, he indicated the paintings, which were attracting a fair amount of interest.

"Come on then, let's go and have a look. If you faff about, someone else'll get there first and you'll miss out on both of them. What?" Nadia protested, when he still didn't move.

A small smile lifted the corners of Jay's mouth. A dry, know-all smile with a hint of challenge.

"Exactly."

Damn, thought Nadia with resignation. She'd walked right into that.

Chapter 45

"THIS ONE," SAID ANNIE. "This one's definitely my favorite. Look at the expressions on those faces—don't you just love the little boy hiding under the table?"

The evening was turning out to be far less intimidating than Annie had feared. Everyone was cheerful and friendly, and the paintings lining the walls of the gallery meant there was always something to talk about. Especially where Clare's pictures were concerned, each with its own cast of characters and story to tell. Discussing the hidden meanings of abstract art would have been a minefield, Annie thought with a shudder, far too nerve-racking and requiring the use of scary long words, but Clare's quirky, comical style meant you could simply enjoy her work.

And everyone did seem to be enjoying it. The man she'd been chatting with said, "And how about that baby with the dummy in its mouth? Fantastic." He glanced at the brochure in his hand. "Clare Kinsella. She's a clever girl, I'll say that for her."

"She is." Annie nodded in agreement as James reappeared with a fresh drink for her, and said, "Oh thanks, darling." Then she blushed, because she'd never actually called him darling before. It had just popped out.

"Dad, Dad." Behind James, Clare tugged his arm in a state of excitement. "Three paintings sold already, isn't that amazing? And an agent's offered to represent me in New York!"

The man next to Annie touched her arm and said, "Sorry, I

didn't realize." Genially he added, "You must be incredibly proud of your daughter."

Before Annie could react, Clare had swung round, her glossy hair managing to swish across Annie's face.

"Oh, please," Clare half-laughed in disbelief, "you have to be kidding. You didn't seriously think she was my mother!"

"Sorry." The man blinked, taken aback by her vehement reaction.

"I mean, do we even *look* alike?" Clare gestured at Annie, with her wavy reddish hair, plump curves, and mortified expression. "Apart from anything else, she's not even old enough to be my mother."

"Clare." James was apoplectic.

Spitefully, Clare went on, "She just looks it."

Annie turned and fled, stumbling toward the door then out of the gallery into the street.

Into the shocked silence, James said furiously, "You've gone too far this time."

"I don't care." Awash with hormones, Clare defiantly stood her ground. "She's after you, Dad. She's like a limpet. I just want her to leave our family alone."

Most strangers would have been embarrassed. Eagerly, the man waited for James to retaliate.

"You clung to Piers like a limpet." James's voice was icy. "The difference is, he didn't want you. Nobody's going to tell me to stop seeing Annie. She's welcome at our house any time and I won't tolerate you speaking to her in that way. In fact," he concluded, pointing a trembling finger at his spoiled, wayward daughter, "I think it's probably high time you moved out." James turned and left, following Annie out of the gallery.

"Oh, for God's sake," Clare sighed under her breath. At least the rest of her family hadn't been around to witness the spat.

"Family tiff," observed the man who had caused the ruckus in the first place.

Irritated, Clare surveyed him properly for the first time. He was incredibly ugly, with the face and neck of a toad. And what he wore was frankly ridiculous, a hideous purple velvet suit with an ultra-shiny gold waistcoat. He was also perspiring freely and the neckline of his emerald-green shirt was damp with sweat. When he stuck out his hand, her first instinct was to pass him a paper napkin to wipe it with.

Gritting her teeth, she forced herself to shake the pudgy hand. Yurgh, wet.

"Malcolm Carter," said the toad. "I like your work."

Double yurgh, was he actually leering at her? Clare, who had been leered at by ugly men before, said briskly, "Well, I should be mingling."

Malcolm blinked. "You could always mingle with me."

I'd rather cut off my own tongue, thought Clare. Honestly, she'd gone to all the trouble of ensuring that only the right people received her invitations; clearly the other exhibitors hadn't been so fussy.

Her gaze flickered restlessly in the direction of the door; no sign of her father so far, returning with Annie. She supposed she'd have to make some sort of apology, just to keep the peace.

"I'm over here," Malcolm prompted. As if she didn't know.

"What? Oh, sorry. It's just that I really ought to speak to the people who've bought my work."

"Speak to me nicely and I might buy something."

What a creep. Clare wondered whatever possessed a middle-aged man to put on a purple velvet suit and think he looked good in it. Moreover, it wasn't even a decent suit. Why should she waste another minute talking to someone like this?

"Look, I'd love to stay, but I need to see that man over there." Vaguely she indicated Jay. "Could you give me five minutes?"

"Then you'll be back?"

"Of course." In your dreams, Mr. Toad.

"You won't regret it." Groping inside his jacket, Malcolm

pulled out a card and pressed it into her hand. "Here, keep this anyway. Don't lose it. We should get together soon. Dinner maybe, next week."

Good grief, was the man insane? How old was he, anyway? At least forty-five, not to mention grotesque. And he seriously thought he was in with a chance?

"Absolutely." Clare flashed her most insincere busy-artist smile, the one involving almost more teeth than she possessed. "I'll see you around. Ooh, must catch up with… um… my friend over there. Bye!"

"New boyfriend?" said Jay.

"You're so funny. I just had to get away from him." Clare shuddered at the thought of being snogged by Mr. Toad and his repulsive toad-like tongue. "So, are you going to buy one of my paintings?"

"Don't be shy. Just say what's on your mind."

"Oh pleeease." Clare clutched his arm. "Go on, you know you want to. And God knows I want you to." Rolling her eyes, she said mournfully, "Poverty-stricken, single mother-to-be, I'm going to need every penny I can scrape together."

She was being deliberately flippant, making light of the situation, but Jay sensed the anxiety beneath.

"Nadia told me. How are you feeling?"

Clare hesitated. How was she *really* feeling? To be honest, now that the initial shock had worn off, the prospect of a baby was no longer as horrifying as it had been. Secretly—and whether this was the hormones kicking in, she didn't know—she was beginning to feel differently about the future. Unbeknown to the rest of her family she had bought herself a book entitled *You And Your Baby*, and had even felt quite maternal toward the diagrams of fetuses at different stages of development, even though most of them looked like E.T. It was all very new and strange, yet at the same time curiously moving…

Except this wasn't the image she wanted to project tonight,

especially not if she was going to persuade Jay to dig into his pocket in order to keep her and her newborn babe-in-arms off the streets.

"Pretty crappy." Clare shrugged bravely and looked resigned. Then she indicated the other exhibitors and said with a rueful smile, "But selling more pictures than those two losers would definitely cheer me up."

—~~~—

"I'm not going back in there," said Annie, "so don't even waste your breath if that's why you've come after me."

"Don't be daft." James had found her finally, waiting at the bus stop opposite the church. She was dry-eyed but trembling and clearly upset.

"She really doesn't like me. Well, that's fine, because I don't like her either. I'm sorry, James, but that's it. Pregnant or not, your daughter is a spiteful cow. And here's my bus, so if you'd just let go of my arm—"

"You're not getting on the bus. I'm taking you home," James said firmly.

"You can't. You have to go back to the gallery. Everyone will be wondering where you are."

"Clare's gone too far this time. I've told her she has to move out."

The bus trundled to a halt, the doors swishing open.

"You can't do that," said Annie. "She's your daughter. And I'm catching this bus."

"No you aren't."

The driver, watching the exchange with interest, said, "Getting on?"

"Yes." Annie attempted to wrench free from James's grasp.

"No," said James.

They glared at each other.

The bus driver, who had young children, said with exaggerated patience, "Right, I'm going to count to three. One... two..."

"Let me *go*," Annie panted.

"I'm never going to let you go." Without even realizing what was about to come out of his mouth, James added, "I love you."

"…three," concluded the driver, and the doors of the bus swished shut. As he pulled away, he tooted his horn and shot them a cheery grin.

"There's no point," said Annie helplessly, scrabbling in her pocket for a tissue as tears began to leak from her eyes. "It's never going to work."

"Let me deal with Clare. She's going through a rough time—"

"See? You're defending her already! She was mean to me *before* she got pregnant. She wants me out of your life and she's not going to stop until she gets her way."

"That's not going to happen," James insisted. "I won't *let* it happen. I've already told you, she's getting a place of her own."

"James, listen to me. Clare might leave the house but she'll still be your daughter."

"Sshh. Come on." Since passers-by were starting to stare and public demonstrations of affection weren't James's forte, he took her firmly by the hand and led her back toward Princess Victoria Street, where his car was parked.

Ten minutes later they reached Kingsweston and Annie's cottage. The sun was setting now. Her hanging baskets needed watering. The look of sadness and resignation on Annie's face clutched at James's heart.

"I don't think we should see each other anymore," she said quietly.

"I love you."

"It's too difficult, too… complicated. Easier to end it now, before—"

"No, listen to me." Vehemently, James shook his head. "I mean I *really* love you. And I want us to be together, more than anything.

You're the best thing that's happened to me since… God, you're the best thing that's *ever* happened to me."

"Don't, please don't. Oh hell, I can't believe I'm starting again." Annie rubbed at her brimming eyes with the scrumpled damp tissue. "*And* my nosy neighbor's peering out of her bedroom window. Nothing she likes better than a bit of drama to gossip about."

"Let's go inside." James climbed out of the car, gazing pointedly at the nosy neighbor as he marched up to the front door. The moment Annie had managed to fit her key into the lock, he bundled her over the threshold and kissed her, hard.

"You're not making things easy for me," Annie protested, when she was free to speak again. "I'm only trying to do the sensible thing."

"Bugger being sensible," declared James, who had spent the last forty-odd years being sensible and now couldn't for the life of him imagine why. "I'm not letting you go and that's that."

Annie didn't speak. She couldn't. James had just told her—*three times*—that he loved her. Theirs had been a ridiculously chaste romance to date. Having both acknowledged from the outset that they were both hopelessly out of practice, all they had exchanged so far had been kisses. She had been simultaneously grateful and frustrated. Young people these days might leap into bed with each other at the drop of a G-string, but she had never been able to do that. Love mattered. It was important to her. Sex with a virtual stranger, just for the hell of it, held no appeal.

Finding James and getting to know him properly, the old-fashioned way, had been a blissful experience. And now she was ready to take their relationship further, in the knowledge that this would only make it more perfect.

Except what was the point, when the relationship was doomed?

Annie blinked, squeezing her eyes shut and willing herself not to cry.

"James. Please." Falteringly, she tried to explain what he was refusing to acknowledge. "I've seen this happen before. My cousin went through it. He met this wonderful girl. She was divorced, with two children. The boy was fine, no problem at all. But the girl turned into the teenager from hell. She refused to accept my cousin and tried everything to split them up. He did his best to win her over, but it was hopeless. After a year, they broke up. Just couldn't handle the stress anymore." Annie shrugged helplessly. "And it's not only them, it happens all the time. If the children aren't happy, no one can be. The family just gets torn apart and everyone ends up miserable."

"I love you," murmured James. *Fourth* time, oh God, he must really mean it. "I want to be with you," he went on, brushing a strand of damp, red-blonde hair from her forehead.

Annie melted; how was it possible to feel so loved and so unhappy at the same time? It was hopeless, a no-win situation. And James wasn't helping, stroking her shoulder like that and kissing her neck.

The thin strap of her turquoise dress slid down and Annie shakily exhaled, each kiss setting her skin on fire.

Oh, who was she kidding? Of course she wasn't unhappy. At this moment in time, how could she be?

"Not fair," she whispered, trembling with lust and anticipation as the second strap slipped off.

"Just trying to cheer you up." James smiled and pulled her closer. Hmm, he was definitely managing that.

Annie gave up and kissed him back. Oh well, plenty of time later to be miserable. She was certainly overdue a bit of cheering up.

"Only if you want to," he added. Dear James, so gentle and diffident, as considerate of her feelings as ever. He really had no idea how attractive he was.

"I want to," Annie solemnly assured him. Taking his hand and leading him toward the stairs, she added with a mischievous smile, "In fact, I insist on it."

Chapter 46

"I DON'T KNOW WHAT's happened to Dad and Annie." Nadia was puzzled. "One minute they were here, and the next they'd vanished. I hope nothing's wrong."

"Probably just got bored." Clare shrugged, her eyes narrowing as she watched another group of people drift out of the gallery. "Like them. God, what a bloody waste of an evening this has been."

It was nine o'clock, and everyone was starting to leave.

"Don't say that. It hasn't."

Truculently, Clare snapped, "Of course it has. Total disaster. I sold three paintings, that's all. *Three*, for crying out loud." Jabbing an irritable finger in the direction of the other two exhibiting artists, she went on, "*He* sold six and *he* sold eight. God, humiliating or what? And your so-called friend was a fat lot of use." Her gaze narrowed still further as Jay headed toward them.

"Just came to say goodbye, I'm off now," he cheerfully announced. "Great show."

"Thanks so much for coming," said Clare. "I'm so glad you enjoyed yourself. Even if you didn't buy a single painting, after promising you would. Still, at least you got some free drinks out of it, that's the important thing."

"I didn't promise," Jay pointed out. "There were two paintings I really liked, but they both sold before I could get to them."

"Handy, that."

"Look, I'm not going to buy a picture I only *quite* like." Refusing to rise to the bait, Jay said reasonably, "I'd rather wait. Maybe we could talk about a commission. Not now, obviously…" He indicated his watch and Clare's lip curled in disdain.

"Oh, *obviously* not now. We're all *far* too busy. In fact you'll have to excuse me, I think Thomas wants a word." She turned and stalked off.

"Oh dear," said Jay. "Not happy."

Nadia pulled a face. "She only sold three."

"Plenty of time yet. It's only the preview night."

"The others sold more."

"Lucky I didn't buy any of theirs, then. Look, I know she's upset. But I'm not buying something just because I feel sorry for her. That would be the ultimate insult."

Nadia sighed. He was right. Hideous memories of the sunken scones she'd once made for the school summer fair came flooding back. The scones had come out like pancakes. When Miriam had overheard a group of her classmates sniggering at them and had promptly bought the lot, her classmates had only sniggered harder and her own shame had known no bounds.

Plus, to be fair, Clare was charging a lot more than five pence each for her creations.

"See you tomorrow." Jay turned to leave. Over his shoulder he added, "At least Robbie's brother didn't turn up."

Nadia watched him go, then made her way over to the desk where Thomas Harrington was talking to Clare. Lurking next to Thomas was the short plump man in the purple velvet suit.

The way Thomas greeted her with an extra jovial, "Nadia, join us!" told Nadia that he was struggling and in dire need of support. Poor Thomas. Owning an art gallery would be so much easier if only he wasn't forced to deal with temperamental artists.

"Great news, great news," Thomas exclaimed, beaming at Nadia. "Clare's just sold two more paintings! We have a collector here with a truly discerning eye! Have you met Malcolm Carter, Nadia? Malcolm, this is Clare's sister."

Nadia shook hands with the man and instantly wished she hadn't.

"How d'you do? Clare has a great talent. I'm just inviting her to dinner," Malcolm told Nadia. "At my house."

Clare's tightly clenched jaw said it all.

"I'd like to discuss her plans for the future," Malcolm Carter went on.

Thomas said with enthusiasm, "I think that's an excellent idea! Don't you, Nadia?"

Clare brought to mind a dog being dragged against its will toward the bath. Nadia guessed exactly what was going through her head. It was school discos all over again, being violently self-conscious and aware of the fact that the slow music had started and everyone was paired up but you. Then, lumbering toward you across the crowded dance floor with a determined glint in his eye, comes the ugliest boy in the school…

Actually, that was me, Nadia realized. She doubted it had ever happened to Clare.

"I've just bought two of your paintings," Malcolm pointed out.

"You've sold five now," wheedled Thomas.

"Five. Phil sold six and Jethro sold eight." Clare's lip curled as she uttered Jethro's name. "He only calls himself Jethro to sound more arty, you know. His real name's Jason."

"So how about Thursday?" Malcolm was nothing if not persistent.

"Thursday. Um…"

"Or Friday. Or Wednesday. Whichever night suits you best."

"D'you know what I really hate?" Clare demanded. "I really hate it that those other two jerks sold more than me. If you bought another painting, I'd be level with Phil." Perkily, she beamed at Malcolm. "So how about it? And we'll have dinner any night you like."

Thomas rolled his eyes. Nadia squirmed; sometimes Clare was beyond belief. Puffing out his cheeks, Malcolm studied Clare for several seconds without speaking.

Then he smiled, and it occurred to Nadia that he was actually a lot shrewder than Clare was giving him credit for.

"You drive a hard bargain. I hope you're worth it."

Clare inwardly shuddered, hoping he wasn't implying what he appeared to be implying.

"Of course I'm worth it." Her expression was serene. "So, which painting?"

He turned and pointed. "The cinema queue."

"I love that one. Great choice," enthused Thomas Harrington, still scarcely able to believe that Clare's audacious demand had been met.

"Credit card?" said Clare.

Malcolm Carter handed his card over to Thomas. When the transaction had been concluded, he shook Clare's hand. "It's a pleasure doing business with you. I'll see you on Thursday. Eight o'clock at my house."

Nadia said helpfully, "She'll need your address."

"Clare has it. I gave her my card." Malcolm paused, gauging the look on Clare's face, then reached into his jacket pocket. "Then again, maybe she'd like another. Just in case she accidentally screwed the last one up and dropped it into an ashtray."

So he'd spotted that. Clare shrugged, unperturbed. "You hadn't bought anything then."

"I've bought three now."

"And I'll be there at your place on Thursday night, for dinner. Just dinner, by the way. Nothing else."

Blinking in his slow, deceptively toad-like manner, Malcolm said, "Just dinner."

Clare smiled. "And I'm sure you won't mind if I bring my sister along."

Oh great, thought Nadia, drag me into it. Although there was a reassuring twinkle in Malcolm's eye that belied his outward appearance.

Malcolm inclined his head and said pleasantly, "I'd be delighted. Actually"—he turned to Nadia—"I believe you know my younger brother, Robbie."

"Trust you to make things complicated," murmured Annie, rolling over onto her side in bed. Her whole body was tingling and alive. The last hour had been, without question, the most perfect of her entire life.

"I'm not letting you go." To prove it, James's arms tightened round her. "Nothing's going to come between us. I just won't let it happen."

The Clare problem was still there. It wasn't going to go away. Annie knew they had to address it.

"We'll still see each other," she told James. "But I don't want to see Clare. I'd rather just keep out of her way."

"She's moving out." Beneath the duvet, James ran his hand over the curve of her hip.

"Even so." Privately, Annie wondered whether that would ever happen. If Clare didn't want to go, he surely wouldn't cast his pregnant daughter out into the metaphorical snow. "You can visit me here," she said with a smile. "I'll be your mistress."

"Married men have mistresses. I'm single. You're single. We shouldn't need to sneak around."

"Come on. It'll be fun. Didn't seem to do Charles and Camilla any harm." Playfully, Annie tweaked one of his dark chest hairs. "If you ask me, having to sneak around is what keeps affairs going. It's the excitement factor. You don't have a chance to get bored."

"I'm never going to get bored with you." James kissed her. "That's a promise. Will you still come to my house?"

"I don't know. Maybe. If I knew for sure that Clare wasn't going to be there." And preferably in a different country.

"I love you. Did I mention that?"

"May have done. I wasn't really paying attention." Annie cupped his dear face in her hands; how could she have thought, even for a second, that giving up James was an option? "It's almost ten o'clock. They'll be wondering where you are."

"Let them." Gathering her into his arms and realizing that he felt miraculously twenty years younger, James said, "I'm staying here with you."

Chapter 47

Malcolm Carter lived in a modern apartment in Capricorn Quay on Bristol's waterfront. The apartment, which was on the third floor, overlooked the harbor. Having welcomed them into his home, Malcolm had left Nadia and Clare out on the balcony with drinks while he put the finishing touches to dinner in the kitchen.

Clare wasn't Nadia's favorite person at the moment. Her continuing refusal to accept Annie meant she wasn't James's favorite person either. The atmosphere at home had been tricky. Nadia, who had been invited along to the Comedy Club by Janey and the old crowd from the garden center, felt that Clare could at least be grateful she was here instead.

"Just be nice to him," Nadia warned now, because Clare was shifting irritably in her seat.

"He gives me the creeps. And I'm not even hungry. We don't need to be here." Clare was truculent. "He's bought the paintings. It's done now. Too late to cancel the check."

Being nice was clearly out of the question.

"At least be polite. He's a collector. He might buy more if you don't antagonize him."

"He looks like a toad. And he fancies me. Ugh," said Clare with a shudder of disgust.

"Dinner's ready, girls." Malcolm appeared on the balcony and Nadia prayed he hadn't overheard. "If you'd like to come on through."

The glass dining table was laden with food. Around the walls, Malcolm's art collection was displayed. No expert, Nadia was nevertheless impressed by the couple of big names she recognized.

"This salmon mousse is fantastic." Nadia ate with enthusiasm to make up for the fact that Clare was picking at hers as if it were sheep's eyeballs. "And I *love* that painting."

"Beryl Cook original. I started buying her stuff fifteen years ago. Cost twenty times that now." Malcolm was wearing a shiny lime-green shirt today and tight magenta trousers. "And the Andy Buchanan oils? I discovered him when he was still at college. Paid two hundred each for five of his paintings. Sold one of them last year for thirty thousand." Proudly, Malcolm added, "I have an eye."

For art, maybe. Nadia thought it was a shame it didn't extend to his wardrobe. Nevertheless, she was impressed. Malcolm clearly knew his stuff.

"And you think Clare could sell like that?" Crikey, this was exciting. Even if Clare didn't seem to think so.

"Possibly. We'll have to see how she goes. It doesn't happen overnight. Some of that work she did for the exhibition was dashed off in too much of a rush. You can't fob the public off with second-rate goods. You were churning them out, not giving them enough thought." Malcolm turned his attention to Clare, who was toying disinterestedly with the dill sauce on her plate. "That's why they didn't sell."

"How kind of you to point that out," Clare drawled.

Under the table, Nadia kicked her. "It's true. You *were* churning them out," she told Clare.

"Everyone finished? Let me have your plates." Malcolm rose to his feet. Patiently he said, "There's no need to sulk. I know what I'm talking about. Look, a friend of mine sells work for clients over the Internet. I'll show you the website later. It can be a great way to launch yourself."

"Patronizing git," Clare muttered while he was out in the kitchen.

"He's trying to help you," Nadia hissed back.

"Trying to get me into bed, more like. I don't want to *be* here."

"You're *lucky* to be here," Nadia whispered furiously, offended on Malcolm's behalf. "Trust me, you need someone like him to advise you. Just because he doesn't look like—"

"Here we go, I hope you like lamb!" Emerging from the kitchen with a steaming casserole dish held between reindeer-shaped oven gloves, Malcolm announced, "It's a tagine. Speciality of the house."

Clare clutched her stomach. She shook her head and said, "Oh God."

Malcolm looked concerned. "Are you OK?"

"No, I'm not. I really don't feel well. Malcolm, I'm sorry, I'm going to have to leave. I just want to go home."

Nadia stared at her. This was Clare all over, it epitomized her total selfishness. If she wasn't happy with a situation, any excuse would do to get her out of it. That she was inconveniencing anyone else wouldn't even occur to her. The fact that Malcolm must have slaved in his kitchen for hours to produce dinner simply wasn't relevant.

"You can't go," said Nadia.

"I need to. I feel really ill. Sorry." Clare was already pushing back her chair, getting to her feet. "I couldn't eat a thing. I feel sick. Nadia, you have to drive me home now."

Nadia fought back the urge to dump the tagine of lamb over Clare's head.

"It's fine." Malcolm nodded at Nadia. "Take her home. It's not her fault if she's ill."

If being the operative word, Nadia thought savagely. It was blatantly obvious that she wasn't.

"Your lovely food," Nadia apologized. "After all the trouble you went to."

"I didn't. The caterers delivered it. Hope you feel better soon," Malcolm called after Clare as she rushed from the flat.

She won't by the time I've finished with her, thought Nadia.

"I'm really sorry," she told Malcolm.

"It's OK. Not the first time I've been walked out on." His face creased into a rueful toad-like smile. "By the way, your sister was wrong about one thing."

"Oh? What's that?"

"I don't fancy her. And I'm certainly not trying to get her into bed," said Malcolm. "I'm gay."

"Blast," said James, putting down the phone and coming into the kitchen. "That was New York. They need some papers faxed through urgently."

Annie was making the sauce to go with their steaks. She added the chopped garlic to the sizzling onions. "Do you have them?"

"They're at the office. Damn, I'm going to have to go in. It won't take long." James paused. "What d'you want to do?"

Breaking into a smile, Annie realized that this was why she loved him. One of the many reasons, anyway. He was so considerate.

"I'm fine. I'll stay here and carry on getting dinner ready. How long will you be?"

"Thirty minutes. Shouldn't take more than that. Are you sure?"

Annie kissed him lingeringly on the mouth. With everyone else out for the evening, she'd been persuaded to come to the house tonight to watch the latest Bond film just out on DVD. They were quite safe, James had assured her. No Clare.

Annie, who had no DVD player at home and adored Bond movies, had happily agreed. And she'd been right about the thrill of coming to James's house; it actually felt deliciously illicit.

"Absolutely sure. You go and do your fax thing. Send my love to New York. By the time you get back I'll have dinner ready."

James gave her a quick hug. "Don't you dare start watching the Bond film without me."

"You're unbelievable," Nadia said furiously. "That poor man. Sometimes you are *such* a cow."

"Oh, stop going on. Nag nag nag. Anyway, I *do* feel ill. And I've got a stomachache."

"Bullshit." Nadia gripped the steering wheel. Clare had always been the same, the world's biggest hypochondriac. At school she had forged sick notes from Miriam practically on a weekly basis.

"I have. It really hurts!"

"Probably because you ate a pound of grapes last night. Right, we're home." Screeching to a halt at the gate, Nadia pointedly left the engine running. "Bye."

Clare looked at her. "Where are you going?"

"Why? What's it to do with you? You're sick, remember. I'm going to catch up with Janey and the rest of them at the Comedy Club."

The way Clare hesitated meant that Nadia knew, just *knew*, she was about to ask if she could come along too.

"And no," Nadia said bluntly, before Clare had a chance to open her mouth, "you're not coming with me. Forget it. You can stay at home and go to bed. That's what sick people do."

Clare stood at the bottom of the driveway and watched the car disappear in a cloud of dust. She'd been about to ask Nadia to stay with her, but since Nadia would only have refused outright, there hadn't been much point.

Which was unfair, because she did actually feel unwell, despite having exaggerated the symptoms in order to get out of creepy Malcolm's flat. The nausea had begun when she'd gazed at the food and imagined it being lovingly prepared by Malcolm's fat sweaty fingers. After that, eating anything at all had been out of the question.

And she did have a kind of stomachache, more of a rumbling gripey sensation than actual pain. Experiencing it again now, Clare turned toward the house. So what if she had eaten a lot of grapes yesterday? And a whole Charentais melon? The *You And Your Baby* book she'd been secretly reading had said that food cravings began at around six weeks' gestation. Having been looking forward to indulging sudden yearnings for strange foods, she felt inordinately proud. Imagine, yesterday she'd experienced her first proper pregnancy craving. If her body was urging her to guzzle far too many grapes, it wasn't her fault.

Honestly, Clare thought, a quick visit to the loo and she'd be fine. Which would mean she could have gone along with Nadia to the Comedy Club after all. Why did she have to be stuck with a sister who was so irritable and selfish?

Letting herself into the house, Clare was expecting it to be empty. Miriam and Edward had gone to the theater in Bath. Tilly was out with Cal, her friend from school. And James's dark blue Jaguar was missing from the driveway. But there was a smell of cooking in the air, and sounds of activity coming from the kitchen.

Ouch, stomach. That *did* hurt.

"Did you forget the office keys? *Oh.*" Annie stopped abruptly in the kitchen doorway. She was wearing a green-and-white-striped apron and clutching a whisk.

Brilliant, thought Clare. Just what I need. She surveyed Annie with contempt.

"Cooking dinner. How cozy," she drawled. "Have you moved in and nobody remembered to tell me?"

Recovering from her initial shock, Annie stood her ground. "I only came here this evening because your father told me you were out."

"Really? Well, now I'm back." Doggedly ignoring the uncomfortable sensation in her stomach, as if her intestines were being slowly squeezed, Clare stalked past her into the kitchen. "Sorry if that's an inconvenience, but I do still live here. I know what Dad said the other day, and I'm looking for another place just as fast as I can. Bet you can't wait," she added, pouring herself a glass of water from the bottle in the fridge. "The moment I'm gone, you'll be able to start dropping hints about moving in here yourself."

Annie watched James's younger daughter lounge against the fridge, slim and elegant in a sleeveless navy top and pale yellow trousers. Oozing confidence and disdain. Tapping her fingers against the side of her glass tumbler. Why did she have to come back now? *Why?*

"I won't be dropping hints. And your father just had to call in to the office. He'll be back soon." *I hope.*

"Marvelous. Could you open the window?" Ostentatiously, Clare raised a hand to her throat. "The smell of that raw meat is just repulsive."

She's pregnant, she's pregnant, Annie grimly reminded herself. She can't help having a sensitive stomach.

"Would you like me to cook you some dinner?"

There, couldn't say she hadn't tried.

Clare's upper lip curled in derision. "Oh, please. Are you *trying* to make me throw up?"

Right, that was enough. Annie deliberately turned her back on James's nightmare daughter and began to stir the pan of sauce on the stove. Clare took the hint, thank God, and stalked out of the kitchen. Shaking slightly, Annie heard her stomp up the stairs. Then the bathroom door slammed shut.

Good.

Annie stopped stirring the sauce. Damn. Now the whole evening was spoiled.

Moments later the hairs on the back of her neck rose as a high-pitched shriek rang out upstairs.

Annie froze. God, what now?

Then she heard another noise, less of a shriek, more of a groan. Alarmed, she rushed out to the hall and gazed up the staircase.

Silence.

Cautiously Annie advanced as far as the bottom step. She cleared her throat and called out, "Are you OK?"

No reply. Did that mean Clare was lying slumped on the bathroom floor, or that she simply couldn't be bothered to reply to her father's beneath-contempt girlfriend?

Then Annie head a low-pitched moan, like the sound of an animal in pain. Racing up the stairs, she hammered on the bathroom door.

"Clare? What's wrong?"

Still nothing. By this time truly terrified, Annie beat the door again. "Clare, please. Can you hear me?"

Moments later, to her intense relief, came the rattle of the toilet-roll holder. Then the loo was flushed. Backing away from the door as she heard the taps running full pelt in the washbasin, Annie nevertheless jumped as the door was finally unlocked.

The moment she saw Clare's ghostly pallor and distraught expression, she knew what had happened.

Chapter 48

"I'M BLEEDING," CLARE WHISPERED, cradling her stomach and swaying in the doorway. "Oh God, I don't believe it. This can't be happening... make it stop... I don't want to lose the baby..." Overwhelmed with shock and grief, she slumped against the wall. Annie caught her.

"OK, come on, let's get you into bed. Which is your room?"

Helplessly, Clare nodded in the direction of the door at the far end of the landing. Together they made their way slowly toward it. Annie hastily swept the scattered clothes and makeup off the duvet and helped Clare onto the bed.

"Shall I phone the doctor?"

"No." Clare began to cry. "I don't want that fat old git prodding me about. I just want the bleeding to stop. Is this a miscarriage?" She raised anguished eyes to Annie. "What should I be doing? Is there any way to stop it?"

"Let me call the doctor." Annie straightened up, but Clare's hand gripped her wrist.

"Don't leave me. Please don't leave me on my own. I'm sorry I was so horrible to you. But... I'm so scared. I don't want to lose my baby." Tears rolled down her cheeks and her face crumpled. "This isn't fair, it's n-not f-f-fair. Just when I'd got used to the idea of a baby... it's like being punished for not being thrilled in the first place."

Having finally managed to extricate herself, Annie was back moments later with the phone. The doctor's answering service put her through to NHS Direct. The adviser at the other end told her to keep Clare in bed and continue to monitor the situation. Tomorrow morning she should see her doctor. Basically, there was nothing else that could be done in cases of early miscarriage. If it was going to happen, it would.

"Oh God." Clare groaned, sinking back into the pillows in despair.

"Is the pain bad?" Annie hated feeling so helpless.

"Not really. Just cramps, like ordinary period pains. I just can't believe it. Three weeks ago I was crying because I didn't want to be pregnant." Clare wiped her eyes with the corner of the dark blue duvet. "And now here I am, crying because I don't want to lose it."

Feeling sorry for Clare had until tonight been something Annie would have put on a par with bumping into Elvis in Walmart. Now, she simply gathered the girl into her arms and let her sob.

"I have to go to the bathroom again," Clare gulped, some time later. "I need a… a pad of some kind. All I've got is loo roll stuffed in my knickers."

Annie jumped up. "Where do you keep them? In the chest of drawers over there?"

"I've only got T-T-Tampax."

"There's a spare in my bag downstairs. Let me go and get it."

When Annie came back, Clare managed a tremulous half smile. "Thanks. You're being really kind."

Annie smiled back. "It's only a pad."

"You know what I'm talking about. I've been such a cow. I didn't want you taking Dad away from us, and I didn't want anyone trying to be our stepmother."

"I wasn't actually planning on doing either of those things," said Annie.

"Well, I'm sorry."

A lump rose in Annie's throat. As if sensing it, Clare pulled a face. "God, this is in danger of turning into *The Waltons*."

"I used to love that program."

Wryly, Clare said, "Except in *The Waltons*, Mary-Beth doesn't get pregnant."

"That'll be your dad." Annie rose to her feet as the front door slammed downstairs. "Let me speak to him."

Two minutes later James burst into the bedroom, his face white and strained. Hugging Clare, he said, "Oh, sweetheart. I'm so sorry."

"Why me, Dad?" Clare was by this time exhausted from crying, but over the worst of the shock. It was happening and there was nothing she could do to stop it. She just wished she could get the irrational thought out of her mind that the baby had decided it didn't want her as its mother.

"These things happen. You didn't do anything wrong. It just wasn't meant to be," said James.

"I know." Deep down, she did know that. "Dad? Annie's been really great."

"She *is* really great." James stroked his daughter's tousled hair.

"Where is she now?"

"In the kitchen. Getting dinner ready."

Clare nodded. "When you've finished eating, could she come up here and sit with me?"

"Of course she will, if that's what you want."

It seemed almost sacrilegious, but Clare realized she was hungry. Adjusting her pillows, she said, "And if there's any to spare, I wouldn't mind a steak sandwich."

There was a good atmosphere in the Comedy Club; several of the acts had gone down a storm and even Josh had earned himself tumultuous applause and requests for an encore. But, although she couldn't put her finger on it, Nadia sensed a change in Suzette. Before, they had hit it off instantly. Tonight, however, she appeared to be holding back, making excuses not to join in with the rest of the crowd. Rather than enjoying the evening, she gave the impression of someone in a dentist's waiting room about to have a couple of wisdom teeth yanked out.

Every time Nadia caught her eye, Suzette hastily averted her gaze. It was most odd and rather unsettling, almost as if she felt guilty about something. But what reason could she possibly have to feel guilty? If Laurie had flirted with her over dinner, she would have told them—that had been the whole purpose of the ploy. And if he *had*, then what possible reason could there be for Suzette to cover up for him?

It made no sense, Nadia thought. She was doubting Laurie again, letting her imagination run away with her. As Josh headed to the bar, she took the opportunity to slide into his seat next to Suzette.

"Hi."

"Oh, hi." Suzette's knuckles tightened around her drink.

"Are you OK?" said Nadia. "It's just that you seem a bit... I don't know... on edge."

"No. I'm fine." Her voice was high. "Honestly."

"Look, is it something to do with Laurie? Because if there's anything you feel you should tell me—"

"Actually, I'm not fine," Suzette blurted out. "I've got a raging headache and I feel terrible. Right here." She pressed her hand against her forehead and briefly closed her eyes. "Really, it's nothing to do with Laurie. I've been hoping it'll go away but it just won't. I think I'd better go home."

Nadia watched her rise jerkily to her feet. "D'you need a lift or—"

"No, no, I've got my car. I'm just going to slip away. A good night's sleep and it'll be gone in the morning... Bye."

Janey came back from the loo. "Where's Suze?"

"Gone home. Headache," said Nadia with a shrug.

"Headache? She didn't mention it before."

"Maybe she was just tired." Frowning, Nadia said, "Did she ever say anything about Laurie?"

Mystified, Janey's eyes widened. "No. Like what?"

"Well, I wonder if Laurie said or did something that she hasn't told me about."

"You mean he might have told her you've got a backside as big as a sofa? *Ow*," giggled Janey, fending off a flying beer coaster. "Come on, give the boy a break. You checked Laurie out and he passed with flying colors."

Nadia gazed thoughtfully at the door through which Suzette had exited and wondered why she wasn't convinced.

Chapter 49

THE HOUSE IN CLARENCE Gardens was finished at last and on the market. Inside, following the departure of the decorators yesterday, the smell of fresh paint lingered. The wooden floors were polished, the windows gleamed, and the official For Sale sign had gone up. Andy Chapman, the estate agent, was wasting no time.

Jay was inside the house checking that everything was immaculate and Nadia was outside watering the garden when Andy arrived at midday with the first potential buyers. Nadia was still busy drenching the nicotianas—poor things, they were parched—when everyone appeared on the sunbaked terrace.

"Well, this is just charming." The wife turned to her portly husband. "Isn't it, Gerald? I can just see us sitting out here. And low-maintenance, perfect. We could cope with a garden like this." To Jay she added, "It's been very well designed."

Nadia felt absurdly proud. This had to be how Clare felt when she heard clients praising her paintings. There really was nothing like a good compliment to give you a boost.

"Nadia designed the garden," Jay explained as Nadia turned off the outside tap.

"You mean you did all this yourself? By heck, and you're only a slip of a thing," the husband exclaimed. This was what was so heavenly about men who weighed almost 300 pounds, Nadia decided. As far as they were concerned, anyone less than 150 pounds counted as a slip of a thing.

"Should have seen the place before she started," Andy Chapman told him. "Nothing but rubble and weeds."

"Is she included in the price?" Guffawing at his own joke, Gerald turned back to Nadia. "Tell you what, love, that's not a bad idea. We could keep you here, put you up in the spare bedroom, in exchange for keeping the garden up to scratch."

"Any time," Nadia joked back. "This is a dream house, I'd live here like a shot."

Too late, she saw the wife give her husband an anxious nudge, terrified that he may have unwittingly offered her the job and been taken up on it.

"I'd like to see the kitchen again," the woman announced to Andy, before Nadia could start haggling over terms and conditions. Over her shoulder she added, "Very nice garden, dear. Gerald, would our pine table go with those tiles in the kitchen? And we have to work out where the piano could go."

"Seemed pretty keen," Andy observed ten minutes later, having dispatched the potential buyers and come back out onto the terrace for a cigarette. "They've just accepted an offer for their place on Frenchay Common. Short chain. Could be promising. By the way"—he flashed a grin at Nadia—"they asked me to tactfully let you know that they weren't actually serious about the room."

"I'm distraught," said Nadia.

"Anyway, next one's due any minute." Checking his posh watch, Andy took several hasty puffs of Marlboro to crank up his nicotine levels.

"He's already here," said Jay, emerging through the French windows onto the terrace with Laurie in his wake.

Nadia's fingers tightened round the garden hose she was in the process of winding up. She looked at Laurie, as disreputable as ever in his scruffy Earl jeans, ripped gray T-shirt, and butterscotch tan.

"Mr. Welch. Right on time. *Excellent*," Andy declared, flinging down his half-smoked cigarette and stepping forward to shake Laurie's hand with enthusiasm.

The expression on Jay's face was unreadable. Laurie grinned at Nadia.

"No need to look so shocked. I can buy it if I want, can't I?"

Only taken aback for a millisecond—he was an estate agent after all—Andy said, "You two know each other?"

"I've asked Nadia to marry me," Laurie replied easily. "Just trying to get her to make up her mind." He paused. "I know how much she likes this house."

Andy could barely contain his delight. "Who wouldn't? This is a superior property." Turning back to Nadia he added, "And what were you saying not ten minutes ago? That you'd live here like a shot? Well, well, this could be the answer to your prayers. Sounds like a perfect arrangement to me."

There was a knot like a tangle of elastic bands in Nadia's stomach. Her and Laurie together. It had been her dream for years. Yet suddenly she was no longer quite so sure…

"Nad? Why don't we take a look round?" Taking control, Laurie relieved her of the hose.

"You've already seen the house," she told Laurie coolly.

"Not properly. Not since it's been finished. Come on." As he reached for her hand, Nadia noticed the absence of the zing of electricity she'd come to associate with his touch. It hadn't happened.

Jay's phone beeped. He glanced briefly at the text message on the screen and snapped it shut.

"Right, I'll leave you to it. Have to go."

"Missing you already," Laurie murmured, American-style, as Jay left.

⁓

"You took it on board then."

Clare, who was painting in the garden, glanced over her shoulder at Nadia and leaned back on her stool.

"Took what on board?"

"Malcolm's advice. Paying more attention to detail." Nadia removed her sunglasses and studied the fairground scene taking shape on the canvas. "This is tons better."

Inwardly Clare glowed, because she knew it was better too. She even felt better, more centered and less panicky. Maybe turning into a nicer person was making her a better artist. Blimey, she'd even admired Annie's new dress yesterday in an almost genuinely sincere way. OK, the dress hadn't been *that* great, but it had actually suited her. And being complimented had cheered Annie up no end.

"I spoke to Thomas at the gallery yesterday. He said Malcolm Carter's pretty well-respected on the art scene," Clare admitted. "He reckons any advice Malcolm offers, I should take."

"Good."

"Anyway, the thought of him doesn't give me the creeps quite so much now. It helps that he's gay." Quickly she added, "But he still looks like a fat toad," because there was such a thing as being *too* nice.

"So. How are you feeling?" Collapsing onto the grass, Nadia popped the tab on a can of lager and offered up the other one.

"Fine." As she took the can, Clare realized that it was true. Let's face it, if her periods had been irregular, she would never even have known she was pregnant. While having the miscarriage hadn't been nice, she no longer thought of it as losing a baby. It had been a minuscule collection of cells barely visible to the naked eye. And although it made her feel horribly guilty to even think it, the inescapable truth was that maybe it wasn't always a tragedy for something like this to have happened.

Clare put down her brush and opened the can of Heineken. God, wasn't ice-cold lager great?

"I'm twenty-three," she told Nadia. "I want children one day. But I'd much rather have them with someone who isn't a complete arse."

"Absolutely." Wiping her frothy upper lip with the back of her hand, Nadia nodded in agreement. "And you couldn't find anyone more arsey than Piers. That wouldn't be physically possible."

"I hate him," Clare marveled. "I can't believe he gets away with *being* him."

"You're well out of it." Wriggling out of her T-shirt, Nadia flopped down in sunbather mode in her lime-green lace bra and white shorts.

"I've still got that check he gave me. I was wondering what to do with it." Resuming work on her painting, Clare said, "Do you think I should post it back to him? Or spend it on really nice shoes?"

"Depends. Would you let me borrow them?" said Nadia.

"Of course you could borrow them."

"Oh well, in that case, that's the silliest question you ever asked. Definitely spend it on shoes."

Clare broke into a grin. "Sometimes you say the sweetest things. Crikey, what's up with Tilly?" Shielding her eyes with her free hand, she watched as Tilly, looking shell-shocked, headed across the lawn toward them.

Encouragingly, Nadia patted the grass next to her. "Tilly, sit down. Are you OK?"

Tilly couldn't sit, she was in far too much of a state. Shock vied with confusion. She felt like a cartoon character in a whirl of befuddlement, with spirals and question marks bouncing out of her head on springs.

"Hey." Clare waved her paint-loaded brush in front of Tilly's pale face. "You can tell us. Is it Cal?"

"What?" Tilly was finding it hard to concentrate.

"Cal. You know, your… *friend*. What happened?" said Clare teasingly. "It's OK, we won't be shocked. Did he try to undo your bra?"

"Leave her alone." Nadia saw that Tilly was trembling. "Tilly? Who were you talking to on the phone when I came through?"

"Mum."

Typical. What was Leonie up to now?

Aloud, Nadia said, "And?"

"She wants me to go and live with her in Brighton. With Brian and Tamsin. For good."

It wasn't so much the unexpectedness of the invitation that had Nadia lost for words, it was the look on Tilly's face. Were those tears of horror swimming in Tilly's huge blue eyes? Or tears of joy?

—⁓—

"This is fantastic," Nadia breathed as the auctioneer called the assembled crowd to attention. "How can everyone else look so calm? What if I scratch my ear and buy a house by mistake?"

"Just don't scratch your ear," Jay murmured.

"But I might not be able to help it! I'm feeling very twitchy. And itchy." Twitchy and itchy. God, it sounded like a couple of cartoon characters.

"You've probably got fleas," whispered Jay. Pulling Nadia in front of him, he stood behind her and held both her hands firmly down at her sides.

Phew, that was exciting. She felt his breath on the back of her neck and the heat from his body against her spine. Even better was the knowledge that, in all honesty, there wasn't any need for him to be doing this, because they both knew she wouldn't really accidentally bid for a house.

The attraction was still there, Nadia thought happily. On both sides. And maybe the time had come at last to do something about it.

Ooh, here we go…

"Now we come to Lot Seven," said the auctioneer, and Nadia felt her heart break into a clumsy gallop, because this was the one

Jay was after. They were here in the Garden Room at Bristol Zoo, the venue for tonight's property auction. When Jay had asked her if she'd like to come along with him, she'd jumped at the chance. The last time she'd been to an auction was during her college days, when she'd bought a portable black and white TV for six pounds, beating off opposition from a fellow student who'd chickened out at five pounds fifty.

Needless to say, the TV hadn't worked.

But here, incredibly, the bids could leap up ten thousand pounds at a time, racing from four hundred thousand to half a million in less than a minute. Just the thought of so much money made Nadia feel queasy with excitement.

"Highcliffe House. Just off the Downs in Sneyd Park," the auctioneer continued. "A detached Georgian property requiring refurbishment but retaining many original features. Potential for re-development. I'll start the bidding at two hundred… two twenty… two forty… two sixty…"

It was like watching the start of the Grand National. Overwhelmed by the speed of the bidding, Nadia's head swiveled around the Garden Room as she attempted to pick out the other bidders. God knows how the auctioneer managed it; some of them were dipping their heads by no more than a centimeter. Close behind her, she knew Jay was doing the same as the bids shot up in twenty thousand pound increments. Imagine, twenty thousand pounds *per nod*…

"Sold," said the auctioneer, with a delicate tap of his gavel and a nod of acknowledgement that, confusingly, appeared to encompass the entire room. "For five hundred and forty thousand pounds."

"Who got it?" Nadia twisted round, her heart in her mouth.

"I did," said Jay.

"Really?"

His mouth twitched. "I always get what I want. Well, almost always."

Nadia's stomach did an excited bunny-hop.

"Mr. Tiernan?" The auctioneer raised his eyebrows, indicating with another brief head movement that Jay should make his way over to the desk by the entrance and indulge in some serious form-signing.

"Fancy a drink when I'm done?" Jay said lightly.

Fancy a drink? She could do with a whole vineyard.

"Why not?" Nadia smiled and felt instantly bereft as he let go of her hand.

Oh crikey, getting a bit carried away here. It was looking like make-your-mind-up time. Who knew where tonight might end?

~~~

Jay took her to Crosby's, a busy, buzzy bar on Whiteladies Road in Clifton. He ordered a bottle of Veuve Clicquot to celebrate.

"You'll have to pay," said Jay. "I'm broke now."

"Don't open it," Nadia told the bartender. "We'll have a couple of lagers instead."

Amused, Jay opened his wallet and paid for the champagne.

"Here's to the new project," he said, raising his glass. "Yours too."

Nadia chinked glasses with him. Apparently, chinking glasses was a dreadfully common thing to do—glasses were only meant to air-kiss—but where was the fun in that?

"My next garden." Her wrist brushed against Jay's, the fleeting contact every bit as thrilling as having her hands held during the auction. Jay's plan was to turn Highcliffe House into four flats and the surrounding grounds into a communal garden. It was larger than the one she'd just finished, but in less of a mess than Clarence Gardens had been.

"Five hundred and forty thousand pounds," marveled Nadia. "That's a lot."

"I'd have gone up to five eighty."

Gosh. When the work was finished he'd probably sell the apartments for over three hundred thousand apiece. Speculate to accumulate and all that. You must need nerves of steel in Jay's business, not to mention the ability to keep a cool head when things went horribly wrong. And he was cool, thought Nadia. It was an attractive quality in a man. Then again, having a body like his didn't do any harm. Or eyes like that. Or a wicked smile so dangerous it should definitely be made illegal—

"What?" said Jay. Oh God, and here he was, doing it again.

"Just wondered where you got your shirt," Nadia lied. The shirt was dark green with a fine red stripe. "It's my dad's birthday soon. He might like something like that."

"Try again."

"What?"

"The truth, this time."

"OK, he probably wouldn't like it. But we're desperate to liven up his wardrobe. If I bought him one like yours, he might feel obliged to wear it a few times, then we'd all compliment him like mad."

"Come on, you know what I'm talking about," said Jay, and Nadia's mouth went dry.

Oh, she did, she did.

Then his mobile burst into life.

For a moment they both listened to it ring.

"I hate these things," sighed Jay.

Taking a gulp of champagne, Nadia thought, don't answer it then. Less than two minutes later she thought, *shit*.

Chapter 50

JAY SLID THE PHONE back into his pocket. "That was Belinda's mother. Belinda's having the baby."

Nadia nodded. Under normal circumstances this would have been good news. But she'd already seen Jay check his watch and heard him say, "I'm setting off now. I'll be there by ten."

Which was, frankly, not what she wanted to happen. It was completely pain-in-the-bottom news.

Although not so painful in the bottom for her as it would undoubtedly be for Belinda.

Oh well, time to put on a brave face.

"You're going down to Dorset."

"I promised Belinda I would. She asked me. It means a lot to her," Jay said evenly. No longer smiling, it was clear that he was reliving his brother's death. The birth of Anthony's child would be an emotional, bittersweet experience.

"Just as well you only had time for one glass." Nadia indicated the bottle on the table, still two-thirds full. "You should go now. Don't want Belinda having it before you get there. Sometimes they pop out like champagne corks."

"I'm sorry." Jay's mouth twitched. "This seems to keep happening, doesn't it? Every time we…" He paused, then shook his head. "Well, never mind. If Anthony was still alive, I'd have something to say to him about his timing."

Except if Anthony *were* still alive, Jay wouldn't need to be rushing off now, would he?

As he stood up, searching his pockets for his car keys, Nadia was appalled to realize she was actually jealous of Belinda. It had suddenly occurred to her that it wasn't uncommon for women who'd loved one brother to transfer their affections to the other. Advice columns were full of such cases, except most of the women writing in hadn't bothered to wait until the first brother was dead.

Even more appalled by the direction her thoughts were taking, Nadia gave herself a brisk mental shake.

"Will you cut the cord?"

Jay looked squeamish. "Absolutely not. I won't be in the room. Bit too personal," he said with a shudder. "Belinda just wants me to be there at the hospital. I'll see the baby once it's washed and wrapped up, thanks very much." Jangling his keys, he added, "Better make a move. I'll drop you home."

It was only eight o'clock, still warm and sunny outside. Nadia shook her head; it would be an easy walk back across the Downs.

"No need, I'll be fine."

"Sure?"

"Absolutely." She did her best to breathe normally as Jay dropped a fleeting goodbye kiss on her cheek. "Good luck."

He pulled out his sunglasses. "I'm going to be an uncle."

"You'll have to set a good example," said Nadia. "Think only pure thoughts, do only good things."

"How dare you?" Jay's dark eyelashes cast shadows on his razor-sharp cheekbones as he smiled briefly down at her. "You know perfectly well I've never had a pure thought in my life."

Nadia watched him go with regret. Another chance blown. Honestly, these selfish sisters-in-law who just *launch* into labor whenever it suits them, popping out babies and wreaking havoc on completely innocent people's lives.

~~~

Nadia was queuing up for popcorn in the cinema foyer when someone pinched her bottom. Whirling round, she said, "Bernie!"

Bernie Blatt, clearly recovering nicely from the recent traumatic breakup with his fiancée, grinned at her, then at the dustbin-sized cardboard bucket of popcorn the assistant was waiting to hand over to Nadia.

"Feeding the five thousand?" Peering about him, Bernie said, "Who are you here with, the bastard or the boss?"

"No one. Just me." Nadia enjoyed coming to the cinema on her own. Which was just as well, seeing as no one she knew shared her taste in films. Laurie, whose all-time favorites were *Star Wars*, *Spider-Man*, and *Dumb and Dumber*, had groaned when she'd arrived home from the property auction and started studying the listings in the *Evening Post*.

"Oh God, she's off again, more arty-farty bollocks with bad subtitles. Nad, don't do it. Why don't we go bowling instead?"

"No. There's a film I really want to see and it's only on for two nights."

Laurie winked at Clare. "Wonder why."

"You can both come along if you want to," Nadia had offered, safe in the knowledge that they wouldn't.

"Hmm, let me see. A once-in-a-lifetime opportunity to watch a crap film where nothing happens and it never stops raining. In a foreign language, so I can't understand what's going on. Color?" said Laurie. "Or black and white?"

"Black and white."

"Thought so. Making it in color would have been far too lifelike. Phew, what an offer. I'll give this some serious thought. Clare?"

Clare said, "I'd rather eat a raw toad."

Laurie grinned and said, "So that's raw toad for two."

"You can't watch a film on your own," Bernie said now. He looked shocked.

"I can. I like it. You get to eat all the popcorn yourself. Anyway," said Nadia, checking the huge clock up on the wall, "film's about to start." She didn't want to miss anything, not even the ads.

"What are you seeing?"

Nadia pointed to the poster behind him. "The new Roberto Benigni."

"You're kidding!" Bernie's face lit up. "Me too!"

This was startling news. Nadia would have had him down as a *Dumb and Dumber* man if ever there was one. Poleaxed, she said, "Really?"

"I'm mad about Benigni. He's a genius." Bernie shook his head in admiration, then whipped out his wallet. "Wait here while I pick up my ticket. We can watch it together. That is, if you want to."

"Fine, as long as you buy your own popcorn." Nadia hugged her bucket possessively to her chest. "Because you're not having any of mine."

They emerged from the cinema two hours later, picked up a pizza, and went back to Bernie's flat in Clifton. It was a hot night. They sat on the stone steps leading down to the garden, divided up the pizza, and washed it down with lager from Bernie's fridge.

"That's the brilliant thing about popcorn," said Nadia. "You can eat masses, but it never fills you up. That was a fantastic film, wasn't it? I really hope he gets another Oscar. I've got *Life Is Beautiful* at home on video and I still cry buckets every time I watch it."

Bernie chucked a curve of pizza crust, boomerang-style, into the yew hedge separating his garden from his neighbor's. Black and white foreign films with subtitles and no discernible plotline weren't his thing at all. His favorite actor was Arnold Schwarzenegger. You knew where you were with a chap like that. Still, no need to wreck Nadia's illusions now.

"Me too." Swiftly, before she could start rattling on about the funny-looking Italian bloke all over again, he said, "So how's it going with you and Laurie?"

Nadia peeled off an anchovy and fed it to Bernie's cat, Titus, who was purring and weaving around her legs. Titus promptly spat it out in disgust. "OK. I'm just not rushing into anything. Laurie buggered off to the States for over a year. Now it's my turn to keep him waiting."

"And the other one? The bloke you're working for?"

Nadia briefly wondered what kind of films Jay liked to watch. "He can wait too. God, your cat's fussy," she complained as Titus sniffed at a mussel before declining it and stalking off.

"So are you," Bernie pointed out. "Know what I think? I think you should chuck 'em both. They aren't the only men on the planet, you know." Clearing his throat, he mumbled, "I've always liked you."

Nadia spluttered with laughter. Then she began to cough, which was the wrong thing to do. Having thumped her on the back several times, Bernie somehow managed to leave one arm draped round her shoulders while the other one slid round her waist.

"I'm serious," said Bernie. "You could do a lot worse."

Oh dear, time to go. Extricating herself from his octopus arms, Nadia said, "Bernie, thanks. I'm very flattered, but we both know you're only saying this because you just broke up with Paula."

"But I'm *not*."

"Yes you are." Breaking into a grin, she stood up before he could try to kiss her—there was a tell-tale pucker around his mouth that indicated this was on the cards. "Bernie, we're friends. Let's not spoil it. And it's late"—she checked her watch—"I really have to go."

Bernie gave up with good grace. "Oh well, it was worth a try. Nothing ventured, nothing gained." Giving it one last shot, he raised his eyebrows and said hopefully, "I'm quite a catch, you know. Sure you don't want to change your mind?"

Solemnly Nadia said, "Quite sure, thanks." She hesitated on the doorstep. "One last thing. That film we saw. Did you really enjoy it?"

Bernie smiled. "You're joking, aren't you? I hated every single bloody boring black and white minute."

"Oh well," said Nadia cheerfully, "in that case, serves you right."

Chapter 51

TILLY WAS IN BED trying to work through her muddled train of thoughts. The train didn't seem to know where it was going; she'd never been more confused in her life.

It was eleven o'clock in the morning. Outside her bedroom window the sun blazed down; it was another glorious day. Everyone else had gone out, giving her the peace and quiet she needed to think things through. Turning onto her side, she reached for Colman, her beloved battered teddy. Colman, who had faded yellowish fur, lopsided eyes, and a floppy left leg that really needed sewing back on, was no looker. Years of being cuddled had left him bald in places. Leonie had given Colman to Tilly on her fifth birthday.

Leonie. *Mum.*

OK, thought Tilly, here we go again.

She was completely and utterly torn. She may love her mother, but she didn't want to live with her. This was her home. She was happy here, happy with her school and her friends—especially Cal—and her family.

But was her family happy with her? For a start, they weren't even really her family. James and Miriam may have brought her up, but she wasn't related to them. And while she knew she loved them, what if they didn't love her quite as much as she'd always imagined? What if they were secretly hoping she *would* go and live with her mother?

How did she know they weren't secretly thinking, God, we've done our stint, it's about time Leonie took her turn?

Tilly blinked back tears. Of course, they hadn't said as much. They never would. But they had their own lives to lead. James had Annie now, and they were so happy together. As for Miriam, surely she'd done more than her share over the years. Bringing up two grandchildren must have been hard enough. And then to find herself saddled with yet another child... poor Miriam must have wondered what she'd done to deserve this much punishment.

Imagining it, hot tears dripped down Tilly's cheeks into Colman's threadbare fur. When she'd told her family about Leonie's plan, she had expected them to react with horror and dismay. She'd waited for Miriam to announce in her customary forthright manner, "What absolute nonsense! Darling, of *course* you're not moving to Brighton, you're staying here with us where you belong. Right, pass me the phone, we'll soon sort this out."

But it hadn't happened like that. Taking the news calmly—a bit *too* calmly for Tilly's liking—Miriam had stressed that it was her decision and hers alone. If she wanted to live with Leonie, then that was absolutely fine. Not that they wanted to lose her, Miriam had hastily added, because of course they'd all miss her dreadfully, but at the same time Leonie was her mother. They would understand.

And that had been that. Hugging her, James had said much the same thing. So had Nadia and Clare, which had come as the biggest shock of all.

Tilly rubbed her eyes. Well, there wasn't really any dilemma, was there? Basically, she didn't have a lot of choice. Everyone might be telling her she did, but it wasn't actually true.

Like it or not, she was going to have to move to Brighton and live with Leonie, Brian, and Tamsin. New school, new town, new people. It was nice that her mother wanted her, of course. But if she was being honest, she found Tamsin a bit scary.

Oh well, so much for making her mind up. Pushing back the

duvet, Tilly stumbled out of bed. She was seeing Cal this afternoon. At least she knew he didn't want her to move away.

Downstairs, Harpo greeted her with a squawk and a friendly flap of his electric-blue wings. Feeding him a corner of toast, Tilly said, "I'm even going to miss you, Harpo," and felt her throat close up.

"I'll have a gin and tonic," Harpo cackled. "Make it a double."

"Bit early in the morning." Tilly didn't even know why she'd bothered making toast, she wasn't the least bit hungry.

"That was the news. And now the weather," squawked Harpo, who watched far too much television.

Tilly wasn't meeting Cal until two thirty. She still had a couple of hours to kill. Tomorrow, Leonie was driving up to talk to Miriam and James about the move before taking Tilly back with her for a few days. Since she and Cal were going to the cinema tonight, it would make sense to get her things together now.

Upstairs Tilly crammed jeans, trainers, Rollerblades, and various tops and bits of underwear into her sports bag. If you didn't fold stuff, packing didn't take long at all. Having closed the bag with difficulty, Tilly promptly opened it again, stuffed in a nightie and a swimsuit and set to wrestling with the zip again.

Her nightie proved to be the straw that broke the camel's back.

"Oh bum." Leaning back on her heels, Tilly gazed in dismay at the broken zip.

The loft was a bit of a memory lane. Thankful that there were no Indiana Jones-style cobwebs, Tilly eased her way past her own cot, dismantled now and propped against the water tank. James had always been the one who could never bear to throw anything away. He'd lugged her old tricycle up here, and the musical mobile that had hung in her bedroom for years. There was even a box containing spare rolls of wallpaper that Tilly only dimly remembered seeing on walls.

Squeezing between piled-up crates of gramophone records and old books—honestly, had James never heard of Oxfam?—she spotted Miriam's cases over in the far corner. Not the huge trunk, she wasn't going on a world cruise. Or the green Samsonite thing; far too posh and bulky.

Tilly strained to see past the Samsonite. There, that one would do. Miriam wouldn't mind. Reaching for the smaller squashy tan leather case, she hauled it over the others then straightened up and made her way back toward the trapdoor.

Back in her own room, Tilly unzipped the case and saw what had been rattling around inside as she'd made her way down the stepladder.

This time all her things fitted easily into the case and the zip fastened without protest.

But how strange. Why on earth would Miriam have left a DVD in there? Surely it couldn't be one of those rude ones?

Of course it couldn't. Turning the DVD over in her hands, Tilly was ashamed of herself for even thinking such a thing. Good grief, Miriam would never have anything to do with mucky videos. Her all-time favorite film was *Casablanca*.

In fact, this probably was a copy of *Casablanca*.

Except it wasn't.

Idle curiosity had got the better of Tilly and now she was wishing she'd never gone up into the loft in the first place.

She almost wished it *had* turned out to be a pornographic film.

Even a pornographic film would have been better than this.

Until she felt the drops soaking through the knees of her jeans, Tilly hadn't realized she was crying again. Rocking backward and forward with her arms wrapped tightly round her ribs, she watched the flickering black and white images on the screen and wondered if she was going completely mad.

How could she be seeing what she was seeing on this video? It was just bizarre, as impossible as going to the cinema to watch the latest Harry Potter movie and suddenly seeing yourself up there on the screen, acting in a film you knew you hadn't appeared in.

Tilly knew what Robert Kinsella looked like. He had been Miriam's husband and James's father. There were photographs of him dotted around the house. This was why it made no sense, no sense at all.

Because the man she was watching on the video certainly wasn't Robert Kinsella.

Jay phoned Nadia the following morning.

"Hi," she said happily. "How are you?"

"Shattered. It's hard work, you know, this giving birth business."

"You poor thing, I hope you had loads of painkillers."

"Gas and air. Pethidine. I passed on the epidural."

"Well done you. And?"

"A boy. Eight pounds, six ounces, fit and healthy, blue eyes, dark hair." Jay paused. "And absolutely huge balls."

Nadia laughed. She couldn't help it, he sounded so perplexed.

"He'll grow into them. What's his name?"

"Daniel Anthony. He was born at eleven o'clock. I've been phoning all the relatives."

"I'm glad he's OK. How's Belinda?"

"Emotional. Happy. She swears he's the image of Anthony, but you know what newborn babies are like. They all just look red and squashed to me."

Nadia said helpfully, "That's because you're a man."

"So I've been told. Anyway, I may be home this evening. If you're free, do you fancy dinner?"

"Could do." Nadia flushed with pleasure.

"Look, I don't know what time I'll be back, so I'll give you a ring," said Jay. "You got home all right yesterday, did you?"

"Absolutely fine. No trouble at all. Actually, I went to the cinema."

"See anything good?"

"The new Roberto Benigni film."

"Who's he?" said Jay.

Nadia smiled to herself. Oh well, you couldn't win them all.

Chapter 52

LEONIE WOULD BE ARRIVING any minute now. Feeling like a dog bracing itself for a visit from the vet—which was ridiculous; this was her own mother, for heaven's sake—Tilly lugged her bag downstairs.

"Darling, you can't use that! The zip's broken," Miriam exclaimed. "Why don't I pop up to the loft and find you a proper case?"

Miriam was wearing a white shirt, an embroidered vest, and a bias-cut black skirt. Her face and hair were immaculate, as always, and diamonds glittered on her fingers.

"I'm fine." Having returned her grandmother's tan leather case, along with the bewildering DVD, to the attic, Tilly had crammed all her stuff back into her old sports bag and fastened it with a sturdy belt. "I like this one."

It was hard to meet Miriam's gaze. She'd found a video that made no sense at all and there was no one she could ask about it. Whoever the man in the video was, Tilly was painfully aware that she had no right to ask prying questions. It was none of her business. She was the cuckoo in the Kinsella nest, a cuckoo about to be gently nudged out.

"Oh, sweetheart." Enfolding Tilly in her scented embrace, Miriam said, "We'll miss you so much if you decide to go. You do know that, don't you? The house just won't be the same without you."

That was the thing about Miriam, she was so believable. When she said stuff like this, it sounded as if she really and truly meant it.

"Anyway." Miriam smoothed her hair and glanced out of the window as a car came crunching up the gravel drive. "Sounds as though Leonie's arrived. Do you want to go and meet her, while I get the drinks organized? It's such a beautiful day I thought we'd sit out in the garden."

"She's here?" In the kitchen, Edward was already arranging glasses on a tray and taking bottles down from the cupboard. Gin, vodka, and Scotch.

Nodding, Miriam impatiently brushed away a tear. "Bloody hell, Edward. How am I going to do this? I can't bear the thought of Tilly going to live with that wretched woman. If I had my way I'd tell Leonie to clear off and never come near us again. But she's Tilly's mother, and if it's what Tilly wants… oh, sod it, I know I mustn't influence her, but it's so hard to try and stay impartial. I just want to *shoot* Leonie."

"I know, I know." Edward put his arms round Miriam. "But Tilly has to make up her own mind."

"She's only thirteen!"

"All the more reason why she probably wants to go. And shooting Leonie really wouldn't help. Tilly might not appreciate the gesture." Edward had a neuropsychiatrist's sense of humor. He couldn't help it.

Pulling herself together, Miriam took a steadying breath. "Right, I'll take the tray. Can you bring the rest?"

"The rest. You mean the ice cubes, mixers, spirits, wine, and orange juice." Edward rolled his eyes. "I'll just carry all that, shall I?"

Miriam said carelessly, "Oh, I'm sure you'll manage, darling. You always do."

"The Mummy Returns," murmured Clare as Leonie came sauntering toward them with her arm slung round Tilly's thin shoulders. "Here we go."

"Now remember what I said," Miriam warned. "No slanging matches. That's the last thing Tilly needs."

"Crikey." Gasping, Nadia peered into the drink Edward had poured her. "Any tonic in this gin?"

"We're going to need something to line our stomachs," said Miriam grimly. "Edward, there's dolce latte and ciabatta in the larder. And don't forget the olives."

Edward hesitated and for a millisecond Nadia thought he was about to tell Miriam to fetch her own bloody olives. But all he said, drily, was, "Just call me Jeeves."

"May as well bring out the cashews as well," Miriam called after him.

"Lovely." Clare grinned. "We'll need something to throw at Leonie."

Nadia gave her a kick under the table. God, this drink was strong, at this rate she was going to end up legless.

"Darlings, here we all are," Leonie exclaimed, descending on them and kissing her elder daughters. "Isn't this lovely? I was just telling Tilly how excited Tamsin is. We just can't wait to have her home with us!"

"If she decides she wants to go," Nadia said evenly, because Tilly was looking like a trapped rabbit.

"Oh nonsense, of course she wants to. Don't you, darling?" Leonie patted Tilly's arm, then dug into her raffia shoulder bag. "Here, I've brought some brochures about Tilly's new school. She'll be in the same class as Tamsin, which is brilliant. No James?" she added, glancing around the table as if realizing for the first time that her ex-husband was missing.

"Dad had a meeting. He'll be here by four." Nadia checked her watch; it was almost that now.

"Oh well, it's not as if we need him." Beaming, Leonie shook back her hair. Silver bracelets jangled as she ran her fingers through the overbleached ends, then swiveled round on her chair at the sound of the garden gate clicking open. "Unlike *this* gorgeous boy. Laurie, how heavenly to see you again!" Leaping to her feet, she greeted Laurie with characteristic enthusiasm.

"I just came to tell Dad he's had a call." As Laurie spoke, Edward returned with a second tray of food. "A Professor Spitz rang from Boston. He'll phone back in an hour."

Edward nodded. Ernst Spitz was an old colleague of his; they had co-written several papers for medical journals.

"Laurie, you can't leave us!" Pouting girlishly, Leonie tugged him down next to her. "Stay and have a drink. How's that silly daughter of mine treating you? Has she come to her senses yet?"

Nadia gritted her teeth. The fact that her mother adored Laurie and couldn't understand why she hadn't taken him back in à flash irritated her intensely. As one who had spent her life flitting from one man to the next, leaving a trail of unhappiness in her wake, Leonie thought it was a completely normal thing to do.

"Still working on her," said Laurie with an easy grin. "She's making me wait. It'll happen."

Nadia felt her shoulders stiffen. Laurie's confidence was annoying too.

"I'm seeing someone else tonight." Defiantly she took another swig of her drink. "For dinner. *And* I might have torrid sex with him, so there." She didn't actually say this last bit aloud, but she was jolly well thinking it.

"Jay? Well, good." Spinning the cap off the vodka, Laurie poured himself a couple of inches and topped it up with orange juice. "I told you you should. Get him out of your system."

"Who's Jay?" Recalling the name, Leonie said excitedly, "Oh, you mean the one with the dead brother!"

"And more notches on his bedpost than Jack Nicholson," said Laurie.

"Ah, but that's what makes them so irresistible." Leonie gave a pleasurable shiver. "You can't beat a good bad boy."

Nadia wondered what she'd done to deserve this. Right, now she was definitely going to shag Jay tonight.

Aloud she said, "Aren't we supposed to be discussing Tilly?"

Her mother nudged Laurie and whispered, "Bad boys are always more fun. Ooh, that reminds me." Turning to Clare she went on brightly, "How's that naughty chap of yours? Piers, isn't it?"

Clare stiffened; Leonie was the only one here who didn't know about her brief pregnancy.

"At last." Miriam sighed with relief as they all heard the front door slam. "Here's James."

It's going to be fun, everything's going to be great, Tilly told herself as she headed back up the garden and into the house. Her mother had said so, she kept stressing how marvelous it would be, especially with someone her own age to play with.

"It's just what Tilly needs," Leonie had explained to James. "She and Tamsin will make a brilliant team. You should see the two of them together, they're as thick as thieves!"

Which, what with Tamsin's shoplifting skills, was actually quite funny, except it scared Tilly rigid. The last time they'd visited a department store, Tilly hadn't discovered the stolen Stereophonics CD in her bag until they'd arrived home.

Anyway, look on the bright side. Like it or not, she was moving to Brighton, and bits of it might be fun. They could swim in the sea, for a start. She and Tamsin could share clothes, borrow each other's shoes, and talk about teenage girlie stuff together.

Plus, Tilly reminded herself, she'd be living with her mother, who genuinely wanted her there. That was the good thing about Leonie; you didn't have to wonder if she was only offering you a home out of a sense of guilt or obligation, because Leonie never did feel obliged. Her mother was a guilt-free zone.

Right. Ice cubes.

She was busy in the kitchen, clattering ice into a tall glass jug, when the doorbell went. Grabbing a runaway ice cube and lobbing it into the sink, Tilly wiped her wet hands on her denim shorts and went to answer the front door.

A man she didn't know was standing in the porch.

At least she thought she didn't know him, but there was something distantly familiar about his face.

The visitor had to be around Edward's age, and despite the heat of the day was wearing an expensive-looking suit, dark blue shirt, and striped tie. His shoes were highly polished. He wasn't carrying a Bible, but Tilly suspected this was his reason for ringing the bell. Anyone this smartly dressed had to be on a mission from God.

Clutching the jug of ice cubes to her chest she said warily, "Hello?"

"Hello there. I'm here to see Miriam Kinsella. Is she around?"

Not a Mormon then, bent on converting them to the Way of the Lord. Tilly wondered who he was. She couldn't put her finger on it, but there was definitely a faint echo of recognition nudging at the back of her brain.

"She is expecting me." As if sensing her doubt, the man said charmingly, "Miriam and I are old friends."

Still mystified, but remembering her manners, Tilly said, "She's out in the garden. If you wait here, I'll just go and get her." Even as she said it, she was wondering if this was the right thing to do. Closing the front door on an old friend of Miriam's would seem awfully rude. On the other hand, what if she invited him to wait in the hall and he turned out to be a con artist, tricking his way in? By the time Miriam got here, he could have made off with the family silver.

As if helping her out of her dilemma, the man said, "Wouldn't it be easier if I just came with you?"

"OK." Relieved, Tilly decided that it would. There had been a spate of robberies in the area recently. The man didn't look dodgy, but that was the trouble with con artists these days, they never did.

She led the way through the house. At the French windows, the man paused. Next to him, Tilly watched him take in the scene. It looked for all the world like the most relaxed and convivial of gatherings, a happy mix of friends and family enjoying drinks in the garden on a glorious summer afternoon. Laurie said something that caused everyone around the oval table to burst out laughing. Nadia was pouring drinks. Leonie, cradling the bowl of olives on her lap, lobbed one in Laurie's direction.

"There she is," murmured the visitor, gazing at Miriam. He shook his head in admiration. "Hasn't changed a bit."

Out of curiosity, Tilly said, "When did you last see her?"

He smiled down at Tilly. "How long since I last saw Miriam? Fifty-two years."

Blimey. More than half a century. The good old black-and-white days, marveled Tilly.

The next moment, prompted by this thought, she realized where she knew him from.

Oh good Lord.

"Come on," said the man, gently guiding her forward. "Time to say hello."

Chapter 53

"WHO'S TILLY FOUND NOW?" Nadia shielded her eyes and peered across the lawn.

"Dad? Is this another stray professor?" said Laurie.

"Never seen him before in my life," Edward protested his innocence. "Probably some door-to-door chap selling conservatories."

Miriam glanced up and felt a chill settle around her ribs. Oh no, it couldn't be, it couldn't possibly be.

But of course it was.

For a moment Miriam wondered if she was about to faint. Her heart felt as if it had been physically wrenched out of her body and plunged into ice-cold water. She'd spent months mentally bracing herself for something like this, but now it was actually happening she knew she was hopelessly unprepared.

"Miriam." The man standing before her nodded and smiled slightly.

"Charles." Hideously aware of curious eyes upon her, Miriam held out her hand for him to shake.

Ignoring it, Charles bent and kissed her on each cheek. Then, straightening up, he said easily, "No need to look so terrified. I don't have a gun."

Now he really had everyone's attention. Miriam pushed back her chair and said, "Maybe we should talk in private."

"I'd prefer to do it here." Charles stood his ground. "Out in the open, so to speak. I think your family deserve to know, don't you?"

Curtly, Edward said, "What's this about?"

"I don't want to." Miriam's face was white, her knuckles clenched.

Charles said calmly, "I'm sure you don't. But I do."

"You can't just barge in here—"

"I didn't barge in, I was invited by this charming young girl." He indicated Tilly, who was looking agonized. "Besides, it can't have come as too much of a surprise. I did tell you I'd be paying a visit." He paused, raising his eyebrows. "In my last letter, remember?"

Miriam remembered the last letter. She had thrown it into the bin without reading it. Ostrich behavior and completely pointless, but it had felt necessary at the time.

Closing her eyes, she shook her head.

"Well," said Leonie, her expression eager, "I'm intrigued! Are we going to sit here like this all afternoon or is some kind soul going to put us out of our suspense?"

Silence.

With a playful glance in Charles's direction, Leonie wheedled, "Please? Before I burst with curiosity?"

"Oh, do shut up," sighed Miriam, wishing Leonie would burst.

"My name is Charles Burgess." The man remained standing. "Miriam and I were married in nineteen fifty."

James put down his drink. "Mum? Is this true?"

Miriam nodded.

"Well," said James, "that's not so terrible, is it?" He looked around the table, wondering what all the drama was about. "Plenty of people get divorced."

"They do," Charles agreed. "But that's the thing, you see. We never did."

James frowned. "But… hang on, this doesn't make sense. My parents married in nineteen fifty-two. I've seen the wedding photographs. That's only two years after—"

"Our wedding," supplied Charles Burgess. "And ours certainly didn't end in divorce. Which I'm afraid makes your mother a bigamist."

Nobody gasped. A wisp of white thistledown drifted idly over the gathered bottles and glasses. A bee settled on the table, briefly investigated a puddle of spilled wine, then flew off again.

The silence was abruptly broken by a snort of laughter. Rearranging her scarlet skirt, Leonie flapped her hands. "Sorry, sorry, but this is just too funny for words. Miriam, my mother-in-law, a bigamist! She dumped her husband, upped and left and married someone else!"

"Leonie." James flashed her a warning glance.

"But don't you see?" Leonie was enjoying herself far too much to stop now. "This is just brilliant. I mean, it was fifty years ago, so basically who gives a toss? But… bigamy! And when you think of all those years of grief Miriam's given *me*."

"Actually, I give a toss," said Charles Burgess.

"Come on." Leonie regarded him with scornful amusement. "It happened half a century ago." As she shrugged, the strap of her frilled top slipped off one shoulder. "It's just not that big a deal."

"Oh, it gets better," drawled Charles Burgess.

Gazing down at her hands, Miriam saw that they were shaking. Defiantly, she reached for her drink and gulped it down.

"I married Miriam because I loved her," Charles continued. "I thought we loved each other. For richer or poorer, until death do us part. When I said those words, I meant them."

Miriam couldn't look at him; she had meant them too. Meeting Charles Burgess at the age of eighteen had been an all-consuming experience. Theirs had been a passionate whirlwind romance. Everyone else had wanted Charles but she had been the one he'd chosen to marry. The trouble was, the fact that he was no longer single hadn't stopped the other girls chasing him. Particularly Pauline Hammond.

Beautiful, predatory Pauline Hammond, Charles's personal secretary and greatest fan. Seeing them together that Friday afternoon, Miriam had died inside. There had been rumors before then of course, endless hints dropped and warnings given. She had done her best to ignore them, hoping they'd somehow fade away, but deep down she'd known the truth, because sometimes you just *did*. And at that moment something had snapped. This was how it would always be with Charles. A married philanderer didn't change his spots.

All the old feelings of jealousy surged up now, as caustic and wounding as though they'd never been away. It was over fifty years since Miriam had felt them—since then, she had made sure she'd never been in a position to experience anything like that again—but now she could actually taste the metallic bitterness in her mouth. This was what had engulfed her as, almost deranged with grief, she had rushed home that bleak wintry afternoon and resolved to escape. And if she managed to hurt Charles even a tenth as much as he had hurt her, then so much the better.

In less than an hour, Miriam had packed and left. Sod him. She would put the marriage behind her and make a new life for herself elsewhere. The only reason she'd even bothered leaving a brief note for him had been because, without it, the police might suspect him of having murdered her. Not that that would have bothered Miriam in the least, but it meant they would also have made intensive efforts to track her down.

"I came home from work one day and she was gone," Charles said now, addressing the assembled group. He added slowly, "And so had a fair amount of our money. You shouldn't have done that, Miriam. That was below the belt."

"Ha!" Leonie whooped with delight. "A bigamist *and* a thief."

"Why?" Miriam bridled. "Why was it below the belt? We were married, weren't we? It was *our* money, not just yours."

Except, she had to acknowledge, it had been mainly Charles's money. She had contributed what she could, but he had earned so much more than her. Then again, had that been her fault? And she'd only taken two thousand pounds, it wasn't as if he'd been left penniless.

"You destroyed my life," Charles continued remorselessly. "I couldn't stop looking for you. I loved you, Miriam, and you did this to me. Everywhere I went, I'd catch a glimpse of a dark-haired girl in the distance and think it was you. But it never was. And every time I thought I was getting over you, something would happen to knock me back. Did you enjoy the video of the wedding, by the way?"

Miriam couldn't speak.

Frowning, James said, "What video?"

"It's up in the loft." Tilly's voice was small. "Hidden in one of the cases."

Everyone except Miriam turned to stare at Tilly, who shrank down in her chair and examined her bitten fingernails.

"Remember Gerry Barker, our best man? Brought his cine camera along and filmed the reception," Charles explained for the benefit of the rest of them. "A week later he was called up for National Service. He came back eighteen months after Miriam had left, brought me the reels of tape. I'm not a crying man," Charles said evenly, "but when I sat down and watched that cine film, I cried."

Miriam looked at him. "How touching. Did Pauline Hammond cry too?"

"Miriam." Charles shook his head. "I never had anything to do with that girl. Either before or after you disappeared. Never."

Anger rose up in her. "I saw you, that Friday afternoon. I came to your office and saw you with her. I was watching through the glass door, Charles."

"Really? And what were we doing, having sex on the desk? Excuse me," Charles apologized to Tilly. "But this is important."

"You had your arms round her," Miriam blurted out. "She was clinging to you and you were holding her. You were kissing the top of her head."

"I know. Because she'd just had a call from the hospital, telling her that her mother was dead. She was distraught," said Charles Burgess. "Her mother was hit by a car and killed. I took Pauline to the infirmary. When I got home I would have told you. Except I couldn't tell you," he concluded heavily, "because by then you were gone."

Miriam couldn't breathe. It hadn't looked like that kind of embrace to her. "Is that true?"

"One hundred percent. I never lied to you then, and I'm not lying now. I spent the next ten years trying to find you," said Charles. "And all that time you were with some other man, spending my money. You married again within... what was it, eighteen months? Quick work, Miriam. And how long have you lived here, exactly?"

The look on Miriam's face told him all he needed to know. He smiled. "Fifty years, then. Nice house." Charles nodded approvingly at the huge ivy-clad property. "Very nice. Must be worth... what, three-quarters of a million now? You always did have good taste." He paused. "So, is this where my money went?"

Miriam knew she should have hired a hit man. "Is that why you're here, to claim your money back? Is that really what this is all about?"

Her brain was racing now; he wasn't getting his hands on this house. One way or another she'd have to pay him off. How much was two thousand pounds in today's money anyway? One hundred thousand? Good grief, would Edward help her out?

"Give me some credit," said Charles. "I don't care about the money. I may have done at the time, but I'm over that now. Besides," he added with wry amusement, "my home in Edinburgh is twice the size of this place. I ended up doing pretty well for myself."

"So what, then?" Miriam regarded him with suspicion.

"You ruined my life, but I never stopped loving you. My wife died two years ago," Charles announced. "That means we're both free to give it another go. I want you back, Miriam. You loved me once. I can make you love me again."

Miriam's stomach lurched. Across the table, she saw Laurie's eyes narrowing.

"Your wife died," she echoed, hazy on the subject of how these things worked. "So you did divorce me?"

Charles shook his head. "After seven years, I had you declared dead."

Heavens, imagine that, thought Miriam. I'm officially dead.

"Look, you can't just turn up like this and say you want her back," Laurie exploded. "You can't do that!"

For a split second Miriam was tempted to retort, "Why not? You did."

But Laurie was on her side. Or, more accurately, his father's.

Turning to Laurie, Charles Burgess said pleasantly, "Of course I can. It's a free country."

"But Miriam isn't free. She has someone." Laurie indicated Edward, who didn't react. "This is my father. He and Miriam are… a couple."

Which wasn't strictly true, thought Miriam with a pang of guilt. Maybe they were a couple emotionally, but not in the physical sense. Laurie knew that.

Charles Burgess nodded and said, "Dr. Welch, that's right, I saw the photograph of you with Miriam in the paper. But the two of you aren't married. If you were," he added, addressing Edward in a reassuring manner, "I wouldn't have come."

"But they're together," Laurie insisted. "They have been for years."

"All the more surprising, then, that they haven't married."

"That is none of your business," Laurie angrily retorted. "Anyway, you're wasting your time. Miriam isn't interested."

"You don't know that. She might be. All I'm asking for is the chance to find out," said Charles Burgess. "I'm here in Bristol for the next week, staying at the Swallow Royal. Miriam, I'd like you to join me for dinner this evening. You owe me that much, at least."

"And what if she says no?" persisted Laurie, earning himself a kick under the table from Nadia.

"Simple, I'll go straight to the police. Miriam will be arrested and charged with bigamy and theft. It'll be humiliating," Charles promised equably, "and the consequences may be unpleasant. Trust me, I'd make sure the case went to trial. And Miriam could end up in prison."

Tilly's eyes were like saucers.

Charles Burgess looked at Edward and shrugged. "Sorry. But Miriam's my wife. Was my wife," he corrected himself. "She was mine first."

At long last, Edward spoke.

"Feel free," he said coolly, causing everyone to stare at him in disbelief. Pushing back his chair and smoothing the front of his shirt, he rose to his feet. "You're absolutely right. I've been asking her to marry me for years and she's always said no. Looks like I've been wasting my time."

"Edward," Miriam gasped, "that's not true! You can't—"

"On the contrary, I can. Maybe you've been waiting for something like this to happen. I don't know. Now if you'll excuse me."

"This is crazy," Laurie burst out when his father had left.

Shaken, Miriam looked at Charles. "I think you'd better go too."

"I'll pick you up at seven thirty," said Charles.

Everyone was looking at Miriam, waiting for her to tell him to sod off.

But it wasn't that simple.

"Right." Miriam met his steady gaze, remarkably unchanged after all these years. "Seven thirty."

"That's blackmail," Laurie muttered.

Charles smiled broadly as he turned to leave. "Maybe. But under the circumstances I think it's fair enough, don't you?"

Leonie showed Charles out of the house. Moments later she called across the lawn, "It's OK, he's gone."

Miriam began to tremble. Unable to face her family, she said, "We need more gin," and headed for the kitchen.

Leonie was there already, switching on the kettle.

"Well, this is a turn-up. How did it feel, seeing him again?"

"Stupid question." Miriam's tone was curt, belying the swirl of emotions she was actually experiencing.

"Who'd have thought it?" Leonie's bright eyes danced. "You of all people, a bigamist. And a thief!"

"Leonie, please don't."

"Not to mention the other business. Poor old Edward, still not having the faintest idea why you won't marry him. Oh God, and did you see the way he pressed his hand to his chest as he stood up? For a second there I thought it was going to happen all over again. I mean, ironic or what?"

Close to despair, Miriam snapped, "Will you keep your voice down?"

"Fine, fine. I'm just saying it would have been a hell of a coincidence, that's all." With a naughty grin, Leonie mimicked clutching her chest. "I mean, first Josephine, then Edward. To lose one member of the Welch family is bad luck, but to lose two is downright suspicious."

"Leonie, shut up."

"Oh, come on, relax. I can't believe you've never told Edward. I mean, it's not as if you did it on purpose. And when you think about it, he was just as much to blame as you."

The kitchen door swung open. In the doorway stood Laurie and Nadia. All the color had drained from Nadia's face.

Evenly, Laurie said to Miriam, "She can't believe you've never told Edward what?"

Chapter 54

NADIA HAD TO SIT down. She couldn't believe what she was hearing. Aided and abetted by Leonie—and also because she no longer had a lot of choice—Miriam was spilling out the whole story. It was no secret, of course, that Laurie's parents hadn't had the happiest of marriages, but none of them had realized the extent of Josephine's destructive ways. Her only enjoyment in life had come from making Edward miserable, whilst all the time she had reveled in her status as the wife of an eminent neuropsychiatrist. Determined to keep up appearances, she had flatly refused to even contemplate divorce. Edward, at the end of his tether, had turned to Miriam for support. Predictably, their friendship had deepened. Within months they had fallen in love and embarked on a discreet affair.

"But not discreet enough," Miriam admitted resignedly. "She found out, of course." (To her eternal shame, thanks to an emerald earring Josephine had found in Edward's bed, but Miriam couldn't bring herself to say this now.) "That was when Josephine called me over to the house while Edward was at work. We were out in the garden and she confronted me. It was awful, she was screaming at me, getting redder and redder in the face, yelling that I was destroying her marriage and calling me terrible names. And because I knew I deserved it, I didn't retaliate, but that only made Josephine more furious. Then… oh God, and then all of a sudden she made this gasping noise and clutched her chest. For about a second, maybe less. Then she just slumped to the ground and that was it." Miriam's dark eyes filled with tears. "She was dead. I checked. There was nothing I could do." She paused, unable to meet Laurie's narrowed gaze. "And then Leonie was there. She'd been visiting, waiting for Tilly to come home from school. When she heard Josephine shouting and came over to see what was going on, she heard everything else too. We rang 999 and I made her promise never to tell anyone about the argument. I didn't want Edward to feel any worse than I knew he already would. I told the ambulance men that Josephine had invited me over to admire her garden… well, at the time I thought that was why she *had* invited me over…"

Nadia was in shock. Laurie's face was utterly expressionless. First James, then Tilly and Clare had by this time joined them in the kitchen and were listening with equal disbelief.

Miriam finally summoned the courage to look at Laurie. "I'm sorry."

Laurie didn't speak. Nadia felt her nails digging into her palms. The silence in the kitchen was excruciating.

Leaping into the breach, Leonie said brightly, "But it's not as if it was deliberate! A heart attack like that can happen at any moment. And Miriam's felt so guilty all these years—that's why she hasn't married Edward, which *I* think is completely ridiculous—"

"I used to respect you," Laurie told Miriam. He shook his head in disgust. "What a difference a day makes."

"Oh come on," began Leonie, but Laurie quelled her with a look. "Isn't it time you left?"

Deeply offended, Leonie held her arm out to Tilly. "Fine. Come on, darling, let's go."

"And someone had better pay a visit to my father." Laurie turned his cool gaze on Miriam. "It doesn't seem fair, somehow, that he should be the last to know." Another pause. "Do you want me to tell him exactly how his wife died?"

Miriam closed her eyes and shook her head. "I'll do it myself."

"Let's get out of here," Laurie muttered when Miriam had disappeared over the road and Leonie had borne Tilly off to Brighton.

"I'll be all on my own," Clare protested as he ushered Nadia toward the door. "Can't I come with you?"

Pretending to consider her offer for a second, Laurie said, "How can I put this? *No.*"

"Right, I'm off." James reappeared, jangling his car keys in an agitated manner. "I'm going over to Annie's."

"Keep your fingers crossed," said Clare.

"Why?"

"Annie may not want you anymore when she hears your parents' marriage is null and void." Clare shot him a mischievous smile. "That makes you illegitimate."

Nadia clung to the passenger seat as Laurie drove at high speed, rocketing through the narrow lanes. When they pulled up outside a wisteria-clad country hotel on the outskirts of Winterbourne he said, "Sorry, I can't face going home tonight. Is this OK?"

Nadia nodded and squeezed his hand. Feeling desperately sorry for him, she could only guess at his sense of betrayal.

"Should have bought one of those houses." Laurie sighed; he had put in an offer on the house in Clarence Gardens, but Jay was holding out for the asking price. "It's mad, having to book into a hotel just to give myself space to think. I keep picturing it, you know." He glanced somberly at Nadia. "My mother arguing with Miriam. When someone dies, you imagine it happening, you go over and over it in your mind. Now it feels like I have to start all over again."

"Come on." Nadia's tone was soothing. "Let's get you booked in."

Laurie looked distraught. "You're not going to leave me here? I'd rather you stayed. I mean, no funny business, just… you know… I could really do with the company."

Nadia's heart went out to Laurie, who was clearly going through hell. How could she abandon him now, after a day like today? Gazing up at the honey-colored hotel basking in the early evening sunshine, she said, "D'you think they sell toothbrushes?"

"Let's just get a room." Wearily, Laurie rubbed his hands over his face. "God, I'm shattered. To be honest, all I want to do is sleep."

This, of course, turned out to be a big lie. What Laurie had really wanted to do was sleep with *her*.

And under the circumstances, Nadia thought some time later when it was all over, how could she have refused?

Well, he'd needed comforting. Cheering up. The reassurance of intimate bodily contact.

And celibacy wasn't easy for girls either.

She lay on her back, catching her breath, and gazed up at the beamed ceiling.

"See?" Laurie murmured against her shoulder. "I knew you could make me feel better."

Then his mouth closed over hers once more, warm and sweetly familiar, and Nadia gave herself up to the sheer pleasure of it. Their bodies fitted together so well, just as they always had done. They knew each other's likes and dislikes. Making love with Laurie had always been magical.

"What?" said Nadia, realizing that he was gazing down at her.

"Nothing." Laurie's green eyes sparkled. "Aren't you glad we came here now?"

Nadia looked at him. "Are you telling me you deliberately planned this? Were you only *pretending* to be upset?"

"Of course not. I didn't plan anything, I swear." Vehemently Laurie shook his head, then broke into an unrepentant grin. "But OK, I admit it, as soon as we pulled up outside this place it did occur to me that this could be my big chance."

Nadia smiled too, because that was the thing about Laurie; he'd always been honest.

"And I fell for it."

"Come on, you kept me waiting long enough. I was starting to get worried, I can tell you. And now there are two things I have to say."

"Fire away."

"I love you." Laurie kissed her again, his gold-blond hair flopping over his forehead. "And I'm bloody starving."

"There's a restaurant downstairs." Nadia squirmed helplessly as he began to nuzzle the part of her neck where he knew she was most ticklish.

"Boring. We'd have to wear clothes. And I wouldn't be allowed to ravish you between courses. I think we're probably safer having dinner up here."

"Less likelihood of being arrested," Nadia agreed.

As Laurie reached across her for the hotel phone, his warm skin sliding over hers, not having to get dressed seemed infinitely preferable.

When he'd finished ordering dinner, Laurie gazed soberly at the phone in his hand. "I should call Dad, find out how he's doing. But I just can't. Not tonight."

"Don't then." Whisking the phone from him, Nadia rapidly punched out her own home number. "They're all adults, let them sort out their own mess—hi, it's me. Anyone shot anyone else yet? OK, that's good. Yes, Laurie's fine too. We're staying at Hutton Hall. He just needed to get away for a bit. We'll be back tomorrow, OK? Call me if anything drastic comes up."

Reaching for the phone, Laurie added, "But only if it's really drastic. All in all, we'd prefer not to be disturbed."

At the other end of the line, Clare let out a squeal of delight. "You sleazebag! You're naked, aren't you? I can tell by the sound of your voice!"

"You may think that." Laurie kept a straight face. "I couldn't possibly divulge that information."

"You finally did it," whooped Clare. "About bloody time too."

Laurie grinned. "I know. Luckily, I was worth waiting for."

Worth waiting for, worth waiting for, oh crikey...

"Hey," said Laurie as Nadia attempted to slide out of bed. "Where are you going?"

His arms closed round her waist before she could escape. It had just occurred to Nadia that her mobile was in her bag on the dressing table, and that Jay had said he'd call. If he was back in time, they'd arranged to meet for dinner. After everything that had happened this afternoon it had gone clean out of her mind.

"Just wanted to check my mobile, see if there are any messages." As she said it, Nadia realized there wouldn't be. Her phone was switched on and her bag was less than six feet away. If Jay had called, she would definitely have heard it ringing.

As Laurie rolled her over, he said playfully, "Who were you expecting to hear from?"

"No one." Actually, it was just as well Jay hadn't rung; she'd only have had to turn him down. Leaping out of bed with one man to rush off with another probably wasn't considered good etiquette.

"Did you sleep with him?"

"Who?" Honestly, how did he do that? Nadia looked mystified.

"Come on, you know who I'm talking about. Your boss. The one I suggested you sleep with."

Nadia shook her head; with Laurie's eyes upon her, it was nice not to have to flounder, debating whether or not to lie.

"No."

"Good." Laurie ran his fingers gently through her tangled curls, pushing them back from her face and kissing her forehead. "I'm glad."

Catching sight of his watch, Nadia said, "Miriam's with Charles Burgess now. I wonder how it's going."

Pushing her back down amongst the pillows, Laurie murmured, "Let's not worry about other people now. I'd rather concentrate on us."

———

Nadia's phone wasn't in her bag. Wandering out into the garden to clear away the debris of the afternoon's drinks party, Clare had begun desultorily collecting up plates and glasses when she heard the familiar chirpy ringtone and spotted the mobile lying in the grass under the table.

Since anything was better than playing at being a waitress—particularly when there was no one else around to shower you with praise—Clare abandoned the glasses, retrieved the small silver phone and answered it.

"Hello?"

"At last. I've been leaving messages for the last hour. Why didn't you call me back?"

Recognizing the voice, Clare said jauntily, "Because this isn't Nadia. You're lucky enough to be talking to her beautiful, far more talented sister. Not that you deserve to be," she went on, "seeing as you still haven't bought a single one of my dazzling masterpieces, but that's just the kind of generous, forgiving person I am."

"Actually, I was thinking about that earlier today. We may be able to come to an arrangement." Jay was certainly sounding cheerful. "Can I have a word with Nadia?"

"She's not here. All kinds of weird stuff has been happening today, you wouldn't believe it. Anyway, Nadia's gone off with Laurie, to stay in some posh country house hotel. She rang not long ago from their room, and let me tell you, they weren't reading the Gideon Bible. Now, what kind of an arrangement?"

There was a pause. Then Jay said, "What?"

"You said we could come to an arrangement. So tell me all about it," Clare prompted. "We're talking about some kind of commission, right?"

"Yes, but—"

"Brilliant! I knew you had good taste. Look, I'm not doing anything this evening, so why not come round and we'll have a chat about it, find out exactly what you have in mind?"

"Well, er…"

"Oh, go on," Clare wheedled. "Everyone else is out and I just hate being here on my own." Innocently she added, "And if you're really good, I'll tell you all about Miriam being a bigamist."

Chapter 55

"So there you go," Clare concluded some time later, having spilled every last bean to Jay Tiernan. "Who'd have thought it? Miriam Kinsella, Bristol's very own answer to Robin Hood! Except Miriam robbed from the rich and gave to herself. And she's having dinner with the long-lost husband right now. I can't wait to see how she gets herself out of this mess. Another drink?"

"No thanks. I can't stay long." As Jay shook his head, Clare wondered why she'd never realized before quite how attractive he was. Except... well, she *had*, of course, but it simply hadn't been relevant then. At first, she'd had Piers. Then she'd been pregnant. After that, there had been Nadia's ambivalent attitude toward Jay, the rules of the game being that you didn't contemplate tangling with anyone your sister might have earmarked for herself.

At least, not if you wanted to keep your various body parts intact.

But now that Nadia had finally made up her mind and chosen Laurie, those rules no longer applied. And Clare was rapidly coming to the conclusion that this might be No Bad Thing. With those warm brown eyes and that narrow curving mouth, Jay Tiernan was really rather gorgeous. And *far* more her type than Nadia's.

"Your turn now." Refilling her own glass from one of the half-empty bottles still strewn across the garden table, Clare shot him a challenging smile. "So, what kind of a commission are we talking about?"

Jay sat back and pushed his fingers through his dark hair. "Well, Nadia tells me you do portraits."

"I do." Clare nodded with pride.

"Are you good?"

"Bloody cheek. Of course I'm good!"

"Right." Jay smiled. "Well, it's a portrait I'm after. It's kind of a family tradition. My mother arranged for me and Anthony to be painted when we were babies, and I was wondering if you could do the same. My nephew was born this morning. My brother's son."

Clare nodded sympathetically. "Nadia told me. How's Belinda doing?"

"Pretty well, all things considered. And the baby's amazing." Jay paused. "So what do you think? Could you manage that, working from photographs? Or would it be too...?"

Sensing that he didn't entirely trust her—portrait work was, after all, a particular skill—Clare leapt to her feet. "Come on, follow me. I'll show you some of my stuff."

Upstairs in her room, she pulled out sketch pads and thrust them into his arms.

"These are good," said Jay. "The only thing that was slightly bothering me is, what if Belinda isn't wild about the idea? I want it to be a surprise for her, but some people aren't keen on having family portraits in oils on permanent display. I mean, I'm more than happy to pay five hundred quid for the painting, but I don't want her feeling obliged to hang the bloody thing on the wall simply because she knows it cost a lot of money." As he spoke, his gaze wandered over to Clare's easel set up by the window, where the current work-in-progress was drying. "That's very nice."

The three-quarters finished canvas, her fairground painting, was, if she said so herself, one of her better ones.

"It's going to be called 'Taken For A Ride.'" Assuming a businesslike air, Clare said, "OK, I have a suggestion. I could do you the portrait in oils or gouache for five hundred pounds, but that's the hard way to get a true likeness. And watercolors always look drippy."

Flipping through one of her sketch pads and showing Jay a detailed drawing of Tilly curled up on the garden swingseat reading a book, she said firmly, "You get a far better result with a pencil sketch. Why don't we do it that way? Then if Belinda isn't wild about it she doesn't have to feel guilty, because it won't have cost you anything."

She saw Jay frown. "Why won't it cost me anything? You have to charge me."

"No I don't. I'll do the pencil drawing for free." Triumphantly Clare added, "That way, you'll have all that lovely money left over to buy one of my fabulous paintings."

Jay regarded her with amusement. "Taken For A Ride?"

"Not at all, I call it a bargain."

Finally he nodded. "OK. You've got yourself a deal."

"You won't be disappointed." Clare shivered with pleasure as her bare arm not-quite-accidentally brushed against his. Closing the sketch pad and throwing it onto the bed, she said invitingly, "Shall we celebrate by tearing each other's clothes off and having wild unbridled sex?" Well, her eyes said that. Her mouth, rather less excitingly, said, "Shall we celebrate with another drink?"

"Better not. I should be getting back." Jay smiled, as if acknowledging the other, nonverbal offer and regretfully declining it.

When they reached the front door, Clare paused. OK, so maybe not sex, but surely a kiss wasn't out of the question? Just to get the ball rolling, so to speak.

Reaching to open the door, she felt her cropped top ride up to expose even more of her torso. Tugging it back down resulted in a tantalizing glimpse of tanned cleavage and fuchsia-pink bra. Clare grinned in apology, then leaned back against the open door and smiled her best temptress's smile up at Jay, who was going to have to squeeze past her before he could get out of the house.

"Well, see you again soon," said Jay. "I'll drop those photos over in the next few days."

"Pleasure doing business with you." Tilting her face up to his, just fractionally, Clare gave him the perfect opportunity to drop a kiss on her parted lips.

Bugger. He didn't.

"Tell Nadia I'll call her tomorrow." Jay skillfully maneuvered himself past her bare midriff.

Clare shrugged. "I'll tell her if I see her. But if she's shacked up in a hotel room with Laurie, God only knows when she'll be back."

—⁓—

The hotel restaurant was the kind of glamorous, sedate place where people murmured to each other and took care not to scrape their cutlery against the plates. The clientele were pretty sedate too, elegantly turned out and quietly appreciative of their surroundings.

It wasn't the place to cause a scene and Miriam was grateful for that. Glimpsing her reflection in the mirror-lined walls, she thought how well she and Charles blended in. To look at the two of them enjoying their dinner, no one would ever guess why they were here.

"Why are you smiling?" said Charles.

"Oh." Miriam shook her head. "It just makes you think, doesn't it? If we look ordinary—the thieving bigamous wife and the husband she abandoned fifty years ago—can you imagine the kind of secrets this lot must be harboring?"

Charles put down his fork. "You've never looked ordinary in your life. You haven't changed a bit." He paused. "Tell me about the man you married. What was he like?"

What had Robert Kinsella been like? Miriam didn't hesitate. "The very opposite of you. A good man. Safe. I knew he'd never let me down. I liked him, so I married him. Then I grew to love him. He was kind and faithful, a wonderful husband. How about you?"

"I was a wonderful husband too. You just didn't trust me."

Miriam's mouth curved at the corners. Without her family looking on, it was far easier to relax. "I meant what was your wife like."

"Ah. The opposite of you. A good woman, safe. I knew she'd never plunder our bank account and run off."

Touché.

"Were you ever unfaithful to her?"

Charles shook his head. "Never. I wouldn't have been unfaithful to you, either. Miriam, when you left, I wanted to die. You ripped me apart. The only reason I didn't stick a shotgun in my mouth was because I kept hoping you might come back. Then I remarried, but it was never the same. There wasn't that spark. My wife always knew she was second best; poor Emily, she lived in fear of you. She was always terrified you might turn up on the doorstep one day, out of the blue, wreaking havoc."

"That's exactly what you did to me this afternoon," Miriam pointed out.

"I know. It wasn't planned, but I'm glad it happened like that, in front of your family. Call it redressing the balance," Charles said easily. "You can't do what you did to me and expect to get away scot-free."

"I don't know that Edward will ever forgive me."

"I don't know that I want him to. Who cares what he thinks? Miriam, I'm serious about this." Reaching across the table, Charles seized her hand. "I know I'm seventy-two with my hair turning gray and my joints starting to play up, but right at this minute, I feel like a twenty-two-year-old. Inside here"—he held her palm against the front of his crisp shirt—"it's the same as it ever was. The moment I saw you, my heart beat faster. It did it then, and it's still doing it now. You aren't married to Edward. You were married to me. When you disappeared, you made a monumental mistake, and I think you know it." His expression softened. "I also think you're beginning to regret it. It's those giveaway big brown eyes of yours. You never could hide anything from me."

"Except myself. And rather a lot of money," Miriam reminded him, which made Charles shout with laughter and diverted attention away from the fact that what he'd been saying was unnervingly true.

Like Robert, her late husband, Edward was charming and well-educated, a true gentleman in every way. But he didn't make her feel the way she did being here with Charles. Miriam thought she'd been doing a pretty good job of hiding it, but beneath the classic black Jean Muir silk-knit, her body was fizzing away like a twenty-year-old's.

"Well?" Charles was still holding her hand, his gaze intent. "Am I right?"

One great thing about being seventy was that blushing was no longer a problem. She hadn't blushed for decades.

"When I left, I did everything I could to put you out of my mind," Miriam said slowly. "I was devastated, but I told myself I was better off without you. And I haven't had an unhappy life," she went on. "Robert was a wonderful man. I have a terrific family. I know I've given Edward a hard time, but we've been happy too. We really have."

Well, apart from the bit where his wife found out about us, confronted me, and dropped dead on the spot... and the fact that in order to punish myself I've never since that day allowed Edward back into my bed.

"I don't want to hear about how happy you've been." Charles shook his head. "It's the future I'm interested in. I'm seventy-two, Miriam. Who knows how long we have left? I want to spend the rest of my life with you."

"Good grief, Charles, haven't you already suffered enough?" Shakily Miriam smiled, though her eyes were suddenly bright with tears.

To think that her entire life could have been so different. If she hadn't met Robert Kinsella, she would never have had James...

"I never stopped loving you," said Charles Burgess.

Miriam was eighteen again, her heart racing crazily and the butterflies swirling en masse in her stomach. Nobody else had been able to make her feel like this. Heavens, poor Charles, what had she done to him? She'd been so convinced that he'd been having an affair with Pauline Hammond—in part, it had to be said, thanks to Pauline herself—that it had never occurred to her that she might have made a terrible, *terrible* mistake.

And what was she to do now? Well, Edward would no longer want anything to do with her, that was for sure. Not after today.

"What are you thinking?" said Charles.

Good question, thought Miriam. She was thinking that maybe she did owe it to Charles to try again, to see if she could make amends for having caused him so much pain. And if they were to try, she would be able to spare her family the shame and humiliation of her bigamy being exposed.

Oh Lord, but could she do it?

Her voice breaking with emotion, Miriam whispered, "It's good to see you again, Charles."

The lines around his eyes deepened as he broke into a smile. "My dear. Not half as good as it is to see you."

Chapter 56

"You can't tell me what to do, you're not my mother!"

"And I'm bloody glad I'm not, you nasty spoiled brat, but I can tell you not to steal money from my purse."

"God, I hate you!"

"Trust me, not nearly as much as I hate you."

The vicious argument between Leonie and Tamsin had carried on like this for some time, insults flying back and forth with such increasing recklessness that Tilly had been convinced it would end in blows. Appalled, she had been forced to witness the battle from the sidelines. Finally, Brian had arrived home and frog-marched his furious crimson-faced daughter to her room.

Twenty minutes later, he had emerged with Tamsin and made her apologize to Leonie. Afterwards, as Leonie had dropped Tilly at the station, she'd said, "That girl's going through a difficult stage." Then, flinging her arms round her own daughter, she had added, "Never mind, darling, it'll be so much better once you're here. Having you to keep an eye on her will make all the difference in the world."

Tilly really didn't see how it could. Tamsin had never taken a blind bit of notice of anything she said. It was a scary prospect, and one that had been haunting her on the train all the way back from Brighton.

This was it now. She was here to pack up her belongings and say her good-byes. On Saturday morning, Leonie would be driving up to collect her and her things, and her life in Bristol would be over.

Tilly wondered if anyone would actually miss her.

Probably not. They seemed to have more than enough to occupy them just now. As Leonie had pointed out with a little too much relish, other people might put up a good front and pretend they were perfect, but it was never true. Deep down, they all had their shameful secrets.

Even Miriam, much to Leonie's delight.

The train pulled into Temple Meads station and squealed to a halt. Peering through the dusty window, Tilly wondered if anyone was here to meet her—when she'd phoned home last night, she had made a point of telling Clare what time she'd be getting in. There was no sign that the hint had been taken.

Oh well.

Hauling her sports bag over her shoulder, Tilly made her way out of the station and headed for the row of bus stops. It was starting to rain, the gray clouds overhead matching her mood. She was hungry, but not hungry enough to queue up at the buffet for a stale bun that would cost a fiver. When she—

"Whaaa!" Tilly shrieked as a pair of hands covered her eyes. Spinning round, she saw Cal grinning at her and threw her arms round him. "Oh my God, you made me jump! How did you know I was here?"

"Rang the house this morning. Your sister told me which train you'd be on. I meant to be there on the platform when you pulled into the station, but the bus was late. I thought I'd missed you…"

Oh Cal, dearest Cal. She was going to miss him too. Terrified that she was about to cry, or say something hopelessly embarrassing, Tilly beamed at him. She was damned if she'd spend her last couple of days in Bristol moping and whining; that was a surefire way of guaranteeing that even Cal would be glad to see the back of her.

"I brought you back a souvenir from Brighton. A key ring!"

"You shouldn't have," Cal said gravely, when she'd presented it to him with due ceremony.

Tilly dimpled. "Why not? You're worth it."

"I meant you should have got me something better. I deserve so much more than a lousy key ring—*ouch!*" He ducked away, laughing, as she hit him over the head with it.

"Come on, let's go back to my place. Are you free for the rest of the day?"

"I'm all yours," Cal teased, and Tilly had to look away hurriedly before the tears could well up. She mustn't, absolutely *mustn't* cry.

When they reached Latimer Road, everyone was out.

Except Harpo, of course, who greeted Tilly with a ribald, Barbara Windsorish cackle followed by a wolf whistle.

"You've been watching too many *Carry On* films," Tilly told him.

"Oooh, matron," squawked Harpo, lovingly nipping her fingers as she fed him a raisin.

"Hey." Cal moved toward her as Tilly's face abruptly crumpled. "Don't cry. He didn't mean to hurt you."

"It's not Harpo." The dam had burst without warning. Tilly sank to her knees, burying her head in her hands. "It's just… oh God… I don't want to leave. I *love* this family. I don't want to move to Brighton."

"Nice pants." Only mildly curious, Harpo peered down at her from his perch. "Shame about the arse."

"I even love Harpo," Tilly sobbed, "and he's so stupid it isn't true."

"Of course he is. There's absolutely nothing wrong with your arse." Cal was by this time kneeling on the floor next to her. Peeling Tilly's fingers away from her tear-stained face he said, "Come on, stop it, there's no need to cry."

Which just went to prove how stupid boys were, Tilly thought helplessly, because there was *every* need. And to prove it, tears were spurting out of her eyes, her nose was starting to run and she was making undignified hurrh-hurrh noises like a lawn mower refusing to start.

"You don't have to go if you don't want to. They can't force you to leave. Just tell them how you feel." Cal gently pushed her fine blonde hair away from her face before it could get entangled with the watery stuff dribbling from her nose. "If you're this upset, they'll let you stay."

Hopelessly, Tilly shook her head. It was true, but it wasn't enough. They might *let* her stay—of course they would, because they were nice people—but the fact remained that they'd far prefer it if she didn't.

Anyway, her mum really wanted her to go to Brighton. She couldn't let Leonie down.

Rubbing her eyes, Tilly sniffed loudly and shook her head. "I'm going." As she glanced helplessly around the room, she spotted the drinks cabinet. Wasn't that what everyone else did when they were going through a rough time? Crikey, at the first sign of tension practically all the grown-ups in this family reached for a bottle to steady their nerves. Maybe it would make her feel better too.

"What?" said Cal, because she was gazing into the distance like a zombie.

"Let's have a drink." Tilly made up her mind.

"I'll get them. Seven-Up or Pepsi?"

"I meant a proper drink." Sliding off the sofa, she headed for the glass-fronted cabinet. There was more in the kitchen, but this would do for a start. There was port. And cognac. And whisky and Cointreau and Tia Maria. Taking out a couple of cut-glass tumblers, Tilly handed one to Cal. "Come on, let's see what's so great about this stuff."

Cal hesitated. "Are you sure?"

"*I'm* sure. It's practically our last night together, but don't let it bother you." Recklessly Tilly sloshed tawny port into her tumbler. "You can wimp out if you like."

—⁓—

God, whisky was disgusting. What a con. It burned your mouth and made you choke and tasted absolutely vile. So did cognac. Who in their right mind would ever want to drink this stuff?

The Tia Maria wasn't much better. Tilly would have given it up as a bad job, but Cal had told her that his mother drank it with milk. This had improved it no end, turning it into a kind of medicinal coffee milkshake. And the port was pretty good too, nice and sweet and tasting of concentrated raisins. It was even better mixed with lemonade.

So was the Cointreau.

By eight o'clock, they were really getting into the swing of things.

"I can see why people do this." Tilly giggled at the way her voice sounded, kind of slurry but precise at the same time. "I feel better already. My knees have gone funny. Have your knees gone funny?"

"My knees are fine. But my hands are hilarious. My fingers feel like… you know, bunches of bananas? Oof, nearly dropped the bottle. 'S empty," said Cal, sounding worried. "Will your grandmother mind that we finished the Cointreau?"

"Noooo. They have to be used up." Vigorously, Tilly shook her head. "Can't let them go past their sell-by date, can you? Anyway, she's got loads. Does your tongue feel weird?"

Cal gave this some thought. "It feels like somebody else's tongue. How 'bout you?"

"Mine too. P'raps they swapped when we weren't looking. You've got mine and I've got yours. OK if I take yours to Brighton with me?" Tilly waggled her tongue at Cal and began to giggle helplessly. This was all right, she felt heaps better now, even if she did have an alien tongue in her mouth.

The next moment their heads jerked up at the sound of car wheels on gravel.

"Oh shit, someone's home!" In her hurry to hide the empty Cointreau bottle, Tilly sent her half-full tumbler of port flying. Staring in dismay at the broken glass and the spreading stain on the rug, she leapt to her feet. "They're going to go mental... oops, *ouch*..."

"Where can we hide?" Cal gazed around helplessly as Tilly rubbed her banged shin.

"Bloody tables, why do they have to have *edges*? No, no, they'll see you under the sofa." Giggling, she dragged him out by the ankles. Outside, car doors banged and there was the beep of an electronic lock. "Quick, out through the side door... we'll jump over the garden wall..."

Jump turned out to be the wrong word, conjuring up as it did connotations of leaping effortlessly through the air like a gazelle. Between the two of them they fumbled, stumbled, scrambled, and finally collapsed over the ivy-covered wall with all the grace of a couple of hippos.

Still, at least the bottles didn't break.

"What the bloody hell's been going on?" shouted Nadia, evidently having discovered the mess in the sitting room. Raising her voice, clearly thinking Tilly was upstairs, she bellowed incredulously, "Tilly, did you do this? Get down here this minute!"

Tilly and Cal, crouching on the other side of the wall, sniggered and tucked their stolen bottles—Harvey's Bristol Cream sherry and Taylor's tawny port respectively—under their T-shirts. Keeping close to the dusty ground, they scurried off down the lane away from the house.

By nine o'clock it was dark and the bottles were empty. Tilly, beginning to shiver, realized she was crying again. It had been like this all evening; one minute she and Cal were snorting with laughter over something or other, the next moment she was consumed with misery and just wanted to die. If this was what drinking did for you, maybe it wasn't so great after all.

"They hate me," she sobbed, using the hem of her thin T-shirt— yet again—to wipe her face.

Clumsily, Cal patted her hand. "Course they don't hate you."

"I've messed up their carpet. They can't wait to get rid of me." Tilly had never felt so lonely and unloved, like a puppy being bundled into a sack. "I'm just a nuisance. Where are you going? To be sick again?"

"I don't know." Cal had heaved himself upright and wandered over to the edge of the bridge. He took deep breaths and said fretfully, "I wish it would make up its mind."

"To be sick or not to be," proclaimed Tilly, who didn't feel sick at all. Her head was spinning, though. Round and round and round and round, like riding on the waltzers at the fairground. If she closed her eyes it was worse. Oh well, they'd finished the sherry and the port. Drunk some, spilled some… whatever, it was gone now. Shifting to try and get herself comfortable, she realized her bladder was full to bursting. That was the bad thing about railway bridges, they didn't come with a loo attached.

"I can't go home." Hot tears trickled down Tilly's cheeks. "They'll shout at me. I wish I was dead."

"You don't, you don't, don't *say* that." Having decided he wasn't going to be sick after all, Cal stumbled back to her. In the darkness, he tripped over her outstretched foot and landed clumsily, more or less on her lap. Wincing and crying, Tilly pushed him off her; he wasn't doing her poor distended bladder any favors.

"They hate me. They'll probably have a party when I'm gone, to celebrate. And if I don't find a loo *this minute* I'm going to wet myself."

"There's the loo." Solemnly, Cal pointed to a small bush. "Go on, I won't look, I promise."

Tuh, did she look stupid? Staggering to her feet, Tilly ignored the bush and reeled to the end of the bridge. The slope leading down to the railway line below was fenced off, but if she clambered over the fence and down the slope she could wee in peace, without Cal being able to see or hear her.

Much more dignified.

Scaling the fence, she landed with a *flumpph* on the other side and crawled to the safety of the wall of the bridge.

"What are you doing?" Cal's voice was raised in concern.

"You know what I'm doing. Weeing in a discreet ladylike manner, without an audience. And you mustn't listen either." Awkwardly, Tilly unfastened her shorts and half crouched, half leaned against the bridge. Balancing herself so that, hopefully, the stream of urine wouldn't go all over her feet, she allowed her muscles to relax.

Oh, bliss, utter bliss…

"Are you OK?"

"Will you shut up and leave me *alone*?" Honestly, do-gooders. How could he possibly think he was being helpful?

"You shouldn't be down there." Cal's voice drifted down to her.

"Don't *fuss*, I'm coming back up now." Irritated by his concern, Tilly struggled to pull her shorts back up—bit damp, oh well—and braced her feet against the stony, sloping ground. Her head was still doing its spinny thing, making it hard to regain her balance. One foot slipped on loose rock and she made a panicky grab for the side of the bridge. The next moment Tilly let out a shriek as she landed agonizingly and awkwardly on her back. And after that she couldn't stop herself falling, rolling down the steep rocky incline, her head bouncing and ricocheting off the ground as she flailed like a rag doll, screaming with pain and terror all the way down.

Chapter 57

Nadia crashed through the doors of the ER like a bullet. The phone call from the hospital had given her the fright of her life.

"My sister's here somewhere, she was brought in by ambulance, they found her on a railway track." She gabbled at the receptionist behind the desk. "Her name's Tilly Kinsella."

Recognizing the name, a passing nurse said, "Oh, the little thirteen-year-old? She's having her stomach pumped just now. If you take a seat, someone will be out to speak to you in a few minutes."

Nadia swung round in horror. "Her stomach pumped? You mean Tilly took an *overdose?*"

The nurse placed a reassuring hand on Nadia's. "She'd had rather a lot to drink. The doctors were having trouble treating her injuries, she was being a bit... well, uncooperative, shall we say? They'll come and have a word as soon as they've finished."

"Can't I see her now?"

"Just be patient." The nurse nodded toward the far corner of the waiting room. "That's her friend over there, the one who came in with her."

Turning, Nadia said, "Cal."

"I'm sorry, I'm so sorry, it wasn't my fault." Cal flinched as Nadia loomed over him. White-faced, disheveled, and evidently still pretty much the worse for wear himself, he wailed, "I told her not to climb over the fence, but she wouldn't listen. And then she fell and landed on the track. I managed to pull her off, but there was blood on her face and I thought she was dead. I had to leave her and run to the nearest house to call an ambulance… I was so scared she'd crawl back onto the track and a train would come… but the doctor says it's just cuts and bruises, he thinks she'll be OK…"

"Cal, Tilly's thirteen. She doesn't drink. How did this happen?" Nadia tried not to picture Tilly, retching and struggling as her stomach was pumped. It made no sense at all.

"It wasn't me." Fearfully, Cal blinked up at her. "Tilly wanted to get drunk. She was just so upset, in a real state. I couldn't stop her crying, then she opened the first bottle and said maybe drinking it would make her feel better. It wasn't my idea, I promise."

Cal was looking terrible, bedraggled and mud-stained. His eyes were red-rimmed. He smelled of alcohol and Extra Strong mints with undertones of vomit.

"Upset? Why would Tilly be upset? *Why* was she crying?"

"Because she doesn't want to move to Brighton. She doesn't want to live with her mother and Brian and Tamsin. She wants to stay here"—Cal gestured dramatically around the decrepit waiting room—"with all of you."

Dismayed, Nadia said, "Are you sure? So why's she going, then? Why doesn't she stay? Why didn't she *tell* us any of this?"

"Because she thinks you want to get rid of her."

"*What?*"

Cal dropped his gaze to the floor. "She thinks she's in the way. A nuisance. She said you all hated her." Defensively he added, "But I told her that wasn't true."

Nadia felt sick. Sick and numb.

The nurse appeared and beckoned to her. "You can see Tilly now."

Cal, almost in tears, said, "I'll wait here."

Nadia searched in her jeans pocket, found a couple of pound coins, and slipped them into his hand. "Get yourself a drink."

Then with a brief smile, she indicated the machine against the wall. "Maybe just a Coke, this time."

The sight of Tilly lying on the narrow bed in the curtained-off cubicle brought a lump to Nadia's throat. The sheets were rumpled, as if she'd been battling furiously with the nurses. Her face was as white as her hospital gown, apart from the bruises and the sizable cut above her left eye. Bending over, Nadia dropped a kiss on Tilly's hot forehead. Tilly opened her eyes and her face promptly crumpled.

"I'm sorry about breaking the glass… the mess on the rug…"

"Oh, please. I can't believe this has happened. How d'you feel?"

Tilly licked her dry lips. "Horrible. They stuck a tube down my throat. I kicked one of the doctors. I've got a headache and my back hurts and there's blood and mud all over my T-shirt." She paused. "I suppose you're really cross with me."

"Don't be daft. You just gave me a shock." Nadia stroked her thin hand. "Tilly, why did you get drunk?"

A closed expression flickered over Tilly's face and she turned her head away. "No reason. Just to see how it felt."

"Cal's outside. He told me what you said. Tilly, is it true?" Nadia gave her arm a little shake. "Are you only going to Brighton because you think we don't want you here?"

A tear leaked out of the corner of Tilly's closed eyes.

"Because that's just bollocks," Nadia exclaimed. "I don't know how you can even *think* it. Tilly, we love you! We'd *all* rather you stayed, don't you know that?"

The tears were flowing faster now, dripping into Tilly's ears. "No one said it. Everybody j-just seemed really cheerful, like they didn't c-care. You all said it was up to me."

"Here, wipe your ears." Nadia grabbed a tissue from the box on the trolley behind her. "Sweetheart, we had to say that. Miriam drilled it into us. She told us we mustn't try and persuade you to stay because that wouldn't be fair on you. Leonie's your mother. If you wanted to be with her, we had to let you go. She said we weren't allowed to make you feel guilty."

"Are you sure? Is that r-really true?"

"Of course it's true! But if you don't want to go anyway, we don't have to worry anymore. You can stay here and we'll *all* be happy." Nadia gave her a hug so fierce that Tilly felt as if she was tumbling down the rocky slope all over again. Half of her wanted to burst with joy because she wasn't unwanted after all.

But there was still an obstacle in the way. In a small voice, Tilly said, "Mum won't be happy. She'll be devastated. She wants us to be a proper family… her and Brian, Tamsin and me. She said she needs me there… oh God, I can't let her down."

Nadia marveled at Tilly's concern for her mother. Well, this was something she could certainly sort out.

"Don't worry about that. I'll explain everything to her. Just leave Leonie to me."

Half an hour later James and Annie arrived at the hospital. The doctor informed them all that in view of the alcohol poisoning and the fact that Tilly had been briefly knocked out following her fall, they would be keeping her in hospital overnight.

Outside in the parking lot, Nadia tried to get through to Leonie on the phone, but the line had apparently been disconnected.

Joining her, Cal said anxiously, "What's going to happen now?"

"Two things." Nadia stuffed the mobile back into her pocket. "Tilly's staying with us in Bristol."

"Ace!" Despite his hangover, Cal beamed with delight. "What's the other thing?"

"Your parents are going to be wondering where you are. I'm giving you a lift home."

~~~

Tilly was moved to the children's ward, the eye-watering amount of alcohol on her breath bizarrely at odds with the bright Winnie the Pooh murals on the walls.

"This place is for kids," she mumbled.

"I've got news for you," said James, as Annie rummaged in her handbag. "You are a kid."

"Here." Annie pulled out a brush. "Let me try and sort out your hair."

Tilly relaxed, enjoying the way Annie patiently unsnarled the tangled bits. James and Annie were such a couple, it was as if they'd known each other forever.

"I messed up your night."

"You're thirteen." James sat on the edge of the bed. "It's what thirteen-year-olds do."

"Are you really sure you don't mind if I stay?"

"Tilly, will you stop this? I was out of my mind with worry when Nadia called us tonight. You're family. You belong with us."

"But I'm not family. Not really. And you've got Annie now, you don't need—"

"You're as much a part of me as Nadia and Clare. Every bit as much," James said firmly. "And you're not going anywhere. Apart from anything else, I wouldn't have Annie if it wasn't for you. You organized that all by yourself."

Tilly smiled with satisfaction up at Annie. "I suppose I did, didn't I?"

"If it wasn't for you," James went on, "I'd still be calling in to that shop every night to buy an *Evening Post* and wondering who that beautiful woman was behind the counter."

"So you see?" Annie grinned at them both. "It's all thanks to you that he stopped going there and started coming to my shop instead."

"Sorry, did I wake you?"

Nadia rubbed her eyes; she'd managed roughly an hour's sleep last night before the doorbell had jerked her out of a terrifying dream about custard and trains and clinging to a hospital trolley as it juddered over broken glass... Oh well, good job it wasn't real.

Jay was, though. It was nine o'clock in the morning and he was here on the doorstep clutching a manila envelope.

"Come on in, I'll put the kettle on. Is this about the new house?"

"Actually, I brought the photos for Clare. Is she around?"

Was he kidding? At nine in the morning? Clare would be out for the count until midday at the very least.

Nadia made the tea and duly admired the photos of the baby. Lots of newborns look like blobs but Daniel, thankfully, had quirky eyebrows, huge dark eyes, and a tuft of dark hair like Tin-Tin. Clare would be able to make him instantly recognizable in the portrait.

"He's beautiful," said Nadia, because you always had to say that about a baby, even if it resembled a pickled walnut in a monkey suit. But actually this one didn't. Daniel was cute, with long eyelashes and dainty fingers and the sweetest pointy chin.

"Thanks. Even if he isn't mine," said Jay. "You look terrible, by the way."

"I'm allowed to look terrible. I have special dispensation." Slumping down opposite him at the kitchen table, she told Jay about last night. "So anyway, it's all sorted out now. Well, almost." Picking up her phone, she punched in Leonie's number for the tenth time. Still the monotone telling her it had been disconnected.

"Problem?" said Jay.

Nadia rubbed her face. "Can't get through to Leonie. I'll have to go and see her, explain what's happened. You don't need me today, do you?"

"I don't need you." Did she detect a smidgen of not-so-hidden meaning in those words? "Where's Laurie?"

"Taken his dad to Kent to stay with his sister. Edward wanted to get away for a couple of days and Laurie hasn't seen his aunt for years. God"—Nadia stretched and yawned noisily—"it's all happening at once. Miriam didn't come home last night. She doesn't even know about Tilly yet."

"You can't drive to Brighton," said Jay. "Look at the state of you."

"Thanks. Flattery'll get you everywhere."

"I mean you're exhausted."

"I don't have time to be exhausted. I promised Tilly I'd get this sorted out… oh bugger." Nadia leapt back as coffee slopped down her front and over her jeans. A fair amount had also splashed onto the kitchen floor.

"Leave that," said Jay as she rushed to the sink for a cloth. "I'll clear it up. You go and take a shower, change into something else. When you're ready, I'll drive you down to Brighton."

Weak with relief, Nadia said, "Seriously?"

"Look at what happened when you picked up a cup of coffee." Jay raised an eyebrow. "Now picture yourself trying to drive a car."

"You'd make someone a lovely wife," said Nadia with a grin.

"And put on something half decent," Jay retaliated. "You look as if you slept in those clothes."

Actually, she had.

"Cheek," said Nadia.

Chapter 58

THE DRIVE DOWN TO Brighton was stress-free. It was heaven not having to be behind the wheel. Having showered and changed into a short white skirt and orange strappy top, Nadia no longer felt like a vagrant. She'd even dolloped on some mascara and orangey-pink lipstick. The Stereophonics were belting out of the car radio, she was in the hands of a skilled driver, and her hair had managed to dry in ringlets like it was supposed to, instead of exploding into a ball of frizz.

Best of all, Jay hadn't mentioned Laurie once since setting out. Or Andrea. Instead, they had talked about Belinda and the baby, Tilly's close encounter with the railway track, and Jay's preliminary plans for Highcliffe House.

By the time they reached Brighton it was almost midday. Yesterday's rain had passed and the sun blazed down from a cloudless sky. As they drove along the crowded seafront, Nadia gazed longingly at the sea, cobalt blue and glittering like diamonds.

"Turn left up here," she directed Jay. "Now right. On to the end. This is their street."

"I'll wait in the Italian restaurant we just passed," said Jay. "Meet me there when you've finished. Good luck," he added as Nadia climbed out of the car.

She smoothed the creases out of her white denim skirt. "I don't need it. Leonie doesn't scare me."

Nadia nevertheless braced herself for the histrionics when her mother found out why she was here. Leonie didn't take kindly to not getting her own way.

Leonie opened the front door and gaped. "Darling, good heavens, this *is* a surprise!" Peering over Nadia's shoulder she said, "Have you brought Tilly with you?"

"No. We've being trying to phone you."

"Oh, the silly thing's on the blink. Don't tell me you drove all this way because you were worried about us." Leonie's eyes sparkled with amusement.

"Not quite." Taking a deep breath, Nadia followed Leonie into the house. "I'm here because Tilly isn't coming to live with you. She doesn't want to. We didn't realize because she didn't tell us until last night. She got drunk and ran off—"

"Tilly got *drunk*?"

"Very drunk. She ended up falling down a railway embankment and almost getting hit by a train. She's in the hospital," Nadia rattled on, "but it's OK, just cuts and bruises, she's coming home today. But she's made up her mind," she concluded firmly. "It's not fair to drag her away. I'm sorry, but Tilly's happy where she is. She's been with us since she was a baby and she doesn't want to move. So that's it, she's staying with us."

Phew. Got it all out in one go. Now all she had to do was weather Leonie's hysterics and make her realize she meant business; no one was about to change their mind.

"Well." Leonie leaned back against the fridge and shook her head. "That's a bolt from the blue." Then she broke into a bright smile. "What a relief."

Nadia thought she'd misheard. Either that or Leonie had somehow misunderstood.

"What?"

"Oh, come on, let's open a bottle of wine! After the time I've had, I deserve one." Gaily, Leonie sloshed Rioja into a couple of glasses.

"You wouldn't believe what's been going on here since I came back from Bristol. I'd suggest going out for lunch, darling, but I have to be here—the telephone repair man's coming round this afternoon to fix the phone. If you're hungry I could defrost a quiche."

"I'm not hungry." Still dazed, Nadia shook her head. "Where's Brian? And... um, Tamsin?"

"He's taken her to Sunderland, the little witch. That's it, she had her chance and she blew it. The police picked her up yesterday—she was with those ghastly druggy friends of hers, causing a public nuisance. Tamsin was caught shoplifting and got involved in a punch-up with the store manager. Well, it was the last straw for Brian. He's had it up to here with her. He phoned his ex-wife and told her she could jolly well have Tamsin back. Of course, Marilyn kicked up a bit of a fuss at first, but when he told her what her precious daughter's been getting up to recently, she realized she'd have to take her. To be honest, it's been a complete nightmare, darling. That girl's totally out of control. You should have heard her last night, the names she called us—and then she *ripped* the telephone socket out of the wall and chucked my CD player through the window! If you ask me, she needs a good slapping. She'll end up in prison, mark my words."

Transfixed, Nadia said, "So why were you so keen for Tilly to move in with you?" Although she suspected she already knew.

"Oh well, it was Brian's idea really. One teenage girl mooching around the place is a pain in the neck. Tamsin kept complaining that she was bored. Brian thought that having Tilly here would improve things—Tamsin would have some company and Tilly could keep her on the straight and narrow. To be honest, I had my doubts from the start, but Tamsin seemed quite keen on the idea. Anyway, she's gone now, so all's well that ends well. We don't need Tilly anymore. Now, shall I pop that quiche in the oven or not?"

Jay was relaxing at one of the steel-topped tables outside the Italian restaurant, drinking a double espresso and reading the paper. His dark hair gleamed in the sunlight. He was wearing a black shirt and his long legs, in cream jeans, were stretched lazily out in front of him. He looked gorgeous.

"That was quick." Glancing up as Nadia approached, he folded the paper and took off his dark glasses.

"I had to get out before I killed my mother." Collapsing onto the chair opposite him, Nadia tore off a corner of the newspaper and began ripping it to pieces.

"It didn't go well?"

"She's unbelievable." Nadia shook her head. "She never wanted Tilly in the first place. They just thought she'd come in useful as some kind of… baby-sitter. Oh, pweeugh." Spluttering in disgust, she realized she'd just helped herself to Jay's sugarless espresso. "Sorry, didn't mean to do that. I just can't get over how completely selfish my mother is. All she ever thinks about is herself."

"But it's sorted?" said Jay. "Tilly's staying in Bristol?"

"Forever. Until she's eighty-five at least. Then we *may* allow her to leave home." Managing a smile, Nadia ran through the details of her encounter with Leonie. When she'd finished, Jay indicated the menu.

"Are you hungry?"

If he asked her if she fancied some quiche, she might have to stab him with a fork.

"I can think of something I'd much rather do." As soon as the words were out, Nadia winced and shook her head. "Sorry, didn't mean it to come out like that."

"Story of my life." Jay's mouth tilted at the corners as he slid some coins onto the saucer on the table. "So what do you have in mind?"

Nadia flushed, remembering that Brighton was practically the dirty weekend capital of England.

"It just seems a shame to come all this way," she told Jay, "and not have a paddle in the sea."

It would have been nice to rip off her top and skirt and plunge into the waves. Nadia conjured up a mental image of herself, frolicking in the surf and looking fabulous. Except her lacy black bra was very obviously a bra and her Marks and Spencer knickers were bubble-gum pink.

Also, it was hard to frolic barefoot on slippery pebbles. And while the water may have looked sparkly and inviting, it was actually bitterly cold.

Jay had wisely waited for her on the beach. When she rejoined him less than two minutes later, he said, "Had enough?"

Nadia suspected he was laughing at her. Oh well.

"It's bloody freezing." Reaching for her sandals, she shivered. "And the pebbles hurt my feet."

"Ah well, that's the thing about the sea," Jay remarked easily. "Sometimes it tricks you into thinking it's more fun than it really is." He smiled briefly. "Never mind, everyone makes mistakes."

~~~

Exhaustion caught up with Nadia on the journey back to Bristol. Last night's lack of sleep hit her like a house brick. It was warm in the car and Jay had turned the radio down low.

Satisfied that she had done what she'd come to Brighton to do, Nadia slept.

"Brace yourself for the welcome committee." Jay woke her with a light hand on her arm, and she saw Clare and Tilly rushing out of the house.

"Is everything OK?" said Tilly, as Nadia jumped out of the car and hugged her.

"Never better. All sorted."

"Was Mum upset?"

"Disappointed," Nadia lied, exchanging a glance with Jay, "but she understood. She's fine about it. Anyway, how are you feeling?"

"Put it this way, hangovers are the pits." Tilly pulled a face. "I don't know how you old people manage it—I'm never going to drink port and sherry and Tia Maria and Cointreau again."

"Thanks for the photos," Clare told Jay. "They're perfect. And the baby is gorgeous. Brilliant eyebrows." Her smile broadened. "You can tell he's a Tiernan—he's going to be a real heartbreaker when he grows up."

Nadia raised an eyebrow of her own; Clare was sounding positively flirtatious.

"You're not leaving?" Clare protested as Jay climbed back into the car. "Stay for dinner, we've got loads."

"I have to get back. Business to take care of," said Jay.

"You scared him off," Nadia observed as the car disappeared down the driveway. "What was all that about?"

Clare shrugged, slightly miffed by Jay's unflatteringly speedy getaway. "Nothing, just being polite. Anyway, he's on the market, isn't he? And you're off it."

Nadia frowned. "What?"

"Well, you've got Laurie now. You're sorted. Like I told Jay the other night—"

"Hang on. You told Jay I was with Laurie now?" Nadia felt as if she'd been kicked in the stomach.

"Well, why not? You *were* with Laurie, at that hotel." Clare was indignant. "You can't have both of them, you know. It's not like when we were kids and you wouldn't let me even *watch* Duran Duran on TV because Simon Le Bon and John Taylor were both yours."

"But—"

"You're not allowed to argue," said Tilly bossily. "You have to be nice to each other. Remember what the doctor said," she smugly reminded them. "I'm not to be upset."

Chapter 59

THE RECEPTIONIST AT THE Swallow Royal buzzed Charles in his suite and informed him that a Dr. Welch was downstairs in reception wishing to see Mrs. Kinsella. Charles looked amused.

"Want me to send him away, darling?"

Miriam shook her head. "No. I'll go down and speak to him."

As she descended the sweeping staircase, she saw Edward waiting for her. Tall, shoulders back, wearing his brown tweed suit and looking more serious than she had ever known him.

It was an odd sensation, seeing him again like this after... what? Three days? Aware that her heart was beating faster, Miriam straightened her own shoulders as she reached the last stair.

"Edward? What's this about?"

He came straight to the point. "Us. You and me, Miriam. I'm here to tell you that if you stay with Charles Burgess, you'll be making the biggest mistake of your life."

Good grief, he was serious. Taken aback by his vehemence, Miriam said, "You don't know that."

"I *do* know. Maybe he loved you fifty years ago, but you've both changed since then. I love you now," Edward said forcefully, "and that's what matters. I'm never going to stop loving you. I'd never do anything to hurt you. Miriam, I don't blame you for Josephine's death. If that was what was stopping you from marrying me, then it's not a problem anymore. Is it exciting being with Burgess?" Abruptly he changed the subject. "Does the sight of him make your heart beat faster? Actually, no need to answer that. I guess it must do. It's been a long time, after all."

"Edward—"

"No, let me say this." His face reddening, Edward pressed his hand to his chest. "I just want to remind you of something, because you may have forgotten. The sight of me used to have that effect on you, Miriam. Remember? In that last year before Josephine died, both our hearts used to beat faster at the sight of each other. And then afterwards, you closed your feelings off. Like shutting a box. You wouldn't allow yourself to remember how you'd felt. And now you've spent the night with another man—"

"I didn't," Miriam helplessly blurted out. "We slept in adjoining rooms, I haven't—"

She jumped as a hand came to rest on her shoulder. It was Charles, confident and seemingly entertained by Edward's outburst. Loudly enough for the receptionist and a group of Australian tourists to hear, he said, "Is this gentleman bothering you, my dear? Shall I call security and have him removed?"

But Miriam barely heard him. As usual, as *always*, Edward was right. She had loved him, pulse-racingly and passionately, until that dreadful day when the lid of the box had come crashing down. And now he cared enough about her to come here and publicly declare himself, which was an astonishingly un-Edwardlike thing to do.

At her side, Charles told Edward, "You're making a fool of yourself, you know. It's all over. I'm here now."

Edward looked him straight in the eye. "Will you keep out of this? It's for Miriam to decide, not you." His face was still red. Despite his stiff-upper-lip demeanor, he looked as if he might explode. As Miriam wondered what his blood pressure might be doing, she realized that Edward's hand was once more sliding inside the front of his tweed jacket; he was either carrying a gun or massaging his chest—

In the garden… Josephine shouting furiously… then gasping for air as she collapsed to the ground…

"Oh Edward!" Springing away from Charles, Miriam rushed toward him. "You're right, you're always right, I'm so sorry!"

Silence. The receptionist, the dapper doorman, even the Australian tourists were agog.

"Meaning?" said Edward, scarcely daring to breathe.

When Miriam finally spoke, her dark eyes filled with tears. "You're the one I want to marry. If you're sure you still want me."

Across the echoing marble foyer, she heard one of the Australians whisper loudly, "Aaaw, ain't that the cutest thing? And they're, like, *ancient*."

Imperceptibly, Edward's arms tightened round her waist before she could race across the marble floor and fell the gawping Australian with a single blow.

Closer to hand, behind them, Charles said evenly, "Miriam, stop this at once. Move away from him." As if Edward were an unexploded bomb.

She shook her head. "I can't, Charles, I'm sorry, but I've made up my mind."

"This is ridiculous." Charles's voice was icy. "You can't do this." He paused. "All I have to do is call my lawyer."

Miriam closed her eyes. If he was serious… well, there was nothing she could do about that. A court case would be awful, truly humiliating; it would leave her reputation in shreds. And she could go to prison; the solicitor she'd consulted in Bedminster had already warned her that this was a real possibility.

But Edward would still love her, and that was all that mattered.

"Fine," Miriam said clearly. "If that's what you want to do."

"Oh, don't worry, it's what I *shall* be doing." With a bitter laugh, Charles raised his voice and addressed their assembled audience. "She's a bigamist, you know. And she ran off with my money."

"*Our* money," corrected Miriam.

"How much?" called out one of the Australians, a fat man in khaki shorts.

"I think I'd like to go now," Miriam said, but Edward held her there.

"In today's terms? Over a hundred thousand," said Charles.

"By the way, I haven't been to stay with my sister in Kent." Edward's tone was conversational. "Laurie and I went up to Edinburgh."

Miriam looked at him. "Did you?"

"Oh yes. Spent a couple of days in the city library up there. D'you know, it's incredible, they have all the old local newspapers stored in a vault. The newer ones are kept on microfiche, but the papers from fifty years ago are still there. Laurie and I had a good look through them."

"What's he on about now?" complained the Australian.

"Sshh," said his wife.

"What's really interesting," Edward was addressing Charles Burgess now, "is that Miriam told me the date she'd left you. So we checked every paper for that week, but there was no mention anywhere of Pauline Hammond's mother being knocked down by a car and killed. As Laurie pointed out," Edward concluded with a shrug, "it's like *The X-Files*. Almost as if it had never happened at all."

Charles Burgess paled visibly. Miriam, watching his reaction, almost laughed aloud.

"Th-that's not true," he blustered. "You've made a mistake."

"Oh, I think we know what isn't true," said Edward.

"You were lying all along." Miriam gazed at the stammering Charles. "Well, I suppose I should have known. You were always so good at it."

"You needn't look so pleased with yourself," Charles retorted, recovering himself. "I can still take you to court."

Miriam, blissfully aware of Edward's arm round her waist, said, "I've already told you, Charles. Feel free. But mine won't be the only name dragged through the mud, will it? The court will want to know why I left you, and I'll tell them. OK, so what I did was wrong, I should have divorced you, but I was only nineteen at the time. I was silly and reckless, but at least I wasn't unfaithful."

"Too right," said the Australian wife, vigorously nodding in agreement.

Charles shot the woman a look of utter contempt.

"And taking me to court isn't going to win me back," Miriam went on calmly. "Nothing's going to do that now, you must realize that. But anyway." She paused and regarded Charles with an air of finality. "It's not my decision, is it? I'll leave it up to you."

"…it's like going on holiday and missing a week of *Coronation Street*," marveled Clare. "You get back and find out that all this… God, *stuff* has happened."

Smiling to herself, Annie finished locking up the shop for the night. Clare was right; who would have thought that yesterday Miriam would have returned with Edward to announce that they were getting married and would be moving into Edward's house?

Or that later that evening, James would have asked her, Annie, to move in with *him*?

Or, most astoundingly of all, that Clare would fling her arms round her and say, "This is brilliant, I'm so happy for you," and actually appear to mean it?

And now this.

"I've been chatting to Dad," Clare had announced when she'd burst into the shop just ten minutes ago, "and I've decided to move out. Not because of you," she added hastily, glimpsing the expression on Annie's face. "I just think it's about time I stood on my own two feet. I'm twenty-three. I need to sort myself out, learn how to behave like a grown-up."

"Well, that's… um, great." Annie wondered why Clare had come to the shop to tell her this. "What'll you do, share a flat in Clifton?"

"That's what Dad said, but I'm not really interested. I quite fancy getting away from the whole Clifton scene… you know, the endless clubbing and wine bars and hooking up with dickheads like Piers. Anyway"—Clare led the way to the car she'd left parked on double yellows—"Miriam was asking Dad what you'd be doing with your cottage and I thought, hey, perfect, this could be just what I need, so that's why I'm here. We'll go and look at it now. If I like it, I'll rent it from you and you won't have to bother about finding a tenant you can trust!"

⁓

They pulled up outside the cottage and Clare bounced out of the car, entranced.

"This is so *sweet*. When I first met you I thought it'd be really grotty, but it's not at all!"

Drily, Annie said, "Thanks."

Inside, Clare rushed from room to room in a state of excitement. Since it was tiny, it took no time at all.

"If I'd known you were coming I'd have tidied up. Sorry it's a bit of a mess." Hurriedly Annie tipped a pile of ironing behind the sofa and kicked a couple of magazines out of sight.

"Ha, you're joking, I can make *loads* more mess than this. And it'll be my very own place, so nobody will be able to give me grief about it." Joyfully, Clare surveyed the sunny glass extension to the living room, not grand enough to be called a conservatory. "I can keep my easel here. Really, I'm turning over *such* a new leaf. No more drinking, no more men, I'm just going to concentrate totally on painting, get my career properly off the ground… Can we look upstairs now?"

Clare was like a whirlwind; Annie struggled to keep up. The bathroom was minuscule but clean. The second bedroom was more of a walk-in cupboard. But the main bedroom was good enough, and the view from the diamond-leaded windows had Clare in raptures.

"This is great, I can see all the way down the lane!" Flinging open the window, she leaned out so precariously that Annie almost grabbed her ankles. "And it's so peaceful, like being right out in the country. Which is just what I need," Clare added over her shoulder. "No distractions, just lots of peace and quiet and—whoooahh, who is *that*?"

Peering past, Annie saw what had caught Clare's attention.

"Oh, that's Danny. He lives in one of the big houses overlooking the village green."

Danny glanced up as he jogged past the cottage, his long hair bouncing off his shoulders and his mouth broadening into a grin at the sight of Clare in her perilously low-cut scarlet top. Without breaking stride, he raised a hand in greeting and jogged on down the lane.

"Danny LeBlanc." Clare gazed incredulously after him. "The soccer player, right? Plays for City." Whirling round, she said, "Is he single?"

"He's so single he has a revolving front door. The locals call his house the department store." Annie gave Clare a please-don't look. "Trust me, Danny's the last man you'd want to get involved with. He's impossible, up to all sorts of mischief—"

"And what a pair of legs. Oh yes, I am definitely going to rent this cottage."

"I thought you wanted to concentrate on your painting, give men a miss for a while," Annie pleaded. Although she already knew it was a lost cause.

"A *while*," emphasized Clare. "I didn't mean fifteen *years*."

"But Danny LeBlanc, he's not what you need. He treats all his girlfriends appallingly."

Clare flashed her a dazzling, supremely confident smile. "That's because he hasn't met me yet."

Chapter 60

"I CAN'T BELIEVE YOU'RE doing this," said Laurie. "I thought everything was fine. After… you know, at the hotel, I thought that was it, you'd made up your mind."

"I had. Only not in the way you thought. God, this is difficult." Nadia rubbed her temples and wished she had some kind of script to follow. "I'm sorry, but it's never going to work. We can't go back to how we were. Everything's changed."

It had taken a while, but she'd finally made up her mind. Everything *had* changed, including her feelings for Laurie. Maybe it had something to do with his devil-may-care attitude toward work—formulating any kind of career plan was seemingly beyond him. Then Jay had given her a cutting from the paper. A local radio station was on the lookout for a gardening expert to fill a weekly question-and-answer slot. Jay had said, "You should apply, you'd be great at that." Encouraged, she had told Laurie, who had laughed and said, "Watch out, Howard Stern, Nadia's after your job," and had then gone on to poke fun at the tiny radio station, telling her she shouldn't waste her time.

Little things, but they added up.

The sun was setting, turning the sky Day-Glo pink on the horizon. As they walked over the Downs, hot-air balloons practicing for the upcoming festival rose from Ashton Court and drifted across the Avon Gorge. Laurie paused to watch a ninety-foot Rupert Bear float over their heads.

"Did you sleep with him?"

"Who?" Nadia was glad of the sun in her eyes. She blinked, hard.

Laurie tut-tutted. "Ewan McGregor. You know who I mean."

"Oh. No, I didn't."

"See? Big mistake. You should have done."

"Maybe, but I slept with you instead."

Shoving his hands into the pockets of his jeans, Laurie smiled slightly. "And you're telling me I was a disappointment?"

Nadia shook her head. "You said I should sleep with Jay to get him out of my system. But I couldn't do that. It wouldn't have seemed… right."

"So you slept with me instead, and got me out of your system."

"It was your idea."

Drily, Laurie said, "Well, remind me never to have that idea again."

"I'm sorry." Nadia hadn't expected to cry. It was pathetic really; how could she get upset about finishing with someone she wasn't even properly involved with?

"Me too. I'm gutted. Still"—Laurie smiled briefly—"I suppose it serves me right for finishing with you in the first place."

"Maybe." Wiping her eyes, Nadia managed a feeble smile of her own.

"If I hadn't, we could have been married by now."

"Probably."

"So it's all my fault."

"Oh, definitely."

"Bugger." Laurie sighed. "And you bring me here to tell me." Spreading his arms, he indicated the Downs. "At least I had the decency to take you to Markwick's."

"What will you do?" said Nadia.

"Get over it, I suppose. In about fifty years." He gave her a tragic look. "Oh, don't worry about me, I'm tough. By the time I'm seventy-six I'll be absolutely fine."

If he was able to joke about it, Nadia thought with relief, things were probably going to be all right. They could revert to being friends—which, seeing as her grandmother was about to marry his father, was just as well.

"There's an ice-cream van over there." As she linked her arm companionably through his, a huge detached house floated across the gorge toward them. "Come on, I'll treat you to a Magnum."

"Sure you don't have to rush off? Isn't Jay waiting for you?"

"Why would he be?"

Laurie raised his eyebrows. "You mean, he doesn't even know he's won?"

Something that felt horribly like panic began to spread through Nadia's intestines. Would Jay react as she had once reacted upon learning that she'd won a pair of lime-green crocheted hot pants in the school raffle?

Aloud she said, "He might not even want to win."

Laurie started to laugh. "Now that's what I call risky. Talk about taking a gamble."

"You gambled," Nadia couldn't resist pointing out.

Laurie's eyes glittered with rueful amusement. "I lost."

～

Andy Chapman from the estate agents had been showing another potential buyer around Clarence Gardens. Even if Jay hadn't let her know this on the phone, Nadia would have been able to tell by the amount of Armani aftershave still lingering as she let herself into the house.

Jay had called to ask her to come and water the garden.

"I'm stuck here at home," he'd gone on to explain, sounding harassed. "Look, can you do me a favor? Andy's left some stuff in an envelope for me in the kitchen and I need it pretty urgently. If you could drop it round, I'd be grateful."

Nadia had spent forty minutes with the hose, watering the parched plants and tidying up the edges of the lawn with her strimmer. Now that she was finished, it was time to pick up the stuff-in-an-envelope, to take over to Jay's house.

And here it was, left on the worktop next to the sink, a white A4 envelope containing... well, whatever it contained.

What was the difference between nosiness and idle curiosity? Well, steaming open a sealed envelope would definitely count as nosiness.

Happily, this one wasn't sealed.

As the contents slithered out onto the worktop, Nadia felt the little hairs on the back of her neck stand up in alarm.

Property details. Well, hardly that surprising, seeing that they'd been left here by Andy Chapman. But why on earth would Jay be interested in details of houses in and around Manchester?

Not the in-need-of-renovation kind, either. Quite the opposite. These were big, glamorous, over half a million-pound properties, four- or five-bedroomed and period rather than modern—in fact, not unlike the house Jay currently owned here in Bristol.

OK, no need to jump to conclusions. Just because he'd asked Andy for these details didn't mean they were actually *for* him. Anyway, why would Jay want to move to Manchester?

Giving herself a mental cheek-slap, Nadia shoveled the details back into the envelope. She was being ridiculous; Jay had just bought Highcliffe House, for heaven's sake. That meant months of work. And he was employing her to redesign the garden. He couldn't possibly be leaving Bristol.

Oh God, could he?

It was only a short journey to Canynge Road. As she passed Bristol Zoo with its crowds of summer visitors queuing outside, Nadia couldn't shake off that on-your-way-to-the-dentist sensation. Turning left onto Jay's street, she realized her toes were scrunched up inside her trainers.

And with good reason. Maybe, telepathically, her toes had known all along.

After a hopelessly girlie bit of parking, Nadia switched off the ignition and wiped her clammy palms on her black jeans. Despite the heat of the day, goose bumps had pinged out all over her arms. She gazed at the For Sale sign outside Jay's house. So it was true, it was really going to happen.

Feeling sick as she climbed out of the car, Nadia clutched the envelope to her chest. It wasn't until she was ringing the doorbell that she realized she'd forgotten to check her face in the mirror. Earlier she had planned to joosh up her hair, take the shine off her nose, and stick on a bit of lip gloss. Instead, she probably looked awful. Oh well, too late now.

Bloody Jay, she could hit him.

Where was he anyway? Why wasn't he answering the door?

When he did, Nadia discovered why it had taken him so long.

"Sorry, sorry... the sticky things kept sticking to the wrong bits... and then I realized I'd put it on back to front... come in, God, this is harder work than I thought." Looking harassed but pleased to see her, Jay ushered her into the hall. Clearly he hadn't had time to brush his hair or dash on a bit of lip gloss either. The baby, naked apart from a disposable nappy dangling from one foot, was whimpering and flailing its legs against Jay's chest. There was an ominous damp patch on the front of his denim shirt. Evidently disgusted at finding himself in the hands of such a rank amateur, Daniel gave a kick that sent the clean nappy sailing through the air.

"Mary Poppins, I presume." Despite everything, Nadia was unable to keep a straight face. In all the time she'd known him, Jay had always been in control of every situation. Nothing fazed him.

Except, it now became apparent, the intricacies of getting a small baby into a disposable nappy.

"Just leave it," Jay sighed as she bent to retrieve the mini-Pampers.

"Bloody thing's stuck together all wrong anyway. And mind your feet," he added as they made their way through to the living room. "The full one burst as I was taking it off. All these weird gel-beads exploded all over the carpet."

"Let me take him." Nadia held out her arms for the baby and Jay handed him over with undisguised relief.

"Watch out, he's like the Trevi fountain. Nearly got me in the eye when he was on the changing mat. I had no idea babies peed every couple of minutes."

"I'd count yourself lucky. Babies don't only pee." Years of baby-sitting during college had given Nadia the advantage; lowering Daniel onto the plastic mat—white and decorated with blue elephants—she deftly fastened the wriggling baby into a fresh nappy. Rummaging in the carry-all on the floor next to the mat, she found a clean onesie and expertly fitted him into it. Each of the snaps between his legs made a satisfying clicking sound as she fastened them. The baby looked almost disappointed, as though she'd come along and spoiled all his fun. Gazing around in search of inspiration, he opened his mouth to start bawling. Locating the bottle of water on the coffee table, Nadia scooped him up and popped it into his mouth before he could get into full swing.

"Has this been boiled?"

"Of course it's been boiled, I'm not completely hopeless." The moment the words were out, Jay ruefully shook his head. "OK, maybe I am. Belinda's over at the house, packing up. She's leaving Bristol. I offered to look after Dan for a few hours." He looked help-less. "I thought he might sleep."

"Babies only do that when you don't want them to. It's their way of keeping you on your toes. Where's Belinda going to live?"

"Dorset. She's renting a place for now, just down the road from her parents."

Bugger. Why couldn't he have said Manchester?

Chapter 61

"THERE'S YOUR ENVELOPE, BY the way." Holding Daniel in the crook of her arm, Nadia nodded at the envelope she'd dropped onto the table.

"Oh right, thanks." Jay paused. "Did you look inside?"

"No!" Nadia hoped he wouldn't start dusting for fingerprints.

"OK."

Flushing slightly, she said, "I couldn't help noticing the For Sale sign, though. What's going on?"

Jay shrugged and pushed his hands into his pockets. "I've put the house on the market. Changed my mind about staying in Bristol."

"What's wrong with Bristol?"

"Just got bored, I suppose. It's not that fantastic."

Stung, Nadia blurted out, "So you're moving to *Manchester*?"

Oh bum. She saw the glint of triumph in Jay's brown eyes.

"X-ray vision, I presume."

"Oh shut up." Crossly, she faced him across the room. "I don't call this very fair. You're employing me. So what are you saying, that I'm out of a job?"

"Not at all." Jay shook his head. "I spoke to the chap I outbid at the auction, and he's going to be buying Highcliffe House from me. I made him promise he'd take you on to sort out the garden. He's a good bloke, you'll like working for him. So you see, it won't make any difference to you. You still have the job."

Nadia wondered how a supposedly intelligent grown man could

stand there and say something so stupid. It would make all the difference in the world. The urge to throw something at Jay—not the baby, obviously—was overwhelming.

"You don't seem very pleased," said Jay.

Nadia's eyes began to prickle. Oh good grief, *please* don't say she was going to cry.

"It's just… you know, come as a bit of a shock."

"You'll be fine." Jay's voice was expressionless. "You have your life here with Laurie. There's no reason for you to want to move anywhere, but when it's—"

"I'm not with Laurie." Nadia heard the words spilling out of her mouth. "We're not together anymore. He's gone to London."

Should she be telling Jay this? Oh well, too late now. Anyway, it was the truth. Honesty was supposed to be a good thing, wasn't it?

And it seemed to have worked for Miriam.

Jay's eyebrows lifted. "He's gone? Whose decision was that?"

Bloody cheek.

"Mine." As she spoke, Nadia felt Daniel's tiny fist curl trustingly round her index finger, surely one of the world's all-time great feelings.

"But I thought… the two of you…"

"I should have done it weeks ago. I think Laurie guessed it would happen. If I'd really loved him, I wouldn't have messed him about for so long."

"He's not the only one you messed about," Jay pointed out.

Glancing down, Nadia saw Daniel's long sooty eyelashes drooping over his cheeks. He was no longer sucking from the bottle. Carefully, she lowered him onto the sofa and wedged him in with cushions, then almost at once regretted it. Daniel had been her shield. Now she no longer knew what to do with her hands.

"That plan went wrong then," said Jay with a rueful smile. "The idea was to open the front door with Dan in my arms. He was meant to be happy and quiet, and you were going to be wildly impressed by my ability to cope, not to mention completely won over by how great we looked."

Why? Why?

"But now you're moving to Manchester. How long's the house been on the market?"

"Couple of days. But there's been a lot of interest."

He actually had the nerve to sound pleased. Nadia felt sick. She'd left it too late.

"I still don't see why you have to go." Oh God, did that sound hopelessly weedy and pathetic?

He shrugged. "There's nothing to keep me in Bristol. Thought I'd give another city a try."

A horrible thought struck Nadia. "Is Andrea going with you?"

"Oh, come on." Jay gave her a be-serious look. "I haven't seen Andrea for weeks. There's only one person I'm interested in. Sadly, she's spent the last few months completely buggering me about."

Nadia couldn't speak. Did he mean her? What if he didn't? If she assumed he meant her and he was actually talking about some other girl, she was going to look *such* a wally.

"What's wrong with your hands?" said Jay.

"Nothing. I don't know." Helplessly, Nadia flapped her huge, out-of-control hands. "I don't know where to put them."

Oops.

Jay's mouth twitched. "I could always take the house off the market, you know. I don't have to leave Bristol."

On the sofa, romantically, Daniel chose this moment to emit a peaceful baby fart in his sleep.

Nadia spluttered with laughter. "Sorry. Are you serious?"

"Well, I'm trying." Jay moved toward her, causing her heart to break into a canter. "Look, I'm not used to saying stuff like this.

Dammit, I'm not used to being in a situation like this, but you must know how I feel about you."

Thank you, God, thank you, thank you...

"I may need another clue," Nadia murmured, and Jay smiled.

Then he kissed her.

Oh yes, definitely worth waiting for. As the fireworks went off and her body swam with joy, Nadia realized that this was what had been missing with Laurie.

Kissing Jay just felt so completely and utterly *right*.

And OK, so maybe there were no money-back guarantees, but that was the difference between men and microwave ovens. Sometimes you just had to live with one and hope for the best.

"You," said Jay, "have been nothing but trouble."

"But now I've turned over a new leaf." Nadia trembled as his mouth slid down to her neck. Jay's hands were warm round her midriff where her shirt had ridden up. As it rode up a little further— not quite of its own accord—she murmured, "Promise you'll take this place off the market."

"I will."

"And don't sell Highcliffe House to that other chap."

"Whatever you say," said Jay.

"That's my bra you're undoing."

"God, is it? Sorry, I'm such an amateur."

Struggling to maintain some kind of control, Nadia panted, "We can't do this now. What about Daniel?"

"He's asleep. This is what baby-sitters get up to when their charges are out for the count." Smiling, Jay murmured, "Didn't you know that? It's practically the law."

"Oh yes, I remember now. Silly me."

Rrrrrinnggg.

"Hell, who's *that*?" Jay turned in dismay as the doorbell shrilled. Loudly.

On the sofa, Daniel's dark eyes snapped open in alarm. Jerked from sleep, he let out a bellow of outrage and punched the cushions with his tiny fists, demanding to be picked up.

"After all these months, you'd think I'd have been due some good luck." Shaking his head, Jay said resignedly, "But no, the moment anything *remotely* promising threatens to happen, some inconsiderate bastard pitches up and starts ringing my doorbell. You know, at this rate we could both be bloody pensioners before—"

"Shouldn't you answer the door?" said Nadia as the shrilling rang out again.

"You'd better do it." Indicating the front of his jeans, Jay said ruefully, "I'm not quite respectable just now. Give me a minute to recover."

Leaving him to scoop up his furiously yelling nephew, Nadia made her way through to the hall. Opening the front door, she was confronted by an irate middle-aged man.

"Is Jay there?"

"Well, he's a bit... um, busy at the moment." Backed up by the ear-splitting wails coming from the living room and simultaneously wondering if she'd ever been happier in her life, Nadia said brightly, "Can I help you?"

"Maurice MacIntyre. I live across the road. My house went on the market yesterday."

"Gosh, what a coincidence." Nadia guessed he was bursting to compare asking prices. She gave him an encouraging smile. "And?"

Maurice MacIntyre gave her an odd look, clearly thinking she was mad.

"Look, I don't know what Jay thinks he's playing at. But I'd like my For Sale sign back."

a walk in the park

"OK, WE CAN SEE it from here." Lara Carson pulled up at the side of the road, buzzed down the window and pointed into the valley below. "See the L-shaped house with the white gates and the green car outside? That's the one."

Home sweet home. Or maybe not. Eighteen years had passed since she'd last set foot over the threshold. Who knew what it was like inside now?

Gigi was leaning across from the passenger seat, breathing minty chewing-gum fumes over her as she peered down at the house. "Does it feel funny, seeing it again?"

"No." That wasn't true. "A bit." Lara gave her daughter's hand a squeeze.

"Are you going to cry?"

"What am I, some sort of *girl*? I'm definitely not going to cry."

They sat in silence for a few seconds, looking at the old house with its ivy-strewn walls, blue-painted window frames and neatly tended garden. "OK, come on then," Gigi said at last. "It's nearly time. You don't want to be late for your own father's funeral."

———

Lara was one of the last into the church. It felt like being in a film. Her high heels click-clacked across the gray flagstones and people swivelled round to see who was making all the racket. Of the seventy or eighty mourners, most were strangers and didn't recognize her, which suited Lara just fine. But there were a few who clearly did. Eyebrows were raised and elbows nudged. She made a point of steadily meeting their gaze before looking away and slipping into an empty pew at the back.

What a weird situation to be in. People were spreading the word about her now; she could practically feel the mini Mexican wave of whispers rolling forwards. Finally it reached Janice in the front pew, flanked by her sisters and wearing an extraordinary feathered black hat. Together the three of them stiffened then turned their frosty glares upon her. With the feathers waving around her head, Janice resembled an angry crow with an acute case of bed hair.

Was it very wrong to think ill of the grieving widow during her husband's funeral? Obviously it was, but where Janice was concerned, it wasn't easy to think of anything nice.

The organ music started, everyone rose to their feet and the coffin was brought in.

Lara watched it being carried past her pew. The weirdness intensified. Charles Carson, her actual father, was inside that coffin.

He was dead.

And she genuinely didn't feel a thing.

—⁓—

Outside the church, Evie waited for the service to end. It was a long shot, but she hadn't been able to help herself. The moment she'd seen the notice in the local paper announcing the death of Charles Carson and the date of his funeral, she'd booked the time off work. The chances of Lara turning up at the funeral might be slim, but it could just happen. And if it did, Evie wasn't going to miss her.

They'd been best friends once. There were so many unanswered questions. Coming here today was an opportunity she simply couldn't pass up.

Not long now before the service was over. From this distance Evie heard the organ cranking up again, launching ponderously into "Guide Me O Thou Great Redeemer." It was hot out here; the sun was blazing down and her hair was sticking to the back of her neck. Pushing open the car door for extra ventilation, she swivelled sideways and swung her legs out, then tipped her left hand from side to side to admire the way the emeralds and diamonds flashed in the sunlight. Was Lara inside the church? Would she be seeing her again for the first time in eighteen years?

Oh well, soon find out.

⁓

The funeral ended. The genial vicar made the announcement that refreshments were available at Charles and Janice's home, and that everyone would be welcome back there, but Lara guessed she probably wasn't included in the invitation.

Luckily she didn't want to go anyway.

From her pew at the back, she watched Janice and her sisters lead the exit from the church. As they came down the aisle, the looks they gave her pretty much confirmed her suspicions. The black feathers shuddered with outrage and three sets of pale eyes ringed with black make-up bored through her. Since now wasn't the time for a confrontation, Lara averted her gaze and waited for the malevolent trio to pass.

The church emptied. She sat and waited a few minutes longer for the mourners to disperse. Soon came the sound of cars being started up and driven off. Finally, when all was quiet again, Lara rose and headed outside into the welcome heat and sunlight of a glorious summer's day.

Everyone had left, apart from a lone figure at the bottom of the driveway. Someone was sitting on the wall next to the open gates; someone with red hair, wearing a cobalt blue shirt and a white skirt.

Which in turn meant she was likely to have moss and lichen stains on the back of it.

Lara attempted to focus but the distance was too great and her superpowers weren't that strong. She hadn't thought to bring her binoculars with her.

But… there was something familiar about the figure that was causing prickles of recognition down her spine. It couldn't be, could it…?

Her pace quickened and the distance between them was reduced. The redhead slid down from the dry stone wall and began to move toward her. Moments later they both stretched their arms wide and broke into a run. It was like one of those slow motion Hollywood sequences that more traditionally featured two members of the opposite sex.

"It *is* you," shouted Lara.

"I *know*." Evie beamed as they collided and hugged each other until they were both panting for breath. "Oh my God, I can't believe it, you're really *here*." She pulled back to study Lara's face. "Your dad… I'm sorry… are you upset?"

"No, no." Vigorously Lara shook her head. "Don't worry, you don't have to be polite. I only came back because of the solicitor. He phoned and said I needed to get myself down here. Anyway, let's not talk about that now." She was so thrilled to see Evie she was burbling uncontrollably. "How are you? You look fantastic! Oh, I've missed you so much. You have to tell me everything!"

It was true, she had missed her oldest friend more than words could say. But at the time she'd known it was the only way. And look at Evie now, eighteen years older and obviously looking older… but at the same time miraculously unchanged. Teasingly, she turned Evie sideways and peered at the back of her white skirt. Thirty-four years old and she still hadn't learned how to keep herself stain-free. "You've got dirt on your skirt."

"Have I? Oh no! How did that happen?" As she always had, Evie seemed genuinely surprised. For a couple of seconds she slapped ineffectually in the general area of her rounded bottom before giving up. "Oh well, never mind, you're *here*. This is so brilliant! I'd almost given up hope, then I heard someone say on their way out, 'Was that her? Was that the daughter who ran away?' So I knew you were in there. Everyone's gone back to the house for drinks. Is that where you're going now?"

"Urgh, no way." Lara checked her watch; almost two o'clock. "I'm meeting the solicitor in his office at three thirty. But I'm free till then. Do you have to be somewhere or can I buy you lunch?"

<hr />

Fifteen minutes later they were sitting at a pavement café by the abbey, drinking Prosecco and catching up. Having spotted the emerald engagement ring, Lara now heard all about Joel and the imminent wedding. Less than six weeks from now, Evie was set to become Mrs. Barber. Joel was the one she'd waited so long for, and she'd never been happier in her life.

By unspoken mutual consent they'd covered Evie's story first, getting it out of the way. Then it was Lara's turn. Evie said, "Tell me what happened," and Lara took a deep swallow of fizzy, ice-cold wine.

"The people at the church, you said they called me the one who ran away. Is that what everyone thought?" She placed the glass carefully in the center of the table. "I didn't run away. They kicked me out."

"I called round to your house to see where you were," said Evie. "Your dad answered the door. He just said you'd gone and wouldn't be coming back. Then Janice appeared next to him and you should have seen the look on *her* face. Like she'd finally got what she'd always wanted. Which I suppose she had. But I'm telling you, it gave me the shivers. I was so worried… you could have been *murdered*."

"I was late home," said Lara. "I had to be back by eleven o'clock and I missed the last bus. By the time I got home it was almost half past. That was when it all kicked off." She didn't go into detail; this wasn't the time or the place. "It was the biggest row we'd ever had. Janice called me some vile names and told me she wished I'd never been born. Dad said I was ruining his life and he'd had enough, he wasn't going to put up with it anymore. He gave me an hour to pack my things. Then he told me to get out."

Evie was appalled. "How could he do that? You were sixteen!"

"Didn't matter." Lara shrugged and emptied her glass. "He wasn't going to change his mind. On the bright side, looking back on it now, I'm glad it happened. Mind you, at the time it wasn't so great. I'd never been so scared in my life."

"You should have come to our house!"

"I couldn't. It was three o'clock in the morning. And I was just desperate to get away. So that's what I did. I sat outside the train station for the rest of the night, then caught the first train out of Bath."

"Where did you go?"

"I called my Aunt Nettie and asked if I could stay with her for a couple of days." Lara broke into a smile at the thought. "That was it, basically. I turned up on her doorstep in Keswick and that's where I've been ever since."

"Keswick? In Cumbria? We had no idea," said Evie. "None of us knew where you were. I kept waiting for you to call or write…"

"I know. I'm so sorry." The guilt had haunted her all these years, but even now she wasn't able to tell Evie the rest of the story. "I just knew I'd never come back to Bath as long as my father was alive. It was easier to make a clean break."

The food arrived, they talked and drank some more, then it was time for Lara to head off for her appointment with the solicitor in nearby Harington Place.

"And I have to get back to work." Before they left, Evie took out her diary and said, "But we're not going to lose touch again. Give me everything you've got... address, email, phone numbers, I want the lot. And you have to have mine too."

Once that was done, Lara walked back to Evie's car with her. They hugged each other again hard.

"You must come to the wedding," Evie begged. "It'll be fantastic. You will, won't you? On the twelfth of August." She squeezed Lara's hands. "Please say you'll be there!"

Acknowledgments

Big thanks to Jeanette and Mike Groark, and Mark Andrews, for the sterling legal advice. Thanks also to Garth Harrison, barbecue supremo, for lending me his stunning home. Thanks are due too to Anne Evans, Lorraine Wilson, and Val Curtis, who deciphered my appallingly messy handwriting and worked so hard against the clock to turn my scribble into a readable, typed manuscript. (No thanks, incidentally, to the Royal Mail, who promptly lost it…)

And finally, thanks to Pearl Harris, private detective par excellence.

About the Author

With over 5 million copies sold, *New York Times* and *USA Today* bestselling author Jill Mansell is also one of the hottest selling authors of women's fiction in the UK. She lives with her partner and children in Bristol and writes full time. Actually, that's not true; she watches TV, eats gumdrops, admires the rugby players training in the sports field behind her house, and spends hours on the Internet marveling at how many other writers have blogs. Only when she's *completely* run out of ways to procrastinate does she write.